Before

EDEN

Before

EDEN

Mark Littleton

THOMAS NELSON PUBLISHERS

Nashville • Atlanta • London • Vancouver

Published in Nashville, Tennessee, by Thomas Nelson, Inc., Publishers, and distributed in Canada by Word Communications, Ltd., Richmond, British Columbia.

Scripture quotations are from the NEW KING JAMES VERSION of the Bible, Copyright © 1979, 1980, 1982, Thomas Nelson, Inc., Publishers.

Library of Congress Cataloging-in-Publication Data

Littleton, Mark R., 1950–
    Before Eden : a novel / by Mark Littleton.
        p. cm.
    ISBN 0-7852-8210-6
PS3562.I7865B4 1995
813'.54—dc20   94-29373
                                                                         CIP

Printed in the United States of America
1 2 3 4 5 6 — 99 98 97 96 95 94

Prologue
The Woman

Voices screamed toward the front of the tiny hovel. I watched from the mulberry bushes, a child, a girl, with long flowing blonde hair and a dirty face. Eleven years old. It was a good guise.

"Come out, Vasro! Come out! We wanna talk with you!"

I peered in through the side window and saw the woman huddled with the child and her husband standing at the door. He held himself very straight, ramming out his thick chest like the stub of a tree trunk. He was a violent man, I knew. But that didn't matter now.

"Do not go out," the woman moaned. "Please, do not go out."

"I have my sword, and a knife," the husband answered. "They won't harm me." He leered toward the door as if to spit into the faces of the four who sat astride lean brown and black horses recently stolen from a larger farm not far away.

"They will kill you and rape me," the wife sobbed. "Please, Vasro. Think of Jolain."

The baby wriggled in the woman's arms. I could see its tiny dimpled face, streaked with the tears it had just shed. I watched the mother again and said under my breath, "He will not listen to her." I sighed, fear gripping me. Why did men never listen to women in this world? Why were women always helpless and at the hands and whims of the men? It made no sense although I knew well the main part of the cause: the curse on all because of the sin of the first two.

"Please, Vasro! Please!" She lanced out her hand and gripped his arm. He shook it off, his thick-muscled brown arms like iron to her touch. As she moved, the necklace she wore dropped out from under the tunic. I gasped. There, shining before me on the woman's chest, hung the white stone.

"I must go out. I am not a coward."

The woman sobbed, and he pushed her away. "Stop crying. I hate crying. Stop!"

He didn't strike her, though, as I had seen so many times in these places. I was thankful for that. Thus, I waited in the shadows. I would have to move quickly, I knew, if anyone was to be saved here. But my thoughts were on the white stone, for I was its guard and protector, and since its theft ages ago I had not seen it. Had Kyrie sent me here at this time to retrieve it, or just to speed it on its way to its next home?

I didn't know. I only knew I had to lead the woman and child to safety and freedom.

Vasro walked back to the door. The men outside were laughing. Four of them, all heavy with swords, knives, and bows—the tools of their craft, which was marauding, looting, pillaging, killing. I knew the husband did not have a chance, but I also knew neither the wife nor anyone else could persuade him not to demonstrate his courage.

"Put the beam in the door when I go out," Vasro said. He opened the heavy oaken wall of wood and stepped out, then closed it gently. I immediately ran to the back window, still hidden in the shadows of the trees. I ran my hands up and down the bark, thinking, planning, pushing my mind to find the one way to save these two. The husband, I knew, was as good as dead. But the woman, and the child, perhaps . . . just perhaps One never knew the outcome of these things. Even in our world, no one knew the outcome of anything.

The four men sat on horseback, their bows strung across their chests. Hatchets and knives in their belts. Short swords at their sides. They were painted, and their hair was cut in odd squarish and triangular shapes. I had already seen them murder two others, rape the women, behead the children, then take everything they could find. Which was little. So much murder for so little.

I could never understand it. To this day, I don't.

Vasro approached the four men. "We have nothing here. Just a house. Look to the west. There's your prey. I am alone. I do not want to fight."

"Ha!" the big one said. His shoulders spanned three or four of my own. He must have weighed three hundred pounds, all muscle. One of the giants, with a shock of black hair, deepset, angry eyes, and a continual sneer on his lips.

The big one cried, "He lies! Let's kill him. There is a woman here. I heard her!"

"There is my wife," Vasro said. "She is not pretty. You would not want her. I am an ugly man as you can see. I have not won a beautiful bride."

"We don't care about looks!" the giant shouted.

The others grunted, and their horses stamped their feet. My own heart beat through my rib cage, and I knew I would have to act. Soon. I raised my head to look inside the window. The wife lay in a corner, cuddling the baby. She was weeping. There was no back door. She would have to squirm through the window, hand the baby to me first. That might be difficult. She might not want to. She might fight me.

I hurried back to the side corner of the house and peered out at them, counting the moments when I should return and get the woman and baby out of the house. When was the best time? I knew it was while they were talking. But we would have to be very quiet. The four men were already restless.

I was about to go back to the window, when the two men on the right and left trotted over to either side of the house and peered back into the bushes. Checking. I ducked down and watched them from behind the thick coating of mulberry leaves, hoping my brown, cloaked form would mesh with the dead leaves around me. The man on my side was scarred and ugly, his head bald with some growth as if he hadn't shaved it recently. He looked down toward me but did not seem to see anything. He turned his horse sideways and nodded to the two others.

Vasro tried to placate them. "I have gold. You can have it. All of it."

"Yes, we will take that," the one next to the giant said. He was not only slim, dark, and small, but also powerfully built. He had a scar across his brow. His chest was bare. He looked and spoke like the leader. I knew of others like him. Rough, uncaring men. No heart. No eye for beauty or ear for music. They lived for murder after murder until they themselves were murdered. Sometimes they welcomed death.

Vasro took a thong off from about his neck. It held a small pouch. He threw the pouch with the coins jingling inside to the smaller, muscular man.

"Very courteous of you, sir," the smaller man said. "We appreciate your generosity." He was fingering a knife in his belt.

The lone killer on my side of the house nudged his horse forward. He was out of sight of the window. I crept back, looked in the small aperture. The woman was standing and caressing the baby. Her eyes flashed in my direction, wild with fright.

I said to her, "Come with me."

She jumped at the sound of my voice, then regarded me with apprehension. "Who are you?"

"A friend. Please come."

"You're a child."

"Not all things are as they appear."

"What is that supposed to mean?" Her fear had suddenly turned to contempt. I had seen this many times before.

"There is not time to explain," I said. "Please come. I will take you to a place where you will be safe. First, put the beam across the door."

"I am safe here."

"Then why are you crying?" Out in front, there was the noise of arguing. I said again, "There is not time. I am a friend, and I will help you."

"How can you help me?"

I held my tongue. "I can take you to someone who will."

"Who?"

"Japheth."

"The holy man?"

"Yes."

"He will not help the likes of me."

"He will. Come."

There was a scream. Then the sounds of a scuffle. A moment later I heard a body thud to the ground. A blood-stifled cry burst from someone's lips. Vasro's. "Help!"

"My husband!" the woman cried. She ran to the door and was about to open it when I whispered loudly, "Bolt it."

She hesitated, then did so.

I stretched my hand out through the window. "Come. There is no help other than me."

She looked frantically from me to the door. Then she hurried across the room. There was a bang at the door, the sound of the men pushing on it.

"Come. Hand me the child."

She hesitated, but as the banging increased, she lifted the baby to me through the window. A second later, she clambered out. The white stone swung into my face, and if I had wanted, I might have bitten it off and taken it for myself. But that was not lawful. Not now.

I gave the baby back to her and took her hand. Saying nothing, we ran into the trees.

I knew the way. She was weeping, and I did not try to comfort her. My mission was to get her to Japheth. We climbed the hill, then descended into the little valley. "My husband," the woman sobbed. "My husband is dead."

"Japheth will help you," I said again. "He is a good man."

"But why will he help me? Us?"

"Because he believes."

"In God?"

"In God."

I felt her shudder. "I am not a good person," she said. I pulled her through the rising mist. We scrambled along by the tiny lake. I saw Japheth's house on the other side. He would probably be fishing now.

We reached the other shore and hurried up to the door. I said to the woman, "Knock, and wait. If he is not here, then simply wait on the stoop here. When he comes, tell him what happened. He will help."

"But aren't you . . . "

"I must go. My duty is done."

"Who are you?"

For the first time all day, I smiled. "A friend."

Her eyes filled with tears. "Thank you, little girl," she said.

"Thank Kyrie," I said.

"Who?"

"God. Thank God."

"I will."

I ran back into the mists and disappeared. I had to get to the mountain before dawn. I had walked for an hour, enjoying the sounds of the woods and trees, when suddenly I felt a presence at my side. I stopped and looked. There was a shimmer. I knew it was one of my brethren.

"Aris."

"Yes?"

"Hurry. We must go."

"Now?"

"There is trouble. Kyrie is . . . " His voice broke, but instantly he regained his composure. I knew it was Rune now. "Kyrie is going to destroy it."

"Destroy what?"

"All of it. Earth. The whole world."

I stared at the shimmer, now able to make out the outline of his tall, radiant form. "He is going to destroy it?"

"Everything."

"But how?"

"We don't know."

"When?"

"We don't know."

"Why?"

"You know why."

I immediately thought of the scene I'd just witnessed and a thousand more like it over the last year. Then there were those before this year, those all the way back to the original pair. Yes, I knew why. I couldn't help but know why.

"But what about people like Japheth? And the woman? And the child?"

"The child will die. The woman, we do not know. Japheth, we don't know. Kyrie is merciful. We know only that."

I sighed anxiously.

"Change. Then come."

I said to Rune, "So Lucifer has won after all."

"We do not know that."

"We do!" I said fiercely. "It was always coming to this. Kyrie has never dealt with him. Kyrie has always given in. And now this is His last giving in that I will be part of."

"Aris. Forget the doubts. Come. We are called."

I sighed again, my childish form slowly metamorphosing. In less than a minute, I was myself.

"So it has really come to the end," I said. "Lucifer has won as he always proclaimed he would."

"The end has not come yet," Rune said. "There is Japheth, and the woman. And others."

"Shem?"

"Yes."

"And Noah?"

"Yes."

I looked across the mountain, seeing as only one of our brethren can see. Through the mists, through the darknesses, all the way to Japheth's home. I could see him succoring the young woman. I knew already the child was ill. I knew that from the beginning. But perhaps she would survive.

Perhaps.

"Hurry!" Rune said.

I lifted my arms, and my wings unfurled about me. They were a vibrant, golden color, and they gleamed in the sunlight. "Lucifer has won," I said again, a thick, raw cry welling into my throat. "And nothing matters anymore."

"We do not know that," Rune said. We mounted into the air. Then I remembered. "Rune, I have found the white stone."

He turned in the air and regarded me with wonder. "It has not been destroyed?"

"The woman has it."

"Then maybe there is much to hope for after all."

"Perhaps."

I looked back on the receding blue orb. And then we were in the tunnel, moving fast. A moment later, I was home.

Once we were safely upon the shores of Heaven, I said to Rune, "I have to go back and watch it, especially if Kyrie will destroy the whole world. I must ensure the safety of the stone."

Rune's eyes softened as he peered at me. "You know you cannot always make sure it will fall into the right hands."

"I know that, Rune. It's just that it startled me. I had not expected ever to see it again."

He smiled, and we both looked across the green pastures and glades of Heaven. So much had happened since that first day when I breathed the life of Kyrie into my own breast . . .

❖

The first time I saw Lucifer, I was so astonished I stepped back several paces and almost ended up in the crystal sea. I gained my reputation from those first few seconds of my creation. "Aris the Amazed," I was called after that and have never been known any other way.

I remember well how the whooshing noise resounded in my ears. Every limb tingled. I felt my eyes, lips, and face forming, then my neck, arms, torso, legs. A moment later I stood. And then I heard a word: "Aris."

I looked up and into the eyes of Kyrie. They seemed to dance with gay pulsations of light, and there was mirth in His voice. "You are Aris."

"Yes, Kyrie." My own voice thundered within me, as if I was enclosed in a huge conch shell, but then it sprang onto my lips and out. I existed, and for the moment a joy jolted through my being like electrical splinters. That was when I looked up and over Kyrie's head into the four-faced, multi-eyed person of Lucifer, the greatest of Kyrie's creative imaginations.

His robe bore every gem—diamond, ruby, emerald, beryl, onyx, jasper, turquoise, lapis lazuli, topaz. A multitude of eyes looked out upon us with grave authority. Four wings graced his appearance and four faces—that of a lion, human, bull, and eagle. He shone against the resplendent effulgences of Kyrie like a clear winter night, all the refractions and color mixing in one glimmering panoply of beauty so amazing that few could look upon him and not gasp with fright, wonder, and sheer ecstasy. He walked among the stones of fire and conversed with Kyrie as if they were doing nothing more important than taking an afternoon stroll. And he stood on the holy mountain, overarching the throne with his magnificent green and gold wings like a worshiper caught in a moment of thunderstruck repose.

In every way, he was perfect. Even Kyrie Himself was no match for the refulgent glories of this, His first, foremost, and crowning creation. At times the rest of us struck me as little more than afterthoughts, beings spoken into existence on the rear end of a short and weary sentence, if it's possible to think of Kyrie as becoming weary.

Of course, we weren't afterthoughts at all. Each of us was unique, the beginning and end of his species. I watched, spellbound and transfixed in place. I stood in the midst of a multitude so vast I could not see the beginning or end of it. It was as if a great general would appear and march by us, his deribboned billions, and review us in solemn cool severity. We were all silent, except for various oohs and startled ahhs as the next and the next and the next beings convulsed into life.

"Uriel."

"Antimy."

"Cologuel."

Kyrie spoke each name, and instantly, the being by that name shimmered as if in indecision and then bolted into bright, bold color and form. Long black hair. Or red. Or blonde. Or yellow, orange, blue. Eyes small and wide. Knobby-nosed. Or flat-nosed, as if punched just before shattering the line of existence with his presence. Tall. Short. They were every possible posture, height, weight, and style. They were all there, blended perfectly. I gazed on the assembly as the numbers mounted. There was no counting them. I did not even try. Row upon row. Face upon face. Chests like burnished bronze. Faces burning yellow and gold and black in the light. Everyone beautiful. Everyone perfect.

There was no sense of time. Each moment sprang new and resplendent, as if no moments or thoughts preceded it.

Lucifer spoke to Kyrie as his multitude of eyes surveyed the form of yet another magnificent being. "He will be Sixth Quarm?"

"Yes," Kyrie said. "All of them in the next grouping."

"It is good."

Beside Kyrie sat another being, a young man, bearded, kindly looking, with white hair and ivory face, a trembling smile on his lips. I knew instantly He was the Son, though I knew little else about Him. For a long time He would remain a mystery in all our minds.

When our number was complete, Kyrie looked out upon us and cried, "My children!"

We answered, "Our Father!"

"We are one!"

Echoing His words, the same expression broke from our lips in pleased chorus: "We are one."

"Watch. And see. And learn."

We stood transfused and spangled with light, our bodies standing in air as if in a stadium with row upon row of seats stretching into the heavens.

He spoke, and suddenly a whole city, the Great City, sparkled white and luxurious before us. Great white golden towers, pillars as high and wide as the sun, forums and gardens and long stately streets, veritable skyscrapers of translucent platinum, crimson and maroon turrets, cathedrals with bulwarks and buttresses like illumined swans at sea, all of it shimmering up before our eyes like a fountain. It stayed rooted in place.

Kyrie uttered so few words, but at each whole panoplies of wonder unfurled themselves before us. How it was happening, I could not know. What power graced those lips!

And at each word, the sizzling lightninglike movements of the Cherubim Lucifer above Him signaled deeper wonder in the enterprise. Lucifer himself spoke rapturously as each new marvel emerged and led us in cheers of praise when Kyrie paused and spoke the hallowed words, "It is good."

Then Kyrie spoke again and the whole rolling, roiling countryside came into view. Here I saw a bower of trees with an altar, and there a glade, dark and green and translucent with beauty. And there streams, rivers, lakes, seas, tinged diamond and sapphire blue in the shekinah light. It all rushed before us like cartooned hounds launching off the edge of the page into oblivion and then finding they have come down on something altogether new on the next page.

He spoke again, and flocks and herds, grazing or running or standing in respectful silence before Him, broke into being. The great brown tufted Dogs of Dallet. The starraxes in the Outer Reaches. The wyxoxen in the Stillnesses. Each honed and carved as if from marble. Each woofing and baahing and mooing and neighing and squirming with life.

The creating went on and on till Heaven shone like a magnet at the center of all things. As He spoke again and again, roads, streets, and byways wrapped the land. He spoke, and trees appeared with all kinds of fruits and nuts. He cried out, and the clouds above broke through the blue, white and billowing.

Every moment was a wonder.

And then, as if it had all taken only moments, it was finished. We sang till our voices seemed to ring down joy from the heavens and inundate the whole land with its cool filtered perfect melody.

When we finished singing, Kyrie suddenly cried, "Go to your homes. We meet in the Temple to play and make music. Now go and return, for then I will give you your instruments."

And so the first moment of creation ended. I sighed, still edgy and blustery with the soaring excitement of being alive and being there and being His. I knew it was good, very good.

Hours later, Kyrie gave me my instrument. It shone in His hands like caged lightning yearning to burn free. As He handed it to me, His fingers touched mine, and I felt the inviolate pulsation of life through those tips as I feel the very pulse of life in my own temples today. He bent close, and I could smell the scent of His great beard, like a thick winter coat. The color slipped off in white dancing spirals of light. Looking into my face, He said,

"Aris, this is yours. As you know, it is a much favored Harpistrer. Use it well. Soon you will compose."

I bowed. Tingles of violently joyous light stirred my lifeblood. A Harpistrer. I had hoped only for a Vinn or a Solem or a Cruke. But He had given me my longing.

"Thank you, Kyrie."

An undertow of emotion bulged tears into my eyes, and I went back to my place with a thankful, teeming heart. I took my seat and watched as each of us of the orchestral echelons were given our instruments. To each, Kyrie gave a special word.

"This Cruke will resound the trills of the Trinity, Terras."

"You have been given a Solem, Deppen. Do not grow weary of doing your best."

"This is a Dollen, my friend Ladna. It will respond to only your most fervent and effervescent whispers, so whisper well."

There was never a sense of boredom or of time standing still. We never knew what He would say or who was next, and we bent to each new moment as if it were our first.

And then the music began. Our conductor, Zarsill, whose thin, wizened face shone with vitality and energy, his green cat eyes taking it all in and pausing as if all the universe rotated on his axis. He waved his baton with a sudden upward stroke, and the mild strain of a Vinn cut the silence like dancing light in the blood. The wood vibrated as the Vinnist whispered, a bold and trim virtuoso named Harras. His long hair was dark, flowing over his shoulders, and he wore his huge, Hebrew nose with an abandoned happiness that I at once admired and praised. He bent to the music like Kyrie Himself bending to the formation of a blade of grass.

I watched in transfixed wonder as the atmosphere above us tingled. Glimmers of light wrangled far out on the edge. The horizon lit, a small burst here and there as other Vinnists joined him. My ears were filled with a distinct longing, a raw consuming hunger to know Him and live in Him and allow Him to live in me. I drank and lived the music as if each note was a replica of myself pirouetting in some sacred dance on the edge of the crystal sea.

We played, and the Crukes interwove a gentle, stirring roll. Our heads swayed with an inner unison, touched to the core by the melody. I looked up, saw Kyrie standing behind it all and next to Him the Son, then plucked the first note of my Harpistrer. I felt the vibration tow through me like an undercurrent, then burst inside till my body swelled and embraced Him in mind and soul. My bronzed arms tensed. I dipped slightly, feeling as if I might weep. My long golden hair fell into my eyes, and I brushed it back.

The music gripped me, held me. I was captured. Imbued.

We effortlessly drew in light, then exhaled in the first stirring strains of a word.

"Yannonay!" The First.

"Lazona." The Last.

"Yannonay. Lazona. Yannonay. Lazona."

Over us all, Lucifer the anointed cherub, each eye fixed on one of us, spoke guiding words to our hearts. "Now softly. Now a build. Now the Vinns. There, watch that, a little lower now. Yes. YES. YES!"

With him and with Kyrie and with the Son, we were one, a single body strung and looped and bound together by music that spindled galaxies and would hie the unborn souls of millions out of their Master's mind.

I smiled deep down in my chest. I looked at my legs, wishing to soar as the fire built underneath us. We were the core of the volcano, boiling towards break, ready to burst. We were the sea in raucous roar. We were roses budding into bloom.

And then we sang. The words burned on our tongues and spewed forth in showers of light. Rivers, spangles, shock waves of light. They danced. They undulated. Figures appeared, creatures of our own imagination: the vast white form of a star's face, kind and grinning; the cool blue of an arm, flexed, bent, stirring toward a smash against the skin of a monstrous drum; the legs of a seraph, glowing and white with righteousness; the leaping edge of dawn over the mountains like a tongue lapping at milk.

And then Him. A world, a universe danced out between the chords. We watched even as our phrases brought forth cool blue orbs huge as galaxies that spun, swayed, then exploded in showers that reflected the face of some terrible being who would exist only a moment. But in that moment that being would experience the breath of eternity.

I laughed. I cried. The galvanizing beauty of it all filled me. Waves of melody, harmony, lystrony, and kemany poured over us like the River flowing from the Tor of Heaven. Music and light shimmered up into the air above us, sizzling, crackling bolts of orange, green, turquoise, and crimson. Words splotched across the sky in iridescent bursts. The mountain of God quaked, and the temple that filled it echoed with the resonances of our composition. The stones of fire themselves exploded upward and over, down and around till all of Kyrie's creation moved to dazzle the melody that pierced our hearts. Our souls shook with delight! Even Zarsill fell back, his mouth agape with wonder. But he kept his station, leaned toward us, beckoned, and called us to greater heights.

Lucifer cried, "Vinns, rise. Higher. Higher. Harpistrers, hold the strain. Feed it out. Let it ride. Crukes, smash your booms in unison till the mountains break! Ah, it is beautiful!"

How long we played, I cannot know. The music filled and throbbed till we became musical renditions of ecstasy itself. Only after the climax when we sat exhausted, beaded with bulbs of light and shaking our heads with wonder, did we stop and Kyrie rise.

"Magnificent," He exclaimed. "Beyond words. Beyond all anticipation. A marvel. You have done all things well!"

We basked in His heat like children before a roaring fire.

Zarsill bowed. We stood. Zarsill gestured toward us, and we bowed again.

Yannonay.

Lazona.

Truly.

Lucifer fluttered above, enraptured, but always proclaiming the grand truth we all knew deep in our souls, "Holy, HOLY, **HOLY** is the Lord God Almighty, who was, and who is, and who is to come!"

We sat for hours, perhaps years, basking in the glow of that composition. And then Kyrie said, "A time of rest. Work at your lessons. There is further to go. We have not struck even the first bold letter of what you're capable of."

I went to my room aflame with will and determination. We would canter the stars themselves, I resolved. And someday I would compose. For Him. For all of us. One day, as Kyrie promised, I would enter the heights of the clouds and behold Him as He is, not just as He chose to appear. I burned toward that day.

That night, I made my first entry in my journal:

> *I am.*
>
> *Just that I can write these words is a marvel. I wonder if each of us tonight sits at a desk and composes what writhes and crackles within us.*
>
> *I am. He is. We are.*
>
> *We made music. We make music. We will make more.*
>
> *I am for the moment overcome with thanks.*
>
> *All is marvelous to the senses, quite beyond the power of language to describe. This evening we sang one new song together on the mount as the stars coursed their rolls. I feel in my deepest parts it is very good, and I live in expectation of joy beyond comprehension.*
>
> *I am.*
>
> *I am. I am. I am. I am.*
>
> *I grow with each repetition of the syllable. His joy is my strength. I speed toward a greater more glorious day than I can ever now imagine.*

I look at these words now and wince. Just a little. Truly, I was a child. But the whole panoply was a wonder. Everything was. How astonishing that it was all snuffed so quickly and almost without remorse.

— 2

Tyree gave me the sobriquet "Aris the Amazed." He stood there in the throng that first day and said my near accidental waltz with the water printed the first smile on his lips. We met and embraced after the first concert. He played the Listrom, a wind instrument that cast out tendrils of sharp green light and formed mouths in the air speaking the bold words of praise that our music accented. I would soon discover he was a quick learner, would soon ascend to the highest among his rank, the Fifth Quarm. When we embraced that first day, he batted my shoulder and said, "We are going to be friends."

"How do you know that?" I said, not knowing what else to answer.

"It's written in the clouds."

I stared at him, then guffawed. "You think so?" I looked up at the clouds crowning the heavens with a misty whiteness and added, "I don't see anything written up there."

"That's true," he said, shielding his eyes in the shekinah light. "But if you look hard you can imagine it. See. 'Aris the Amazed' and 'Tyree the Typical' are friends."

I laughed. I had to admit I liked him. "Tyree the Typical?"

"Yes, that's what they all say about me. When I do something wrong or foolish or otherwise non-heavenly they just say, 'Typical.' So I've gotten that nickname sort of."

"You just made that up."

He blushed slightly. "Just making it all up as we go along."

I grinned. "All right. We'll be friends."

He immediately clapped me on the back. I sensed there was a healthy insecurity to his personality that made him at once bold and then, in a sudden reversal, shy and fearful he'd gone too far. The classic put-his-foot-in-his-mouth kind of angel was not too common, I supposed, but they were there. I couldn't help but like him.

He was tall, with a forehead like granite, sharply square features, ebony eyes, a fall of black hair with a liquid glimmer that gave it a sheen. Why he singled me out, I suppose neither of us quite knew.

It was Tyree who first showed me the white stone. He took me that afternoon through the Glade of Sunder, and we passed from there to one of the Mountains of Hered. We sank through the surface and deep into its core. There, burning with a whitish flame, stood the flower, a diamond white spray of tendrils, smaller than my fingernail. We stared at it a moment, and then Tyree said, "It is the soul of the mountain."

I had already heard of souls. They were the living elements of material things, the part that knew Kyrie. I had never seen one, not this close.

The bud stretched and breathed in the still light of the center of the mountain. It was its own light. Behind me, there was a creaking noise, then the sound of steps. Tyree straightened up beside me. "He's coming," he whispered.

I waited in silence. Moments later, a tiny figure not much higher than the flower itself appeared. He stood next to the bud. He was armed with a sword and dagger, but also carried a hoe and a small shovel. He tipped his helmet to us, then loosened the soil around the flower with the hoe.

Tyree bent on one knee and stooped over to speak with him. I knelt down beside Tyree.

"You are Sember?" Tyree said.

"I am," the tiny but august angel answered. He was clothed in a blue tunic. His thin golden band crown sparkled in the light. He bore a firm, unstudied look. I knew of such tiny angels, of course, but this was also a first-time experience for me.

"It's beautiful," Tyree commented, motioning to the flower. Sember said nothing.

I drew closer, bent to sniff the fragrant petals. It was surrounded by a mossy loam, nestled as it was in the center of the small pile. It had no stem.

"So you guard the flower?" Tyree said to Sember.

He nodded. "Aye. And water it, tend it, nurture it."

"You are the husband-angel?"

"Aye. Many others there be among us."

"At the heart of each mountain?"

"Aye." Sember's red hair gleamed in the slight light. I strained to see around me. The roof of the mountain hung over us like a vast silent globe. I looked up and could feel the mountain breathing around me. With each inhalation, the flower gleamed brightly, and with each exhalation, the light aroma waned, as if drawing back into the petals. It calmed me with a settled, firm feeling of joy that, like the earth, felt fixed and secure in place.

"It's very old," Tyree said. "They were created even before we were. They hold the secret names. Each contains one. When the flower is removed from the mountain, the mountain becomes one with Kyrie, and the flower becomes brittle. It then closes upon itself and hardens. It becomes a white stone."

"White stone? The white stone?"

"The one."

We all knew about the white stone, though I did not know where they came from. And I had never seen one. I did not think any of us had ever seen one, and I was certain no one ever held one, for by it he would have wielded tremendous power and influence over all creation.

On each stone was written a name, one of Kyrie's secret names which no one knows. When Kyrie gave someone the stone, that name became known to him alone. He could use that name to call on Kyrie, or speak in the stead of Kyrie, or even act on Kyrie's behalf without having to consult with Him beforehand. It was a sacred trust.

"So Sember here is guarding one of the great relics of all time," Tyree said.

"A mountain has to die to make one, though," I said.

"The mountain doesn't die. It simply hardens, never moves again."

"What good is that?"

Sember looked up at us. "It's a symbol," he said.

We both looked at him. I regarded the tiny angel, thinking he would make an awesome enemy despite his size.

"It is a symbol, as are all other of Kyrie's works."

Tyree lay his hand on the ground and said, "Step onto my hand so we can speak face to face." Sember stepped onto his palm. Then Tyree lifted him up.

"Kyrie speaks and acts in symbols," Sember said, "so that nothing is lost. Nothing is an end in itself. We see it all about us. I have had much time thinking about the symbolism of this lone flower here at the heart of this huge mountain, that I can assure ye."

"And what have you learned?"

"Nothing is lost. All is conserved. Nothing is gained that can be lost. Nothing can be lost that will not one day be found. Nothing can be found that will not change the finder. Creation is easy, but eternal creation is manifestly difficult. All flows together. All is one, and yet nothing is alone. We are part of Kyrie, and yet Kyrie is above and beyond all of us. Kyrie gives, but what He gives we have the opportunity to give back. We . . ."

"You speak in circles!" Tyree cried. But he grinned at me and said, "The second friend."

I smiled and Sember laughed. "Aye."

Tyree grinned. "And what would happen if I plucked up this little gem and made it my own?"

"You would have me to wrestle with," Sember said. "I should think that would be pause enough."

"Yes, I think it would."

Tyree set him down, and I felt the mountain moving and us moving with it.

"Where is the mountain going?" I asked, regarding our new friend with admiration and kinship.

"To drink," Sember said. "At the River."

"Of course." There was a reverence as both of us responded to Sember's words. There was only one river in Heaven. It proceeded from Kyrie's throne and wound all through the land, sending its tributaries all through the Outer Reaches and elsewhere. To drink its liquid refreshment was life itself.

The mountain rolled and surged underneath us. Tyree said, "I guess we should just enjoy the ride."

"Definitely."

Sember said, "Would you like me to show you what else we have down here?" His R's were spoken with a burr, and as he walked off, I noticed his straight up and down, all-business stride, and I knew he would not flinch in the face of danger, however precipitous. He led us to what he called "the teeth of the mountain," high, shimmering white cliffs that studded the perimeter of one of the inner pools where mists rose and strange new fragrances titillated my senses. He then took us to the "skin" where upon inspection we could see the first spores of fluff that broke into down on the outer surface.

Finally, we stood on the outside lip of the mountain and watched as it drew in great draughts of the river. There were no lips as I normally thought of lips; the mountain merely slid up to the edge of the riverbank and drank. Then, as if charged with an inner excitement, the great beast flowed away, gathering speed, giving us a few gentle bucks on the way. The earth parted before it and closed behind it like water, and I felt around and below me an inner hum like singing. Then it struck me: the mountain was singing one of the very hymns that Kyrie had composed and we had played on the Mount that morning.

I looked at Tyree, and he raised his eyebrows with recognition. "A regular dance tune," he said.

Sember laughed. "Aye, it's an anthem Kyrie has taught them. They sing it constantly now. I sometimes find myself as lost in the tune as I am in my work." He leaned on his hoe and grinned. "Aye, he's happy," Sember said. "I love to see that."

I felt the soil slither under me.

"He's playing now," Sember said.

Almost losing our balance, Sember led us back down into the bowels of the mountain. When we reached the white bud and stood around it one more time, I noticed that its light seemed to dance and spiral in response to the humming undertow that had gripped us.

Moments later, we passed through the outer skin of the mountain and then stood on it. Looking over the gathered mountains, many of them drinking at the River, I thought of the great peace of that flower at the heart of a formidable giant like this mountain.

"I wonder how many of those flowers there are," I said.

"Hundreds, thousands, billions," Tyree answered. "But there is only one white one. Every one is its own unique color."

He looked off toward the mountain and said, "What I would give to gain one of those. Great power it holds, perhaps greater than any other."

"They are not for us to own!"

"But it's all right to dream about, isn't it?" He could obviously see my concern and added, "Don't worry. I'm not going to steal it. It just marvels me, that's all." He looked off over the vast reaches of the mountains and the plain before us. He placed his arm on my shoulder. "Look at it, Aris. It is Heaven, and it is ours and we are all one and nothing can take it away."

I noticed a tear in his eye as he spoke, and I said, "You weep."

"It's just so beautiful." He wiped away the tear. "Come, let's fly. Let's fly faster than the light itself."

In a moment, we were in the air, launched straight toward the Great City and moving as fast as thought itself.

3

Later that evening as Tyree and I walked along the pleasant paths of the city, exchanging thoughts, marveling at our performance and Kyrie's unpretentious enchantment, we naturally edged around to the subject of the Cherubim, notably Lucifer.

"What exactly does he do?" I asked Tyree, as if he should know everything I didn't. The experience with the white stone, though, had taught me something.

"He proclaims Kyrie's plan and person. Instruction, to some degree. He will teach us the canons of our kind, illumine the glories of Kyrie's character, and reveal the deep things of God. Not something I'd like to be entrusted with."

"He obviously takes it seriously. All those eyes."

"With which he beholds the infinite grandeurs of his Master." Tyree grinned at me blithely. "I'm sure he misses nothing."

"He gave me quite a scare."

"You were only three seconds into your journey." Tyree laughed. "You should have seen some others before you. Fright, astonishment, awe, terror—all those emotions coursed their eyes and visages. I found it quite an entertainment, and I wonder what others will say of me. I just stood there, my jaw open, unable to speak."

"Tyree the Tongue-tied, perhaps?"

He chuckled. "No, I don't think so."

"And the One next to Kyrie?"

"The Son?"

"Yes. Who is He?"

"No one seems sure. He is very quiet."

"Is He one of us?"

"Kyrie has not said. I know one thing: some will not like Him getting a great deal of acclaim when He does so little."

"Oh, I'm sure all will receive their just acclaim." I was always one to put a balancing touch on every statement.

"Except you," Tyree said. "You can be sure if they leave one out, it'll always be you."

I glanced at him quizzically, and he laughed. "Just joking." We walked through the Great City, talking, laughing, tasting here and there one of the delectable products of heaven: the pastries of Quolm, the fruits of the Climmer, Degate, Plumino, and Vias trees, the sweets of the Street Salom.

"*Lucifer* means 'light-bearer,'" I commented to Tyree as we came back to the subject.

"He reflects and refracts God's glory," Tyree answered—he was looking up at something in one of the clouds. "He bears the luminous light of Kyrie's wisdom, love, justice, and righteousness like a lone sentinel on a high hill. He is to exposit it all to us over time. In fact, I understand that he knows things about Kyrie that none of us will ever comprehend. Though that is only a rumor I have heard discussed. Lucifer is the highest and . . . Oh, and here is another friend, Rune."

Tyree called over a very tall, angular Archon with a mane of blonde hair, sparkling green eyes, and a haunting look of calm solemnity. I knew immediately he was an angel like us, but of one of the higher Quarms. I decided to speak only when spoken to. Tyree said when he came near, "Break out of your meditations and give Aris the Amazed your warmest embrace."

Rune gave me a hard, friendly grip with a twitch of a smile on his face. He carried a Cruke, a tympanic instrument that produced a muted rhythm to the music. It was not a drum as such, as you did not beat upon it with sticks but rubbed it with your fingers in a circular motion. The effect was an emotional incandescence of intense longing not unlike the cry of a desperately hungry doe or kitten. A single pass on the instrument and one might be smitten with tears of passion or enkindled with a strange leaping desire to course the whole of Heaven in one magnificent burst of energy.

Rune said to Tyree after embracing me, "I see you have already tampered with his name. What's next—his visage?"

"No, Kyrie has already given him a fine one," Tyree said. "Though I wager I'd do something about that nose!"

It was true. I did have a rather large nose, but Tyree added, "Actually, I wouldn't mind exchanging noses. But of course, then I'd have to be a Vias Tea Pot, which this late in the day I don't think I'd enjoy."

We all laughed and continued down the path as it wound in and out among buildings. We passed through several parks and spent time ogling displayed pieces of art of all kinds that had already been done on that very first day. Tyree then invited us to his quarters.

Like most angelic quarters, Tyree's featured marvelous translucent barriers that conveyed the light of Kyrie while providing a deep, unbreachable, and unequivocal privacy. There were various articles of furniture—a desk, chairs, shelves with a small library, balconies opening onto vistas of the parks below, a garden with many of Heaven's most wonderful plants—the Vias Tree, a Climmer, Gomerels, Balsirils, Dergens, Foorenoos, the succulent Avises, and many others. All this was given and created that first day along with us, and the knowledge of it was infused within us so that it was as if we'd been there for centuries, even though the first day of Heaven had not yet passed.

Rune and I took our seats, and we each examined the others' instruments, offering to play on them parts of the piece we had played earlier. Then we moved on to the more momentous discussion of what we would do with the rest of our day.

"Let's take a jaunt," Tyree offered when Rune finished his rendition on his Cruke. "The Outer Reaches, perhaps? Or the Stillnesses? What is your preference?"

"Not me," Rune said, "I need to adjust to this already overstimulating assault on the senses."

I said, "And I think we should stay where we are and practice for tomorrow's performance."

Tyree nodded resignedly. "I see I have two very serious brethren on my hands. Well, so be it. A cup of Coller then?"

Coller was a kind of tea, something we frequently drank not because we were thirsty but because it was one more way to stimulate worship and an appreciation of Kyrie.

Rune stood and walked over to the library. I knew what would be there: the books of our law, atlases, dictionaries for the many tongues of our worship, lexicons, many of the stories that had already been written that very day. Each day would see a complete change in this respect with the addition of new books that we were expected to consume in our own time, journals, craft and artisan manuals—it was really quite amazing the way it worked in Heaven, with each library stocked with new pieces daily.

Tyree walked off to prepare several cups of Coller while Rune and I examined books in the library, then headed out to the balcony. As we watched the throngs pass through the golden streets, I leaned over the railing and I told him about the white stone.

"I have heard of it," he said. "I understand we are soon to dedicate one at the Temple."

He was a picture of deep thought standing on the balcony ledge holding his chin in his hands. He was one whose meditations would always seem far higher than my own. I sensed that in the coming days I would learn much from him.

"Do you have a question for Him?" I asked.

"A question?"

"When we meet on the Mount of the Assembly."

He nodded reflectively. "Many. Though I would not go to Him—or Lucifer, for that matter—with nonsense."

I gazed at him quizzically. Suddenly, I realized with a vague crackle of fear that what he said was true. The Mount was for questions and talk, teaching and discussions. But I certainly wouldn't want to raise an issue that others thought to be nonsense, even though I wasn't sure what would be defined that way. I said, "What would be nonsense?"

"Anything they deem as such." He regarded me gravely. "I suppose we don't know what nonsense is till it leaps out into the light. So it very well could be out of your mouth before you've had a chance to realize the mistake you've made!"

"You mean we'll never know what real nonsense is till we speak it?"

"Precisely."

"But how can we hope to learn anything if we're afraid to speak what's in our minds?"

"You saw him," Rune said with a sudden grim fervor that amazed me. "Lucifer, I mean. I realize we're all Kyrie's special creations and that this is all new and so on, but I don't think Lucifer is one who will abide fools."

"Kyrie didn't create any of us as fools, though, surely!" I was astonished at his candor.

"Kyrie can create us any way He likes," Rune said.

I stared at him. He went on, "We are here for His pleasure. And whatever pleases Him is surely what we are. If He likes fools, then certainly He has created a few to give Him pleasure. You, or I, or Tyree, or any one of us could be the cause of the laughter of Heaven, and we'd have no recourse but to accept it."

I said, trying to be a bit more lighthearted, "Rune, you're getting a bit deep here. And anyway, if He created us that way, wouldn't we take joy in being fools? Wouldn't that be our purpose and our destiny, and therefore a source of complete satisfaction and fulfillment?"

Rune leaned over the railing and looked down below. Tyree's rooms were high in the air and as I leaned out too, I whistled. "It's a good thing we can fly."

"Yes," Rune said, pursing his lips thoughtfully. "But I hope that He has not created me such."

"As what?"

"A fool." He turned to regard Tyree coming through the doorway to the balcony. I wondered if he already thought I was one. I liked his serious air, but I thought he might be a little too calculating for my taste.

"Coller tea for everyone," Tyree said. I took the cup gladly and sipped at it. It was my first taste of the elixir, and a memorable one. Immediately, my mind was seized with pleasant thoughts—in contrast to what we had just been discussing.

Rune also sipped at his tea, but his face took on no readable expression. I said nothing while all three of us drank.

Tyree said, "So what were you discussing?"

I didn't answer, but Rune said, "Our terror that we might find ourselves the object of Kyrie's jest."

Tyree's eyebrows wrinkled with consternation and he turned to me. "Translation?"

"Rune hopes he is not destined to be a fool for the pleasure of Kyrie, Lucifer, and the rest of us."

Tyree grinned immediately, a keen look splaying across his face. "Rune a fool? Impossible! It would be easier to believe that Aris here was a seraph in disguise than that! And I don't think any of us think he is a seraph!"

I smiled.

Tyree grinned again, but Rune remained sober and direct. "You do not know whereof you speak," he said.

Tyree immediately rejoined, "Are you unhappy with your position?"

I watched eagerly to see what Rune would say. He simply shook his head. "I think we need to discuss another subject."

"Rune the Reluctant," Tyree suddenly said. "It fits, doesn't it, Aris?"

I looked at my two new friends, then put down my Coller with a tinkle of cup and saucer. "I think you've given out enough nicknames for one day."

"Yes," Tyree said, looking at Rune with bright, pleased eyes. "I've got to come up with something better."

We talked on the balcony for awhile. When Rune finished his tea and set it down, he said, "Now to practice."

We picked up our instruments and began to play. The song hallowed the room with a beauty that was indescribable yet something so palpable that I found my heart beating in precise unison to the tune. Soon we began to sing.

And a moment later I heard it. The whole city, all of us, our voices trimming the air above us, joined. We were one. The music filled us, and suddenly we knew we were no longer practicing but making the music of Heaven. We played and sang and the song spiraled out over the city till it glowed with a radiance as if it in itself had become form, body, and mind. Our hearts and souls were carried up, and from each room the music rose till all of Heaven chorused together.

At that moment, I wondered what Kyrie must be thinking. I couldn't imagine. But I knew He was pleased. Very pleased.

4

The Mount of the Assembly is located in the recesses of the north. That is, Heaven, being north, west, south, and east, stretching for seemingly infinite distances in all those directions, has many specific mapped areas that we travel in. The far north—unlike yours, which is covered with ice, a land of mountains of ice and snow—is replete with gigantic mammoth projections through the bluva of Heaven that reach high into the sky lit by the holy shekinah light of Kyrie. In the daytime, the mountains jut into the sky like great tents filled with spices and delicacies. They invite you every moment to come, look, see, live. Every angel enjoys flying or walking among their granitic enchanted faces, finding treasures, jewels, fruits, streams, and elixirs too numerous to recount.

We met on the Mount, the highest peak of those mountains—it soared many billions of feet into space and would make your Everest look like a day-old anthill in comparison—each day for worship, songs, speeches, discussions, and so on. And what happened that first day was nothing less than another marvel in a day of marvels.

Lucifer gathered us. We flew to our places—those who could not fly climbed on the backs of others who did. The teeming masses of Heaven assembled in all our robust finery. It was an explosion of color, costumery, and heady visages. Seraphs mingled with the lowest among us. Cherubim flapped their wings and nestled down on the mountain grass as if this was nothing more than an afternoon picnic. There were no assigned places, as there were in the Temple. It was first come, first served. And yet all were deferential.

"Would you like to sit here? I can make way."

"No, I'll take a seat over there."

"But surely, if you prefer . . . "

We were a world of good manners, good spirits, and good makers of splendor and song. We sat before our Master, all of us gathered on the sides of the Mount, stretching to the very top. Kyrie, the Son, Lucifer, and their entourage stood at the bottom in the combed valley of pale beeches, evergreens, and lofty oaks. Kyrie's face shone with an obvious glad sense of accomplishment. His first words were, "It is very good, my children. Very good indeed." And we all felt a deep sense of amazement and pure undistilled rhapsody.

Lucifer took up his station before us, all of his eyes like gentle but industrious fingers wordlessly complimenting and encouraging us. His four faces shone, and his hands were flywheels of expression. Before he even spoke, we were captivated, rooted to the mountain as hairs upon a stallion's back.

"Today we have begun," he cried, his wings lifted in jubilant epitome to our own rising acclaim.

A cheer rose up from our numbers. "Alleluia! Praise Kyrie. Alleluia in the highest!"

Once we settled down, Lucifer cried, "Today Kyrie has begun the grand adventure. And we are His champions."

Another cheer went up and could not be stalled for many minutes. But Lucifer, himself basking in the wonder of it all, spoke on. "There is much to do, peaks to climb, heraldries of music that none of us yet knows is possible. But we will make it so!"

More cheers erupted, and it seemed that this meeting would never end for the cheering. But why should it have been stopped? We were a happy, lively, rollicksome band, the crown of creation, Kyrie's heart and desire.

Lucifer cried again, "We stand on the beginning edge of forever. And surely this will never end. Let us press on toward the mark set for us by Kyrie at each of our separate moments of creation, that mark which said: Holy, Holy, Holy is the Lord of hosts. Heaven is full of His glory. And we will achieve it!"

My own eyes teared at the words. Tyree said to me, "I told you Lucifer was one to be reckoned with."

But Rune added, "Just don't let him ask me to say something!"

I smiled. Our camaraderie was sealed. We stood poised at the edge of eternity, already launched and speeding toward our destiny with sure and certain strides. We would never be stopped. We would never stop!

There were other speeches that evening. We dined on the resplendent seven brooks of the Mount, each a stream of purest living water and each a flavor that invoked the profoundest worship. We walked among the valleys and the glades and then came back for more speeches, more drinking, and more of Kyrie, Lucifer, and all. It was wondrous elation, and I wished it never to end.

But it did and we sped back to our cities, and there we celebrated again. The streets danced with the cheering and friendship of our multitudes. I felt in my deepest parts that surely nothing could veer us from our mark.

And yet, even then, I sensed something wrong. An undertow. The slightest of impressions.

And Tyree's comments about the white stone. Would he—or anyone—try to steal such a thing? It seemed incomprehensible to me. Heaven was just created. We were all new. And perfect.

Yet the question grated on my heart, spawned by Rune's curious comments: could I be destined for something Kyrie knew and planned, but which I would loathe with every fiber of my being?

For we were at His mercy. Even then I knew that. I could feel it in the air and in those eyes that Lucifer kept fixed on each of us.

I told myself it was nothing. Yet from the first day, the very first, there was this tiny corrosive dripping in the back of the mind. I wouldn't find out for many days how serious it was. But it was there, from the beginning. Perhaps a flaw of creation. No, that couldn't be. Something more. Something I still struggle to understand.

5

The next concert seemed to be going well, until Zarsill started in on a particularly difficult passage, one that most of us struggled with the evening before to perfect. There was a sudden flutter of wings around Kyrie's throne, and Lucifer rose up before us. He said, "Keep practicing, champions, you will soon compose."

Zarsill, the under conductor, said, "It is not correct." He was a thin, slim Hauker with sharp blue eyes and an angular look. Very intelligent. He had been the only one to conduct us in the temple so far.

"I realize that," Lucifer said. "They're trying. Let them please try it again. Have patience, conductor. All good things do not come to pass in a moment."

We went back over the portion, but Zarsill was not satisfied. "It is not correct. Kyrie requires perfection."

Lucifer nodded and bid him go on. But I detected some strain between Lucifer and Zarsill. After all, Zarsill was being hard, unnecessarily. It was a difficult piece. I only hoped no one would make mention of my mistakes, a few hums here and there where I was yet unsure of the rhythm and the accentuation.

Zarsill tapped his signet ring and we came to attention. "Kyrie requires perfection," he said. "We must offer to Him only the best, most fragrant of our worship. Now, begin."

Kyrie Himself sat unperturbed on His throne, the Son in quixotic silence next to Him. There was no indication from either that all was not well. Zarsill settled down and we played it again. There were many mistakes. It was a difficult section. No one claimed that it was correct.

"It is not correct," Zarsill cried again, throwing up his arms, this time a harsh edge to his voice. "We will keep at it until it is correct."

Suddenly, Zarsill focused on one of the angels sitting before me. He played Harpistrer like me and had been struggling, quite visibly. His name was Marras. Zarsill pointed to him.

"You are missing your cue repeatedly, Marras. You must do better."

Then his eyes grazed over the panoply, millions of us. How he could select one or two like that was beyond me, but he did.

"Haffir!" he cried.

A lean, tall Kinderling stood. "I am trying, Zarsill."

"Not trying hard enough." Zarsill pounded his foot on the ground. "We will do better. Now!"

"Of course, sire," Haffir said.

I could see he was frightened. Zarsill was a dominating, potent presence, a real martinet. The weight of his disapproval crackled the air with tension. Both Marras and Haffir were flustered and unsure of what to do.

"Play it again, each of you," Zarsill intoned. "Alone."

Marras went first. His notes rang true in the first few bars, but after that he was clumsy, as if his ear had gone deaf. He was obviously unprepared. My arms shook with the anxiety of what was happening.

"Again!" Zarsill cried when Marras was finished. "This is despicable."

"I have not had time," Marras wailed.

Zarsill bore in, leaning over the podium, his mane of white hair like a patch of weeds, his eyes afire. "You have had time enough!"

Marras played again, but his fingers trembled so badly it was worse. I swallowed, sinking down in my seat, hoping Zarsill hadn't noticed my own mistakes.

"Argghhh!" Zarsill cried with gnashing teeth when Marras was finished. He turned to Haffir, and the tall Kinderling performed just as poorly. Zarsill looked apoplectic.

"All of you!" he cried. "All at once. Now!"

Vinnists, Crukers, and those in the Harpistrer section struggled to get the notes right. The air filled with smoke and incense, spirals wisping off in one direction or another, nothing under control.

"Sire, we need time!" Marras suddenly exclaimed. As Zarsill expostulated, Lucifer's many eyes seemed to rest on different members of the orchestra; one set focused on me and I could feel the pulsation of their sobering inner consciousness. But it was a look of affection and kindness and I felt drawn to it.

"Kyrie demands perfection!" Zarsill shouted suddenly.

It was then that Lucifer rose before us. His form like a mountain, His faces granitic, there was sudden and complete silence. "Conductor, peace!" Lucifer said, low and credible. Zarsill turned, his face inflamed. But he didn't speak.

"This is not a place or time to embarrass individuals," Lucifer said to all of us. "We will be patient with one another." He did not seem to be looking at Zarsill. He went on, "Take time to practice. It is a difficult piece. There is no reason to rush things. To be sure, Kyrie requires perfection, but perfection does not come without work and effort. Do not use Kyrie's desire for perfection against yourselves. It is meant to be a goal, not a goad or a knife at your throat!"

The great Cherub fluttered back down to his position over Kyrie, and we went on to a second piece. His wings fluttered up every now and then, but he said no more. I wondered in my heart if this difference between Zarsill and Lucifer boded well. Lucifer was wise, perfect in every socket, no one could compare to him. He had not been abrupt or demanding, like Zarsill.

It was a small matter. But after that many praised Lucifer for his wisdom and his gentility. I heard several of our number say, "He should be the conductor, not Zarsill."

And others: "He is very wise. I will listen to him next time."

I thought about these things and wondered. What did it all mean? Surely, Kyrie would not allow there to be a rift between Zarsill and Lucifer. But it appeared that He would say nothing.

Then came our next practice. It was much the same. More of Zarsill's harshness. Another example of Lucifer's patience and goodness. At the end, Kyrie stood. He towered over us, his robe unfurled like a great banner, shining like molten metal, silver and gold and platinum. Spangles of light shimmered from his brows and lips. The matchless glow radiated off Lucifer, and there was a moment when I bowed in worship at the majesty of Kyrie's countenance. Pinwheels of light refracted off each of Lucifer's gems, and he appeared even more majestic than Kyrie. But then Kyrie spoke, and His voice, like the music at the heart of a mountain, bent us in toward His love and His compassion.

"It is not good that brothers be parted by words," He said. "I would that you would all agree and that your hearts be knit as one. Do not let passion overtake you. There is much time. I desire perfection, but not at the expense of dignity and respect for one another. There will be no more altercations.

Zarsill, please understand. You are now under Lucifer's authority. Play well. But do not play to the misfortune of another."

We returned to our quarters to work on the piece, but when I reached my place, Tyree and Rune, my two friends, stood there in the light, waiting. Tyree clapped me on the back. "It was only the grace of Kyrie that kept me from being selected today. And Rune, too. So what was it that kept you? I heard those little slips."

"They weren't little slips," I said. "They were rather large ones, I thought. Real blooming bruisers!"

"Ah, a truly humble member of the Harpistrer section," Tyree said, grinning and leaning on his Listrom. I hoped he would not give it so much weight that its thin neck would snap.

"I was trembling," I finally confessed.

"So were we all," Tyree said, glanced at Rune, then shot me his winning smile.

We all entered my room. It was spare, with a desk, a couch, some chairs, a small library. Not as beautiful as some, but I needed little. My heart was in my music and I did not care for lavish quarters. I suppose most of us didn't, either, or there would have been more.

Not that Kyrie did not provide us with beatific, worthy surroundings. Any one of our rooms would put an earthly mansion to shame. The whole structure consisted of light, precious gems, translucent silver and gold, an "eye-full" to say the least. It appeared like burnished bronze in the shekinah light shining from Kyrie throughout our land, and to look upon even the ignoblest of my treasures would have spirited your own eyes from your head. But for each of us, our quarters were not a place to sleep or rest as such, they were simply a place where we could be private, practice our music or hone our crafts, if we were craftsangels, and meditate on the glories of creation.

We sat and talked late into the evening of music and crafts, instruments, and the pleasures of Heaven. It seemed that we could never get enough of it, back then.

— 6

Our practices began going well after that, until there was a problem among the Crukers in which the instruments seemed to be making a whining noise as they rubbed their fingers along the surface. The Cruke was known for its ability to fan a melody with a subterranean blend of mewing that gave a heart-wrenching flavor to certain pieces. The whine disrupted the music so that it lost its eerie-sounding mew and was replaced with a mind-numbing squeak not unlike a fingernail on a modern chalkboard. It was disconcerting to say the least.

There were only three musicians with the problem, but it won them no little jibing and jesting from their fellows, and some harsh words from Zarsill.

When they were called up to the front to have their instruments inspected, a great silence came over us. One of the Kinderlings, who was named Tallis, appeared embarrassed and fearful by this breach of confidence. He apologized profusely, but Zarsill simply took his instrument and scrutinized it in the light.

"Looks right," he said, tapping its surface and moving his own hand in the circular motion that produced the mewing sound. "Have you been cleaning it properly?"

All three of them nodded their heads.

"Anything unusual about where you keep it?"

"Always in its place on the wall," all three of them answered promptly.

As Zarsill moved his fingers over all three of the instruments, they each made a mewing sound perfectly in tune. There was obviously nothing wrong. He sent them back to their seats. Then he motioned for us to begin again, and we slipped into the piece effortlessly. All went well until the Crukers sounded up again. And there was that tawdry little scritch! It was deplorable.

Zarsill called them up again. His exasperation was obvious. Nothing would reveal the answer to the mystery. Zarsill looked at their tunics, the way they sat, how the instrument lay on their laps. He even made them clean their fingernails.

None of these measures corrected the problem. When they were in front, they played well. When they went back to their places, the horrid screak resounded till it was as if you heard nothing else.

The whole lot of us were getting rather unnerved about this. It was then that Lucifer stepped in. The instruments were brought to him, and after eyeing both them and the musicians, he asked to see their hands. All of his eyes scrutinizing the small hands of the three culprits, he said immediately, "Have you drunk from the River today?"

All three of them had. Lucifer looked again at their hands and said, "Do you drink by cupping your hands?"

"Yes," all three chorused back.

Lucifer said suddenly, "That explains it. They are Kinderlings, who have very white, porcelained hands. With the drinking from the River, their hands were cleaned and polished to a mirror sheen. The hands reflect the light of Kyrie's presence, and on the especially clean hands of a Kinderling it acts much as a chisel acts on stone. It touches the surface of the Cruke at the same time the hands do and produces the squeak."

"Then why doesn't that happen when they're up here?" Zarsill asked, obviously as nonplussed as the rest of us.

"Because you had your back to Kyrie when you did it, and you do not have the same hands," Lucifer said. "And because when they took the instruments back, they sat in your shadow."

"But what should we do?" the Kinderling named Tallis asked.

"Rub your hands on the grass by the River when you are done drinking," Lucifer said, almost chuckling to himself. "And turn your chairs slightly out of the direct flow of Kyrie's light."

It worked. It was a simple problem, really. But no one saw the answer except Lucifer. It was marvelous.

The experience, though, that cemented Lucifer's reputation in the eyes of many was the difficulty about seating arrangements, differences between members, and rankings. Though we were all divided into Quarms, with leaders of each Quarm, there were literally billions who did not know how we were to relate to one another, settle arguments, order ourselves in assembly, and so on. Kyrie infused us with the knowledge of courtesy, kindness, compassion, and goodness. Few truly turned disruptive in any sense. But it all came up one day when several in the Listrom section became confused about seating. Everyone started just taking it as it came. But naturally certain seats became favored over others and there were disputes.

Two angels, one named Vara and a second named Ellicance, argued over a seat. It was not a vicious thing, just a mild difference of opinion. As others became involved, with one saying, "Ellicance was seated here yesterday next to me," and another, "You are incorrect about that. He was over here," it got to be quite a matter.

Zarsill almost lost all patience and cried, "Just sit anywhere." But there were only so many seats and extras. Different persons tried to step in and settle the matter. Zarsill stood at the podium, tapping his baton impatiently, and Kyrie looked on, saying nothing. As the misery grew, Lucifer suddenly shot forward and hung over the crowd now involved in trying to settle the matter.

"What is the problem?" he asked, not defiantly or angrily, more a simple empathetic chuckle that such a thing could be a problem.

"I was sure I was seated here yesterday," Ellicance answered, and Vara replied, "And I am just as certain that it was I who sat there."

"This is not a thing to dispute over," Lucifer said, "but then we can understand the problem. Each of us has struggled to remember where our particular seats are, and in this mass, it is supremely difficult. I have a suggestion."

Lucifer outlined his solution to the problem: "We will divide you into sevens, seventies, seven hundreds, seven thousands, and seventy thousands, with different leaders in each grouping to solve problems, answer questions, give orders and directions, transmit plans of action, and so on. There will be a lieutenant over a seven. Within the seven there will be a peacemaker and arbitrator. There will also be an encourager, a royster, a variance, and a rick. Each one of these will have different duties within the seven to help you all agree and be one. You will elect those officials within your seven, and all will agree on the selections."

He then broke us down into the respective groupings. I, Rune, and Tyree were each in a different group of seven. I was elected a peacemaker, one who would settle all "matters of disagreement," as Lucifer put it.

The plan was brilliant. It worked beautifully.

As we spent the rest of that day embroiled in discussion and elections, a most wonderful sense of unity and commitment to one another came over us. Our camaraderie increased. A feeling of order and control lifted us. We had a sense of direction now, as if by organizing ourselves, goals, priorities, and real vision had materialized.

It was quite an achievement, and we owed it all to Lucifer. He (as well as Kyrie) seemed pleased with the whole procedure. It rooted us all deeper into the conviction that we truly were destined for glory and that problems could be solved with finesse, expedience, justice, and fairness.

It was at that time that Lucifer also began teaching us the great truths that Kyrie wanted us to understand and know about Himself and His creation. Lucifer spread his wings so widely they seemed to encompass us all, and we felt like a small intimate little group as he explained to us the concept of God's holiness.

"Kyrie is holy in His most basic character. It means that He is utterly separated unto good, righteousness, justice, and truth. There can never be a breach of this holiness. He is impeccable. His character is unbreakable. For as long as we exist—forever—He is bound to truth, righteousness, justice, and good. His holiness guards us against any whim, any sudden change, any new direction that would put us in jeopardy."

There were many lectures of this sort that left us exalting Lucifer in ways that might not have been wise. But who could help it? He was an excellent teacher, musician, and leader. None would deny it. He ended that particular talk with these words, "What is our purpose? To serve. But more than that. To know. To know and love Him who is gracious and Almighty, He who knows all and is in all, He who is ubiquitous and knows our thoughts before we even think them. Our purpose is to learn of Him and so to love Him all the more."

Lucifer encouraged us to take advantage of every good thing in creation and to meditate on its meaning and purpose. It was at that moment that Tyree said to me, "I should think we might like to go riding on the Dogs of Dallett. That will teach us something about real speed, if nothing else!"

I had heard of the dogs but knew little about them. But Tyree—now an encourager as I was a peacemaker—said that we could go immediately after the fellowship on the Mount. Rune joined us, and even as Lucifer continued speaking, we planned our journey to that forest where we would see one of Kyrie's most compelling creatures.

7

"It's quite an adventure, I hear," Tyree said to Rune and me. "They have races, you know."

We were soon flying over the city toward the Stillnesses in the south. It was not long until we dipped down and landed on pure green fields of grass. A herd of brown, marvelously muscled creatures grazed to our left, and Tyree immediately led us over to them.

"I've never ridden one myself. Someone told me about it. You know throughout the Reaches and Stillnesses there are fascinating herds and bands of these creatures. Each one offers a solid lesson in Kyrie's character and persona. So they're worth studying. But most of our brothers and sisters just like to ride them, or so I hear."

We ambled down, and Tyree immediately began talking to one of the herds-angels. The beasts were much larger than earthly dogs. They had two heads, both of them projecting from a single neck. Their jowls were red, and they panted in the light, slathering out their long crimson tongues and grabbing up tufts of grass with relish.

Tyree shambled over to us and said, "All arranged. Pick out your steed and we shall run them a good pace."

We strolled in among the creatures, touching one here and there on the back or head and looking all around for the best looking ones. They were all magnificent, with bright, frolicsome eyes and tautly knotted legs and shoulders as if speed and running was all they ever longed for. They were all obviously eager to give us a ride.

I half expected them to chirrup and talk to us, but they didn't. I quickly found my mount, a robustly muscled dog with thick shoulders and two wide wagging tails that lashed the air like serpent's breath. I caressed the beast's neck and shoulders and kneaded them a moment as if to make my seat more comfortable. Tyree and Rune continued wading in among the throng of dogs as if there were one and only one destined for each of them. When they each finally settled their respective selections, they led the dogs over to me and we all mounted by leaping up onto their backs.

Immediately, the dogs took off on a romp through the fields. I bumped along, my lower teeth clacking against my uppers, and kept up with the other two easily. I suspected Tyree was holding himself back, though, and I decided to give him a run for his wings, just to see what would happen.

The dogs bounded over the fields in long, stretched out leaps, barking as if nothing in existence paralleled the sheer exuberance of their running. I gripped the wad of fur at the back of my steed's neck and held on. The dogs' faster gaits were smooth, almost like a horse's in the canter and gallop stages. I leaned forward and whooped as we zoomed over a hill and rollicked down toward a leafy wood at the bottom.

"There are trails the dogs know," Tyree cried. "Hold on."

Moments later we shot inside the wood, steaming along like fevered sharks through water. The dogs checked, veered, angled, and swept along through the woods with leaves and branches tearing at my shoulders. It was marvelous, the wind in our faces like fondling fingers, cooling and tickling, the breath of the dogs coming in chuffs like a modern fire-powered locomotive. The dogs' feet barely touched the ground. We seemed almost airborne as they leaped—forty and fifty and sixty feet at a bound—and gamboled along like young greyhounds after a speedy, succulent rabbit.

We journeyed for miles, breaking in and out of the woodsy areas, flying over the fields with their feet padding the ground silently. The dogs knew the trails well, and ducked under branches low enough so that I could remain seated without having to bend at all. They did not tire, in fact, their energy only seemed to increase as we whizzed on.

In a few minutes, we caught another group of angels, breaknecking along as if there was nothing else in all the universe to do. We passed them with cries of "Alleluia" and "Praise Be!" Passing them, Tyree gathered Rune and me together and threw down the challenge: a race all the way back to the herd.

Rune didn't seem too eager for this, but I liked the idea. I smiled at Tyree's enthusiasm. Everything to him was new, alive, sparkling with revelation and passion. In a way, I wished I was like that.

Then Rune suddenly "Hallooed!" and bolted his dog forward and soon barrelled down the slope toward the woods. He was far out ahead of us before either of us had the wherewithal to follow. I grabbed a tuft of hair and urged my beast on. Instantly, he flattened out into a romp down the hill to the meadow and then into the woods. Tyree shouted out behind me and brought up the rear.

The dogs appeared evenly matched. We soon caught Rune in the woods, but couldn't pass because the trails were narrow. This time I had to duck and scrape by the large branches that hung over our path. Any moment I knew I'd be either skewered or bounced off onto the dirt trail like a misthrown ball. I held on, gasping and hunched over forward, like a jockey in the race of his life. Or a charioteer in the Roman games.

We jetted out of the woods and into the open range. Now was my chance to take the lead. Tyree yelled out behind us, and soon his beast's double-mouthed panting was right in my ears.

"I'm going to beat you all!" he cried.

I leaned forward and urged my dog onward. The leaps were even greater now, seventy to eighty feet at a crack. Rune was still ahead.

And then behind us we heard more shouts. In moments, a group of about ten other angels, sisters and brothers, galloped into view. They caught us and whisked by, laughing and shouting. At least half were maidens.

I called to Tyree, "We can't let them beat us, can we?"

"Of course not," he answered. "Let's show them what these dogs can really do."

As if suddenly propelled forward by mythical afterburners, the dogs turned on full power. Seconds later we caught the crowd, burning along like lit strings of dynamite. Another wood lay before us, and though there were several trails, we all headed to the one directly ahead. There was no way we could fit abreast, so everyone jostled for the lead to get in first.

Tyree ripped up the turf a few paces behind the leader, a grizzled, dark African with a wide smile. I was back in the pack and Rune just behind me. I tried to get an edge ahead of one of the maiden angels next to me, but she gave me a fierce, determined look, and I wasn't sure whether to push ahead or hold back.

The leader hit the trail just ahead of Tyree, and all of us angled in to slot ourselves in some kind of order. The maiden opposite me wouldn't budge. When we hit the trail, we collided. I fell off backwards into the trees, but the sister wasn't so lucky. She pitched backward into the head of the following dog, and then crunched to the ground underneath the feet of the others.

I cried out, "Stop, there's been an accident," and everyone pulled up. My tunic torn, I ran through the brush to the sister still on the path. She looked unconscious.

Tyree and the others gathered around. I pulled her head into my lap and held her. She had beautiful golden-brown hair and lovely tanned cheeks, crimson lips, and strong straight eyebrows. "Her name is Cere," one of the males said.

I said her name, and then Tyree pushed through the crowd with Rune and stooped down. "Is she all right?"

The sister opened her eyes then and looked around at the throng about her. "I fell off," she said.

I nodded. "Are you all right?"

"Is everyone here?" she asked suddenly, her eyes wide.

The group around me nodded their heads as one. "We all stopped the moment we thought you were hurt."

"So everyone's here?" she said again.

"Yes!" I said emphatically. "Are you . . . "

But she cried, "Good," sprang up, leaped onto her dog, and was off with a shout of glee. Everyone looked at everyone else, mystified, and then realizing what had happened, we all jumped aboard our respective steeds and sped after her.

Tyree shouted at me, "I'm going to catch her if it's the last thing I do."

"Me too," I yelled back. We lashed the air with our arms. It was all out, frenzied, delirious, maniacal steeplechasing.

Rune was right behind us. "Imagine that," he called, "the first pretense."

"I think she knows how to win," I called to him.

"It was brilliant," Rune answered. They were words not too common on Rune's lips, and I stifled a rolling laugh.

We all dashed through the next meadow and to the next wood, getting closer to Cere. It was flat out, manic bluster, and in the end we only caught her when she had reached the herd, dismounted, and sat on a stone, her legs crossed and a "What-are-you-so-slow-for?" look on her face.

When we all reached the end, everyone clamored for Cere to explain herself, but she just said, "I saw my opportunity to win, and I took it."

"Then you're not hurt?"

"A little bump on the shoulder, a knot on the head or so. Nothing dramatic."

After several rounds of hearty backslapping, we lolled on the grass watching the dogs. Cere overflowed with talk about the race and how she'd gotten the idea to play hurt—she said, "I knew I couldn't win otherwise, but I saw one of the dogs do it in their own races. One of the smaller ones. I was watching them on several occasions and saw him do it, so I thought I'd try it."

"You convinced me," Rune said. "Caught us completely off our heads."

"It was excellent," Tyree exclaimed. "I should have thought of it myself."

"But we wouldn't have stopped for you," I added.

Everyone had a good laugh.

8

Cere was a lithe, springy angel with large round eyes and full lips. She laughed readily and joined our threesome with unabashed enthusiasm as if we were all meant for one another.

With her we plunged into our learning with new zest. She seemed to have a hold on the meaning of things far better than any of us, and it was providential that we became friends. It also turned into an occasion to see Lucifer once more in action. As we talked, sucked on stalks of grass, and lazily observed the dogs at rest, Cere started us off with the comment, "They are so perfectly constructed."

"As are we all," I said, not trying to outdo her. I continued, "Just what do these dogs teach us of Kyrie's glory?"

No one answered right away, and we all four sat there thinking. "Why not ask Lucifer?" Cere suddenly said.

"Not me," Rune answered. "When I go I'm going to go with something incredible, not trivialities."

"This isn't trivial," Tyree answered. I was beginning to feel excited. "This is part of our purpose, isn't it?" Tyree said. "Surely Lucifer would not upbraid us for coming with a real question. And there always has to be a first time for everything."

Cere gazed at us with an impish look on her face. "I have spoken to him."

Instantly, we all leaned forward with rapt excitement. "What was it like? What happened?"

"It was . . . " She licked her lips and rolled her eyes upward as if savoring the experience. "Momentous. That's the word. Marvelous, perhaps. Indescribable!" She laughed, a tinkling, happy laugh. "It was wonderful. He is so kind and understanding and doesn't play like you're a dolt, and he knows all. He is the height of chivalry, and has a deft, eloquent tongue for illustrations and stories that rivet the truth in your mind! And he told me to come to him as often as I like."

"Then let's go," I said, feeling in some ways as if I was suggesting that we go tear down the Temple. Rune and Tyree looked at me skeptically, but Cere stood and held out her hands.

"Come. The best time to go is when you think of it. You needn't think twice. He wants us to come and talk. So let's do it."

My heart pounding within me, we all rose. I had never done this before, and I wasn't sure I wanted to after all. But Rune and Tyree were suddenly all for it.

Cere cried, "To the Temple?" ready to mount into the sky.

"To the Temple," Tyree answered.

In only minutes we alighted in one of the porticoes of the Temple. It was quiet. There was no concert going on, and little activity disturbed the silent corridors. Soon we walked into the Temple proper, where the altar of incense stood, and the mercy seat with the two cherubim hovering over it. Lucifer was speaking with several angels who had come in to worship. Kyrie was hidden by Lucifer's wings, but we knew He was there.

We bowed and stepped forward, our heads bent in respect and prayer.

A moment later, we stood before them, alone, an awe gripping me that I'd never felt before. Lucifer's eyes regarded us with a look of quiet confidence. "Sit," he said. "And make your request."

Incense rose in streams of smoke about us. We bowed low and Lucifer said again, "What do you seek from Kyrie?"

Cere said, "Your grace, we come with a question for Kyrie of how one of His creatures teaches of His glory. We were riding the Dogs of Dallett and wondered what exactly they teach, if anything."

Lucifer turned his attention to her, and all four sets of eyes leveled solemnly on her. At that moment, I had another chance to gain a truer picture of this august and powerful leader. He was robed in a cloak of rich and refractory jewels, each a burning orb distilling the light of Kyrie underneath and splitting it into an array of rainbowed beauty. His four faces were benign, a soft light emanating from each one like a huge glowing diamond. His eyes took you in so that you felt thralled in an ineffable joy too great to hold and you had to look away for fear of implosion. His wings ranged over us like a tent, and their feathers were serpentine, each carved of a resplendent multicolored jewel. Dragon feathers. Underneath were hands that lay open and extended, as if appealing to us to listen and agree and join the worship.

Lucifer, after a pause, said, "What they teach is the perfect meshing of form and function and the thrill of the chase, the brilliant muscular body of the beast himself and its eagerness to run and to run well. All of that shows Kyrie's character as One who creates perfectly, form and function blended masterfully with each muscle, limb, and organ. It shows His wisdom as He imbued it with beauty, and His grace as He bedecked it with qualities far beyond that of others. He could have made the creature a speck of dust or a drop of quicksilver, but He chose to make it brilliantly fast and marvelous, thus showing us once again His masterful touch."

We thought about this and I just gulped. All that in few sentences. It was astonishing. Tyree stammered, "Is there anything else?"

"Certainly," Lucifer answered. "The more you delve into it the more you will understand. Were you to dissect the creature—I don't recommend it; they don't enjoy such procedures—"

We all laughed at the humor of it, but Lucifer went on, "You would find how various muscle groups work together, how limbs and organs function. You would see the perfection and symmetry of the being and once again realize how great our Lord is. And nothing is the same. No duplicates. For instance, notice the brown sheen of their fur. Each one is a little different, and that speaks of Kyrie's ability to make utterly unique creatures. He doesn't ever do the same thing twice. No two hairs in all the universe are duplicates. He makes each blade of grass singular and individual."

He raised the eyebrows of his human face dramatically. "And think of the power Kyrie has given these beasts. They could all munch you up in one red piece!"

We laughed at that.

He smiled and continued, "But it is power under control. These beasts are disciplined, they know their limits, and they live within them. That tells you much about Kyrie's nature. He is omnipotent, but it is omnipotence wedded to perfect wisdom, discipline, and control. Imagine if His power were out of control! We couldn't exist!"

Cere said, her fine, angular face a vision of curiosity and the illumination of discovery, "Yes, and there's the dog's limbs and the way its body rides as he runs or walks or eats. If one limb was out of place, or an ear was placed on a flank or the eyes were pressed out of the head and into the chest, it would look ridiculous. But at a word, Kyrie has brought them to life with flawless design. He's even created us with an ability to appreciate such beauty. But I wonder if He designs it all in his head before He speaks or how that works."

"Bravo!" Lucifer said. He looked at Tyree. "And what do you see?"

Tyree said, "I remember the first day as we watched and He created each of us. Kyrie just moved from one to another, singing out the names and—presto!—there Rune was, or me, or you. He does it effortlessly."

"And does not grow tired," Rune added. "Never."

Lucifer seemed extremely pleased. "Indeed." There was a pause after Rune's answer, and Lucifer regarded me with a cool precision, as if weighing what he would say next and alternately striking and then discarding a hundred thousand possibilities.

"Aris," he said. "I have a question for you."

I gulped, but masked it as best I could. "Yes?"

"If Kyrie is infinite, how can He be here, among us?"

I glanced around at my comrades, wishing one of them would answer for me. But no one did.

"That is an appearance of reality," I said. "It's not all of Him."

"But I'm telling you, He is here now. I am protecting and shielding Him from you because that is the way He chooses it. But the Him that is here is all of Him."

"All?"

"Yes."

I stared at Lucifer. "I don't know what you mean?"

"Kyrie in His whole person is here right now. When you worship Him, you worship the entire Kyrie, not an apparition or appearance, not a part of Him."

"And He is nowhere else?"

"I didn't say that."

"Ah." I smiled. This was getting out of my depth. I said to Rune, "You must have an answer to that."

"Kyrie's omnipresence," Rune said. "He is present everywhere in His entire being at all times. He is not diminished by His presence in a body, nor is He lessened by taking on form for our pleasure or instruction. He is ubiquitous yet wholly individual in every place that He is, which is everywhere."

"So He is really here, but He is everywhere else too. And not in pieces either." I liked the talk. It was fascinating, and I felt as if I was learning a deep secret that few of our number would ever learn.

"Reality is theology," Lucifer said. "The knowledge of God is the only knowledge. He is everywhere present and present everywhere. There is no place that can hide from Him, no resource that He has not searched out, known, understood, and owned. This is His glory. This is why we worship."

I swallowed, then stammered, "But how can He be in all places at once when we have seen Him sitting on His throne before us?"

Lucifer's wings seemed unsettled a moment, then he raised them high above us as if he would fly. Then he said, "This is the great mystery. How, it is not possible for us to know. Only that it is truth."

I gazed long into his eyes, and then his wings fluttered as if to shield his eyes from us. "I have enjoyed being with you," he said. "Kyrie's spirit goes with you wherever you are. You do not need to see Him to know that He is present. He is ready to speak and to listen at your desire."

A moment later, I nodded to Cere and the others. We stood, bowed, then walked reverently out of the Temple, being careful not to break the silence.

When we were outside, Cere immediately said, "That was very . . . "

"Extraordinary," I said when she didn't complete the sentence.

"No, far more. Scintillating, perhaps. No. Impressive? Not enough. It was beyond words."

"Yes," Rune said quietly.

Tyree gazed at us, a look of wonder in his eyes, too. "One day we will know as Lucifer knows. And he has four heads!"

I laughed, then said faintly, "That will be quite a day to behold."

"I think we should all retire to our quarters and meditate on this," Cere said, her face blanched almost white as if a great fright had come over her. She was disturbingly beautiful in such reverie, and I was drawn to her.

We parted, a hush upon us. I returned to my quarters and sat down, thinking. Lucifer's words, "That is the great mystery," kept rebounding in my mind. What did it mean? And could it be understood?

One thing was sure—for many like me, Lucifer had become the mentor and model of all thoughts, words, and deeds. We aspired to speak and teach and learn and direct as he did.

9

The time flowed by with more talk of Kyrie's spiritual immensity and Lucifer's grandiose gentility. We all marveled at the intricacies of our own individual beings and gladly spoke of our discoveries to one another. Kyrie told us we were reaching a point in our musical abilities when we could compose on our own, first as a unit and then individually. "Composition," He said, "is a marvel and an ultimate joy, but it must be entered into with gravity and a sense of reverence."

No one complained, of course, that we were not yet composing. It appeared difficult to me. I had no idea where to go in a kind of spiritual "ad lib" on even the written themes and the current material. But I knew I would gladly try and enter into it with the same privileged awe that we all brought to everything else.

At the next practice, though, Kyrie did something that changed forever the way we looked at things. At the time, I did not realize the import of it. What He did was introduce the Son as His equal. Kyrie stood out before us and gestured to the Son to stand. Until then, few of us knew the meaning of His presence. He remained silent at most of our gatherings. But now Kyrie was definitely instituting a change.

"This is My Son," Kyrie said, motioning to the figure beside Him. "You will accord to Him all that you would to Me. Worship, love, adoration, all can be directed to Him as you would to Me. He is My equal, My greatest friend, My first love. I have anointed Him as Messiah for all ages and times, and you will address Him as Messiah. In every way He is as I am and we rule as coregents among you. He will have many duties among you, so welcome Him and love Him with all your hearts as you have loved Me."

For the moment, we all seemed awestruck. But then a great shout went up: "Messiah! Messiah! May your reign and power only increase!"

The Son stepped forward. His white, lamblike hair and beard, His eyes golden and alive like lightning, His face like bronze burning in the sunlight—He was a towering figure of power and synergy. Love radiated from Him, and I was immediately smitten with a desire to cry out again, "Messiah! Messiah!" But I said nothing and wondered what others were thinking.

He simply smiled out upon us, a smile that was at once full of joy and yet reverential, ebullient but also deeply unpretentious. He said, "My Father's words humble Me. I wish only to be your comrade, mentor, ally, and prince. As you have treated Him, so treat Me. If I am silent, it is only out of deference to My Father and those He has appointed in high positions. Do not take My silence as disapproval. My eyes see only the goodness etched into each of your souls. I know you as My Father knows you, and in this I rejoice. Attend to your music and work, and I will work beside you and with you. All exists to the glory of Kyrie and His Son! Thanks be to God!"

Another cheer went up, and spontaneously we began playing, the music filling the air like incense.

But the Son waved His hand for quiet. "Today we dedicate a precious gift of our realm to the Temple," He said. "Today we hallow the White Stone in its proper place. Sember?"

A procession began with the Son at the head. We marched to the Temple in long lines behind the hallowed stone. Once in the Temple, the Son performed a rite of dedication. He held the stone up to Kyrie on the palm of His hand.

"This stone signifies the authority of Kyrie," Messiah said. "Only those will hold it to whom Kyrie has extended His scepter." At that moment, Kyrie stood. Above Him Lucifer fluttered, and he moved out before Him, but Kyrie shook His head. Lucifer, moving like lightning, the fiery wheels under his body spinning with a roar through the Temple, returned to his position over Kyrie.

Then Kyrie extended the scepter to the Son. "This is My beloved Son," He said, "in whom I am well pleased. This day You and You alone shall hold the white stone in Your palm."

The Son bowed and gripped the white stone in His right hand. Light poured from between His fingers like the sun shining in its strength. And for a moment, Father and Son blended, became one, lived and breathed in perfect unity, and then they were themselves. The whole scene enthralled us, and a cheer went up that shook the stones of the Temple.

❖

Afterward, I thought only what a marvelous occasion it all was. But

Tyree caught me on my way back to my room and said, "How do you think Lucifer will take today's events?"

I did not detect any undertone of diffidence or ambivalence in the proceedings, so I said, "As he always takes things, I suppose—with perfect finesse and aplomb."

"We shall see," he said. I caught him before he moved away.

"What do you mean? Do you think Lucifer will not like it?"

"Until now it has been understood that he was Kyrie's archangel. But now there are two Kyries. That makes him number three instead of number two. And Kyrie has extended the scepter to the Son and given Him the White Stone."

"I don't think it should matter that much."

"Neither do I. But that may not be what Lucifer thinks. Number two doesn't feel like a long way from number one. But number three, I suspect, feels like whole universes."

I shook it all off. "I don't think Lucifer will be upset. Why should he? He still retains his position and all rights to it."

"We shall see."

Tyree left me feeling vexed and worried.

Then something happened at our next recital.

It was a small thing, at the time. But looking back, I can now see that it was the beginning of the great misfortune that befell all of us through the invasion of evil into our perfect universe.

Once the rankings, seatings, and other rather mundane assignments were made, we felt much more ordered and organized. No more disputes about one's place.

But then at a practice session, Zarsill instructed us in a very difficult passage. It required a hallowed hum beneath mounting adagios in the text. The hum was mellow, quiescent, an almost translucent sound version of what we saw every moment in the shekinah of Kyrie's glory. It called for the most meticulous of controls. We struggled with the passage, and it kept coming out wrong.

Zarsill fidgeted about, looking for a means to show us what he wanted. We went over and over the tune, until Zarsill wiped his brow in frustration and dropped a silken mantle to the floor. It floated in the air a moment, little billows forming on its surface as it slid down through the air, first one way then another.

Zarsill suddenly skewered the wrap with his baton and flicked it into the air again. We all watched in silence as the mantle banked again, drifting and gliding in different directions until it sank to the floor. It was as if every pair of eyes was transfixed on the mantle.

Then Zarsill said, "Play it like that!"

It was a magic moment, unforgettable, one I knew we would discuss for eons if something else didn't come along.

But suddenly Lucifer coughed and moved forward. "Our august conductor has given you a brilliant illustration," he said, "but it will not help you in the playing. The hum is to be executed more in a sprinkle than a single flow. Think of it as a whole sky full of cut and quartered mantles floating down, each one of you playing that sprinkling of sound and light, and that should make it work. A veritable sky full of silken confetti!"

Zarsill looked flustered. It was the second time he had suffered something of a rebuke at the hands of Lucifer. Why Lucifer singled out this moment, I do not know. But Zarsill immediately protested.

"I was only trying to make it more graphic," Zarsill stammered.

"I understand that, and you made an honest, worthy attempt at it. But you did not take it far enough! I stepped in because I wanted them to see the picture in all its fullness." There was an undertone of the adult teaching the child in Lucifer's speech. All of us sensed it and realized the rightness of his suggestion. Zarsill was clearly out of his element and range.

"Sire," Zarsill answered again, "I was only . . . "

Before he could speak any further, Lucifer said rather tersely, "Peace, conductor. Do it as I tell you. I know you have reasons for why you said what you said. There really is no further need for discussion. Please continue with your ministrations."

"I was only trying to picture it," Zarsill muttered.

We sat there, unsure of what to do, when Zarsill tapped his baton on the edge of the podium. "Play it as Lucifer has asked. Ignore what I just said."

A frustrated sputter suddenly leaped from Lucifer's lips. "Zarsill, your words do not have to be ignored! There is no reason to make an issue of something for which there is no issue. I do not like this contradictory tone of yours. Please move on with the playing."

Zarsill turned to face the Cherubim, his wings lifted high above us, his four faces etched with something that I would later come to realize were the first vestiges of anger.

"On the contrary, Sire, it is you who are contradicting me!" Zarsill said with sudden force and ferocity.

At that moment, Kyrie stood, His great torso emerging from behind the wings of several Cherubim. He said, "Lucifer, a word with you."

There was a suspenseful conference in which Lucifer fumed and sputtered and we all felt very uneasy, I extremely so. Zarsill waited on the podium, his head bowed. Someone whispered to me, "It is not Zarsill's fault."

And then behind me, others began talking in low whispers, "Lucifer is the one who is pushing it."

And, "I think this is all nonsense."

I do not know whether Lucifer heard any of this discussion, or that at that time Lucifer's awareness was akin to Kyrie's in terms of omniscience. I sensed his "adjustment" to Zarsill's illustration was well taken. But all this sudden verbosity was strange and strangling. Our communion, I felt, was scratched, though not shattered.

Moments later, Kyrie sat and Lucifer said to Zarsill, "Please continue with your ministrations. You have done well. We needn't discuss this further. Just remember that it is I who advises you in these settings."

"I will not forget that," Zarsill said shortly. He turned to us and we began playing, this time with better result. I'm not sure any of us really understood the point of the argument. But I sensed that some change had occurred in Lucifer and perhaps Zarsill.

I sought out Tyree, Cere, and Rune afterwards, and we discussed the situation at some length. Cere only commented that there was obvious tension between Zarsill and Lucifer and suggested they should talk things out. But then I said, "What did Kyrie say to Lucifer that turned him around?"

"Perhaps He rebuked Lucifer himself!" Rune immediately responded.

"Would He do that?"

"Not in a belittling way, certainly," Cere answered. "But it was obvious Lucifer was a bit cowed."

"He made it clear who was in charge, though," Tyree said.

"Everyone knows he's in charge," I shot back, not sure why this aggravated me. "He had no reason to light on Zarsill about a minor point, really."

Tyree's lips were set. "Something stinks in the realm of Heaven."

We were all flabbergasted at the next practice when Zarsill suddenly informed us, "I have been unduly harsh at times with you and for that I am sorry. We wish to continue now without further interruption. However, I must make it clear at this juncture that Lucifer is in charge—he always has been, but it's more formal at this point—Lucifer is in charge of the selection of the material to be played and all ultimate refinements of the production. His word is law. I have been unnecessarily remiss in making this clear to you, and for that I apologize."

He paused and an audible sigh broke our silence. Then Zarsill said, "Today we will continue with a new piece written by Lucifer himself."

This time there was a real gasp from the orchestra. Composition, even for Lucifer, hadn't yet been allowed, or so we thought. This heralded a new day for all of us.

Someone asked, "Does this mean that we shall all compose?"

"Soon, I am told," Zarsill said. "Right now, only Lucifer will do so. He wants to keep control of it, to ensure quality and execute the purest and most vibrant innovations. But he will grant that permission soon, and perhaps even earlier to certain select musicians in whom he sees particular promise."

I was stunned. I looked across at Lucifer, his great wings hovering over

Kyrie and the Son, his many eyes blinking and flashing in mute satisfaction that his way had been won.

But at the same time, something else in me wanted to be one of the "selected." I knew composition was difficult, but I yearned to be one of those who would ascend to such a position.

We learned later that evening that in many other quarters—among the artisans, the herds-angels, the builders, and others—a similar point had been made. Lucifer held the reins of power over all of them and had appointed deputies to carry out his bidding at every place. I wondered if this was good, but I quickly realized that Lucifer's wisdom and desire for a central authority had to be the right course. Otherwise, Heaven would soon be chaos.

But something else in me wondered if the appearance of the Son as Kyrie's equal had not forced these issues.

__ 10

The next days were a tumult of activity, practice sessions, journeys about the interior of Heaven and the Great City, and concerts, concerts, concerts. Each day brought with it new music that we learned and performed to perfection. My Harpistrer ran hot with the racing of my fingertips and vocal hums, so hot in fact that it was recommended I visit the Outer Reaches where the trees were grown that were used in the making of a Harpistrer and pick out a specimen for the myrrin—angels in charge of carving and fashioning the instruments—to work on. I said of course I would, and hoped Tyree and Rune might like to come along.

It was during this time that I began examining and evaluating my surroundings, my fellow Harpistrers, the orchestra and choir itself. I couldn't help but notice who occupied the first chairs of each section, though. I learned our own virtuoso was a wise and seraphic angel, full of glows and trembles, named Harkriss. He played magnificently, certainly better than I at times, though most of us were on an equal footing. What I marked right away was his instrument.

A hallowed spell emanated from that device, as if possessed by the Spirit Himself. At times I found myself listening to its melodies and forgetting my own playing. Frequently, Harkriss was asked to perform alone, a solo within the greater harmonies of the full orchestra. He tore into his task with a smooth, almost casual distinction, as if he himself was part of the music. I could not help but wonder what that Harpistrer could do in my hands.

Of course, I thought little of this as anything but childish musings. I certainly did not "lust" after that particular piece, nor did I covet it. I simply wondered.

That night, I settled down for a quiet evening in my room, but I was interrupted when someone appeared in my doorway. I did not know him. He introduced himself as Dosrin. Slight-shouldered, diminutive, pale blondish hair. He did not look formidable. I invited him to sit.

"I have come on an errand," he said.

"Yes?"

"There are those who have noticed."

I waited.

"Noticed your playing. The Harpistrer comes alive in your hands. Something marvelous to watch. I applaud you."

"Better to applaud Kyrie."

"Of course. But it has been noticed by some."

Again I waited. His terse manner made me feel restive, an uncommonly strange feeling for me.

He smiled, then rose. "That's all. I was sent to tell you."

"Thank you." I didn't know what else to say. "Thank you for telling me."

"That's my duty."

He walked to the door, then turned. "You should be given a better instrument," he said.

I didn't know what to answer. I finally stammered, "The one I have is excellent. And I am soon traveling to the Outer Reaches to select ... "

"Yes, of course. All that. But you should be playing a tested piece."

"What do you mean?"

He smiled. "Just an opinion. I must go now."

I watched him leave, feeling troubled, another new sensation. I resolved to talk to Tyree and Rune about this visitation, and then someone else. One of the cherubs perhaps. Lucifer? I wasn't sure. I felt a strong desire to go directly to Kyrie or the Son. But could I do that?

I didn't know and resolved to find that out, too. I felt I should go out to the land of the myrrin as soon as possible now. Not knowing what Dosrin meant by a "tested" instrument, I felt this business must be taken care of immediately.

That afternoon, I decided to visit the myrrin, make my choice of a new Harpistrer, and see how things looked. Once there, I quickly selected a new Harpistrer, though I didn't want to part with my old one.

By now Lucifer controlled everything that happened in the making of worship to Kyrie. Zarsill had been consigned to simple genuflections on the podium, all in obeisance to Lucifer.

I was surprised. But I certainly understood it. Lucifer was politic in his suggestions and intonations. His own compositions were all we were playing now.

And behind it all, Kyrie was strangely mute. His own presence seemed to shrivel as Lucifer's grew, as if Lucifer was drinking Him dry, taking all that He had done and making it the possession of Lucifer and company.

And Kyrie was silent.

It irked me, tore at my insides like a jaguar. Why silent? Why did He let it go on?

That day Lucifer recited all the special arrangements of the present piece, a song of praise that seemed a bit stilted to me. I did not understand the logic behind many of the new measures, but Lucifer was imperious in his tone and the demand that we conform absolutely to his directions.

One of the Harpistrers stood and said, "Sire, these lines are impossible. They cannot be done on a Harpistrer."

"They can be and they shall be," Lucifer said. He seemed almost frolicsome in his rapture at all the new activity under his tutelage.

"But sire, this line here requires a hum that is too low in range for a Harpistrer to manage."

"Then we shall invent new Harpistrers."

That was how I learned about the instrumentation houses. In a matter of hours, Lucifer began setting up a process to transform the present Harpistrers into far more agile and flexible instruments, even though I did not think it was possible. Some things were simply impossible to do no matter how hard you tried.

There were other objections, but we began playing and soon dove into the performance with gusto, even though it sounded raw and unwieldy to my ears. The piece did not have the melodic qualities of the usual compositions Kyrie gave us.

It was when the noise had reached its greatest cacophony that Kyrie suddenly stood. He rose right through the wings of the Cherubim. I wondered if He had gone asleep, but I know that is impossible. It's just that He'd been so quiet all through this that many of us had ceased to think of Him as being present.

He said, "It is dissonant."

"Of course," Lucifer cried immediately. "That is just the point. A new variation on the old themes."

"But it is dissonant and does not ring true to the instruments, the musicians, or the performance. There is no harmony. There is no distinct melody."

"Do you doubt me?" Lucifer answered. "This is what we need! Don't you agree?"

There were cheers from the orchestra and those who were watching, as well as from other quarters.

Kyrie gazed at us and then at Lucifer with dismay. "I have allowed these exercises for a purpose. You have wanted to compose. I have allowed you. Now I see that we are not yet ready for that step."

Lucifer's wings rustled, and I detected a deep disturbance. "I had thought we were doing very well."

"I am not pleased," Kyrie answered. His towering body and the robe that clothed Him shimmered in the light. Kyrie turned to the Son: "What do You think?"

"I agree that it is dissonant. Perhaps we have allowed things to occur too quickly. I felt before that we were not yet ready."

"Yes, I can see that," Kyrie said. He looked at Lucifer. "Perhaps you should go back to the older compositions."

He began to sit again, but Lucifer cried out, "Then it is all to no purpose!"

"No," Kyrie answered. "All has purpose. Nothing can be done in My realm without purpose. There is time yet, to grow, to learn, to appreciate all the depths and heights of music. I will teach you. But we cannot continue as we are. It will lead to an unhappy end."

Lucifer rose up before Him. Both of them were like jewels, gleaming with an awesome stillness. For a moment, I thought Lucifer was confronting Him. But then the great archangel descended.

"There is delight in obedience," Kyrie said slowly, firmly. "There is great comfort in the knowledge of the holy. I bid you to seek that comfort. All, I bid you, seek and find. There is nothing I will withhold."

Lucifer's light flickered as the Cherubim settled back into position. Kyrie sat down on His throne and all the Cherubs cried, "Holy, Holy, HOLY!"

But Lucifer's own voice was stilled.

Zarsill mounted the podium, suddenly alive again. He tapped for our attention. We all turned from the remarkable scene to our right around the throne and gave him our focus, though deep in my heart I wondered what had happened. A rift had formed between Lucifer and Kyrie. That it could happen was astonishing, for Lucifer was the ultimate protector of all that Kyrie was and is and would be. He taught us the great truths. But how would he do that now?

I heard someone say behind me, "Kyrie was unduly harsh with Lucifer. There was no need for it."

And another, "I thought the composition quite good."

And a third, "What will become of us if Lucifer and Kyrie are at odds? How will we perform?"

Zarsill immediately called for a piece that we all knew, had memorized and played frequently, one of Kyrie's favorites. We began, the melody mounted and soon we were lost in the harmonies, our hearts bending to our work like high wheat in a summer's breeze. For the moment, we seemed joined and one again. Even Lucifer, I noticed, threw off his mood and listened. I could tell as his wings riffled about him, still overarching Kyrie like a tent. Kyrie Himself smiled and clapped at certain crescendos. At the end, Zarsill bowed and we were in our element, alive once again and springing, gasping for great quaffs of the air that illumined us. We drank the light as living water and grew still and satisfied in its fragrance. We knew Kyrie was comforting us, and in that we rested, a quiet, happy throng of angels on the way to the heights.

As the stillness around us grew, Kyrie spoke to Lucifer and the great Cherubim announced to us, "We shall have a procession down the streets of gold and into the Temple. Go, don your finest robes. Come with your instruments. The whole of Heaven shall display itself before Him in the Temple, and we shall all live before Him as children in freshets of shekinah glory."

I returned to my room once again to mull over the events of the day when there was a bright knock at my door. It was Dosrin.

— 11 —

"As I told you before, you have been noticed," he said, greeting me warmly and gesturing to be let inside. I wasn't sure that I should let him, but the natural deference and courtesy accorded to all angels overcame me and I opened the way. He took a seat. "There is a way," he said, "that you might procure a tested instrument."

My heart sank. "I do not see why or how," I said quickly. "I have already been to the Outer Reaches and commissioned the myrrin with a new one."

"Pish," he said with a wave of his hand. "The myrrin have become old and crotchety already. They do not know the newer ways."

"The newer ways?"

"Of course. We have now in development instruments that far outshine anything a present Harpistrer can produce."

I remembered how Lucifer had spoken of new instruments and had appointed deputies and others to oversee the production. I had not yet seen any of them. In fact, I assumed that was all shut down with Kyrie's edict about composition. But Kyrie had not expressly forbidden the making of new instruments.

"The newer Harpistrers can at once support two lines of hum and project several trails of colored light all at once."

"I cannot produce two lines of hum." I did not say this as if embarrassed. It simply was not done that way.

"You will," Dosrin said. "It will be taught. There are many new things we all must learn. Lucifer is an apt teacher, and he is already training those who will ministrate this service. We'd like to think of you as an applicant."

"I will not be a part of disobeying Kyrie's orders."

He smiled sweetly, almost too sweetly. Condescendingly. I did not like it. "There is no thought of disobeying Kyrie. All work of composition has been halted, even by Lucifer himself. We . . . "

"Who are you aligned with?" I asked suddenly, anger steeping within me.

"Kyrie, of course."

"Kyrie?"

"Certainly. Now as I was saying . . . "

"What do you mean, Kyrie? How can you be serving Kyrie when all you are doing is thwarting His efforts?"

He shook his head sadly. "You have been misinformed. Even today an important understanding has been reached between Kyrie and Lucifer. There are no factions, no serving one over the other. Kyrie has granted to Lucifer all he wishes. Moreover, Kyrie has seen fit to elevate Lucifer even more so that all deputies and ministers previously appointed must also be retrained and reappointed in proper sequences. There is no difference in this matter between Lucifer and Kyrie. They are one in mind."

I stared at him as if struck. I did not know what to say or add. Finally, I just muttered, "Let me think on this. I do not know whether I wish to part with my given Harpistrer."

"There will be other opportunities," he said, rising. "All decisions do not have to be made in one day. Thank you for listening to me." He held out his hands as if to embrace me, but I turned and went to the door.

He said to me in the doorway, "Let's be friends, Aris. I am not against you. We are one, and as one we shall succeed."

"Yes, I do believe that."

"Then count on it."

He left and I returned to my seat more convinced of doom than before. But Dosrin had been cordial. And I knew of no deception in these matters. Why should there be? There weren't two sides established in any sense of the word. There was the procession tomorrow and greater tidings for all of us I was sure. I decided to look to that and hope for a better day.

The procession began magnificently, a veritable parade of figures from every part of Heaven. The Kinderlings led it, myriads of them, their tall figures cutting a wide swathe through the streets, their instruments in hand, or if they were artisans, then pieces of their work. Flocksangels followed them with their flocks of sheep, goats, wyxoxen, starraxes, the Dogs of Dallet—all the panoply of Heaven's creatures marching to the grand anthems of our race.

Kyrie, the Son, the Cherubim, and the Seraphim stood at the head of the Temple so that everyone passed by them. Cheers went up regularly as we passed, and a wonderful sense of camaraderie enveloped us all.

I marched among the Haukers, of which I was one. Rune was with the Kinderlings, and Tyree among the Serren. I did not see Cere, but knew she had to be among her kind, the beautiful Dillassen, dancing their way along and spreading petals of rose, hyacinth, fractire, and lemmentine across the path.

Then as we reached the turn in the street where we would march before Kyrie and his ensemble, there suddenly went up a great shout from our group. "Lucifer! Lucifer! Lucifer!"

I was dumbstruck. There had been cheers all along, though sporadically and not in unison. This appeared to be planned. I did not like it. But many of my brethren joined in, eager to make their voices heard as if by Lucifer himself.

Behind us, though, the myrrin, their dark dwarfish faces thunderstruck, began chanting, "Kyrie! Kyrie! Kyrie!"

And soon the two groups engaged in verbal battle, each outshouting the other. "Kyrie! Kyrie!"

Then: "Lucifer! Lucifer!"

Others behind and in front of us joined the shouting till the two chants split the air like star fire. I did not join either group, as many of my brethren did not. But I watched in dismay as the two groups challenged and goaded one another in a sickening display of disunity.

As we passed, Kyrie stood and raised his arm. "The Anthem," He cried. "Sing the Anthem."

It was our national song, if you want to think in such terms, but called "The Celestial Anthem." It went on for many verses and told the great deeds of our people and our race and of Kyrie and even Lucifer. New verses were always being added. The voices struck up the song. Those shouting "Kyrie" or "Lucifer" gradually silenced, and we all stopped in place, our voices rising and lifting aloft the names of our heroes and great ones.

My own eyes misted as we sang, and I could see in Kyrie's eyes that He was deeply moved. Our energy seemed to mount as we continued, and all races, angels, brothers, and sisters sang so that separation and division vanished. A lump hardened in my throat, and I felt myself carried aloft, winging on a wind of change and freedom and hope. All things were returned to normal. Even Lucifer was strangely quiescent. He did not move, his four faces forward, no emotion registering.

Then Kyrie sat, and we continued. No more cheers for Lucifer or Kyrie erupted from our numbers. I found Cere, and we spoke quietly together, enraptured as was everyone with the sudden new sense of communion.

"It is over then," I said.

"I think perhaps it is," Cere said. She had been weeping, and I hugged her hard, praying that she was right.

"We shall see," I added.

"I wish it was as before," she said and bit her lip. Rune joined us then from the Kinderlings and grasped us hard, spanning his arms over both our shoulders.

"It was good," he said. "That singing brought us together. It's what we must remember. Not what divides us. But what unites us."

We could not find Tyree, and soon we were walking through the golden streets in great crowds, all singing the Anthem and rejoicing together that our world had been put right.

"Kyrie knew what to do," they were saying.

"The procession was just the thing."

"But there was a moment when it almost all came apart."

Yes, it had, but Kyrie had restored it. My trust in Him leaped, it seemed, to a higher level. I felt stronger and no longer afraid for what might happen. At least in that moment, our world was true and no longer split into twisted shards.

12

The next morning, with the increasing light of Kyrie's glory, Rune and Tyree arrived at my door.

"He's really pulled us into something this time," Tyree said.

I looked at Rune questioningly, and he said, "You really must come and listen. I'll only ask you this once. After that it's up to you."

I followed, and minutes later we gathered in the quarters of Zarsill.

"I'm not sure I'm interested in this," I said rather skeptically.

But Tyree pushed me inside. "Don't fret. It'll be ten minutes of blather and then hours of discussion. We can leave after a courteous listen. Then we can go run the dogs or something."

I didn't laugh and sat irritably against one of the walls, my heart dull and draggy. Tyree sat next to me, while Rune, after making sure we had some refreshment from a great bowl of Viasian Tea, took a place in the middle.

"There is, as most of you already know," Zarsill was saying, "a movement afoot that is gaining in prominence and importance among our numbers. This is not, I repeat, *NOT*, something with the purpose of undermining the efforts of anyone, Michael, Lucifer, Jonquin, or any of the others, and especially Kyrie.

"The main point concerns our unity, the force of our strength. Some advocate that our music move toward more complexity rather than the simplicity we have known till now. Things are moving far too fast. We seek a bold unity that shall supersede the power of any individual but that grips us all.

"This, as you may guess, will not be easily attained."

"Not easily attained," Tyree mimicked to me with gravity and a raising of the eyebrows.

"Quiet," I said, still trying to understand what Zarsill was talking about.

"As you may guess," Tyree said to me with an imperious air, obviously imitating the staid Zarsill, "none of it will be reached without effort, that is to say with ease, or to use a better word, easily."

I glared at Tyree, then quickly regained my composure. "Be quiet, Tyree, or I'll leave without you."

He whispered, "That will not be accomplished without the exercise, or shall we say, the ease, the fluency, the very flowingness of angelic potential."

I smiled but turned my face forward. For all his smart-alecky cuteness, Tyree could sometimes zing off a good one. But at the moment, I wanted to hear the lecture and not his banal additions to the record.

Zarsill continued, " . . . that has not been witnessed before, but we anticipate it will augment our aptitude on the symphonic platform."

"Indeed," Tyree intoned, "I anticipate this will all most assuredly accentuate our adroitness with alacrity."

"Shut up!" I said to Tyree. "He is the conductor. You have no right!"

Tyree looked at me stiffly, then said, "Okay, I'll be quiet."

Zarsill continued, "We seek this unity at the expense of all else, life, instrumentation, personal desire to compose, even the altogether individual expression of our own capacities. This is our ultimate goal, and may it come upon us with posthaste."

"If not posthumously," Tyree added, and I gave him a gentle sock in the arm. Sorrow for what we had lost welled over my spirit, and I couldn't speak for a moment. Tyree nudged me.

"What is wrong?"

I shook my head, not able to speak.

"Are you all right?"

As I shook my head all the more emphatically, Tyree grabbed me at the arms. "Come on, you're getting out of here."

I released myself from his grasp. "I'm all right. Just a little emotional."

Tyree peered into my eyes a moment, then he said, "I'm sorry. I make light, and I shouldn't. Everything Zarsill says is patently true. It's just he can be so verbose. If he'd only simplify it for us plebeians."

I replied, the emotion wearing away, "We are not plebeians."

"Just trying to make you feel better."

Tyree's obvious repentance was touching, and I loved him for it.

There was intermittent clapping, and when the clapping died down and Zarsill decided to take questions, I stood to leave. Rune was immediately at my side.

"Stay just a few moments longer."

"I don't want to hear this, Rune," I replied. "I need to get out and think."

"Maybe you have a question."

"I don't."

"Certainly you do. You're full of them."

"There are none that he can answer."

Tyree regarded us both soberly. He finally said, "Look, let's hear some questions. It can't be worse than it's already been, and maybe something will come up that really makes sense. I for one would like to hear it."

I stared at Tyree, surprised and even awed.

That turned us to the first question asked. One of the Haukers present said, "Zarsill, what is to prevent Lucifer from seceding?"

There was some clapping, and Zarsill motioned to someone else on the platform. I hadn't noticed him before, but then I realized it was Michael, one of the great angels who stood before Kyrie. I had always known him to be a trusty and worthy spokesman of truth.

Michael stood. "There is nothing to prevent Lucifer from seceding."

A gasp went up from the crowd, but Michael held up his hand. "Except one thing."

We all leaned forward as one, as if to hold onto whatever would slip from his lips and make it a lifeline to real hope.

"That one thing is Lucifer's heart. He knows Kyrie as none of us know Him. He knows Kyrie's mind and soul and the fact that Kyrie longs for nothing more than a new unity married to perfect freedom and joyful composition, as well as all the other innovations that different quarters have seen, proposed, and ratified. Only Lucifer can prevent Lucifer from seceding."

"But is not Kyrie all powerful?"

"He is."

"Then why doesn't He just stop him?"

Michael glanced at Zarsill, and Zarsill indicated to him to speak. It was clear that while Zarsill did the speaking at this meeting, it was Michael who was the real authority. "Does being all-powerful mean that Kyrie can simply stop someone who in his freedom of will chooses wrong?" Michael asked. "Obviously, Kyrie has the power to do that. But His power is christened and governed by any number of other qualities, attributes, and virtues that we have not yet had time to teach in their fullness. Kyrie is holy, and His holiness dictates that He not only protect those who might be harmed by someone anywhere anytime, but it also requires that He give each creature the freedom to make honest, uncoerced choices. In other words, in creating Lucifer a sentient, moral being, He has to also be fair in the game of life and let Lucifer be Lucifer, no matter the pain involved."

Another angel, this time a staid Kinderling, queried, "But does that make sense for all of us? What if Lucifer drags others of us into this quarrel? He seems bent on it. What if it happens?"

Michael replied, "Like it or not, each of us must make that choice. It is part and parcel of our being."

"Do you mean to say," the same angel added, "that any of us could follow Lucifer into a doomed feud with Kyrie?"

"That is true."

Another gasp shot out from our astonished faces, and I found myself quivering with emotion as I listened. If what Michael said was true, then each of us stood in great danger. That is, unless Kyrie was able to stop Lucifer and whatever hordes he might enlist in his quest.

And that question was the one that nagged at my soul. I finally stood.

"Michael, I respect you greatly for coming here and speaking to us. My question though speaks to the heaviness in my own heart. I am wondering if it is possible that Lucifer could actually overthrow Kyrie."

Michael blinked only slightly, then he said, "I do not believe he is able."

"But do you know?"

"No one knows until it is done."

I quaked on my feet, and with shaky legs sat down. Instantly, I leaped to my feet again. "Just one more question."

"Yes?"

"If Kyrie is omnipotent, is Lucifer also omnipotent?"

"That is not possible. Two beings cannot be omnipotent at the same time. It defies logic and good sense. Either both are equally potent, which I might call 'equipotency,' or one is omnipotent and the other isn't."

"Kyrie is omnipotent, though."

"Yes."

"Or so He claims."

"Yes."

My disquiet magnified all the more with that last yes. Kyrie claimed to be omnipotent, but was He truly? He could create, yes. He had fashioned our whole world. We had seen much of it happen before our eyes. One angelic being after another was created out of nothing. But did that require omnipotence? And did that prove He was indeed all-powerful?

I tried to reason it through in my own mind, and I realized that I had no real proof of Kyrie's statements over Lucifer's. Perhaps even Lucifer would soon maintain that he was the omnipotent one. And then it was one's word against another. How could we tell the truth? There were only two possibilities: through mortal combat or through one acceding to the other.

If the latter was the course, then it would appear that Kyrie was far less powerful than Lucifer. He had acceded everything so far. It was Kyrie who was constantly giving into Lucifer's demands, not the other way around.

On the other hand, if Lucifer did have absolute power, then why did he even have to request anything from Kyrie? Why did he not simply take it?

If Kyrie was omnipotent, then his restraint with Lucifer was a sign of His patience, goodness and kindness, and ultimately of His love. Perhaps He was hoping Lucifer would improve.

Again on the other hand, perhaps His restraint was a sign of His weakness. He had to give in to keep Himself alive!

That thought was so grievous to me that I winced while sitting there, feeling more and more lonely as time went on.

What would a world be like governed wholly by Lucifer? Already I'd seen something of his favoritism, his pragmatism, his "get-my-way-at-any-cost" attitude. Who would live and enjoy such a world?

But if Kyrie was truly weak, then how could He govern? And how could I give Him my final and ultimate loyalty? He was little more than just another one of us, only bigger. And all the more a target of derision.

It came down to a basic choice: either I was to trust Kyrie, believing that

He was all He said He was. Or trust Lucifer, believing he was who he said he was.

Which to choose?

I suddenly realized Tyree was looking at me. He was saying, "This is very bad, Aris. I don't think Kyrie should allow it." Another change of direction. He was becoming a little too mercurial for my ability to follow his switch turns.

"But obviously He does."

"Maybe Kyrie cannot stop it."

"Or maybe He doesn't want to." I gave Tyree an inquisitive look, hoping he would come up with another alternative.

"Or maybe Kyrie doesn't know what to do," Tyree said. "In which case, He's far less a presence than I thought He was."

"Do you really think Rune considered Zarsill's speech that weighty? It was fine, well-meaning, but certainly not weighty. Michael was weighty."

"Yes, but there's something else there, something else going on that Rune has not let us in on."

"But what?"

"I'm going to find out."

13

A day later, Tyree caught Rune and me and led us out into the streets. "I've been watching this place for several days," he explained. We had decided to visit the tallurgers not far from the Temple district. "First we'll take the tour on the inside," he said, "but then we move on to what they're really doing."

We arrived at the main shop on Tither Street not far from the Temple. The street blazed with the light of the main Temple where Kyrie sits and rules, and I frequently covered my eyes just to see from one end of a street to another. Tyree led us along, like some river scout spotting starraxes or wyxoxen in the Outer Reaches. We went into one of the shops and a tallurger named Soskin greeted us.

"I'd be glad to show you around," he said. He showed us several of the brethren working—they were mostly Lippings, though I spotted a couple of Kinderlings in the back. We all marvelled at the intricate work that went into forming the various instruments, including the Listroms and the Crukes. Soskin was well-informed and seemed pleased to be showing us around. It was not a formal visit anyway, and clearly he was quite eager to guide us.

We completed the tour without any amazing revelations.

"Now the real work starts," Tyree said as we stepped out.

I turned my face to the light and let its warming rays refresh my face. "The real work?"

"Come on." Tyree led me around through the streets to the rear of the workplace. "Did you notice the cool, airy feel of the workshop?"

I hadn't thought about it, but I had noticed how cool it was inside. Rune was a little tight-lipped about it. "You certainly haven't come out with something heaven-shaking," he said a bit acidly.

"Don't worry about that," Tyree said. "I'll soon have your eyes ripping out of your head. That cool, airy atmosphere in there I think means only one thing."

"What?" Rune and I asked together.

"A cave or deep hole underneath. I think there's something else under the shop that they don't want certain of us knowing about."

He studied the ground around the workshop, and then finding no entrance, he watched different brethren who were coming and going on the street.

"What are you looking for?" I asked.

"All in time," Tyree said, squinting at the door of the small shop. He crinkled his brows with stern watchfulness. He said to us suddenly, "Now watch."

It was one of those places where most of us obtained the tunics, robes, belts, and epaulets that we wore when not playing in the orchestra. Nothing about it looked particularly strange. But then two angels—Haukers—stepped out, talking animatedly.

"They always talk very fast when they come out," Tyree whispered. "One of them anyway. But the other doesn't seem to be listening. I think it's a little diversionary tactic."

"What do you think's going on?" I asked. Even Rune bent down with us to watch.

"I don't know," Tyree said. "I've never been inside. But I think it may be something the likes of us are not to know about." Suddenly he nudged me. "Him," he said.

I let my gaze fall upon a tall, stately Kinderling wearing nondescript brown robes and a worried look. His eyes shifted quickly about, and he hurried by the clothing shop without turning to peer in. Tyree started to say, "Just a ruse. Keep watching." A moment later, the Kinderling turned around, then tromped into the shop, closing the door quietly behind him.

"Quick!" Tyree said. We rushed across the street in just enough time to see the angel descend a stairwell in the back of the shop. We waited in the shadows outside the shop, taking in some of the new sights along the street—a Hauker with several Liminnines on his back and an obvious member of the myrrin playing a Cruke in front of a shop full of Harpistrer bows. None of us was sure when the shifty-eyed Kinderling would appear again, and we all stepped inside the shop to see what was there. The Kinderling appeared only minutes later. The three of us acted as if we were shopping for new tunics, and Tyree cleverly said to me, "It looks excellent on you, Grago. I'd get that one without any more hesitation."

I was so caught off guard that I didn't respond till he made eyes at the row of tunics at my fingertips. I pulled one out and tried to put it on as the Kinderling scurried by with a clopping sound of his sandals. I didn't notice till I had my arm up one sleeve that the tunic was almost four sizes too small. Tyree led me with his eyes back to the short, plump Hauker brother who appeared at the counter. He had not been there before, until the Kinderling came back upstairs, and we walked over to him. Tyree said with surprising ease (though I should have not been surprised by now), "We'd like to see a tunic in my friend's size. We didn't see anything like it elsewhere."

"Make that two," Rune said. I turned to look at him with surprise and he gave me a little shrug. When the Hauker disappeared into the back, Rune whispered, "I can play your little spy game too, Tyree." It felt good to see him getting involved with our little caper instead of standing on the outside looking in and critiquing us all the while.

"It only comes in one size," the brother said grumpily after returning. He went back to his reading.

Then with that intuition which continues to surprise me, Tyree whispered to him, "We'd like to go downstairs."

The brother eyed us both skeptically, then said, "Who sent you?"

Tyree answered without hesitation, "Soskin."

The angel blinked and looked at the door of the shop. "I hadn't expected so many today."

"Soskin has had many visitors and they'll all be coming through in a while, I think," Tyree quickly said.

"All right, go ahead. We have nothing to hide, you know."

"Of course," Tyree answered. He winked at me.

We walked over to the stairwell, and with a chortle, Tyree stepped down into a black murk that took some mental adjustments. We angels are not used to the dark. I said, "That was easy."

Tyree said, as if he'd been doing this kind of thing all his life, "They're all new at these things. No one has perfected a security system."

Rune remarked, "It certainly does look suspicious."

When we reached the main floor, Tyree turned and motioned to be quiet. "I'll do the talking," he whispered. "I think I have the play of this place now."

We plodded on until we heard whirring noises ahead. Then some tamping and banging. We moved along a tunnel—with dripping noises here and there plop-plopping around us—and soon found light.

"I think we're right under the Cruke shop, wouldn't you say?" Tyree commented, looking up at the dark crystal ceiling. The under cave had obviously been hewn right into the gold and crystal walls. There ahead was another workshop about forty or fifty yards long, narrow and well-lighted, with tables and tools up against the wall. Light sifted in through apertures in the ceiling which I thought must have doubled as airholes along the street. Several angels bent over their tables, working on variously shaped tallurgin objects.

Tyree stepped closer to one brother standing at a table looking over a long flat piece of something I didn't recognize. It was very flat, but I thought it might be a slide for one of the Listroms. When we drew closer, though, I saw it was far too flat. We watched him a moment, then strode right up to him. He was trying to bend it into a circle.

"Fine piece of craftship," Tyree said matter-of-factly, and caught the brother unaware. He almost jumped, then eyed us unhappily.

"What do you want?" he said.

"Are we able to take one away today?" Tyree said.

The tallurger bent to his work. "Of course not. We've only been working on these for a few days now. Can't expect miracles, you know. Haven't even arrived at a final form. Strange business if you ask me. I'd rather be making normal Listroms, if you get my meaning. Not these trickster types that everybody seems to be clamoring for."

"Well, I'm not one of them," Tyree said.

"Of course you aren't," said the tallurger. "What, did you think I'd mistake you for one of them? Ha!"

I noticed Tyree looked a bit deflated by that remark, but he pressed on without a hitch in his speech. "Can I try one?"

The worker waved us over to another bench. "A few of those are almost finished, though it's beyond me what good they are. The noises they make are little more than squeaks."

Tyree touched one of the flat pieces of tallurgin and then grasped it. It sprang slightly and had rough, uneven edges. He turned it into a circle and said, "Something like the rim of a chariot wheel," he said.

"I thought they were strictly fire," Rune said, obviously interested.

"But the wheel rims themselves," Tyree answered. "What the fire attaches to."

"Of course," Rune said, a little stung. I didn't like the way he reacted to every little joke as a personal affront. But if he was becoming a little sensitive, maybe it was because neither I nor Tyree had given raves about the speech that Zarsill made the night we heard him speak.

Tyree allowed the strip to whip back in his hand as he held one end. A springy, musical sound erupted. By holding the end at different points—so that the length of the "playing part" was augmented or diminished by his action—it made different sounds.

"Rather a hard thing to play with so much whip action," Rune commented.

"Perhaps it's only for our virtuosos," I offered.

The worker just shook his head. "We're just trying different things now. No one has agreed about things. Are you inspectors?"

"No, just interested members," Tyree answered.

"Sixth Quarm?" the angel asked.

"Fifth," Tyree said, giving me and Rune a gulping look.

He held up the strip again and let it dangle. There were other pieces on the table: a crystal that came to a sharp point and produced a jingly, pleasant sound when tapped; a length of wood with a bit of crystal rammed through the end that tinkled gently but not very loudly as you tamped the other end on the floor; and several other objects that offered no clue as to their use.

"You hold it like this?" Tyree asked as he held up the thin strip of tallurgin.

"No, it needs a handle. I'm only making the shivery parts that you have there."

Tyree asked, "And I suppose you whip it like this"—he shook it in his hand as it made its gangly noise again—"or perhaps like . . . ?"

"No, I'm told it's for several purposes. Don't expect me to figure them out."

"Oh, I see. For the times ahead."

"Of course." For a moment, he eyed us suspiciously. "Ethher let you down here?"

"Yes."

"Who sent you?"

"Soskin."

He gave a little snippy grimace, then turned back to hammering on another of the thin strips in his hand.

"What do you call it?" Tyree was looking hard at me, the tallurger simply bending over the piece and not paying much attention to the conversation. "What do you call it?" Tyree asked again.

"Right now? A Hodda."

"Invented by Hodda, the famous Cruker, no doubt?"

"That's what I understand." The tallurger eyed Tyree and me once more. "Aren't you supposed to be in and out very quickly?"

"Yes, I know." Tyree said. "We'll order four, two for me and two for each of my friends."

"It's one per person at this point."

"Then one for each of us."

Above us, there was the sound of a loud crash, and the walls of the room shook. The tallurger snorted with disgust. "I keep telling them this place is unsafe, but who's going to listen to me?"

"Sure you can't make me two?" Tyree said to the tallurger.

"And what would you be doing with two, my friend? Twirling them in each hand? I don't think so. No, I've got to turn out four of these a day and it's making my back hurt. And you're making my head hurt."

"We'll be on our way."

"And don't come back too soon. These things take a lot of work, you know. Tell Lucifer that, would you?"

"Certainly."

When we reached the tunnel, Tyree slowed his pace. "Lucifer?"

I nodded. "And those things do some kind of double duty—but what?

Are they really instruments? They don't seem to have anything near the finesse of the instruments Kyrie has approved. And I didn't know he was allowing us to do such experimentation—especially underground."

"I know," Rune answered.

"We have to let Kyrie know about this," I said.

Tyree answered, "I should think Kyrie already knows."

"And will do nothing about it, I guess," I remarked with tight lips.

Rune immediately broke in, "Kyrie has all things well in hand. The kinds of problems we're witnessing are not solved in a minute."

"Of course," Tyree said. "When in doubt, do nothing."

I detected the sour note in his voice and was about to speak again, but then I decided to say nothing. We hurried on through the tunnel to the stairs and then up. Etther—we assumed that was his name—was with a customer, and we just left saying no more.

Out on the street, Rune made both of us stop. "Don't you think we should do something?"

"You heard him," Tyree answered. "Lucifer's behind it. And Kyrie has not commanded us not to make new instruments. So Lucifer's only doing as he pleases. That's it in a sentence."

Rune's features twisted, and I could see tears in his eyes. "It's just that I see all of it coming to pieces now. There is nothing we can do about it. Not a thing."

"If Kyrie would just do something," Tyree mused matter-of-factly. "If Lucifer's involved in this, then you can bet there are many others, and it's very well organized. And have you come to any conclusion about what the double duty is on those instruments down there?"

We both stopped to look at him and said in unison, "What?"

He looked at us with slit, unhappy eyes. "Think about it. Think about it a long time."

_14_

The gathering on the Mount that evening held an undercurrent of tension and anxiety. Undoubtedly, most of those present knew now about Moddo and the things that had happened among the myrrin. Surely there were problems in other places. Just because I had not heard about them did not eliminate the probability that these things were happening all over the realm.

Kyrie appeared to be in a somber, quietly observant mood as He sat on the throne before the gathered billions. Describing that scene is almost an impossibility. The Mount rose up before Him, stately and grand in its sweep and splendor. The round rocked sides of its face provided places to sit, stand, and watch so that any position you took gave you a full frontal view of the assembly. In the crowd of angels that fluttered to the Mount's hewn seats, there was a distinct feeling of being face to face with Kyrie even as you stood there miles above or below Him.

The Mount was actually a single sort of hump-backed mountain with two great mounds like a camel, and thus He could sit on the one side and face us all on the other. It afforded a perfect meeting place, allowing each of us to see Him as if we were alone in conference.

Lucifer and the other Cherubim hovered over Him, their wings beating a slow rhythm that marked time to a perfect pulse throbbing somewhere at the back of our collective consciousness. The many eyes of the Cherubim roved among us, and I caught several at different times looking at me as if measuring my thoughts.

Kyrie's robe filled half the mountain, and the molten glow from His being reflected off the jeweled tunics of the Cherubs so that the mountain seemed full of light, light so beautiful and surpassing that one was soon lost in it, alternately worshiping and then basking in the gilt that set our faces ablaze.

As the jostling and movement settled down, a silence came over us. For the moment, we were one, united in purpose and soul. Slowly, almost imperceptibly, the first notes of a beloved song wafted through the air. Soon, our lips moved, and we began singing with the Cherubim the anthem that had become our daysong:

> *Holy, Holy, Holy, is the Lord God, the Almighty.*
> *The whole creation is full of His glory.*
> *There is no one like Him, before Him, or after Him.*
> *He is, He was, and He is to come.*
> *Alpha. Omega.*
> *Lazona. Yannonay.*

Our muted, low singing filled the heart so that a majestic intersection of mind, emotions, and will roiled there like an undertow in the crystal sea. The emotion built. Our voices rose. The song lifted higher and higher. Kyrie Himself closed His eyes. The Cherubim swayed to the stark, almost strained syllables of speech. We climbed on the rungs of a ladder, higher, higher. Our voices melded, became one, a chorus of voices flowing together like a beatific river of light.

We held it and held it and held it. The notes seemed to go on forever. There was no endpoint. Our voices lifted and reached. The fragrances of our breath mingled. We were Kyrie's. He was ours. We were in Him, and He was in us.

The melody sprang out against the perfect harmony. We rose higher on each of those holies:

> *Holy. Holy. Holy.*

I stretched my limbs, lifted my arms. I could feel the dancing spirals of light before my closed eyes. I grasped at air, stood on tiptoe, reached. My voice seemed about to break. I had never sung like this before. We were worshiping Him now, plunging to the very marrow of existence and then breaking forth to the outermost edge of consciousness.

It was a wonder.

And then it ended. The music broke off.

Slowly, slowly, I relaxed, let my arms go slack and then to my sides. I came down on the heels of my feet, opened my eyes. The whole mountain burned with flame.

I felt everyone releasing the moment. No one said a word. No one needed to. We had climbed a new pinnacle.

The silence grew out upon us, and the flaming mountain slowly slipped back to a bright, celestial glow. I finally sat down and realized Cere had joined me on my right, and Tyree and Rune on my left. I looked each in the eye, smiled ever so slightly, and gazed forward. I did not want to lose what we had just claimed.

Finally, Lucifer broke the silence. "Once again we have worshiped. And it has been magnificent in His eyes. Alleluia."

Our raw voices responded, "Alleluia," almost a gruff, bled sound to what we had just produced in our singing.

All of us looked at Kyrie seated there, His face like lightning held in flash, His robes like a flowing river of resplendent colors. His gaze spoke of pure joy. His eyes were grave but open with love. And His lips spoke, "Well done!"

Our chorused shout must have shaken the very heavens: "Hallelujah!"

A moment later, a very different tone came over us. Lucifer flew forward, rose up before us, and as if he himself would reap our worship, he said acutely and with an almost savage, guttural agony, "There are differences among us!"

We instantly quieted and stared back at this multifaceted creature who suddenly appeared so stern and all-powerful.

"There are disputes, problems, discussions that have separated friends and leaders. There are those who talk in quiet tones about choosing one or the other. It is not so. There is no choice. It must stop."

I sat there, swallowing, trying to regain my composure.

"What you have just witnessed is what Kyrie desires, that we truly be one as we have just sung and worshiped as one. But there are those who would destroy this. To you who would destroy, know this: Kyrie is against you!"

The words struck me like sewage in my gut. I wanted to vomit up all the dread thoughts that had so recently gored my soul and hide them away, never to think them again.

"No good can come from this," Lucifer said. "No good. Know this: that Kyrie is against those who would make war with others. There is deceit.

There is testing of one another. There is pretense. All this must stop. Kyrie is against those who practice these things."

The silence around me was one of deep conviction, awe, and fear. The words, "Kyrie is against you," drilled through my soul. I felt a cold, pallid hand grasping my heart. Its weather crowded up into my mind until I felt like some dead thing, discarded, heaped into ruin in a waste place. I resolved in that moment not to listen to those who would tear down.

Lucifer paused and hung there in the air high above Kyrie, but closer to us. His eyes seemed to look directly into my heart. I quivered. But as I returned that terrorizing gaze, I saw something else. I did not then know what it was. Even now I'm not sure. Maybe it was ambivalence, a cool, calculating inner restiveness. And I knew in that moment that Lucifer did not want to say the things he was saying.

I wondered about it. How it could be?

I had no answer.

But I knew in my soul, something dark and terrible reigned in our midst, and no words from Lucifer or anyone else would still it.

Worse, this dark thing was also inside me.

15

That evening Tyree came to my room again. He was holding what looked like a sawed off Harpistrer in his hands. It was of wood, but sharp at the ends, certainly not playable. He immediately handed it to me.

"Your new instrument," he said.

I studied the instrument, then handed it back to Tyree. "As a Harpistrer, it is useless. I cannot play it."

"It does more than play."

"Yes, I am sure of that," I said. I knew what this was now.

"It is a weapon, Aris," he said quietly. "For your protection."

"I rely on the protection of Kyrie and the Son, Tyree."

"That's good, but it may not be enough."

I held out the Harpistrer/weapon to him, and when he didn't take it, it clattered to the floor inside my door. He fixed me with his eyes, then shrugged. "You can use it or not use it, it's your choice. There will soon come a time when all of us will be forced to make choices."

"Then you know this for certain?"

"I can read the times."

"Then you have made your choice?"

"No. I have made no choice. I just want to be prepared. I had hoped you would also see it that way."

I gazed into his face and it was tight, pained. Then I looked down at the floor and I saw blood dripping down. I gasped. "Tyree, you're wounded."

He blinked and started to stumble. I caught him and dragged him into my room, onto the couch.

"What has happened?"

"I was ambushed," he wheezed.

"Why?"

"I took the weapons without authority. Lucifer's." He winced. I began applying cloths and bandages to the long slice on his upper leg. "It's not a bad wound," he said and smiled wryly. "And anyway, we're immortal."

"But we can be wounded."

"In body as well as heart."

I looked into his eyes and saw the pain there. "I do not want to choose between them," he said. Then he lay his head back and fainted.

I wrapped his wound and went out to find Cere and Rune. When we returned, Tyree was sitting up, the weapon in his hand. He jumped when we opened the door, and then he blinked. "This time it's real friends."

He told us about the ambush and how he'd stolen the Harpistrers from the shop but was caught on the way back. "There is a lot of mischief going on," he said. I could see he felt better. "We've got to stick together."

We all agreed. "No one makes a decision about this without letting each of us know," Cere said.

Rune nodded. "We cannot let our friendship dissolve no matter what happens."

"But can it survive?" Tyree said, still wincing with pain.

"It has to," I said.

We took Tyree down to the River that evening, and when he bathed, his wound was healed.

"Maybe it can still be recovered," Cere said as we all sat on the bank.

"I don't think so," Tyree answered, laying out and looking up at the clouds that covered the home of Kyrie. "It's too far gone. Those angels who attacked me were grim. And angry. We will each have to make a choice. Lucifer is pushing for that now."

"We will each do what we have to do," I said grimly, trying to be steadfast without indicating any signs of weakness.

"I still think Kyrie can do something," Cere said.

"What?" I asked.

"Call a halt to things. Peacemake. Something."

"There is one thing you are all forgetting," Tyree said.

"What is that?" I answered.

"We are made for worship. And we have all ceased worshiping."

We all looked over the River in silence. It was true. The worship of Heaven, which was Heaven's primary activity, had ceased.

"I know what I will do," Tyree said, standing.

We all turned to him, standing ourselves.

"We must protect ourselves, and I for one will get a good weapon."

Rune nodded. "That is probably wise."

Tears slipped down Cere's cheeks, though. "Much as I hate to admit it, I think you are right."

I sighed and said, "I am going back to my room. To think."

We parted, agreeing to decide nothing without informing the others.

16

Later that evening we met on the Mount again. Lucifer made some introductory comments, then said that Kyrie needed to speak to us all. Kyrie stood and began. His tall, imperial presence quieted us, and I opened my heart to listen to Him raptly. I did not see Tyree, though I'm sure he was there. Rune sat some ways off to my left, and Cere a little beyond him. I wondered briefly what thoughts coursed through their minds about all that was happening. But I chose to wait to speak to them until I was sure what Kyrie planned to do. The Son sat by, rapt, attentive, but quiet.

Kyrie began with the words, "I am not a taskmaster. I am not a tyrant. I wish for all of us only harmony, fellowship, and truth. But if I must decide between fellowship and truth, I will choose truth. We cannot survive without it."

He paused and there was an awesome silence, as if each of us pondered in the depths of his heart the freighted words. He continued, "I know that you have questions and points of dissent. I wish to encourage you. We are one, and questions are only a means to illumine truth. I implore you, do not withhold your questions. Come now, and let us reason together. Let us speak our minds, and let us consider the consequences of actions taken without full knowledge. There is power in truth. There is power in unity. But disharmony will not destroy us, and falsehood will not shackle the truth.

"This day I come before you without regret. There have been disagreements. But they can be resolved. One must decide then—for truth and unity and friendship and fellowship, or for lies and death and hatred and Hell.

"I warn you: there is no going back. Once cast, the die is set. If you choose to rebel, it is your choice and you must bear the consequences. Those consequences are separation from Me and all that is Mine forever. If you choose to rebel, I will act, far more forcefully than I have until now. Ultimately, you will each face a final judgment for your deeds in the spirit. I will not tolerate the disruption and destruction of My family."

There was a steady silence as He gazed out upon us, His eyes seeming to meet each of ours. In them I saw pain, but I also saw resolution. For the first time I sensed what a formidable enemy Kyrie would be. It occurred to me that rebellion was the most foolish of choices. Certainly there was room for negotiation, a middle way. Kyrie had left that open.

At the same time He had made the choice clear: Him and all that was His, or Lucifer and all that was his.

As Kyrie sat, Lucifer ascended once more into view. His wings spread wide. Every jewel glinted in the light. My own eyes revelled in the pleasure simply of staring at him. He was light and beauty itself. His eyes were wide with a determination similar to what I had seen in Kyrie. I wondered if they had reached an agreement. We remained quiet. I noticed some brethren carrying the new instruments I had seen in the cave under the Cruke workshop. I was not sure what it meant, but I was sure it did not augur well.

Then Lucifer began to speak. His mellifluous voice trumpeted out over us. The cadence was slow then fast, beguiling, holding. He began, "Kyrie and I have had negotiations. I understand now that we are given leave to compose. We have the right to make our own instruments. We are privileged to eat of the Tree of Life and all the trees as much as we like. We are afforded great new freedoms in our choices of quarters, and we are free to barter away our possessions in exchange for other possessions, as well as rankings, privileges, powers, dominions.

"We personally are given supreme power to further organize and assemble our entourage. We will be doing this shortly.

"We also . . . "

The use of the "we" astounded me. At first I thought I was hearing things. But then I realized Lucifer was using it of himself. I had never heard anyone use it except Kyrie alone, and then only rarely when He spoke of Himself, the Son, and the Spirit. Kyrie seemed to take no notice, though, and I contented myself that this must also have fallen within the negotiations.

"We have privilege to leave the mercy seat and comport among you. We will be engaging this privilege soon as well.

"But . . . "

Lucifer paused and sighed, as if despairing. I instinctively leaned forward to hear his next words. Kyrie's attention was riveted to Lucifer's human face. We held ourselves as if between breaths.

" . . . it clearly does not go far enough."

Immediately, figures arose around me, each of them holding a weapon.

"Hail, Lucifer!" many cried.

"Lucifer reigns!" others shouted.

There was momentary pandemonium. Kyrie sat rooted to His seat, unmoved, saying nothing.

As Lucifer continued, for the first time, I noticed dangling from his multifaceted garment a lengthy diamond blade. "So long as there are three rulers among us, there will be strife, blame, and tragedy. It is I who have organized your ranks. It is I who have settled disputes. It is us who now propose the innovations that will make our music to soar in the sky. Therefore, it is us who should reign. Alone!"

Another cheer went up, and angels held their new instruments high above their heads, shaking and brandishing them like the weapons they were. I stood only to see Kyrie's face.

At that moment, Kyrie stood. "So you do not agree to our conditions?"

Lucifer cried, "No! Never!" His own excitement was palpable, emanating from his visages like sparkling water. Angels danced and spun in the air. The sky was full of smoke, tendrils of light, and the booming of drums.

Kyrie called for silence. When the myriads quieted, He said, "And you do not agree as we spoke earlier?"

"Never!"

More cheers.

"And you intend to secede?"

"We want our own place. We shall have it."

A chanting went up. "Lucifer! Lucifer! Lucifer!"

But underneath another, even louder cry. "Kyrie! Kyrie! Kyrie!"

When quiet prevailed, Kyrie said, "Where will you go?"

An even greater quiet befell us. We stood, transfixed. Kyrie remained standing. His powerful limbs lay at his side. He wore no sword or armor. Lucifer's eyes blinked, as if unable to make a response. Everyone seemed locked to that single moment, that question.

Then Lucifer said, "On the contrary, where will you go?"

Kyrie said immediately, "No rebels will remain here. You must make your own world, your own place. You shall not take this one."

"You are able to make another place. You should do it!" Lucifer cried. More cheering.

"And you are not able?" Kyrie asked.

"I am not a Creator," Lucifer retorted. "I am a Ruler!"

Cries cut the air once again. Lucifer cried for calm, and then as if gripped by an unseen hand, we all stood still, our eyes forward.

Kyrie's voice rang across the mountain like a bell. "If you rebel, you will die. Only judgment and Hell await you. That is my final warning."

He knelt down on one knee and drew a long line on the mountain in the small valley between us and Him with the Cherubim. Then He stood and said, "All those who are with Me, will step across this line to My side of the mountain. And those who are with Lucifer, remain. This is not a choice to be made quickly. I give you one day to deliberate. Tomorrow I will return and we will make our choices. Until then, you are free."

With that Kyrie and the Son slowly ascended before us into the heights of the clouds. We all stared after Him, and then I felt the hard fingers on my waist release.

"The coward has departed!" Lucifer cried. "Who is with me?"

"I am!" shouted one.

A second voice resounded.

In moments, the whole mountain jangled with their shouts and cries.

I could not see Rune, or Tyree, or Cere. I wanted to know what they were thinking. So I left the mountain, still in tumult, and returned to the Great City. I thought to go to my room, but instead, I went to the Temple.

All was silent, cool.

I walked into the holy place and saw the altar of incense, its smoke still going aloft. No one was there tending it. I walked past it to the mercy seat. The two Cherubim protecting it had disappeared, though I was sure they were simply out at the Mount. Surely, they had not already defected.

I touched the altar. Behind it the great throne sat still and silent. I listened as if to hear voices, but none came to me.

My heart was cold, dank, dead inside me. I knelt at the altar and bowed my head. "Kyrie," I whispered. "Kyrie."

No inner voice resounded. I waited.

"Kyrie, help me."

I heard a commotion behind me and looked up and around. Others came in behind me: the Cherubs, the Seraphim, the seven. Others. Multitudes. We all gathered around the altar. The Cherubs took up their station over the mercy seat. We all fell to our knees.

"Kyrie." Whispers. Heartfelt pleadings.

"Kyrie!" Weeping. Cries.

"KYRIE!"

I looked up at the throne, expectant, shaking. He did not appear.

And then He did. Suddenly He was among us, walking, stooping, our size, no longer the majestic. Now the crushed. But valiant.

He touched my head. "Aris, you are doubtful."

"Yes, Lord."

"Hold fast to what you have been given."

Behind me He spoke to another. "Ressir, you are afraid."

"Yes, Lord."

"Keep in My shadow and you will no longer be fearful."

"I will."

Then I heard Him speak to Rune. "You have such impossible questions, My son."

"Yes, Lord."

"They will all be answered. But not today."

"When, Lord?"

"When the time is right."

Still He walked and touched and held. Then I heard Him speak to another: Cere. "You are worried about your friend, Tyree."

"Yes, Lord."

"He is still in My hands, but he wishes to be released."

"Please hold him tight, Lord."

"I cannot hold him unless he chooses that I hold him."

"But why?"

"That is my way."

"Yes, Lord."

And another. "You are angry, Jarus?"

"Yes."

"Do not sin."

"Yes, Lord."

He spoke with each of us. And in the end, we worshiped. He was no longer the majestic. He had come down among us, spoken, nourished us. For the moment, I was unafraid. But I knew His words were right. "Hold to what you have been given." I repeated it over and over. "Hold to what . . . Hold to . . . Hold . . . "

Then He was gone, and a wailing arose among us and we all knelt and prayed. My heart was still cold. I could not worship without Kyrie there. But I had worshiped when He spoke to me. At least Lucifer hadn't taken that away.

And still the doubts looked high and unrelenting.

I knelt a long time. Soon, I smelled fragrant breath. It was Cere. And behind her, Rune.

I looked at them and mouthed the name, "Tyree?"

They shook their heads. Cere finally said, "We do not know. He could be here, but I have not seen him."

I clasped their hands. We wept quietly, then walked slowly out of the Temple with all the others. Many faces looked downcast, despite Kyrie's visit. I saw no one smiling. There was a fear in our souls. And yet, I could also see resolution.

And hope.

Outside the Temple, I looked at the sky. The clouds high overhead where Kyrie dwelt were the same. I wondered what was beyond there, and why He had hidden Himself again. I had no answer, but I prayed that He would soon return. Before tomorrow.

We walked in silence to our own places. As we reached Rune's turnoff first, he suddenly said, "Let's go into the Outer Reaches and talk, and think. There will be quiet. I'm sure the myrrin would welcome it. They are steadfast, and they might have some good word to give us."

"I agree," Cere answered. Her willowy body looked malformed suddenly, as if broken in twain.

I only nodded, and then Cere and I walked on.

When we parted, she said, "Do not despair, Aris. Kyrie will yet save it."

"Lucifer is not to be turned," I said sadly.

"Perhaps. But there are many others whom he thought would join him who have not, many I thought would join him. But they were there in the Temple. I heard Him speak to them. The Temple was nearly filled a few moments ago. I'm sure Lucifer is counting on great numbers to defeat Kyrie. And maybe he does not have them after all."

"We shall see."

"I love you, Aris."

"Yes, I love you, Cere. And Rune."

"And Tyree," she said, filling in the gap that I left.

"And Tyree."

"Kyrie loves Tyree, too," she said.

"Then how can He let him make such a perilous choice?"

"Because it is a choice we all must make. Sooner or later."

"Better to be later."

"Better to be sooner for me." She grasped my hand. "There is much to hope in. I have felt nearer to Kyrie in these last minutes than ever before."

I nodded. "Yes, it was startling."

She left me and I stepped into my room. I was about to cast off my cloak and hurl myself into my garden to weep and pray some more when I saw him lounging on my couch. Tyree. He was smiling broadly.

— 17

I was so stunned, I couldn't speak. And then it all came in a rush. "Where have you been? We were looking for you! What did you think of Lucifer's challenge? Do you think Kyrie can win? Are you for Kyrie?"

Tyree grinned wryly and motioned me to sit. "It's been a long day. I feel as I've been running the Dogs of Dallett for hours."

"You've been riding?"

"Yes. And thinking. Telling myself it is all just a game."

"But it is not a game, Tyree."

He stood and walked over to the bookcase, turned around and leaned against it. I saw his weapon lying on the couch, one of the slinky pieces of metal like a sword. It would not have much effect against a sword like the one that Lucifer wore, and I wondered for a moment where Lucifer had gotten it.

"Yes," he sighed noisily, fingering the backs of my books. "It is not a game."

I finally decided to sit down. After clumping into one the soft chairs, I motioned for him to sit. "What have you decided?"

He gazed at me as if trying to decide what kind of response I would make to whatever he said, alternately taking one course and then another in his mind. Finally, he said with a weary blink of the eyes, "I can't make up my mind about this. It's all so very . . . difficult."

"You realize your very destiny is at stake."

Suddenly, he was angry. "Of course I know that! Do you think I'm blind? Sometimes I wish it wasn't between Kyrie and Lucifer. Sometimes I just wish I could rebel alone. Go out in flames of glory."

I forced myself to answer calmly. "But why?"

He raised his head and the anger vanished. "Just for the fun of it, maybe. To see what everyone would do." He laughed wryly. "That would be something. Everyone thinking it was Lucifer or Kyrie and nothing else, and here this Tyree stooge has gone off in a wholly different direction. It might be fun."

"Fun?"

"I could go for some of that. We haven't forgotten how, have we?"

"You don't really think that."

I refused to let my eyes fall. He couldn't return my gaze. I knew he probably thought already I was against him, and I didn't want him to think that. "There is time," I said lamely.

"Not much."

He sauntered about the room, fingering this, picking up that, finally standing over the weapon he'd given me. "You didn't bring your weapon today," he said suddenly, spinning around and facing me with it in his hand. "You should have."

"I'll have no part of weapons. I've already seen what they can do. How is your leg?"

"Fine. Like new. No pain or anything." I didn't know why we were being so distant, edging around one another like two wrestlers in a match. I was so glad to see him, and yet I knew I was acting as if he were an enemy.

Finally, his eyes met mine and I could see the terror in them for the first time. "I've been offered a principality, Aris. Rulership over a seven hundred."

I was shocked, but I said, "I suppose you should be glad."

"I'm not."

"Why?"

"It complicates things, makes it all the harder."

"You really think you'd take that?"

"It's something I didn't expect, that's all."

"So that's it. Lucifer swings his little bauble before you and you're hooked."

"Not yet." He gave me a surprised, repentant look. "Why are you so against me all of a sudden?"

I sighed, realizing he was right. I was on edge, too, stretched by all these tense arguments and differences in our ranks. "Let's sit and drink some tea."

His lips twitched with the first real smile of the day. "That sounds excellent."

As we drank, we joked about the Dogs of Dallett and other things. He told me of his caper that day with them. There had been others, just riding and riding like there was no tomorrow. "It was as if we all thought it would be the last time ever," he said. It was the old Tyree again, relaxed, cool, friendly. But after several minutes of such talk, he confessed, "It has me, Aris."

"It has you?"

"What they're offering. I'm nothing. I'll never be anything. With them I'd be something."

Now I was stunned. "You are Fifth Quarm, Tyree. A member of the orchestra. You are my friend. You are not nothing."

"I mean in . . . in . . . I don't know what I mean. It's tempting. Very tempting."

"Everything of value isn't balled up in being important."

"I know that."

I shook my head with renewed anger. "Only over a seven hundred? Who has rulership of a seven thousand? And a seventy thousand?"

"Better angels than me," Tyree said, raising his eyebrows as if joking.

I didn't take the bait. I said, "Why didn't you hold out for one of them, or are there others who had to be sucked in for those higher privileges?"

He flinched and murmured, "You make it sound so crass."

"It is."

He turned to me wearily, chewing his lip. "And what about you, Aris? Your doubts? Are you throwing everything in with Kyrie, no questions asked, no positions retained, no gifts, no nothing?"

"No, I receive the right to serve Kyrie and be with Him and know Him. That's enough for me."

"You don't think that." His tone was querulous. "You never think that. You are always walking around saying how Kyrie does nothing about this and does nothing about that and how He just lets Lucifer run Him down day by day. You have no respect for Him yourself!"

"That was yesterday. Today is today."

"So what happened? He offer you a stroll in the stones of fire?"

I looked away, angered, stunned at how nasty he could be. But immediately his eyes fell and he shook his head. "I'm sorry. I'm sorry! I don't know what to think about anything anymore. I need . . . I need . . . I don't know what I need."

I finally said quietly, "Cere and Rune are worried about you. We're all worried about you."

He shook his head and grinned sorrowfully. "And I'm worried about you."

"About what?"

"That we'll all go different ways."

"There are only two ways to go."

"Yes. But we can still end up on the same side for different reasons and our reasons . . . can be reasons that divide."

"But still on the same side, Tyree!"

He looked away. "Nothing works, Aris. That's the thing I can't get rid of. We're all alone in this no matter how much we want to feel a comradeship about it. We're alone. Absolutely alone. And it is our choice. Our own. No one else's. I can't choose for you, and you can't choose for me. And don't you understand, Aris? I don't want to have to choose!"

His last words were little more than a bleat of anguish. I stared at him and swallowed. His face was contorted with pain.

He grabbed me and shook me. "I don't want to have to choose, Aris! I liked things as they were. I love Heaven. I love the orchestra. I love simply running off and hauling down a starrax or leaping on the back of one of the dogs. Why does it have to end?"

"If only Lucifer had not . . . "

"It's not just Lucifer, Aris. That's the point. It's all of us. It's like the day by day things aren't enough. We have to have some excitement, so we cook up a rebellion to still the ennui."

"I haven't been bored, Tyree."

He pounded his hand on the back of the couch. "I don't know what to think anymore, Aris. That's why I'm rambling. It's all twisted up inside me."

I nodded, and for a moment we gripped one another at the shoulders in a violent embrace. Then he let go.

He started to leave, his shoulders hunched, defeated. I said to him when he reached the door, "What will you do, Tyree?"

"I don't know. No one knows."

"Kyrie knows."

"I suppose. But what does that matter? He knows everything but does nothing. So what good does it do?"

"Just grant one thing, Tyree."

"What is that?"

"Come with Cere and me and Rune to the Outer Reaches. Tonight. Just come. Even for a few minutes. They want to see you. Please."

"I'll think about it." He went to the door, picked up his weapon, then discarded it. "This will be of little use for most of us, I suppose, now that some have real weapons."

"We'll be in the land of the myrrin, Tyree," I called as he went out the door.

He didn't respond.

18

Cere was way out ahead of us, spiraling, pinwheeling, and headrolling along in a shimmer of sparkle and cool green twirls of light. We'd almost caught her with a straight shot when she hit a Lader Hole—something like worm holes of sci-fi fame—they really do exist, at least in Heaven—and zipped out the other side before I found the entrance. Rune and I stood near the entrance, panting.

I kicked at the black with my foot, trying to strike the side or lip of the Lader Hole. How was it that Cere had found it so easily?

Finally, Rune and I dove into the Lader Hole. In a moment we were singing along, my veins tingling with the speed, faster than light itself. How it did that I don't know. But such Lader Holes were all over Heaven, and they made exiting and entering very simple for those who used them.

The lights danced in my eyes, and I passed close to hundreds, thousands, of new, bright heavenly orbs, all of them moving in place to the music that held them on the mark. The acceleration was a marvelous sensation, as if I'd spattered into a thousand pieces and each piece had a mind of its own, jostling about and juggling, trying to come back together in some gruesome form. You wondered how you came out in one piece at the end. But you did, and I guess that was all that mattered.

Seconds later, we spat out on the other side and a pair of hands grabbed me before I could protest or even clear my head with the dizzying sensation of arriving in the Outer Reaches still intact. "You two are slow," Cere said, laughing.

A moment later, Rune ripped out and stood next to us, our feet firmly planted on the murky dark bluva of that part of Heaven.

"Look at them," Cere said, giving us both a little flick of her hand to turn us toward the bright blue stars in the sky. "Starraxes."

"They weren't here when I was out here before," I said, gazing heavenward. Even in the shekinah light, they were visible. Great rolling blue orbs with a trail of crimson following.

"They graze all over," Cere said. "Would you like to see them up close?"

"Sure," I answered and glanced at Rune.

"Why not?" he said. I sensed we were all trying not to speak of or even think about the great decision that was to be made tomorrow. This was just a little relaxation. We needed it, and I decided not to protest or hesitate in lieu of more pressing matters.

The starraxes moved with surprising speed, as if the great beasts were concentrating on some mental objective far off to the very edge of the Outer Reaches. They flowed along in a herd, not unlike the buffalo did on earth, their great heads heaving and snorting, almost frenzied with the lust for more speed and a louder rumble under their hooves.

I noticed a small group of myrrinin sitting nearby, their dwarfish faces all dark, but they were not scowling, simply embroiled in some discussion. I walked over to them, wondering if Tyree had arrived and if they'd seen him. I described him, gave my name, and they introduced themselves.

"No one from the Great City has been out since this morning when . . ." The leader's voice trailed off.

I asked, "What do the myrrin say about Kyrie's order?"

"We are pleased, and chagrined at the same time," the leader said, a stout, plump angel with shaggy wings and a punched-up nose that gave him a pugilistic look. He was gentle, though, I could tell, and probably a wise leader to the others. "Pleased that finally these troubles are reaching an end. Chagrined that it has come to this."

"What do they say of Lucifer's challenge to take Heaven from Him?"

"We are ready to fight." For the first time, I noticed the spears lying on the ground. Obviously the myrrin had fashioned them from the same wood used to make the Harpistrers, though I was sure it was only the extra remaining pieces, not the notches themselves. The myrrin were a rigorously honest folk and would not have countenanced my query, if I made it, about where the spears had come from.

I only nodded and said, "We were watching the starraxes."

"Very frisky, them," the stocky angel said. "We have been watching them, too. All of creation seems to be coming apart, but they remain one."

"That is good," I answered. "If Tyree does arrive, tell him we went up to view the starraxes more closely."

"That I will do," the angel said.

I returned to Rune and Cere and told them what I had discussed with the Myrrin brother.

"They are a sober, steadfast folk," Cere said. "I would not be surprised if not a single of their number went to Lucifer."

"I wonder if Lucifer wants them anyway," Rune mused.

"He'll take everybody he can get," I said, a hint of bitterness in my voice.

"Let's go have a closer look," Cere said, throwing her hair back and revealing her pretty ears and lobes.

We leaped into the sky and drew closer to the herd. The beasts were tawny and brown, while the light they threw off would blind me if I looked at them directly. It was necessary to use peripheral vision to get any sense of the creatures' weight, height, and great heaving propulsion. The big lugs sported two curved horns on their heads, a wooly shock of hair on their chest and thighs. Their six feet rumbled on the bluva with a tooth-rattling tremor. Rune and I followed Cere out, until we found the herds-angel behind the flock. He held in his hands a bolo that shimmered with the light of three red flaming balls.

Cere introduced us all, and the angel said, "I am Hara, and this is Terra." The angel had two heads, one blonde, one dark-haired, and a great black and blonde beard covering both of them as well as in between. Both were powerful, with strong chins and large noses. The one named Hara turned to his monstrous charges and grimaced. "Some of them have been getting out of hand. I have to watch them closely. No time for sitting and staring." He was a stocky, burly fellow. He held a staff in one hand and the bolo in the other. His two heads moved independently, and sometimes they spoke with each other, as if he were two different beings.

We watched the herd run and felt the thunder under our feet as their hooves pocked the bluva.

"Does one ever separate from the others?" I asked.

"Yes," Hara said with a nod. The head with the blonde hair regarded me. The other continued watching the starraxes. "Occasionally. That's what the bolo is for. To bring him down and get him back on track. They make a nice mark in the sky." He leaned on his staff and smiled. "Very persnickety beasts, they are. You think you've found a good patch of ground for them to graze, and they turn up their noses to it. And then you can't find anything but some thin lean grass and they smack it up. Funny, they are."

We watched with attentive eyes as the herd circled. Finally, Rune said, "Well, we really should get back down to talk."

I nodded, but Hara answered, "The choice today?"

"Yes," Cere replied. "There is much heartache."

"Do you know who you'll choose?"

Cere looked at me and then Rune. "I think we are all for Kyrie, but we all have doubts. Lucifer has done some marvelous things. It should be easy, but it isn't."

He looked off past the circling herd and growled, "It's a terrible shame, it is. No one of my kind likes this sort of thing. We like it all clean and straight, no hard questions. Just plain answers. Now we must face the hard questions."

"Are there those who would follow Lucifer?" I asked.

"There are," he said. "Not us. But there are others."

"Why?"

He drew a deep breath and chewed his upper lip. "I'm just glad Terra and I agree about this, I am." He glanced at his other head, and then said, "We agree about most things, we do. He doesn't like to do the talking. But we have had a heated discussion or two, we have. It seems that most of those who favor Lucifer think he is a better leader, with greater organizational abilities and so on. Neither Terra nor I agree to that, we don't. Others have been offered special places and positions. They're the most opportunistic. I think their reasoning is the worst. Several, Lucifer has touched in a personal way, he has, and they feel an intense debt owed to him. Why they can't see Kyrie behind it all is beyond both Terra and me. But then each of us must decide for themselves. Sometimes I think it's just the glamor of having to make a choice that has gripped them, it has, and they are casting a vote against Kyrie because they disapprove of His actions in some way, even though they have no great love for Lucifer either. So I judge it, I do."

The reasons were becoming more apparent. Power, position, prestige. Nothing real complicated. Personal loyalty.

After listening to him, I thought of my own doubts and difficulties with Kyrie, especially His reticence. That was no reason to cast my lot in with Lucifer.

Still, what I really wanted was to give myself wholly to one or the other. That seemed the real choice: to whom could I give my absolute and unwavering loyalty? And it seemed to me that the answer was neither. That was truly troubling.

Cere talked more with Hara, and Rune and I watched for several more minutes, when suddenly Terra broke into the conversation. "Hara, this is a good time for us to go meet with the myrrinin. These folk can watch the starraxes while we go down."

"I think not, Terra," Hara answered. The two heads faced one another, and I wondered whatever would happen if they truly disagreed about something. "They are not trained."

"Needn't be, they don't," Terra said. "Come. Let's go and get this over with now, I say."

He turned away and Hara looked back at us. "Could you stand for awhile? We would only be gone perhaps an hour. There is no one else, there isn't one."

I looked at Cere and Rune, then said, "Of course. Three of us ought to be able to handle it."

"Good, then it's settled." He handed me the bolo and Cere the staff and then sped away. Just before getting out of earshot, he cried, "We will be back shortly, we will. And thanks heartily."

I smiled at the burst of energy he departed with and turned to my friends. "I suppose we can talk as much here as anywhere."

"For me, it's simple," Cere said. "Lucifer has done nothing to attract me, and I have no reason to leave Kyrie. Though I wonder about some of Kyrie's judgments, not one has proved untrue yet, so I'm fixed."

Rune sat down crosslegged on the bluva. It was a little like sitting in midair, not hard to accomplish as once you are set in one place it becomes as firm and stable as any other.

Cere remained standing. I whirled the bolo about in my hands. "The more important question is," I said, "what will become of Lucifer and his followers. What will Kyrie do with them?"

"Give them their own place, I expect," Rune said. "What else is there to do?"

"Destroy them," Cere suddenly interjected.

Both Rune and I gave her our abrupt and complete attention. "Destroy them?"

"It's a possibility."

"And what about destroying all of it and just starting over?" I said. "That's a possibility too."

"Indeed it is," she said. "We have never seen Kyrie angry."

"Does He ever become angry?" Rune asked. His blonde hair shimmered in the starlight, and the shekinah gave his tunic an eerie shade. He looked like a classic ghost of earth's lore, though there are no ghosts as such there, and there are certainly none in Heaven. He looked grim and sober. "For if Kyrie were ever to become angry, what would happen? Who could oppose Him, or stop it?"

"He expresses every other emotion, why not anger?" I replied.

"Well, we haven't seen it," Cere said, putting the brakes on our train of thought. "So who's to know? I should think that if He was going to get angry, He would have done so by now. With Lucifer's tricks and all."

"If Kyrie gives them their own place, what's the possibility that they would be able to cross over to us?" I asked again. "And starting personal battles and such? It seems to me that if He creates another place, He would have to make them utterly separate and make us forget each other, or some such thing. Otherwise, there would undoubtedly be war between us."

"Lucifer cannot create from nothing like Kyrie, can he?" Cere said.

"No," both Rune and I answered, but I added, "I don't think so."

"No, he cannot, I am certain," Rune said. "That's why he wants the present creation. It has to be. So that makes sense."

"If he can't create," Cere responded, "then he is in a powerfully bad fix because if he doesn't get what he wants from Kyrie—namely the whole of the present creation—what can he do?"

"I think Lucifer may have other mini-rebellions on his hands, too," Rune said dourly. "Once they find out he cannot create—"

"They must all know that now," I said.

"Perhaps," Rune answered. "But they are counting on Lucifer's personal power, aren't they? If not, what are they counting on?"

"Their power in numbers," Cere said.

"But what will Lucifer do if . . . " I started to say.

Suddenly Cere looked up and remarked, "Look at that starrax!"

We all turned our eyes to the heavens and noticed one of the beasts plummeting away from the herd in the direction of the edge of the Outer Reaches.

"He's heading right for the darkness," Cere said. She stood and wiped her brow, then visored her eyes with her right hand.

"It probably happens all the time," I said. "He'll come back."

"No," Rune answered, always one to take the least happy course. "I don't think he'll turn. This is what the herds-angel is for. To stop him."

"We must get Hara and Terra!" I cried.

"There isn't time," Cere said. "Come on, we have to stop him."

"And get trampled in the process," Rune answered matter-of-factly. But he motioned for me. "You get that bolo going," he said. "Cere, you have the staff?"

"Yes."

We flew closer, just behind the raging starrax. Gesturing to me over the noise of the beast's hooves, Rune shouted and pointed to the free end of the bolo, "Let me grab this end and hold on. Get ready. You'll have to throw it. I think we're in for the ride of our lives." He called to Cere, "Hold onto one of the thongs of this bolo. It'll take all three of us, I warrant."

I began to whirl the bolo as Rune and Cere held on. "All right, here goes," I shouted above the din.

We darted out toward the beast, and immediately it saw us. Roaring with a sound that shook the bluva all around us, my own head seemed to rattle from the vibrations. The starrax shot off to the left, obviously leaving its chosen course and then whipping back around, ahead of us, coming back onto the alleyway like a ballet master.

"If I only get one foot, get ready to have your nose rubbed off!" I cried.

The beast ran hard and I could hear him breathing faster, great chuffs like chomps out of the black. I just hung onto the end of the bolo, whirling it as fast as I could.

"He's getting closer to the edge!" Cere screamed. "Throw it."

"I'm holding on," I heard Rune say, and then under his breath, "This is not what I was made for."

I cast out the bolo as hard as I could. The three balls clanged together, then skittered under the beasts hooves. I missed.

Drawing the line back in, I cried, "Let me try again."

"Do hurry!" Cere yelled.

We wheeled up behind the starrax, now turning its head and looking back at us, then plunging ever more fiercely ahead. I whirled the heavy bolo and Rune ripped it forward, getting as close to the beast's backside as we dared.

The bolo sang in the air, and the beast bellowed. The trail of its light zigged and zagged. I tightened my body with the tension. I didn't relish being pulled all over Heaven by that thing. Luckily, we could always let go of the bolo. But I knew we couldn't let him go off the edge.

I whirled the bolo harder and banked in toward the galloping beast. "If I can loop two of his feet, he'll probably roll. That's the best. If I only get one, we'll be dragged."

"Then get two, at all costs!" Rune shouted, terror on his face.

The bolo sang. Then with a lashing rip, I let go. The bolo spangled out to maximum stretch underneath the starrax. Immediately a ball caught and wound around a hoof.

"Got one!" Cere yelled.

Immediately, we were jerked through space with each lumbering stride of the starrax. My upper teeth cracked against the lower as my jaw jounced to the rhythm. The two other strands of the bolo were still revolving, sparks flying.

"Pray that we hook into another!" someone shouted. I prayed.

Almost instantaneously, the two other loops caught, one on each leg. The starrax tumbled.

"Hold on!" Cere cried. I gritted my teeth.

The starrax rolled, bellowing with rage, and we three were flung over and under the motion like clamshells in storm surf. I bit my tongue. My heels nicked first the back of my head, then my toes smacked into my eyebrows. I was going every which way. I couldn't see a thing. We were all balled up under the starrax's feet.

The beast got another foot free. We were coming up on a giant piece of a bluva-dust balled into a cold flat rock. I knew if we hit it, both I, Rune, and Cere could be crushed.

"He's going for the rock!" I screamed.

"I know. Hold on!"

"We'll be blasted to dust!" Rune shouted.

"Just hold on, I'm trying to direct him."

The starrax churned his legs viciously. A mighty hoof flung Cere into my chest. As we knocked, a second hoof slammed Rune's chin, turning his head. His neck was close to cracking. I just had time to reach up and pull him back before a second blow struck.

"Rune?"

No answer.

"Rune!"

The three legs scraped at the air, looking for hold. We were going into the rock. With a twist, I jerked Rune to the side and up onto the starrax's flank. With a horrifying thud, the starrax smashed into the rock, all six legs going slack for a moment. The three of us were thrown free.

I was dizzy, could hardly get my legs. But I stood wearily. The beast turned, rods of light shaking from his mane and horns like shards of shattered light spoor. The two eyes met mine and he stamped his foot.

"He's going to charge!"

Rune was unconscious. Cere was hurt. I tried to lift them both. I couldn't. Unconscious weight is the worst weight. I slapped Rune's face. "Rune, wake up!"

The beast snorted, then threw off the remaining coil of the bolo. There was nothing else to do. He had us. I screamed for help, not expecting any to appear.

The beast galloped out toward us, the heavy hooves quaking the rock like chips of slate. I grabbed under Rune's arms, dragging him backwards. I was too tired. Cere gave me a lift, but she was still dizzy.

The starrax bore in, gaining speed. I drew back, hoping to dodge out of the way at the last second.

Then like a bolt crackling with thunder, something screeched in by me and struck. An arm clamping the great horns, he tore the beast aside, twisting the thick neck like so much rope. The beast snorted, then fell. I couldn't see who it was—but I grappled with the starrax, wrapping the bolo again around three hooves and tying him up.

Seconds later, I looked up into Tyree's eyes. He was black with dust and feathers from the beast.

"Guess I missed all the fun!" he said with a grin.

I breathed out heavily. "Thanks. We were crushed for sure."

"You would have been all right."

"You saved us, Tyree."

"Yeah, guess I did."

I laughed and clapped him on the back. "Thanks, brother."

"Anytime, brother!"

We hurried back to Rune and Cere. She was patting his face and speaking to him. Rune rose slowly, still dazed, his eyes blinking.

I dusted off his head and beard. He didn't resist. I was worried, but then suddenly he threw his hand out. "Hey!"

We let him shake, and gradually he came back to full consciousness. When he saw Tyree, he smiled faintly. "Well, I guess it all came off as expected, except Tyree appeared like the Spirit out of nowhere! I thought you'd be here, Tyree. But not like this."

"I'd never miss a moment like this one," Tyree said. He grinned and shrugged. "You would have done the same thing."

For a moment we all stood there, grinning, not knowing what to do. Then with a clap, our four palms came together.

Realizing there was more to do, we turned around and regarded the beast, now on his side, his chest heaving.

"Now we get him back into the herd," Cere said. "You want to do the honors, Tyree?"

Tyree shook his head. "I'll watch this one." But a moment later, he pitched in.

Together, we rolled over the panting beast and pulled him by his tied legs. I leaned over and for the first time caught a whiff of his exhalation. Such breath! That alone could blow a valve at the bottom of creation! No wonder Kyrie didn't want these things loose. I breathed through my mouth and leaned into the work.

We dragged the huge living carcass backwards. Cere motioned to Rune to get around back and push.

"Let's just hope he doesn't get free till we're ready," Tyree said with a wheeze, "or we'll be leaking this stench all over Heaven for a month."

I was panting hard again as we tugged on the line. "How much does one of these monsters weigh?"

"You don't want to know," Tyree coughed.

We dragged the raging starrax back up to the herd. We weren't sure whether to release him, but then Hara and Terra arrived, aghast, but pleased that we'd stopped the roamer's mad drive for the edge of perdition. He said he'd be able to get him back now, and we dusted off our hands and helped him loose the beast.

Hara held one rear leg and I grabbed the other. In a matter of minutes, we set the animal free. It rolled onto its feet and shot away like a pig out from under an iron, and we all had a good laugh. I sighed. "So much for our relaxing little talk in the Outer Reaches."

"We still have time," Cere said. "Let's go down, visit the myrrinin, and then have a repast."

"Good idea," I tuned in.

We all burned through the sky down to the ground. I felt good and that whatever happened now would be right. Tyree was with us again. There would be no breaking this alliance.

19

When we sat Tyree broke our silence immediately. "Well, what has everyone decided?"

"For Kyrie," Cere said without hesitation.

Tyree smiled. "That's one. What about you, Rune?"

The tall Kinderling didn't answer right away, and his pause threw me off. I was expecting from him a quick answer, and in favor of Kyrie. But perhaps I had misjudged him all along.

"There are good reasons on both sides," Rune began, a slight tremble in his voice. "Security, a sense of place, a high degree of assurance, a feeling of loyalty, nothing unexpected with Kyrie. It could be a very stable life situation with few questions, perhaps at least fewer than there are now. It might be a dull existence, the kind I'm most attuned to. And yet . . . "

I stared at him, trying to gauge what answer he would now give. That he'd even been considering Lucifer's course astonished me. He had seemed so firm before.

"And yet?" Tyree asked.

"And yet, with Lucifer there is some intangible, some strange excitement, I don't know what it is. Innovation is perhaps the thing that he would stoke far more brightly. A sense of adventure, that seems sure. Better organization perhaps, better communication. I'm not sure. I'm not convinced these things are real, or that Lucifer is better able to achieve them than Kyrie. But my heart says something is missing here. If Kyrie is correct, then ultimate dissolution awaits those who fall in with Lucifer. But is Kyrie able to bring it about? I know He's omnipotent. But what have we seen of that? How do we know it's that much greater than Lucifer? Kyrie says it is. Lucifer himself taught the dogma to us. And no evidence shows that Kyrie has ever deceived us. Except His actions in dealing with Lucifer. So slow. So undecided. So hesitant. I should have squashed the boaster the moment he started in with his demands. Maybe He even regrets that He didn't. I don't know that I would have proven all the more decisive. But it's Lucifer's decisiveness that attracts me. Kyrie is slow, plodding, methodical. He takes so much time to solve a single problem. It galls me. It riles me. It makes me nervous."

He sighed. We all waited for more of whatever he had to say. But he was finished. I said, "So you are going to join Lucifer?"

Rune shook his head. "I don't know. I don't know. That's the bite of it. No matter how many times I argue it in my head, I end up tangled. I can see both sides, and I can see neither. What most worries me is that even if I join Kyrie now, who's to say I wouldn't join a second rebellion, or a third, or a fourth? What's to prevent angels from running off left and right, seceding till He's down to one left? And then none? He must act. That is what I desire. Then I would feel more compelled to trust Him."

I said, "But Kyrie is acting. He has drawn a line that we can cross over to one side or the other."

"That is not action," Rune said. He stood and began pacing. "It seems to me that Kyrie is asking us to trust Him before He's done anything to prove He's trustworthy! He wants us to come along with Him on a promise—no, not even a promise. On the basis of the fact that He is Creator and Lord and Master. He has promised us nothing. What if tomorrow He decides it really all was a bad show and He destroys the whole creation—that is, if He can do that now. I'm not convinced He can. But that's an arguable point.

"For me, I wish He would prove He is trustworthy now. I wish it was settled and . . . "

"And then there would be no choosing," Tyree said.

We all looked at him. Tyree gave us his sober look. "The dilemma you're feeling is the same all of us are feeling. Kyrie has turned the whole process on end. I'd think there'd be a duel, Him against Lucifer, all of us watching, all of us in the gallery, and then at the end, we'd choose the victor who would already be quite evident.

"But Kyrie has done the opposite. He says, 'Choose Me now and I will show you all that I can do, and I will be the victor in the end.' That's wonderful talk, but it makes things difficult for us in the ranks."

"That's it," Rune said. "Why didn't I think of that?"

"You did," Tyree said. "You just didn't put it into the right hole."

I interjected, "But isn't that the same thing that Lucifer is asking?"

Rune started to speak, but Tyree interrupted, "I think we all know very well what Lucifer is able to do. It is he who organized us. It is he who has built a chain of command and a sense of individuality in each of us. It is he who has fostered innovation and change and trying new things. So that much is clear. To a large degree with Lucifer what you see is what you get."

"But wasn't all that Lucifer did," I asked, "ultimately through Kyrie? When he was not opposed to Kyrie?"

"How do we know that?" Tyree said. "Yes, Kyrie speaks of His Spirit as touching each of us, but I have seen nothing. There is no one sitting here talking to us. As far as I'm concerned, Lucifer acted on his own in every instance, just as we act on our own."

"So you are for Lucifer then?"

All three of us turned to look directly at Tyree. He leaned back on his hands, and Cere sat down. She said, "Tell us the truth, Tyree. What are you thinking?"

He rolled his head back so that we could see only his neck and chin and the tip of his nose. Then he shook his head as if it ached. He twisted it around and then stopped, resting his eyes first on me, then Rune, then Cere. "Why is it so important to you?"

Cere, always decisive, always with a ready answer, said, "Because we don't want to lose a friend."

"What makes you think it will be loss of a friend?"

Cere suddenly looked dumbstruck, and I couldn't help but laugh, because all of us had been assuming that. She said, "I just thought it would come to that."

"But who says it has to—that is, if I join Lucifer, which I have not said I will do yet—why does my or anyone's joining ranks with Lucifer mean we will all cease to be friends?"

I struggled in my mind for an answer, but Rune spoke up. "Lucifer wants creation for himself and his loyalists! If that isn't war, what is?"

"But Kyrie drew the line on the Mount," Tyree answered. I wasn't sure if he was arguing from the heart, or if it was just debate. "It is ultimately Kyrie who has provoked all of this. Lucifer has not drawn a line. Lucifer has not demanded that Kyrie and anyone else leave. He has only asked for all that anyone would ask for, given his station and power."

"It is Lucifer who has made unconscionable demands," Cere said. "You have heard what he asks for. More, more, more. Where does it end? He will not stop until Kyrie and the Son are driven from the universe, because Lucifer does not want anyone else to rule besides him."

"Lucifer does not want simply to be a servant, a worshiper," Tyree said, his face turning red with fervor. "It is Kyrie who made us servants, ministers to Himself. How arrogant is that? What right does Kyrie have to make out of nothing sentient beings with hearts and souls and minds and then turn them into slaves." I was surprised at Tyree's apparent strength in tone, considering his words with me earlier. But I realized perhaps he had worked these things out in his mind now. Or perhaps he was simply boxing with the air to see what he did think!

"I don't think we're slaves," I said.

Cere stood. "You have bought into everything he says!" she cried. "Lucifer will stop at nothing short of destroying Kyrie. That is the ultimate issue."

"It is not!" Tyree was on his feet now.

I stood between them. "Cere! Tyree! We are not at war!"

"Yes, we are," Cere yelled.

"Indeed, you are the one who started it!" Tyree yelled back. "Just like Kyrie Himself."

"Everyone, listen!" Rune exclaimed with his gravelly voice. "This is not a battleground. Let's sit and talk sensibly. These are not times to fight."

Cere unclenched her fists and sat, looking away from all of us, her face hot with anger. Tyree just shrugged and slipped down to the ground. My heart was quaking. So this is what it had come to.

I said quietly, "Can we talk about this without going for each other's eyeballs?"

"I can," Tyree said evenly.

"It is not an issue that one should be able to discuss passively and dispassionately as if nothing were at stake," Cere said. "I am angry, and this has only made me angrier. Lucifer is a liar and . . . "

"I take offense at that," Tyree said. "He has been open and honest about everything."

Cere seethed, "Like the agreement that he and Kyrie supposedly made, and then he reneged on the Mount this morning?"

"The only agreement made was the one forced on him by Kyrie," Tyree answered firmly. "It was right for Lucifer to cast it all aside as it was bogus and false. It was dishonorable."

"I don't think Kyrie would say that," Cere said.

"All right, all right. Let's be friendly about this," I said, jumping in again and hoping not to leave these two friends forever committed to the other's destruction. "Let's get back to the issue. We were asking . . . What were we asking?"

"I have not decided for Kyrie or Lucifer," Tyree said. "I raise these issues because they are the very things I'm battling within myself. But I wish that we could all agree to the same side."

"You wish that we would all go one way or the other?" I said, astonished.

"I would. Whatever happens after tomorrow, I do not think we will be anything other than enemies if we join different sides of this argument."

"I will not leave Kyrie," Cere said. I wished more of her gentleness would show, but she appeared to be bitter about this. I touched her arm, and she did not flinch away. She said, "I have struggled with these matters, too, believe it or not. But I do not think Lucifer is honest. He has not been honest with Kyrie, and that is the ultimate test in my mind. How can we have any assurance he would be honest with us if he has been dishonest with the one person who can punish him for that dishonesty? With us, there will be no fear on Lucifer's part. He can deal with us with impunity once the choice has been settled. That gives me great fear. I do not trust Lucifer, and I will not join him."

Rune said, "I only wish I had more time."

I laughed. "That is the very thing you were complaining about Kyrie— that He takes too much time doing everything!"

"Yes, I am very much like Kyrie in this matter."

We all had a nervous chuckle.

Tyree said, "I suggest we go to our rooms, think, meditate, pray if we want, and then come together again before the meeting on the Mount. What do you say?"

"My frazzled emotions agree," Cere said.

I nodded, and Rune lamented, "I fear this shall be our last time together ever again."

I looked at him and noticed a tear in his eye. I grabbed Cere's hand and Tyree's. He took Rune's, and she took Rune's other hand. I said, "Let us covenant this day that we shall never be enemies, no matter what choices we make this evening."

"I do," Rune said.

"I also," Cere answered.

I waited for Tyree, and he said, "I shall live in hope of that."

And I completed the circle. "And me also."

Cere was weeping and Rune had tears in his eyes, but I gripped their hands one more time. "All will be well. You will see." Tyree gripped my hand tightly but would not return my anguished gaze.

A moment later, we leaped into the air and sped to the first Lader Hole on our way home.

—— 20

Soon we stood at my door. "I will leave you," Tyree said. "Time to think. We all need it."

"And pray, Tyree."

"And pray."

He regarded me fondly. "I love you, Aris. And I will not cease to be your friend no matter what happens."

"I hope."

He grabbed my hand hard, then left.

I felt relieved that I finally had some time to think. I sat down and stared out into my garden. My mind was a glut of ends, beginnings, and in-betweens. Kyrie had spoken of Hell and judgment. In our language, Hell meant "black darkness." All of Heaven was filled with the shekinah glory of God, and darkness was its opposite. Absence of Kyrie's light. But I had never seen darkness. Not even at the edge outside the Outer Reaches.

Judgment had a much clearer meaning, though it referred to an act I had never witnessed. It signified being brought before a court of law that rendered a final verdict on what should be done with someone. That much I understood. But again, all that it involved eluded me. How was I to make a decision when I hardly understood the things about which I had to make a decision? Rune's complaint that he needed more time glared in my face all the more ominously. Kyrie had given us a terrible task.

That much, though, was plain and without murk. What I had to choose was clear: Lucifer, Cherubim, ruler of Kyrie's creation, anointed, he who walked with Kyrie in the stones of fire, protector of God's presence.

And Kyrie: Almighty, Lord, Master of creation, omniscient, omnipresent, infinitely holy, just, loving, compassionate, gracious.

And yet, so many of these qualities were just words. I'd never seen Him actually act entirely in that character trait.

Or had I?

There was His reticence to speak when others were leading, presumably under His guidance and direction. His respect for others and His ability to let them be themselves. So there was one. He did not infringe on others' rights when He gave them a position of authority.

On the other hand, there was the altercation on the Mount last night. He had responded to Lucifer's requests . . .

Requests? Is that what they were?

Now I was getting tangled up again. But *requests* was the wrong word. *Demands* was better.

Legitimate demands?

Perhaps. From a certain perspective. Outrageous, audacious, brazen, even disrespectful demands, from another.

What was Lucifer's gripe anyway? Position? He had the highest in creation besides Kyrie and the Son, who in a sense did not even hold a position. Position was too mundane for Him, too plebeian a term. He was beyond position.

Then prestige? Again, Lucifer had the greatest prestige of all of us. Only Kyrie and the Son had more, I suppose, and again that was debatable. I did not think of Kyrie as if He had prestige or was a "prestigious presence," or some such terminology. Kyrie was the Creator, God, Potentate, something completely removed from creatureliness.

Holy might be the word. Completely separate unto Himself. Different in a billion, a trillion ways. Wholly other.

What was left? We did not have possessions as such, none worth coveting. Unless you considered worship a possession. But that was more of a right—in Kyrie's case.

No, it couldn't be quantified as a right. It was far more. Worship for us was a—what? Duty? No. Joy? Yes. Privilege? Undoubtedly. But something more. In a way it defined us. Worship was who we were, it was the meaning of our whole existence. It was why we existed. We lived to worship. It was something we offered freely, without solicitation, in joy, with abandon and beyond.

Worship? Was that what Lucifer wanted?

But why? It made no sense. Lucifer himself was a worshiper. He gained his fulfillment through worship. Personal satisfaction, personal elevation, personal joy and jubilation—if that was what he wanted—could come only through worshiping Kyrie. To cease worshiping Kyrie was to reject his own being and destiny, to throw it away with both hands. And in exchange for what? Judgment and Hell, as Kyrie had said.

Nebulous as those ideas were, they did not compare to what Lucifer had with Kyrie rather than without Him.

So what did Lucifer want? Power? He had authority, supreme authority. But power—to create, to change, to give, to take away—ultimately only Kyrie had all that. Lucifer himself said he was a Ruler, not a creator. He could not create out of nothing. The only creating he would do was with the raw materials Kyrie gave him—Heaven and all it held. If Lucifer lost Heaven, where could he go—and with myriads (or so it looked) of roiling savages bent on sucking from him the life only Kyrie could give limitlessly.

What was it? What did Lucifer crave?

The Son?

Yes, it had all started there now that I thought about it. When Kyrie had revealed the Son as coregent, coequal, then Lucifer began his sorry carping.

The Son. Great mystery there. But even if jealousy was the problem, there was still Kyrie Himself. The Son and Kyrie together threw up two powerful walls to what Lucifer wanted.

And what was that?

There was only one answer: he wanted to be Kyrie. He wanted to have everything he perceived Kyrie having—power, prestige, honor, worship, holiness, omniscience—all of it.

But how could he become Kyrie? More: how could he think he could become Kyrie?

Was that the final "it" I was looking for: Lucifer wanted to become Kyrie?

Clearly, if that was it, he thought somehow he could attain it. And yet . . . And yet . . . How could Lucifer think that? It was a piece of foolishness too vast to touch. How could Lucifer believe that he could be Kyrie? It would mean at the base of it that he must strip Kyrie of all His power and place immediately. That meant either to imprison Him or kill Him.

But that in my mind was inconceivable, monumentally laughable, ludicrous, the stuff of daydreams so farfetched no fully conscious person could give them credence.

So it had to be something else. But what?

I could think of nothing.

Still, if that was what drove him, was it reasonable—intelligent in any sense of the term—to choose following him over Kyrie?

And that brought it all back to the main question: Why should I follow Kyrie? Reasons seemed plentiful on the surface of things: He was Creator, powerful, a Lord, omniscient, holy.

But what did all those things add up to? They were terms in my mind, yes. But in many ways, I had not seen them in action. There hadn't been time to "prove" them, for that was what I really needed.

So it all came down to one thing: could I trust that Kyrie was indeed all the things He claimed He was without yet seeing any of it? Or at least, most of it?

Time . . . Time . . . Time . . . That was what I needed. There had to be a way to get it.

I had settled on this thought when there was a knock at the door. When I opened it, there stood Dosrin. Smiling. Wearing a multijeweled cloak. A shimmering sword on his hip. A hand extended.

I said, "I'm sorry, Dosrin . . . "

"No trouble," he answered and walked in without my leave. "I have come to make you a bold offer."

"Who sent you?" I said immediately, feeling angry and violated.

"Friends."

"Ah, friends. Who might these friends be?"

"Anonymous friends."

"Friends aren't anonymous."

"Forgive me, Aris. May I sit down?"

I felt myself giving way. "Please."

He sat, then fixed me with his attention. "The first seat among Harpistrers is yours."

"It is to my knowledge already filled."

"It is now open."

"And what authority gives you the honor to present this to me?"

"I think you know what authority, the only authority there is in Heaven at the moment."

"So you must be offering this to me because of Kyrie's desire?"

"No. He is not our authority."

"Zarsill, then?"

"You make me laugh, Aris. It is our dear master, Lucifer. He alone has the authority to proffer this, and he has chosen to offer it to you, pending of course your decision to join with him in this glorious battle for our freedom from coercion."

His statement incensed me. "How have we been coerced?"

"The tyrant Kyrie . . . "

"So He is a tyrant now?"

"Aris, please, there is no need to be defensive. We are brothers. We are discussing a matter of importance. Let us be rational and speak in a friendly manner. Sit, and let's talk. I know it does not always appear that He is the tyrant that He is, but I most sincerely assure you He is a dictator who does as He pleases, and no one has yet seen fit to oppose Him until now. But a champion has arisen, and he will secure not only our freedom but the permanent displacement of Kyrie from a position of authority."

"So Lucifer's going to—what—murder Kyrie?"

Dosrin laughed, a sweet but understanding laugh which I would probably have interpreted as condescending had I not been so aggravated.

I said, "Then what will he do?"

"Offer Kyrie a titular position. Perhaps an emeritus kind of thing. Something that will allow Him to be involved as much as He liked. We have no intention of killing Him. Good heavens, angel!"

"Oh, so Kyrie will content Himself with cleaning the streets?"

Dosrin laughed again, a laugh that was too hale and hearty. It rang so false I wanted to strike him, but I just sat there, glaring at him, the rage settling inside me like a coiled spring of flames. "Kyrie will have anything He wants. Lucifer will grant Him nothing but the best."

"And you think Kyrie would settle for that?"

"Why not? He's an intelligent, pragmatic, reasonable artiste. Why not?"

"Artiste?"

"Creator. Whatever. That's Kyrie's real strength: creation. Why not let

Him create away, do all the creating He wants. We could employ Him in that capacity and release Him to His own activities whenever He wants."

"A kind of consulting capacity?"

"Certainly. Why not? I hadn't thought of that. But it's possible. Anything's possible."

"I think you are insane."

For the first time, his demeanor fell. He fidgeted a moment, then stood. He seemed at a loss for words, but then he composed himself. He stammered a moment, then said, "We had hoped not to have to show you this. We had hoped you would be reasonable. But I think you had better come with me to see something singularly important and devastating to the regal claims Kyrie continues to voice."

"What are you going to show me, a new instrument that doubles as a weapon?"

"Oh, no, you will find this most compelling. Come."

— 21 —

Dosrin licked his lips dramatically. I saw the pride in his eyes. But I did not understand precisely what he could be proud about. He had not communicated very effectively, that was certain. But I realized this did not matter. Maybe he thought that his communication was far above the likes of me, and that what I didn't understand was both a sign of his erudition and of my ignorance. He said gravely, "Give me a moment."

He disappeared and I waited anxiously, rapping my fingers on the arm of the couch. Moments later he returned. "Come," he said. "We will see something that will alarm you."

We went out of the room and into the street. I followed him. We journeyed through the city, bright and redolent in the light. Minutes later we stood in one of the towering prayer centers. He led me down into it, long corridors, straight lucent walls about me till we came to a narrow wedged area. He stepped onto it, then slid inside. I followed, my heart beginning to pound harder as we came closer to what I imagined was his goal, though I had no idea what it could be. Soon we were poised on the edge of a room, looking in.

Dosrin motioned for me to lie down next to him. We both peered over the edge of one of the walls. There in the middle of the room was an angel bent on his knees by a small altar. He was praying. It was not a particularly unusual sight.

But suddenly as we watched, he stood and cried, "I swear, I will never again fight You on this. I swear! Please let me go!"

The cry was a wail. It cut me to the heart. The brother was in pain. I started to speak, but Dosrin motioned for me to be silent. "Watch," he whispered.

As the angel walked about the room, I noticed a vague clanking sound and could not see what was the cause. Then my eyes fixed upon the chains on his feet. I had never seen such a thing. Manacles cut out of crystal. The crystal was jagged, mean-looking, obviously disabling.

He dragged about in the chains, crying out now and then, "Please forgive me! Forgive! Just this once! Please!"

The room smelled dank. Around it settled an aura of darkness. Dosrin nudged me. "Let's go," he said.

When we stood outside the building once again, I said, "That is a horror."

"You have not seen anything," he said. "Come."

We wound together through the streets. Heaven was a beautiful, perfect realm, and I could not believe that within it could be a creature like this one, unforgiven, broken. I wanted to discuss it. But Dosrin refused to speak. He only said, "Wait till you've seen all of them."

Minutes later we stepped into another tall structure, mounted up several floors, and then secreted ourselves into some cavity between rooms. Dosrin said, "We can see him. He cannot see you. Do not be afraid."

I had never felt fear in all my travels in our realm, except that fleeting fear occasionally sensed wrangling some beast, like the starrax affair of that morning. Other than that, the only fear we knew was respect for the Master. Now an icy gasping fear clutched at my throat. What had happened to the angel in that room? And what was Dosrin about to show me?

My vision cleared. There before me stood a haggard Kinderling, his beard a tangle of unkept hair, his eyes sunken and cold, almost dead, his limbs thin and bedraggled. He was naked, standing before us, looking into a mirror. Spittle dripped from the sides of his mouth. He jerked about with strange quirky motions. He was clearly insane.

I listened and he spoke in clucks and growls and hideous sudden tinny squeaks. Occasionally words of our language punctuated the flow. "Friend, please friend . . . escape . . . merciful . . . the kingdom . . . " Nothing made any sense.

I watched with growing horror and revulsion. But suddenly he seemed to see us. A guttural shriek broke from his lips. He charged at the mirror and splayed out upon it like some hairy insect. He beat against the wall, till his hands were red with pain. And then he fell, quivering to the floor.

"Lost . . . forgotten . . . unforgiven."

I picked up those few words. They made sense of his condition. He had done something, I supposed, to deserve this, though I had never heard of an angel being punished for an infraction. We did not sin. I knew of no one who could have done something to deserve this.

The angel lay on the floor, writhing, his hands reaching out to some unknown, unmentioned person in the sky above him. Then with a loud shriek, he rolled over and sobbed. "Bones . . . " Guttural shrieks. "Bones . . . bones . . . " More shrieks. Then, "Blood." The word short and clipped. He succumbed after that and lay there silent.

I turned to Dosrin, aghast. "How can this . . . "

He put his finger to his lips. "One more demonstration," he said. He led me into the depths of a third building where angel brothers lounged and drank and talked. We did not speak to any of them, and they did not seem to notice our presence.

Dosrin led me deep into the under levels of Heaven. Of course, I had been to these regions. They were no different from those on the surface. Their light coursed their crystal just as brightly. Heaven was layer upon layer of structure and even where the earth lay, below it lay other structures. We were in some ways not unlike one monstrous city from the very core of itself out.

We journeyed down toward the core. I had not been there before, and an excitement gripped me at the sight of the intensity of the light there, as if Kyrie concentrated it more at the center than on the circumference. I remained appalled, though, at what I had seen. I did not think Dosrin could show me worse.

He led me through a doorway that opened upon a small plain. We walked through a field and soon came to a brilliantly green meadow. There in the middle stood a hovel, the light encrusted like dirty diamonds.

He took me to the fence. Then we saw them. Six of the brethren on their knees, bowing and whispering, "You are worthy. You are worthy. You are worthy." They didn't stop. Just the same mantra over and over.

I found myself growing angry at the being who had foisted this upon six of my brothers. What was the point? A recitation of three words ad infinitum? It was truly ad nauseam. I stifled the vomit in my own throat.

After watching this go on for ten minutes, Dosrin led me away, and he took me to the air above, winding over the tops of trees and dodging groups of brothers like gulls on the way to their various destinations. When we alighted, he merely said, "So what do you think?"

"It's an abomination!" I said without hesitation. "Who ordered these atrocities?"

"Who would you think?"

"I don't know—First Quadrant tyrants?"

"Try again."

I didn't want to suggest it, but finally I said, "Lucifer?" More a question than an assertion.

"Never!" Dosrin cried.

"Then who?" I asked again. "This is impossible. Nothing like this was ever seen in all of Heaven."

"Think. There is no one else who could have ordered it."

"Then who?"

"Kyrie. And the Son!"

I stood there stunned. It was more impossible than any of the other answers. How could that be? I said, "But that is ludicrous! How could Kyrie and the Son order these things?"

"We don't know," Dosrin said. "We only know that they did."

The bile burned the back edge of my throat. I was going to be sick. My mind was afire with anger, a desire for vengeance, a need to tear those brothers out of their prisons.

"What can we do?" I said again, still trying to calm the raging in my soul.

"Now you understand Lucifer and those who follow him. Why we meet and discuss. There is something terrible in Heaven, and it must be eradicated. Quickly."

I stood there dumbfounded beyond thought. Finally, I forced myself to say, "Please leave me alone."

"We will be talking," he said, then turned and was gone. I knew, though, what I had to do. Cere, Rune, and Tyree had to witness these sorry spectacles. I would find them and take them there immediately.

22

I could not locate Tyree or Cere, but I found Rune in his quarters. I had my Harpistrer, afraid to leave it in my room. As I spoke, his eyes dimmed, and a dark look came over his face. The glow drained from his cheeks. "I did not think they would show you," he said.

"Then you have seen these things?"

"Not the same, but others."

I plucked my Harpistrer with frustration, sending out a bottom line of light that I kicked across the room with my foot. It shattered on one of the walls in a splattering of blue, green, and purple. The picture in my mind crashed against the images that I had just seen that afternoon.

He commented, "There is such beauty. And next to it, such horror."

"But what can we do?"

"I think Kyrie must be confronted."

"I'm not sure that was Dosrin's desire or plan, as yet."

Rune gave me a sorrowful look, then said, "Perhaps we should do something about the brothers in pain."

"Yes, yes! Let's go to them, talk to them. Perhaps we can help. After all, we are peacemakers."

"I think you are right." He rose and shook his cloak, then put it on. He looked resplendent, regal in the new cloak, and I commented to that effect. He only said, "It is raiment undeserved when there are such hideous vestiges of want and agony in Heaven."

"But it will be made right."

Rune nodded. We stood in his doorway, and then we were off.

"I hope I can remember the way." I led him through the streets, and soon we wound our way to the place of Dosrin's first example, the angel who cried out for forgiveness. I was sure I had the right location. But when we reached the spot, there was no one there. We looked all around.

"But it was here. I am sure," I told Rune.

"Perhaps he has been removed. Perhaps Dosrin has gained audience with Kyrie and secured his release."

"But Dosrin told me of no such efforts."

"Surely he would do that, though, wouldn't he? Even if he is for Lucifer. He would not leave that angel like that. I did find it hard to believe that Kyrie would cause someone to remain in such a condition."

I thought about it, still embarrassed that we had found the room empty. I did not even see the crystal chains anywhere. Whatever had happened, they must have been taken with him. "That must be it," I said. "We'll find Dosrin and discover what happened. But for now, I'll take you to the second location."

At the second spot, though, it was the same. No one about. I wanted deeply to talk with these brethren. Find the cause of their pain. Free them, if I could. But he had also been removed.

Finally, we strode into the meadow. Again, it was empty.

Rune just sighed. "We must get back in time for the gathering."

I said, "Yes, but how can I choose for Kyrie with these pictures in my mind? He is a demon, a murderer!"

"If you cannot find them, how can you prove you saw them?"

"I don't know. How can anyone prove anything? All I know is that I saw them. I was not dreaming, or in a state of rapture—how could I be?—and witness that?"

I gazed with great anxiety into his cool green eyes. As our eyes met, he returned my gaze. For a moment we were one, then it passed. I felt the anguish splitting my features.

"There is more talk now than ever," he said quietly, "of the disgruntlement, of anger, very disturbing anger. It seems that many are for Lucifer."

I nodded unhappily. Dosrin had confirmed the reason for it, though I had obviously seen it manifested elsewhere.

"If what you saw is true, then such anger is understandable," Rune said. "But why are the three places you visited now empty?"

"Perhaps Kyrie has taken care of it."

"Perhaps."

I could not be sure, though of one thing I was sure: Kyrie, if He was the author of such behavior, was no longer worthy of my worship.

Rune shook his head. His golden hair, combed across his forehead with a silver diadem holding it in place, splayed out in the gathering dark, made him look terribly sincere and solemn.

"I don't understand it," Rune said. "Something has gone wrong. I might have thought Lucifer was capable of such things. But not Kyrie."

"That is what troubles me," I said. "It is no small wonder that Lucifer and the others speak in closed circles of grievances. What is it that Lucifer wants, Rune? You know these things better than I."

"No one seems to know. They can't explain it. Or they refuse. The word seems to be freedom."

All my meditations on the issue had led me nowhere, though I knew what freedom was. But there were different definitions. The way I'd understood it put it as power, the power and ability to do what you wished, but what also was right, what benefited all.

There was another interpretation, though, one certain others used, Lucifer among them. He called it the right to do anything he pleased without limits. What that meant, few of us understood. How could there not be limits? It was like asking a Harpistrer to do what only a Vinn could do or a Cruke.

"Freedom," Rune murmured. "Is that what you want, what I want?" He looked down the street we stood on. Then he said, "I don't think Kyrie did these things that you saw."

"You don't?"

"How would it be possible—to enshroud a brother in pain so great he is like a horror beyond redemption? Kyrie do such a thing? No."

"Then who?"

"It may be something quite beyond Kyrie's control."

I shook my head. "If Kyrie did not do it, then Kyrie can make it right again." I tried to speak confidently, though my own doubts lay deep down in my soul, like some kind of otherworldly sludge. It always seemed to come back to Him, no matter what the issue or problem. I said again, "He will know what to do."

Rune sighed. "I suppose." He placed his hand on my shoulder. I felt the weight of his heart pulsing in his fingers. Even the light that normally burst from his blue tunic seemed gray, dusky.

I grasped his hand. "Are you discouraged?"

He nodded. "Very."

I gripped his hand and our eyes met, then we turned back to the city, having seen nothing of what Dosrin had shown me. In the distance, we made ourselves see to the very edge of Heaven. For a moment, a roiling sea appeared to lash up and over the edge, then all was quiet. I felt the tingling of Rune's fingers. He appeared more burdened than I had ever seen him. I whispered, "It will be all right. Kyrie will solve it, as He has solved everything."

Rune tilted his chin and sighed. "They've come to me, Aris. Lucifer . . . "

"What do you mean?" I made him look at me and I searched his eyes.

"I've had thoughts, strange thoughts, Aris. I don't know what to do."

Our fingers meshed. For a moment, there was that wonderful coursing of beat with beat, blood with blood. Then a dissonance.

"Who? Who is 'they'?"

"You will find out," he said and stood. "I must go." He gazed long into my eyes. "We must hold together, Aris. A darkness is coming." His voice seemed to scrape at something deep inside himself.

"We will."

Rune turned to leave. "We will talk again."

I saw him to the edge of the city, and then we parted. Just before leaving, he shouted, "We will compose a memorable one together someday."

"We will." My throat felt constricted, scratchy.

As he wove along through the street, his great shoulders slumped, his hair looked dank. He disappeared in a smoky vibration of light. I held my breath, hoping he would return and tell me more. But I knew I would soon find out. Whoever "they" were would soon come. I felt it in my bones.

— 23

I sat in my room, thinking more about the recent events and the oncoming gathering on the Mount. What was I to do? There was one last thing I had to do before making a decision. That was to speak with Kyrie, alone, direct, no questions held back. I had never spoken to Him that way, not singly and sequestered off from all other outside influences. I resolved to go to the Temple and call upon Him. I would make plain my fears, worries, grievances. I would hear Him out.

I stood and was about to leave when there was another knock on my door. The two brethren who stood there stepped into my room uninvited and said tersely but plainly, "You are invited to speak personally with Lucifer."

I did not hesitate. "Take me to him." For the moment, I felt bold and unafraid.

In seconds, I stood in a distant chamber, not sure where I was. It was a lavishly decorated hall, with numerous instruments on the walls, fine jeweled furniture, a high ceiling, crafts work everywhere. But the room shone little next to the superlative Lucifer. He lay on a huge couch, his light-drenched, multifaceted body curled about him and his eyes closed, his wings furled, only one face looking out at me. All else was in repose.

He motioned for me to sit.

I trembled, remembered my manners and bowed briefly. "Cherubim."

"Yes, child. You have many questions." The voice rasped, as if he had been speaking to others endlessly all the past hours.

"Not so many that they cannot be easily answered by such as you."

The light flowed from him like liquid fire. He shone and shimmered, and his gleaming features up close were hardly less majestic than at a distance. His movements were fluid, utterly fascinating. His whole form was a vision of power, intellect, elegant beauty. I don't know how in his presence I answered so effortlessly. But there was something close and intimate about his look, as if he understood things about me that even I didn't understand.

"My deputies tell me that you are proving a hard case," he said simply and did not elaborate.

"I do not think of myself as a case, Sire."

"Indeed. But why are you so adamant? You do understand that we harbor no harmful intent to Kyrie, only that we all recognize our particular gifts and that His is creation while mine is rulership."

"How do you know that Kyrie does not think He is also a ruler?"

"You do not know Kyrie as I know Him," Lucifer intoned. His voice was mellow, as if gently caressing my mind into submission. "Kyrie does not like to rule. He likes to create something and then allow it to develop on its own. It's a sorry way to run things, especially when so many souls are involved. I have tried to persuade Him that a firm hand is necessary, but He does not agree. And of course you have seen the results."

"Results?"

"Separation of friends. Arguments. Disputes. Factions. Little clans here and there and everywhere. It's appalling. It will take me some time to get things in order once this little mock line-drawing contest is over. Of course, no one will join Him, and that's the tragedy of it. He will be mortally hurt, and I will have been the one to have shown Him and He'll resent me. It makes for bad relations all around. I do not like it. But then I did not provoke it."

"You think no one will join Him?"

"No one who has truly understood the stakes and consequences. Of course, there will be those who out of plain blind loyalty will stick to Him. That's normal and to be expected. What is not to be tolerated is His use of them against us. We have made small, almost trivial demands that He has rebuffed. Why? Because He is arrogant. It would be simple if we could all just agree. And isn't that what real fellowship is about—many fellows living together in harmony and agreement to the basic principles of things? That is what I desire. That is what I will establish, once this difficulty is surmounted. And then we will truly be on our way, composing, making music, and practicing a hundred other noble arts that He has not yet thought of, but which I have lobbied Him to establish for nearly every day of my reign.

"Now, Aris, I have offered you the first Harpistrer chair for a simple reason. You are creative, you have been doggedly circumspect about your music and practices, and it is my conclusion that you will continue to do as well and show a good example to the others. You fully realize there are many who desire this position, but I have reserved it for you."

"What makes you think I even desire such a position?"

"I should think anyone of your stature and wisdom would. If you don't, perhaps then we need to discuss what you do desire. I am your servant, longing only to fulfill whatever longings you have. If I am mistaken in this assessment of the circumstances, I am most remiss. Certainly, I do not want to force upon you anything that you do not desire."

My mind told me that Lucifer wielded a deft hand and was exceedingly sure of himself beyond anyone I had ever known in Heaven. He was sharp, as they say, and I, for one, could hardly keep ahead of him. But something troubled me beneath all the friendly, kindly words. I could not yet put a finger on what it was. His self-assurance, perhaps. That splendid, oh so confident savoir-faire that inscribed every syllable he spoke. Even Kyrie did not seem to have it in the abundance that Lucifer did. And yet beneath it all, something was improper, something disconnected. What was it?

Part of it was that he played on me as I played on my Harpistrer. He made his music by making me want what he wanted. And he expected me ultimately to do as he desired.

"You are silent, Aris? Is your mind once again corkscrewing among its thousand thoughts and contra-thoughts, arguing through each point till no point makes sense anymore?"

"I was thinking, yes."

"About what?"

I was not sure how to answer. To be bold, to speak directly to him was one course. But on the other hand stood the wisdom of diplomacy and reservation and keeping your own counsel. I said, "I was wondering about why you want me so much to make the efforts you have made to get me."

"Every soul has infinite value in our realm," Lucifer said. "To lose one is to lose too many."

"But why do you want me? I'm not particularly significant."

Lucifer's laugh was immediate, a self-effacing titter. Or so it seemed. "You do indeed have a poor opinion of yourself. Perhaps I should take it to heart and treat you as you would treat yourself."

"That is not what I meant."

"Then what do you mean?"

I struggled for the words. My mind seemed filled with the clattering of a hundred loose ends of thought, unable to connect. What was it I wanted to ask him? My thoughts roved back to the previous hours' and day's ruminations. I thought of Dosrin and the hopeless cases he had shown me, and then the startling absence of those same brethren when I came around with Rune. I thought of Kyrie and what He must be thinking, and of His words to me in the Temple of only hours ago.

As I thought of Kyrie, picturing His face, I realized most of all what I wanted from Him was the knowledge of what He wanted for us. For us. And for Himself.

And then I knew what it was I wanted to ask Lucifer.

"Sire, let me ask you one more question, and I rest with that."

"Go on."

"What do you want? Why have you allowed things to happen as they have? Why do you oppose Kyrie, and what is it you hope to gain?"

"That is the most multifaceted single question I think I have ever heard." He glanced at his deputies in the room and everyone laughed. I did not, though I ejaculated something that sounded like a laugh for convention's sake.

"But you ask a good question, and I can answer it in a syllable: peace. I seek peace for all of us. That is your answer complete."

"Then you are not at peace?"

"Not so long as my brethren suffer, live in fear, and fail to achieve all their great potential as inhabitants of Heaven."

"I see." I stood. "It's a worthy goal, I guess. As worthy as any. But the next question in my mind is this: How do you gain peace by making war?"

As if anticipating that question, Lucifer said, "Peace can only be gained when those who destroy peace are fully restrained."

I nodded. "Thank you for seeing me."

"I am willing to see all who come with honest, open questions and willing hearts."

"Of course."

I was led out and soon was back at my own quarters with the two deputies who had not yet introduced themselves. Their faces were dark as they stood in my doorway, and suddenly the taller one said, "You will not disappoint him."

I returned his gaze and noticed his hand on his sword. I had no weapon. I said, "I think many are bound to be disappointed by whatever happens this evening."

"But you will not disappoint *him*," the shorter one said, this time more roughly.

I swallowed and realized suddenly they were strong-arming me. "I will try to do what is right."

Both of them stepped forward, glowering. "There is no right, my friend," said the taller. "There is only will. You will not disappoint him, I say, and I am ready to defend him at whatever cost."

"Aye, and myself, too," said the other.

I started to speak, but both of them drew closer. "You have seen his love. You have heard his intent. What argument do you have left?"

I could feel the tall one's breath on my cheeks, and I did not like it. I stepped back.

"The fact is that you have no arguments left," said the shorter one. His face was dark, his eyes black. He slowly drew his sword a few inches and then shoved it back.

I stood my ground. "Brethren, I assure you, I will try to do what is right."

"And right is to please him. Mark it."

They both glowered at me again, and then turned and left, no more words spoken.

I sat down trembling and said to myself, "What am I to do? It should be plain by now, but I do not know who to believe. No one. Like Tyree said, I am alone and I must make this decision alone."

I stared at the walls and then at the open door. I stood and walked to it, to shut it, and then I knew what there was left to do. The Temple. And Kyrie.

__ 24

We were alone. I had passed numerous revelers in the streets, angels appearing on the way to parties and celebrations. Most of them seemed committed to Lucifer. I wondered how many, if any, of my brethren had permanently aligned with Kyrie. It looked hopeless. If everyone had gone for Lucifer, then some compromise was due. Perhaps Kyrie would step down. That might make it all much easier. But what then? That is what I came to find out.

"Kyrie," I said to the figure on the throne, still as regal and holy as ever. The Cherubs around him looked stalwart, unswerving also, though I sensed a certain air of despair. Though not from Kyrie Himself.

"Yes, my son."

"I come to you because . . . because I am confused."

"And fearful."

"And fearful, yes."

"What gives you fear, my son?"

I wanted to be as direct as possible. Nothing held back. "I have seen things, Lord, seen things that should not be. Angels in agony. One seeking forgiveness for crimes I do not know about, but seemingly repeatedly rebuffed and turned away. Another afflicted with madness. Spittle on his lips and cheeks. A mockery of angelic demeanor and privilege. And others, seemingly lost in meaningless repetition of words of worship, as if they were coerced." I paused, but He did not answer; He only continued regarding me gravely, behind His eyes the light of life and power beaming brightly. "Lord, what are these things?"

"They are deceptions. Ruses to move half-committed or questioning angels toward Lucifer."

"So they are not true?"

"They are not true."

"You have not imprisoned anyone, or coerced angels to live in some obsequious slavish worship that is ultimately meaningless."

"I have not."

"Then who has?"

"Those who would persuade you to distrust Me."

I knelt, my head bowed, hardly able to look Him who is goodness itself in the eye. For a moment, I felt ashamed of being so easily drawn in to a sham. And yet, I knew deep down the question was forming—why should I believe Kyrie over Dosrin or others?

He was looking at me, waiting. I said, "I'm sorry, Lord. I'm trying to collect my thoughts."

He said, "You are wondering why you should believe Me over others?"

"Yes." I was startled, though I knew that He knew my thoughts, or at least I believed He did.

"There are only three ways to judge it. Either I am lying, or I am insane, or I am telling the truth. Are there other alternatives?"

I thought about His words, then said, "I suppose not, Lord."

"Then you must judge. Do you think I am insane?"

I didn't. That was one thing I never could believe of Kyrie. He was the most rational of all of us. Lucifer, I might suspect of madness, in both senses of the word. But Kyrie was the gentlest of all beings, calm, righteous, just. No, I did not believe He was insane.

"No, Lord. I do not."

"Then: am I lying? And what is My reason to lie?"

This was more difficult. If He had imprisoned such creatures and left them in mortal agony, then He had something to hide. On the other hand, He would probably have very good reasons for such conduct and would not be afraid to explain Himself. I said, "No, I do not think You are lying."

"Then what other course is there?"

"That You are telling the truth."

"Good. We have made some progress. What else is there in your mind?"

I said almost immediately, "Lord, where is this all going? If Lucifer rebels, can he be successful? Can he defeat You? Would you be content to put Yourself under his authority? What if I joined forces with Lucifer? What awaits me?"

"Judgment, Hell, and eternal death."

The answer was so quick, so final, I felt in shock. After mulling over this word of terror, I said, "But if that is so, why do they still choose to rebel?"

"They do not believe that will be their end."

"So there is some question about it?"

"In their minds, yes. In My mind, no."

"But what if they war against You and win?"

"They cannot win."

"But what if they do?" I insisted.

"You must trust that I know whereof I speak. They cannot win."

"Then what will happen?"

"That, My child, involves many possibilities, all of which are plausible until they come to pass. I have always known what will happen, and that is why I say that what awaits them is judgment, Hell, and death."

"Then what if they don't rebel?"

"All things are possible to him who obeys."

I felt as if we were speaking in circles, and I was not sure how to untangle myself from them and get to the final bold truth that I needed to grasp to exit me from this turmoil. Suddenly, I blurted, "Lord, why should I trust You?"

"There is only one reason to trust anyone, and that is if he has proven trustworthy in the past and speaks truth in the present."

"But in some ways it appears that Lucifer is also trustworthy."

"Then you must choose between us."

I leaned forward and looked Him directly in the eye. "Lord, whom should I trust?"

"Whom do you want to trust?"

"You."

"Then choose to trust Me."

I sighed. "That's the whole issue, Lord. I don't know whether I should trust You in this because I'm not sure You know what You're doing. It seems to me that You repeatedly allow Lucifer to shove You around. There is confusion. Disorder. You take so long to act in many cases. I feel at times You are confused Yourself, and Lucifer seems so sure of Himself."

"What you are saying is that you wish to trust Me, but you do not know whether I will prove trustworthy in the long run. You do not know for certain that I will cause all things to work out together for a good result."

"Yes, that's it precisely."

"But if you knew all that, it wouldn't be trust. It would simply be a rational response to fact. There is only one choice: to trust now and believe that your trust will be proven right in the long run, or to wait and see until all has come to pass and then to determine to believe. But that would no longer be trust. As long as there is a future, there must be trust. Only when there is no future does trust become meaningless."

"You mean ultimately I have no choice: to either trust You or Lucifer, but it all comes down to trust?"

"Yes."

"And what if I trust now but cease to trust later?"

"If you trust Me now, you will be confirmed in your trust as you see matters unfold day by day. Trust only grows, it does not diminish except to him who has not really trusted, for the first act of trust gives way to opportunity to see things happen that will give him more reason to trust. Only with an untrustworthy object does trust diminish, and that until it is no more."

Each time as Kyrie spoke, I felt myself growing stronger in the resolution that I should choose Him. And yet I realized that the final consideration was what Cere, Rune, and Tyree would do. Cere was sure. That seemed to seal it. Either we all went for Kyrie, or we were divided. And if divided, then all unity was broken. Our friendship could not withstand the break. We who joined with Kyrie would be enemies of those who went with Lucifer. Unless I also chose Lucifer.

But that seemed impossible now.

"Lord, what will my friends do?"

A look of compassionate concern flitted across His features. He said, "Only those who govern the future can tell the future. Are you able to govern it?"

"I don't think so, Lord."

He smiled. "A wise answer. He who knows he is weak and ignorant is wiser than him who believes he is strong and discerning. But I will tell you this: every choice made this day is a choice made with eyes and heart open. There are no deceits that have held except for those who choose to hold them against truth."

"So my friends will do as they do so without force or fabrication?"

"All are wholly responsible for the choices they make."

"You do not make it easy, Lord."

"Nothing is easy. If it were, it would most probably not be worth doing, or pursuing, or creating. Only omnipotence can make such things appear easy."

"But they are not."

"They are not."

"Then why don't you stop Lucifer?"

"And what do you think would be required to do that?"

"Put him in his place. Or demote him. Or, I suppose, You could eliminate him entirely."

"Putting him in his place or demoting him will only anger him all the more and leave him that much more committed to his desires, as well as those who follow him. Elimination of a moral, spiritual being is impossible. I created him to live eternally."

"Then . . . Then imprison him."

"Only to have another arise who will take his place in a line of rebellions."

"But if . . . Then what is there to do?"

"To allow him the freedom I gave him at his creation."

"What freedom?"

"To obey Me or rebel against Me as he decides is best."

"But why must we have such freedom?"

"Without it, you are no longer angels."

"But wouldn't it be better?"

"No."

"It's better that your own creations rebel against You?"

"Better that they have the choice than that they have none."

"But why?"

"That is for the future, my son. What you must learn."

I closed my eyes and sighed, realizing our conversation had reached an endpoint. I simply said, "Thank you, Kyrie, for hearing me."

He smiled affectionately. "Thank you for hearing Me."

I stood and turned toward the back of the Temple.

25

Already, angels filled the air in the direction of the Mount. I wanted to find Cere and Rune, but I had no idea how to locate them in the crowd. The streets suddenly filled with angels of every race and kind. Those who could fly were offering help to those who couldn't, and I offered a ride to one, a Hauker named Stara. He mounted my back, and we were on our way.

The Mount came into view, and I said to Stara, "It is a grievous day." He was friendly faced with dark eyes and hair. We did not talk much. I could see he bore a great inner weight of grief over what we'd come to, and I wondered briefly if he knew what decision he'd make. How many had Lucifer come to as he'd come to me? How many were swayed by his fine words and genial personality? How many had gone to Kyrie and spoken personally of their own fears and questions?

Each of us was free. The lines drawn were clear. If anyone failed to understand the meaning of "judgment, death, and Hell," he had only himself to blame for not seeking a conclusive definition. We were on our way to make a perfectly rational, simple choice. And it all seemed to come down to a simple issue: what did I believe was the truth? And who did I believe had it?

Even with all words spoken and evidence offered, I still felt torn. I knew now I could not let others' choices affect mine. Tyree, Rune, Cere, and hundreds of others whom I knew and cared about had to make their own choices. I was responsible for mine. I could not use the excuse—if that was what I would need in the end—of following another into the path of perdition.

But I still did not know what the path of perdition was. Yes, Kyrie had made it plain from his side. And so had Lucifer. To follow Lucifer invited death and Hell—according to Kyrie. To follow Kyrie meant second-rate or third-rate citizenship in a world where Kyrie was little more than a figurehead—according to Lucifer. I had more reason to trust Kyrie. But the way to a real future seemed to lay with Lucifer. I had stronger evidence that Kyrie spoke truth. But Lucifer offered something more—innovation and adventure. There was certainly no proof that Kyrie had lost stature in any way since the inception of our kingdom. But Lucifer grew with every new pronouncement. And he had charisma, audacity, panache. Kyrie was so plain next to His chief deputy.

But there were Lucifer's deputies. "You will not disappoint him," gave me the shudders. Why did Lucifer on the one hand show himself so kindly, gentle, and gentlemanly, and then allow his deputies to virtually strong-arm me to the door? That made little sense. And if it was all a deception—the events involving the unforgiven brother and the lunatic and the six prisoners—I had to keep coming back to why Lucifer would authorize such a foolish hoax. He was far more intelligent than that, or wasn't he?

On the other hand, what if it wasn't a fraud? Then either Kyrie lied, or else He did not know what was happening in His own realm. Either way, it canceled Him as a worthy object of my devotion.

The problem was I had no reference point with which to settle all these matters. It was literally now or never. And it could not be never, so it had to be now.

I hated the fact, and I hated, momentarily, both Lucifer and Kyrie for imposing it upon me. I wanted to go back to my compact, tight little world of concerts and travels and jokes and friendly romps among the Dogs of Dallett. I resented it having to end.

Then there was always the possibility that maybe it wouldn't end. Maybe this little choice would accelerate the joys of Heaven beyond anything that I'd yet experienced.

Something told me, though, that that would not be. The end result of this "choice" would either be an immediate winner or all-out war which neither side had hope of winning.

I set Stara down on the Mount and then bid him a quick adieu, no questions asked. I sat down where I was, enclosed my knees in my arms, and huddled there, waiting. I did not want to speak to anyone. I did not want to think. I wanted the moment to come, and then I would see what I would do. Somehow I felt it would come to me in that moment.

26

I listened as angels gathered around me. There were different comments all around, some in whispers, some spoken outright.

"I think Kyrie is wrong in making us do this."

"It's really Lucifer's fault."

"It's good. It'll settle things once and for all. Then we can go on."

"There are many better ways to work this out."

"Like what?"

"Certainly Lucifer and Kyrie could think of one or two."

And, "Anyone who goes for Lucifer has to be insane."

"I say the same of Kyrie."

I realized there was as much confusion among our numbers as there was certainty, and there was some encouragement in that. But I simply huddled more tightly in my position, hoping everyone would ignore me, wishing this decision was something far in the past, that we had lived through it, and now all was well.

But there was no sense in wishing.

A moment later, I felt someone at my arm. "Hello, Aris." It was Cere.

"Cere, how are you?"

"I'm fine." Her cheeks were wet. I could see she'd been crying. I touched them, and she nodded. "I'm not fine. The end of all things has come."

"Perhaps a better beginning," I answered, trying to instill my tone with genuine optimism.

"You don't believe that."

I looked across the Mount. Myriads of my brethren and sistren stood or sat, talking, staring, waiting. I recognized many. There were instruments visible, too, and some wore real weapons: swords, daggers, spears, bow and arrows.

"No, I don't believe that," I said with a sigh.

"Have you decided what to do?"

"I was hoping it would come to me in these last hours. It hasn't." I turned to look into her eyes. Her blue, kinetic orbs smiled back at me and I felt relief that at least one of our number had not had such a bad time of it. "Why has it been so easy for you, Cere?"

She flicked her hair back and hugged her knees next to me. A soft, lovely fragrance drifted from her hair to me, and I felt myself bathed in it a moment, lifted into forgetfulness. She said, "It has not been easy, though I have known all along that I could not follow Lucifer, not like this."

"You believe that Kyrie speaks the truth then?"

"Yes."

"Has anyone come to you, tried to persuade you against your desires?"

"Yes."

"Dosrin?"

"Others. I spoke even to Lucifer."

"I think he must have talked to every one of us."

"Yes, and I spoke with Kyrie. I believe Lucifer thinks he is in the right. But I detect a strong underpinning of pride in everything he says and does. He cannot change course now because he is too proud and set in his desire. He believes he can defeat Kyrie, if it comes to battle; but he thinks Kyrie will settle for something less. He is a negotiator at heart, and a risk-taker. I have never felt love from him toward me, or really any other. Kyrie on the other hand . . ."

"You believe that Kyrie loves us?"

"Yes."

"Then why would He put us to this test?"

Cere leaned back, using her hands behind her as supports. "One chooses to love just as much as one chooses to be loyal, or to rebel."

"What do you think I should do, Cere?" I studied her face and eyes as she prepared a response. I sensed she wanted to give me a real piece of wisdom but found it hard to find the words for the right piece, if there was one.

"What did Kyrie tell you?"

"Many things, but nothing that seemed to seal me in my conviction. I left Him feeling as confused as ever."

"And Lucifer?"

"My problem is not so much rejecting Lucifer as it is accepting Kyrie. Lucifer seems to me to be ambitious beyond sense. He wants to enlist me as one more body in his army. Kyrie, on the other hand, gives me far more credit than He should. Something in me wants Him to tell me what to do. But He will not. He seems to have cut every line binding me to Him so that I am completely free in my decision to choose Him. Lucifer wangles and connives and persuades. Kyrie sits back and waits, giving me no directive so that I do not feel coerced in any sense. I don't understand it."

"You want Kyrie to lay it all out plain and pretty so that the answer is obvious?"

"I suppose."

"But if the answer was obvious, then how would it be a real choice? Then you are compelled by all those forces to make your choice the only reasonable way. Kyrie wants to free you from all that."

"But why?"

"So that you will have chosen Him for only one reason."

"And what is that?"

"Because He Himself is worthy. Not His deeds. Not what He can give you. But He Himself alone."

I shook my head. "I still don't understand, Cere. How is it that you understand these things and I don't?"

She laughed. "I don't say I understand them. I only say this is the kind of thinking that has influenced me. I believe that Kyrie is worthy of my loyalty and love because He is Kyrie, and nothing more. Lucifer, on the other hand, is a ruler; Kyrie is God. Kyrie is a creator; Lucifer, the creature. What Lucifer has done is suggest that he is greater than Kyrie because of what he does. And I cannot agree to that."

"It makes some sense. But I wonder . . ."

"Oh, look," Cere said suddenly. "Kyrie and the Son and the Cherubim and Seraphim have arrived and are seated. Things will begin." She paused. "You wonder what, Aris?"

I could see the white stone on the signet ring on the Son's finger. For a moment, I thought about Tyree's revelation. Would he really try to steal it? And what would the consequences be? "I wonder what virtue there is in choosing to make no choice."

"I don't know whether that is possible."

"Neither do I."

"Just remember what Kyrie says: 'All things are possible to him who loves God.'"

"I will remember that."

She stood. "I'll go now. There are several I promised to sit with as we wish to cross the line together."

"Please go then," I said.

She gripped my hand. "I love you, Aris. I hope we will be together on this. But if we aren't, I will not cease loving you all."

"Thanks, Cere. I . . ." I looked up into her eyes feeling as if this was the last time I'd ever look at her like this. "I love you, too."

"Adieu."

"Good-bye."

__ 27 _____

The seven angels who stand before Kyrie blew their trumpets, and we all turned our attention to the small group on the other side of the mountain. Kyrie, the Cherubim and Seraphim, and Lucifer and his deputies. Lucifer no longer stood as the anointed cherub. Neither did he protect and defend God's glory as before. He hung separate and apart, the air filled with the vibration of his wings and the lightning movements of his person. There were two other Cherubs who had joined him, and they fluttered about him as if they were the covering Cherubs of Kyrie. Seven deputies stood before Lucifer, each with a trumpet in his hand and a sword on his belt.

Michael spoke first on Kyrie's side. He stepped forward, his short-cropped dark hair gleaming in the shekinah. His long sword glimmered, every one of its encrusted jewels a beacon. He said, "You know the purpose of our gathering. The line has been drawn. Today we each make choices that determine our individual destinies. Kyrie will withdraw to the right, Lucifer to the left. You will each come forward and announce your choice verbally. You can come in any order you desire. If you wish to hold back until others have shown their choices, you are free to do so. No penalty will be ascribed to those who choose last. Nor will any special recognition be attached to those who choose first."

He paused and looked around, and I trembled slightly, wondering what would happen. Then Michael said, "Those who choose Kyrie do so with full recognition that all Heaven is His to give and parcel as He sees fit. To choose Kyrie is to choose life and goodness and the right."

He paused again and regarded our mass with singular compassion and friendship. "Those who choose Lucifer do so at the peril of Kyrie's wrath and ultimate judgment, death, and Hell." He paused and looked out upon us regally, his great sword shimmering. Then he said, "These are the warnings. Lucifer now wishes to speak."

Michael made a hasty but elegant exit, and Lucifer's bold voice rang out: "My friends. I grieve that this is where we find ourselves today. But be that as it may, we must make a choice fraught with peril. I personally bear Kyrie no ill will. We feel only that great changes are necessary to felicitously

augment and nurture our enterprise. These changes have not been authorized, and our frustration has led us to this moment. I bid you, choose wisely,
choose happily, choose fortuitously. Despite Kyrie's dire warnings, I have
no apprehension of judgment, death, or Hell. On the contrary, we begin a
new day with a grand anticipation of even greater glory. We will build a
new world together, and make it our own. Kyrie, of course, is always free
to join us as spectator and support. Toward those who choose Him we bear
no malice. Our numbers, however great or small, will forge forward to bring
about the innovations we have spoken of. Though it might have been better
had we remained united, I am confident this change will enable us to reach
all of our respective potential and become the great organ of music and art
that was always conceived.

"I bid you to make your choices with utmost care. I promise you glory
and a new heaven."

Lucifer continued for nearly an hour until his speech turned into a
harangue against Kyrie and His tyranny. He ended with the words, "We
must break this yoke and live free. Freedom is the greatest good, and nothing
must be allowed to exist which will stymie it. I bid you, join me and gain
the great freedom we all desire."

Immediately, gleeful cheering went up from our gathered horde. It was
obvious that many had already made their choice for Lucifer. In fact, I
sensed that Lucifer's audacity and boldness were built on the hope that most
of us would indeed follow him. There was no evidence that numbers would
run against him. I realized this posed a precarious twist to our proceedings.
What would Lucifer do if numbers so obviously went against him? Clearly,
he did not think this possible. And that might have been evidence of the
pride that Cere had spoken of.

After Lucifer finished, Kyrie stood. There was some cheering, but He
quieted it with a wave of His hand. "My children, we gather here today to
make decisions that will stay with us for all eternity. It is with sorrow that
I proceed from here because I know that after today many of you who have
been friends will become mortal enemies. I adjure you to understand that
all Lucifer has told you are abject lies . . ."

Immediately, Lucifer shot forward as if to clip Kyrie, but two of the
Cherubs protecting Kyrie restrained him and he was repulsed. Kyrie said
again, "Lucifer has told lie after lie, and in his pride he believes he can defeat
Me. He cannot . . ."

"Lies!" Lucifer screamed.

"Make your choice at peril of your own lives," Kyrie cried.

"He lies!" Lucifer screamed again, and his deputies drew their swords.
Immediately, the seven were at Kyrie's side, their own weapons drawn and
raised.

Lucifer spun back and forth in the air, the wheels of fire underneath him
like lightning. He screamed, "Treachery! Lies! Falsehood! Kyrie deserves
to die!"

Michael held up a flaming sword, larger than anything Lucifer carried, and cut a swathe in the soil. "Choose you this day whom you will serve, angels! Choose today. Lucifer or Kyrie. Now begin, and may wisdom and mercy be with you."

Lucifer and his entourage drew back from the line to the left. There was an immediate rush to the line with hundreds, thousands shouting, "Lucifer! We choose Lucifer! Lucifer reigns!"

First, of course, were the deputies and others already aligned with Lucifer. But then many others from our ranks rushed toward the crease in the soil. Soon, the left side of the mountain began to fill with a roaring, cheering mass. As each new angel stepped to the fore, cheers went up as he shouted, "Lucifer!" Some offered variations. "Lucifer only! There is no other!" And, "I choose Lucifer and spit on Kyrie!"

It was obvious the friendly decorum that Lucifer had spoken of was utterly false. These angels were prepared for their words. They did not approach the line to spout friendly aphorisms.

Soon the crowd thinned, though, and others began stepping to the line who chose Kyrie just as firmly. There was anger in many of their voices, but with each Kyrie pronounced a blessing.

"Carrorr, take your place among the blessed."

"Still your anger, Zol. There will be time yet for anger."

"Find peace, Arranid. Your heart is now free."

Back and forth it went, and as I watched, it appeared that for every one who chose Lucifer, two turned to Kyrie. Lucifer's anger only grew with each new chant of the divine name, and I wondered if he would endure it to the end.

Gradually, the number of those left to those who had spoken dwindled down to just a few. I had seen Cere make her choice for Kyrie. Rune, also. Tyree still hadn't spoken. Nor I.

As others stepped up to the line, I knew I had to make my own decision, but I wanted to wait for Tyree. Not that his decision should influence me. I thought perhaps I could influence him—by waiting.

In a few minutes, Tyree walked over to me. There were only several hundred of us left, and Lucifer had garnered about a third of the myriads. He sputtered and fumed on his side of the mountain, sending his deputies this way and that to count and get exact numbers, though I knew that was probably impossible.

As each deputy homed in with his new count of a class (Kinderlings, Haukers, Dominions, etc.), Lucifer lashed about with his sword.

On the other side of the mountain, the masses waited with much greater patience, Kyrie seemingly taking no concern for the resultant numbers. He knew it already anyway, before any of it had ever happened. This made me in turns angry and bitter, and at other turns amazed and almost worshipful.

I watched Tyree from the back. With each sounded choice, he cheered, "That's it!" And, "Bravo for you!" And, "Give it your best, angel!" And he was doing it for both Lucifer and Kyrie choosers. It didn't seem to matter to him.

I finally pumped up my courage and walked over to him. "You're behaving oddly."

"My trademark," he said. "Yes! Another one for Lucifer! Tremendous, two more for Kyrie!"

"Tyree!"

"Yes! Lucifer! Yes! Kyrie!"

"Tyree!"

"What?" His tone was irritable.

"What are you doing?"

"Cheering on the deciding masses, what do you think?"

"Tyree, what is going on? You're cheering both sides!"

"Of course. They're getting to exercise their freedom. They're showing their true selves. They're being who they were created to be!"

"You sound bitter."

"Ah, a truism. For once, someone speaks a truism."

"What's the matter, Tyree?"

"Oh, nothing you'd be concerned about. You're too sick with worry over which decision to make."

"That's not fair, Tyree."

"Oh, isn't it? While everyone labored over their choices this day, has anyone realized what has truly happened?"

"And what is that?"

"The joy is gone. It's all ruthless politicking and deal-making and overly sincere handwringing about how Heaven's been ruined. But still we must make this choice. I hate them all!"

"Tyree, you can't act like this!"

"Can't I? Watch me!"

"What are you going to do?"

"Stage my own rebellion, what do you think?"

"And who will follow you?"

"Me, that's who!"

"Tyree, think. Choose Kyrie and live. It's that simple."

"Is that what you're doing?"

"Yes! YES!"

"Then do it!"

I stood there, unmoved. There were fewer and fewer left. It was dwindling down to the last stragglers. I knew none of them, and they each seemed to step up to the line with disillusionment in their souls, casting their votes with a whisper or a murmur.

In moments it was down to the two of us. As if all of creation turned on our choice, both sides began cheering for us to join them. Lucifer was quiet, and Kyrie gazed at us with those kind, worn, and benighted eyes.

"Okay, Tyree, then together."

"Together?"

"Yes."

We both stepped up to the line. For a moment, all was hazy in my mind, and I didn't know what to say. And then just as suddenly, it was clear. My voice chimed out over the chasm. "I do not wish to make a choice!"

Immediately, behind me, "And I, too." It was Tyree.

As if all the realm was stung with a plague of silence, no one spoke.

Finally, Lucifer said, "What means this impudence?"

"No impudence, Sire."

"It is impudence. You must choose now, or be banished from both realms forever!"

"Hold!" Kyrie cried suddenly. Every face turned to Him. He looked out upon us with interested eyes. "You both choose to make no choice?"

"That's it," Tyree said. "Choosing not to choose. Our decision is to make no decision."

Kyrie smiled. I was surprised, but He regarded both of us with keen interest. "You understand, Aris and Tyree, that you fall under the protection of no one?"

I hadn't thought about that, but I said, "I understand, Kyrie."

Tyree nodded. "I'm willing to accept that position."

"And that someday you still must choose between myself and Lucifer, or perhaps someone else."

"I understand."

"Then why do you choose not to choose now?"

It struck me that Kyrie had not asked Tyree any of these questions. I wondered why briefly. He repeated His question and I said, "I don't know, Kyrie. I do not feel I can choose either at this time, that's all."

Kyrie looked slightly flummoxed, I suppose as much as He can take on such a look, and then He nodded His head, smiling. "Perhaps there is wisdom in this refusal to choose. So I applaud you, Aris, Tyree, for your courage. You stand there alone, at the whim and mercy of both Myself and Lucifer. So now I shall render judgment.

"You are both free to course Heaven and the domain of the Lucifer party. When such a time comes that you are prepared to make a choice, you shall make it then. And, for your lack of trust and your ambivalence, you shall pay a higher price: you shall be judged all the harsher for your slackness. But your judgment you can bear. Go now, trek the realms, learn, and finally you shall see what no other has seen."

It was a surprising, elevating judgment. I bowed my head and said, "Thank you, Kyrie." Tyree's arm shot up and he yelled, "A wonder!"

And then all over creation, the tumult rose.

28

With sudden fury, Lucifer yelled, "NOW!"

The Mount convulsed, and the earth quaked beneath us. Someone ripped my Harpistrer from my hands and crushed it under his feet. A tall, blonde angel stabbed at my face with a burning object.

Somehow I flinched out of the way. I grabbed his arm and turned it. The burning thing came down into his thigh. He screamed, "Yiiiii!"

I twisted his arm around behind his back and held him. Then I stared at the scene around me. The whole Mountain had become a mass of tearing, screaming angels. The Mount was a roiling, thunderous wound of angels striking, hitting, smashing, stabbing.

Swords swung in the air. Armor clashed and clacked. Steel on steel rang all over the mountain. I saw Michael and Lucifer battling, with many running to either side. The whole Mount had gone crazy.

A moment later, another angel came at me. I let go the one I held and grabbed his sword. Immediately, I undercut into the other's legs. He crashed to the ground, both legs severed. As he moaned, I swung at another running at me and he cut at my arm. I screamed with pain as a long gash cut me to the bone.

As I fell, I held up the sword, and the diving angel was thrust through. He rolled over onto the grass, moaning.

The pain blistered my mind and I could hardly see or think. I wondered what had happened to Tyree. But the battle surged and raged around me, angels fighting in one-on-one or two-on-two combat in little pockets. Slowly, I rose to my feet, found another sword and began swinging.

Then there was a shout. "STOP!"

Kyrie.

We straightened at His command. For a moment I felt paralyzed in place, then realized no one could resist His word.

He spoke again. "Those with Lucifer, step back to the left of the Mount."

Enraged, choking spirits rushed across. My broken adversary gave me an angry grimace, but he returned to his place, his legs already healing. I panted, and then Tyree came up next to me, his hand gripping my shoulder and bleeding light onto my tunic. I turned. "You're hurt."

"It's nothing," he whispered.

Kyrie stood in the gap between the two huge companies. "This will not go on," he shouted.

"Then give us our own place," Lucifer shrieked from the head of the angry throng. Already, I could see their light had turned to a dusky gray. I was so startled, I looked down at my own jeweled tunic. But it shone as brightly as silver in flowing water.

"So be it," said Kyrie. "Be gone and find your own place. You will have to make your own way. You will garner no help from Me."

"We do not want a new place. We demand Heaven!" Lucifer cried.

"It is not yours to take," Kyrie answered.

The forces behind Lucifer gathered, their light like smoking flax. Lucifer looked up into the sky, to the clouds, and drew his gleaming sword. "I will ascend to the heaven of heavens!" he shouted. "I will raise my throne above the stars of God. I will sit on the Mount of the Assembly in the recesses of the North. I will ascend above the heights of the clouds. Who is with me?"

The voices of myriads joined his own. Kyrie stood His ground but looked up at the clouds where His own abode lay. To penetrate that was to destroy the heart and life of Kyrie Himself forever.

"I will make myself like the Most High!" Lucifer screamed again, and a trillion voices joined his. "I will take your realm, and your followers, and your body and cast them all into Hell. I will reign. Who is with me?"

Again, the swarm of voices filled the air with its heated, malicious rasp.

Kyrie motioned to His Cherubs, and they winged aloft toward the clouds. Michael and the others joined them. Then Kyrie Himself rose in the air and disappeared behind the clouds with the Son behind Him.

"Follow me!" Lucifer shouted.

I, along with Tyree, watched in amazement. And then with a bold cry, Tyree said, "This is it! This is what I've been waiting for!"

He launched into the air toward Lucifer and the others. I leaped at the last moment and caught his feet, dragging him.

"No, Tyree. Not now!"

"Yes. Let go of me."

He shrugged me off, and I fell back.

"But why now?"

Behind him the sky was black with the soaring soldiers of evil, their shrieks and war bellows filling the air.

"Why now?" he said to me. "Because now I see what Kyrie is. It was plain all along, I just didn't see it."

"And what is Kyrie?"

He was already screaming through the air. "A tyrant," he cried. "A lone, majestic, all-powerful but ultimately weak tyrant who will not stand the test!"

And he was gone. They all soared into space toward the clouds where Kyrie had entered. Swords gleamed in the light. With crashes and thuds, the tumult began, and soon Lucifer was lashing out close to the very clouds themselves. The clang of blade on blade resounded, and on the ground those who could not fly fought. I was caught between the two, both using me as a dodge.

Then with a foundering wail, I heard Lucifer crash into the clouds.

It was as far as he got.

As if struck by a giant invisible sword, lightning flashed and Lucifer with his minions were hurled back. They rolled and clattered through Heaven as if pitched, their bodies colliding and their brazen cries clotting the air like wisps of hay. Their ability to fly fled them, and they crashed down into the sides of the Mount in the North. I watched in astonishment as they lay there dazed and disheveled.

The forces on the ground fell back, retiring to the Mount and stronger positions, all of them aghast at what had happened. I stood there, panting and holding my own sword to deflect any blow that might come from behind or before.

But it was over. Though Lucifer was on his feet again, he could not leap into the air. He stood rooted to the ground, gnashing his teeth and screeching out spirit-curdling threats that now sounded empty and miserable. He could not fly and he could not move. So it was with the rest of his followers. They were spiritually chained in place.

Kyrie appeared a moment later, and his defenders joined him on the Mount.

"Release us!" Lucifer screamed, his voice now more like the bleat of a wounded sheep. It was almost piteous.

"You have defied My power for the last time," Kyrie said. "If you will not stop, you will be permanently removed from Heaven. Only during assembly will I allow you to come here ever again."

"Murderer! Liar!" Lucifer screamed. "Cheat! Thief!"

"It is you who are the murderer, and the liar, and the cheat, and the thief!" Kyrie said, without raising His voice. "I have made My decision. You shall not come into the Great City, you shall fly only in the air below the clouds, you shall not approach the throne except at My bidding. If you trespass the lines I have made, you shall no longer call this realm home. You will be banished from it forever!"

"We will make our own then!"

"You are not able!" Kyrie boomed. "You have seen fit only to steal and pillage and plunder what already is. You continue to transgress all limits and laws that I have set. If you do not stop, you will be banished forever. You have seen My power. You cannot breach Heaven. You cannot ascend above the heights of the clouds. And you cannot long defy Me."

"But we will continue!"

"At your peril. You and all who follow your ways! From this day forth, you are no longer Lucifer the lightbearer."

"I am Archonix, the first!"

"You are not! You are Satan, the adversary, and so you shall be called!"

Lucifer shrieked. His teeth gnashed and his very cloak seemed to molt. His visage darkened, and the jewels that covered him broke and shattered in a sudden, cataclysmic wrenching of light and darkness. He blackened in the onrush, and his form was transmogrified. Where jewels had been, there were now scales. Where the four faces had looked out on the world, there was now a single snout and eyes. Where light had flowed free and marvelous, there was nothing but green slime and black. His voice roared, and the mouth, with its ugly, twisted, blackened teeth, was that of a dragon.

Beside him another transformation took place. Among the fallen angels and cherubs and seraphs and dominions and principalities, feet turned to cloven hooves, bright iridescent wings to gossamer batskin, and handsome beauteous faces to contorted beaks with slithery tongues and gnarled speech.

"He has made us monstrosities," they cried.

But Lucifer calmed them. "We are the brave. We are the valiant. We shall resist. And we shall win!"

"You cannot win!" Kyrie answered.

But Lucifer stood his ground. "All you have proven, Kyrie, is that You are a tyrant. Nothing more. Yes, You have the power. Yes, You have the means. But You are little more than a petty tyrant. You have shown yourself utterly unable to solve our problems. All can see it. And who will long to follow You then?"

As if the thought had wings, it lodged in the air and rang throughout our ranks. "Tyrant!" they called.

Something within each of us reeled, staggering with the exclamation.

"Fool!" Satan cried. "He who reigns without heart or soul!"

Among Kyrie's ranks, some screamed for revenge, but the thought was planted, and I could see it held. It sucked the air out of me like a snake, and for a moment, I could not think. Somewhere deep inside I knew what Lucifer, now Satan, said was powerfully convincing. Kyrie had shown His power. And that was all. What of love? And grace? And goodness? And compassion? And justice? And righteousness?

"Yes," Lucifer cried again, as if realizing he had stung Kyrie to the quick. "You have proved nothing except that you are a petty tyrant. You may reign. You may lock us up. You may oppose us. But no one will love You or worship You as You desire!"

The taunt song went up. "Tyrant! Tyrant! Tyrant!"

"You have solved nothing. You have only made it worse," Lucifer chanted. "You are the greatest of all fools, for You have fouled Your own nest!"

Kyrie, anguish splitting His features, waved His hand. Suddenly, the Son sprang forward, a great sword in His hand. He swung, and as if caught on the upcurve of a tidal surge, all of the enemy including Satan were thrown back a thousand paces to a second mountain.

"We will fight you!" Lucifer screamed. "No one loves a tyrant!"

Kyrie waved his hand again, and the Son's sword flashed. Another hurricane was unleashed. Lucifer and all of his were cast back miles into the Stillnesses.

Another wave, and another sword sweep. Till the hordes stood on the edge of the Outer Reaches.

"You shall not pass beyond the lines I have set unless I call assembly," Kyrie roared, genuine anger creasing His visage. "And then you shall speak only when spoken to. This is my judgment!"

Lucifer shrieked, but before the guttural cry reached his tortured lips,

Kyrie thrust His hand out, the Son's sword sang in the air, and all of them were cast over the edge. Their screams cut the stillness like flung cinders, but in a moment, all was quiet.

There was a vast brooding silence. We stared aghast at what had happened. Satan and his hordes were truly purged.

Then behind me a quiet, lonely weeping broke through the ranks. Slowly I turned, and I saw Rune and Cere. They were weeping, as well as others. All of us had lost dear soulmates and friends. I blinked, and my heart quaked.

I knew Tyree had been among them. He had made his choice.

My head was dull as lead. And heavy.

Rune held Cere, his right hand still clinging to his sword at his side.

"And Harras, Plun, Siminar, Cardoyle. All of them," Cere said, wiping her eyes. "Lost forever."

My eyes burned, and I tried to make sense of all that had happened. Why had Tyree acted now? There was no reason. Kyrie had given us time.

But the force of Rune's and Cere's words wore at me. I sank to my knees and wept. "Tyree, please make it not so. Please, not you."

Moments later, Kyrie walked through our ranks, touching one here, speaking there. "Be still."

"Be strong."

"Listen to your heart."

"Hope in God."

"Keep trusting."

But angels pulled away from Him, and soon He stood alone. "My children," He said. "Do not grieve. It can yet be made right."

Kyrie could not calm us. I sensed that something more terrible than anything yet had happened. If Kyrie Himself was stymied, if He had indeed "fouled" His own nest as Lucifer had said, what was left?

Slowly, many among us turned and began walking back into the land, toward the Great City. Our shoulders were hunched in sorrow. Our eyes wet. We wept together, and all around us the voices of Heaven rose with distorted, chilling cries of anguish. Many friends and loved ones had been wrested from us, and now they were gone forever.

A cloudy bitterness gripped my soul, and I looked up. Kyrie stood before us, looking off over the edge into the abyss. His hair blew back in the breeze, his cloak wafted out behind Him like a flying mantle. The Son stood next to Him, the great sword cleaving to His hand.

Then both turned. There were tears in their eyes also.

A moment later, Kyrie cried, "My children. I weep for My children!"

Nothing more. Slowly, as if driven by an unseen inner power, we turned and rushed to Him, His great arms enfolding us like chicks under a hen's wings. Together we wept for the souls that had chosen darkness over light.

29

Over the next few days nothing changed. We returned to our orchestrations. Those who played, played gloriously. I was given freedom to continue playing even though I still had made no final choice.

At first we pretended the division among us was the natural and normal consequence of rebellion. But soon we learned the truth. Lucifer and his followers had no power, no experience, no ability to make their own instruments, or a stage, or music, or anything. Beyond the edge of the Outer Reaches, in the great black, they had found nothing.

Some tried to attack again, in smaller groups, a lone angel here and there. But such deeds were quickly discovered and their kind routed out, back beyond the Reaches. Many of our number lived in despair, and there were those who claimed that Lucifer had been right all along. Though Kyrie could not be beaten, He had proven Himself a tyrant. He had been unable to find a creative and equitable solution to the problems of Heaven. For all His wisdom, He was as stymied and impotent as the rest of us.

Of course, there were plenty of arguments against this, but I admit in my own mind it seemed so.

In the end, Kyrie called an assembly of the loyal. "It hasn't worked," He said with a sigh. "We must find another way."

"Forgive them and start over!" shouted Emerie, a stalwart, if sometimes lenient, member of the Risomer section. "Give them another chance."

"They have been given many chances," Kyrie said. "All Lucifer did was keep pushing beyond the limits."

"Maybe then the limits were too great," some said.

"In that case, what are we to have—total anarchy?" Kyrie for the first time seemed as frustrated as we were. "There have to be laws. If they will not obey the smallest and slightest laws—and I have not given you many— they will repeatedly infringe and even desecrate others' rights. I cannot allow them to destroy others for the sake of their own desire for complete freedom. After all, freedom is not the ability to do anything you want, for even omnipotence is held and limited by its own holiness and truth. Lucifer wanted My place and I could not abdicate, for he would have ruled you with a tyranny far beyond anything you think I have done. And he would have disobeyed his own laws with impunity, calling others to account but not himself."

There was a great silence among us, but suddenly I lifted my hand and said, "What if we give them their own place, not unlike Heaven, with the freedom they want and then see what they make of it?"

"That would be possible," Kyrie said, "but I have to think of them, too. If I gave them their own world, they would soon lay it waste with another rebellion and another as those who have power seek to gain what Lucifer started with. I would soon be having to create whole new universes for each angel I have ever created."

"Well, why not?" I said. "If that's what it comes to, then so be it. It's worth a try."

"And what if it doesn't work—and I assure you it won't. For I have made you a social race, and you naturally desire company and friends. If each wants to be ruler over all others, who is to follow and be the friends they desire—unless I am to make them friends with automatons who obey their every whim?"

"Nothing works," someone said.

"No," Kyrie answered. "There is a way. The greater problem is you and Me. What are we to do? You are confused, feeling I have betrayed you. You want to worship and love Me and My Son, as I wish to love and nurture you, but we are at odds. Many of you no longer trust Me as you once did. You obey. You will remain loyal. But it is a hard, not a soft, loving loyalty. And that is what I desire."

No one said anything in response, for all recognized His words were true.

Finally, someone said, "Perhaps you can eliminate them entirely."

Kyrie shook His head. "That is impossible. They are eternal creations. They cannot be destroyed or effaced. Furthermore, who is to say another from your number will not arise and lead a second rebellion, and then a third, and a fourth, till I am left without a single one?"

"Then confine them forever in the darkness," Lasmine answered. I always thought of him as a uniquely sage and confident player of the Limminnine, that instrument which when blown produced notes that sent wonderful odors and savory smoke into the air.

"I have thought of that," Kyrie said. "And perhaps it will come to that. But for now I think it will be better to let them have their say. "

"But why?" cried Hersilie, an agile member of the Star Section whose drums sent great shudders through the whole heaven. "They will only continue to attack us and wound us and steal our playing pieces."

Kyrie nodded. "Those who attack and steal will be ferreted out and removed. They will not pass into Heaven again. But I cannot eliminate them or annihilate them. I can only draw lines beyond which they cannot go. I must be very sparing in what lines I draw."

We stood in abject silence. It seemed impossible, even foolish. We knew now Lucifer would not be stopped short of chains or complete erasure.

"If we can't start over, destroy them, or change them, what can we do?" I said, more to myself. But it came out clear to all around me, and we all looked into Kyrie's gentle eyes.

For a moment, I relaxed and it was as old times, Kyrie teaching and us learning at His feet. Yet, if Lucifer had done nothing else, he had managed one thing: in every breast hung a seed of doubt that would surely flare into rebellion once again. For though Kyrie had solved the immediate problem of Lucifer's rebellion, He had not solved the greater: why we should trust Him and love Him and worship Him forever, as He desired?

To be sure, we feared Him. Lucifer had shown that. But fear is not love, and terror is not worship. Kyrie wanted love and worship, but now it looked impossible. In every mind the words had formed: "Tyrant. Master. Enslaver. Dictator." Somehow those perceptions had to be erased, but how?

I felt sick at heart. Our world was crushed, beaten back by a word.

Kyrie gazed out upon us in a brooding silence. His cloak riffled around Him like an unwavering bolt of silvered lightning. I waited. We leaned forward, in anticipation of what He might say. The Son whispered into His ear and He nodded.

"There are not many choices," He said quietly. "They must live. I will soon reveal to you more as time moves on. For now, be patient."

Then Hersilie stood up erect and muscular. "Kyrie, if you knew this would happen, why did you create them?"

Kyrie made a wry smile. "That is part of the quest," He said. "Understanding that will drive you to despair and to glory. But that understanding cannot come in a day." He turned, then said, "We will play again soon, and I will reveal to you My plans."

I could see that Lucifer had hurt Him. And I grieved in my heart for where it would lead.

Rune, Cere, and I walked out together. My friends were quiet. "Have you been to the River?" I asked.

They nodded. "We felt the need to wash. After all the fighting."

We walked together, pulling at branches, leaves, sucking a bit of Lemur Grass whose thick, green juices energized the thoughts. We said nothing more till we came to the edge of The River and stepped in.

We bathed our wounds and healed. But the flow of crimson light was not completely stanched on any of us.

— 30

The evening came when Kyrie gathered us all on the Mount, including the followers of Lucifer. Kyrie looked august and resplendent in his purple robes. The lightbearer, now a dragon, refracted Kyrie's own light marvelously. His green scales shone against the refulgent glory of Kyrie. But his beauty was gone. I suspected also that his wisdom and perfection were as greatly affected as his being. But I could only wonder at that. All his followers had become deformed monsters: snakes, coiled and malevolent; trolls, warty-nosed and violent; goblins, like gray-skinned banshees; and every other imagined being, ugly, revolting, with none of the beauty that once marked them as citizens of Heaven.

Kyrie began from the throne, "I have decided to take an entirely different action." The flowing purple about Him rippled as He moved before us, only partly different and yet wholly beyond any of us.

We waited, still and silent.

"I will let you test your theories, Lucifer, and all of you, those of you at least who believe you have a better way and that I am a mere tyrant. But it will all happen on a new stage, a new performance area, in fact a whole new world. You shall be witnesses now as I create once again a world where beauty, goodness, love, and compassion reign free." He motioned to the Son, and suddenly Messiah stood.

From the two sides of the Mount we watched, and Kyrie began. Messiah spoke. "Let there be light."

Immediately, far off in the spectacle of darkness beyond the Outer Reaches, a light source wobbled into being, starting first with the slightest point of light and growing. The light was sheer white, as the shekinah of God, and not as powerful. But it contained a warmth, a steady blissful shining that aroused the emotions and made us peer all the harder.

Messiah stepped out into bluva and took the dancing orb in His hand. Batting it back and forth between His hands it grew and grew. Messiah Himself seemed far larger out there in the recessed black than He did up close, but I paid that no attention. I was entranced by the light and its uncanny ability to elicit the strongest emotions.

He juggled the light until on its lower half another orb appeared, but this one black. Then with a massive swipe, Messiah separated the black and the light. The white light and black darkness circled, fused, became one and then revolved. For a moment, the light was hidden by the black and then the black hidden by the light. He set it spinning out there in space and then blew on it with His breath.

It enlarged, grew taller, deeper, wider, until the black spaces beyond the Outer Reaches shone with the mixture of light and darkness, something we'd never seen before. In Heaven, there was light, the shekinah of Messiah. Beyond the Outer Reaches there was dark. But here was a magnificent blending of light and dark into a whole.

The building and forming went on for the whole of the day, and Messiah sang the Song of Light and Darkness until the golden light and cool dark spanned from the depths of the dark to the heights of the clouds. We could see the light shimmer and dance and flow and it was like our own waters, the river of light that we called "The River of Heaven." The darkness also was waterlike, smooth, flowing, ebony, and velvety with a silence that comforted those who looked upon it.

Messiah said, "Day and night. It is good." We echoed back against His voice, saying, "It is indeed good."

One heavenly day had passed. We continued to watch.

The second day, Messiah took the light and darkness and said, "Let there be an expanse in the waters, and let it separate the waters from the waters."

With His hands He plucked the sphere out from the light and darkness and held it. A claylike substance oozed out between His fingers, and then

He made the globe spin slowly. As it did, the empty spaces on it sucked up the waters that were left, and soon it turned into a diamond blue pinprick of reflected light in the darkness. Then Messiah sang the Song of the Expanse and Waters again, and as the song mounted our hearts became one to the music. The orb grew until it filled the sky.

Above it was the expanse of the waters, and below it the expanse itself. Messiah called the expanse Heaven. And He said, "It is good." And we echoed against His voice, "It is indeed good!"

Another day passed, and we watched and sang and waited as Messiah prepared for the next step.

The next morning we watched as Messiah puckered the planet with His fingers until the waters separated into their own places, and He said, "Let the dry land appear."

It was brown and beautiful and loamy, and Messiah nicked the sides of the planet with His fingernails, forming rivers and mountains and hills and valleys. He turned it in His hands and set it rotating slowly against the light and darkness, and the Song of Light and Darkness broke onto His lips as He carved away at the orb with His hands and fingertips. It took form, and here and there we could see the different lands and the different seas. It was blue, and it was beautiful.

When He finished, Messiah cried, "The waters shall be called seas, and the dry land, earth. It is good." And we repeated the chant, "It is very good."

A third day passed, and we continued to watch, held in the grasp of Messiah's creation and music. Even the legions of Satan were quiet and said nothing until the moment when Messiah spoke, and then even they echoed the words, "It is good," as if entranced.

When morning came, Messiah said, "Let the earth sprout vegetations, plants yielding seed, and fruit trees bearing fruit after their kind, with seed in them, on the earth."

Before our eyes, the Song of the Trees began again and as Messiah sang, the air above the land rippled and resonated, and suddenly the first mark of green set down on the earth. A moment later, the earth spewed forth in tiny gusts, and out of its bowels appeared trees, fruit trees, bushes with berries and nuts, long yellow fields of a thin stately grain. Other furrows burst forth as He sang and the ground erupted with every manner of vegetation imaginable: peach trees and apple, hay and alfalfa and cotton and peanuts, potatoes and artichokes, wheat and rye and oats, beech trees, evergreens, oak, maple, and walnut, papayas and rutabagas—all of it in a surge of life and art. My own stomach growled at the thought of so much food and so many delectable treats.

Yet, this was different. It was material, of earth and substance, grainy and gritty and soft and smooth, all of it mixed together but each piece separate and real, singularly beautiful. I crept closer to see the substances that the earth sent forth, and I saw all that man would later name alfalfa and wheat and corn and apples and peaches and plums and hazelnuts and almonds and potatoes (underneath the ground). And I reveled in the sheer majesty of creation for Messiah was creating something far in excess of our own world. It was so lavish, so luxuriant in its effortless assemblage, so many different crops and vegetables and fruits and nuts and berries that one could not help but marvel at the imagination of Messiah's work. Where had He envisioned these things? What thought had gone into it? And what was the purpose? Was this Satan's new world?

I could not believe it, for this was far superior in sheer variety to anything we had seen in Heaven. Though the Tree of Life gave forth twelve kinds of fruit, here in this world there were already hundreds of different kinds, and I wondered what beings He would populate it with to enjoy the grand banquet table He was setting.

The wind sifted through grass, the earth shimmered—first brown and then burst forth all the more green and lush. The wind of Messiah's breath swept over the exterior of the globe, and everywhere it seemed, even the mountain tops, the vegetation lashed up into the air. Finally, the globe was covered in the fine green mantle, and the blue of the waters and green of lands gave the globe a wonderful glow in the light.

Messiah said, "It is good." And this time our rumbled, echoed response slashed the air. The excitement only grew.

The evening came and another day began.

Messiah spoke, "Let there be lights in the expanse of the heavens to separate the day from the night, and let them be for signs, and for seasons, and for days and years; and let them be for lights in the expanse of the heavens to give light to the earth!"

Immediately, Messiah whisked out of the air two shining white clots of light from the expanse of light and gripped them in either hand. He crumpled them together till their heat was white hot, and one He squeezed harder till the light compacted and strengthened. Then He hurled it out into the dark where it leaped and cavorted and then stuck, moving though at an awesome speed through space. And the blue planet moved with it.

Then He took the other orb and kneaded it in His hands until the light waxed and waned and soon a silvery mirror appeared in His hand. He whipped that out against the dark where it winged close to the blue planet and held in place, turning about it slowly in the air.

He spoke again and the expanse of light shattered, its specks of light clattering about the heavens in every which combination. Here, six together, and there nine, and there a hundred. They formed into great circling masses in various places till the whole heaven rang with the melody of their singing. Messiah hearkened the Song of the Stars, and this time we began to harmonize with Him till our mingled voices seemed to dance and spiral and pirouette, and the beauty of the melody lifted up into the heavens where they echoed back.

Tears burned into my eyes as I watched. Messiah said, "It is good." And we echoed in response, "It is indeed good."

The fourth day passed.

The following morning, Messiah began again. He cried, "Let the waters teem with swarms of living creatures, and let birds fly above the earth in the open expanse of the heavens."

Out of nothing a form burst forth, flying. It was an eagle, not unlike the third face of Lucifer when he was a whole Cherubim.

As the air crackled, more creatures broke forth—cormorants, sparrows, bluebirds, eagles, vultures, hawks, jays, robins, albatrosses, gulls—the great and small, winging their way through the heavens, their chirping, cheeping, guttural cries filling the air with joy.

Then in the seas, other soundless explosions of iridescent beauty surged the waters. There a salmon. There a trout. And there a barracuda. The great sea monsters appeared, and the whales, and porpoises, and the great sharks. Dark blue, green, orange, the colors setting the seas swirling with the colors and the song of their untamed squeals and shrieks and shrills and cries.

The whole earth flew with the fliers and doves and sparrows and mites, and the sea was filled. Messiah sang the Song of the Birds and Fish, and He said, "It is good."

Our immediate cry resounded throughout heaven, "Indeed it is good!"

A day passed.

One more morning Messiah set to the work of creation. He said, "Let the earth bring forth living creatures after their kind: cattle and creeping things and beasts of the earth after their kind."

The earth puckered and ripped and boomed, and here, there, and everywhere beasts and brutes and tiny trites appeared, scampering here and lumbering there and clopping beyond. What man would call horse, ox, cow, buffalo, rhinoceros, hippopotamus, lion, tiger, grizzly, squirrel, and raccoon appeared with a hundred thousand other creatures, all of them a romping, rollicking swarm.

Messiah pulled up wads of dirt, threw them into the air, and more creatures appeared: moose, coyote, antelope, gazelle. They leaped out of the air, took their stand on the ground and immediately kicked out their heels, skidded at the tufts of dirt, and splayed out in all directions, gamboling on the earth like frolicsome, overjoyed, throbbing engines of glory.

Messiah smiled and He threw up tufts of grass, and out of them sprang two moles. Out of another tuft tore rabbits and mice and leopards and lemurs. All were clothed in splendid light, dark, speckled, and spotted robes of their own fur.

I stared as the creation went on and on, Messiah singing the Song of the Beasts and Animals, and every kind of living thing bursting out of blank air before my eyes like so many coins out of a machine. It was marvelous, incredible, wholly astounding, and for a moment I worshiped. I knew then that there was no one like Kyrie or Messiah, no one who had ever been, not Lucifer, Michael, Tyree, Cere, or Rune, or anyone. Not even myself.

And I loved Him for His beauty and His awe-inspiring creative genius and the love that shone in every hair and nose and pair of eyes that He created. And I loved Him for the glory that He caused to live before our eyes. And I loved Him for the imagination and power He displayed, and the grace that led beasts to scamper about robed in beauty. And I loved Him for Him.

And Kyrie and the Son sang the Songs again and again, and the Son said, "It is good, but it is not finished."

As if the marvel was not already great enough, Messiah knelt in the dirt and touched the surface with those gentle hands and fingers. He spoke softly, but the joy and ebullience shown in His face as He fashioned something in the soil. The earth glowed with a sentient light as He shaped it, kneaded it, loved it, and graced it. In a few moments, Messiah stood over the form. It twitched, a knee shot up, an elbow quivered. Slowly, the being rose, took Messiah's hand, and was pulled to his feet. He stood in front of Messiah, a lithe, naked form, modulant, sibilant light emanating from his face and chest. He was a marvelously simple, expressive creature with eyes like an angel's, a regal nose, and pink, friendly lips.

The creature stood and did not move, did not seem fully alive. Then Messiah bent over and touching His lips to that of the creature, He breathed into it. Instantly, the creature's face lit with a bold, tranquilizing gleam, and he appeared robed in wondrous light. He was no longer naked, but enfolded in shekinah glory.

Messiah said, "Man," and He began a new song, the Song of Man.

As He sang, the man turned and looked about, stooping to test the feel of the soil, plucking a leaf from its stem, running his hands over bark. Messiah walked with the man, and together they spoke quietly. Finally, the Master of Creation said to the man, "It is not good for the man to be alone. Therefore I will make a helper suitable for him."

Two by two, Messiah brought the animals to the man and he began naming them, noticing that each was male and female. "Lion and lioness. Bull and cow. Stallion and mare."

"Are they suitable?"

"I think not, Lord."

Each time He questioned the man, He grinned broadly, and Adam seemed filled with an unutterable joy.

Adam said, "Elephant."

And Messiah asked, as if He enjoyed hearing the response, "Is this one suitable?"

"No, Lord."

"What is wrong?"

"Far too big, Lord. And gray. I am tawny. And I walk on two legs."

"Yes. You are learning."

The man took his time selecting names, seemingly out of the air, but each a singular description of face and form. All the beasts of the farm and field he named, but obviously none was appropriate as a mate.

"Chimpanzee."

"And this one?" Messiah asked.

"Not so different," Adam answered. "But still very different."

"Indeed."

Among our numbers the mirth rose, and we were soon joining in the celebration of the Selection of the Mate, but as each new pair of animals appeared, Messiah, like a child in a field of dew, awaited the man's verdict with a kind of quiet glee.

"And this one? And this one? And this one?"

"None is right, Lord."

"You have found none suitable to yourself?"

"None," Adam said.

"Then I shall fashion you one from your own being."

Messiah waved His hand over the man and he fell asleep. We watched in silence as Messiah removed a rib from Adam's chest and began to form another creature, as beautiful and delightful as Adam himself, but appropriately complementary in every detail.

As Messiah labored, I marveled at not only the love and grace with which He fashioned Adam's mate, but His humor. I had never seen Him in this guise, as if the material creation elicited from Him a fallow amusement and merriment that even Heaven hadn't. I could see the love He held for each of His creatures. For into each He had poured a piece of Himself, and in each was a picture of some characteristic that, if grasped, would reveal more of His eternal person.

Even Satan's vast hordes seemed fascinated with the process of creation, as if in analyzing it they could discern the source of His power.

When Messiah finished—after quite a long time—fashioning the mate for the man, He awakened him and brought her to him. Instantly, the man was transfixed. She was clothed in the same shekinah glory as the man, and her form was elegant, lissome, and breathtaking. The man himself was stricken dumb at first, and then he cried, "This is now bone of my bones and flesh of my flesh. She shall be called Woman, because she was taken out of man."

Then Kyrie appeared and said, "Be fruitful and multiply, and fill the earth, and subdue it, and rule over the fish of the sea and over the birds of the sky, and over every living thing that moves on the face of the earth." He looked upon them as a father gazes upon his newborn child.

"Behold, I have given you every plant yielding seed that is on the surface of the earth, and every tree which has fruit yielding seed; it shall be food for you. To every beast of the earth and to every bird of the sky and to every thing that moves on the earth, I have given every green plant for food."

Then Kyrie this time looked high into Heaven, past the gathered angels, past the Outer Reaches, all the way into the Great City. Out of it, He suddenly plucked the Tree of Life from its soil there in the great square. He immediately planted it in the middle of the garden and said to the man, "This tree you shall eat of and gain life eternal."

Moments later, He reached in the darkness of the great pit and drew forth another tree, one that I had never seen or known of before. He set it in the center of the garden and said, "From every tree of the garden you may eat freely, but from the Tree of the Knowledge of Good and Evil you shall not eat, for in the day that you eat from it you shall surely die."

The man and woman gazed first at the Tree of Life on one hill in the garden, and second, the Tree of the Knowledge of Good and Evil. Both bore luscious, golden red fruit. From each tree emanated a welcoming, extravagant aroma not unlike that of the apple in blossom.

The man said, "But why is this Tree here, Master? Is it not fraught with danger?"

"Yes, it is indeed," Kyrie answered. "The second Tree will ascertain your loyalties so that the other, the Tree of Life, can grant eternal life and fellowship with Me, or if you fail the test, it will ensure that you will not secure eternal death."

Kyrie Himself walked with the man and woman and spoke of their work and their beauty and of the power of obedience. His joy and theirs was unparalleled, and I could see in Kyrie's eyes the pride of His work, another inkling of character that I was yet unsure how to read.

As the day drew to an end, Kyrie stood on the hill with the man and woman under the Tree of Life. He said, "It is very good."

Night fell and we retreated from our lookout upon the new world. Kyrie gathered us in Heaven on the Mount. The man and woman slept, something we had never seen in our world, their beautiful bodies curled together in an embrace of love. And Kyrie, with the Son now sitting beside Him, said to us, "Here we will test the theories of Satan and Kyrie. Here we will see the outworking of good and evil. Here we will witness the glory of God and the ignominy of Satan. Here you will see why it is that Kyrie honors obedience above sacrifice and servanthood above rulership. You will go down and look and watch," He said. "As you watch, you will learn all the truth about Myself, and about yourself, each of you, and about goodness and love and grace and sin and brokenness and redemption. You will see. You will find the keys that hold. And you will learn the joy or horror of your choices."

Each of us stood transfixed as Kyrie spoke.

A second later, He drew a doorway in the air, and beyond it a causeway down to the planet and to Eden. "By this door you shall come and go," He said. "By this door, you shall see the other world. Enter only if you desire."

He turned away and immediately an angel—a tall Kinderling named Marid—stepped up to the door. "Can I step through, my Lord?"

"Before you do, one more thing," Kyrie said. "This earth is the battleground and the field of play. This is the schoolroom and the worship chamber. Here you will see as you have never seen before. And here all choices, all desires, all lusts and hungers shall be measured, weighed, understood, and judged. It is now up to you. I shall work around and within. Satan shall also do his own bidding. I will not hinder him except as he trammels the limits I will set. I will not allow evil to run free at all times. Nor will I intercede in every situation to bring about a favorable result.

Watch, look, study, and learn. Then we shall truly understand the nature of this conflict, why it was waged, and why it was won."

For a moment there was silence, then Satan screamed, "I will ruin You!"

"Indeed, you shall try."

"Not try! Succeed." His minions screeched with him, brandishing their weapons and dancing in place on the Mount.

"We shall see," Kyrie answered. "Do not try to trespass My boundaries or you shall be eliminated from the gates, confined to the pit, and heard of no more."

"We shall see what we shall see," Satan shouted.

"Still the proud one," Kyrie answered. "Then do your worst."

"Ha! I will ruin you!"

"Away!" Kyrie cried, and with a wave of his hand the soldiers of Satan disappeared beyond the Outer Reaches. I turned and stared at the spectacle of earth, its planets, its sun, its rulers, and its citizens.

Kyrie turned to us. "Now go, and observe, and learn!"

Immediately, He disappeared from view. I thought He must have gone above the heights of the clouds, or the Temple. But I stood there, my body still quaking with the echo of the words I had witnessed still in my ears.

A moment later, Marid and others flew through the doorway. I only stood there, contemplating my position. Kyrie had given me something He'd given no other angel. I resolved in that moment to learn and study and glean every vestige of truth I could from this and all other aspects of that world.

I stepped through the doorway.

— 31

I stood in greenery unlike anything in Heaven. Lush trees and plants surrounded me. In the distance I saw beasts not unlike some of those in heaven. I recognized immediately that Kyrie was with me, at my right hand.

"Kyrie, what is it called?"

"Eden," He said.

I liked the name. In our language it meant "delight." The rustle of the air through the grass and trees almost made me laugh.

"It is so beautiful."

He smiled. "Come."

I saw the creatures, this time much closer. They were not at all like us; He called them flesh and blood. "You are light and spirit," He said. "They are flesh. But they are much like you. They are more limited, yes. But also in some ways less limited. They are bound to earth and cannot rise beyond it."

"And through this you will show . . ." My voice trailed off. I didn't see how.

He turned to me. "You continue to have your doubts, Aris?"

I nodded.

"You must learn to trust Me, Aris. I cannot make you do that. You will only learn through choosing. In that way, some doubts are good."

I leaned up against a huge frond on a fern in Eden, wondering. Then I saw them.

He said, "Come. Look."

The creatures were beautiful. He told me again that the man's name was Adam, and the woman He called Eve.

Kyrie said to me, "They can reproduce themselves. Their numbers will only increase until the end of the age. I have never done that before."

"They can reproduce themselves?" I said uncertainly.

"I will take a special hand in each individual, shaping him or her," He said. "They will be fearfully and wonderfully made, and you will see their glory. But they will start out helpless. It is a way to learn . . ."

"Trust," I said, with a sardonic smile.

"Already you are learning, Aris." He touched my shoulder and gripped it. I liked the way He smiled at me. Did He know how close I'd come to going over?

Soon, others of our number crowded in, watching. Kyrie spoke with them, taking each aside and explaining, answering questions. When I wanted to talk, He was there immediately.

Behind me, I heard Lucifer snicker, but I said nothing. After a glance around, several of my friends disappeared.

32

I looked forward to that first venture into Eden, alone. I wrote in my journal,

> It's a wonder. I don't know where to begin. I journey along the paths of the realm, careering far into marvels not unlike the stones of fire, the assembly in the north, and the musical landscape of a light symphony played against a billion spinning orbs.
>
> Ah, I am piling up words.
>
> The first thing I noticed is the Tree of the Knowledge of Good and Evil. He has set this tree in the center of the garden, a beautiful, fruit laden specimen with an odor like the nectar of Sillid from the nesting place of a Seraphim.
>
> But what is this test? Tyree already told me that it's just like Him to take away with His right hand what He gives with His left. He said it's the story of His whole attitude. He tried to persuade me to join them.

Ah, Tyree. Will I ever win you back?

Yet, to what? To my own indecision? No, but I do not want you to perish, if that is what it will come to. Tyree, Tyree. I loved you. I still love you. And yet, you are one of them now, perhaps forever.

Eden. The marvel. The crowning touch of His hand. The illimitable grandeur of His finest composition. Music is our language and our glory. Creation is His.

I tried sitting upon a lion today. He could see me, though he seems not to know the difference between me and others. I am weightless to him, a glowing ghost.

The lion ran through the wood, his mane blowing back into my face. Others of us gamboled among the animals and flora. It was a romp. The Garden is a true paradise, second only to our Paradise, though in ours such things do not seem as solid. Or as beautiful.

Sometimes I wish I was one of them. Free. Clothed in shekinah glory. Able to partake of the fruits of this world, so vast, so plentiful.

Satan has been here, scowling, angry. He does not like it at all. He says it is an affront to him, a sidebar creation Kyrie is using to shame and exploit him. He will not play the game that Kyrie plays.

But I do not believe him. I think he will try something, though I do not know what. He spends much time observing the animals, studying them, I suppose, to understand their habits and ways. He has restricted his own followers to mere observation till he has decided what to do with this place. They are eager to speak and converse with the woman and man. But they seem oblivious to us. I do not think they can see us. Certainly not touch us. We are invisible to them.

I will watch and wait. What Kyrie is doing I do not know. If this idyllic setting continues, I think we shall all become beguiled by it and live in it with no more thought of Heaven. I do not think that is what He wants.

I keep coming back to the trees. The woman and the man do not seem to realize the import of the Tree of Life. They have not eaten from it.

By the same token, they avoid the other tree.

On the other hand, Satan spends all his time by it, looking it over, thinking about it. He muses, sitting there on a limb or huddled upon a rock. For all his dragonish form, in this world he can seem to take any form he wants, and so do most of his minions. He is, for now, not unlike the man, having taken a form similar, but with a cloak of jewels, not of glory, as they wear. The jewels shine too, and he calls himself the "angel of light," which is similar to his other name, Lucifer. But he loathes the name Satan, undoubtedly because Kyrie gave it to him. Among his followers he goes by Azraith.

I will sit here among the flowers and watch the tree for now, watch Satan. He knows I am here and has gestured angrily in my direction. But I do not wish to talk to him or disturb him. I simply want to watch.

33

Satan was hidden among the trees, watching. I, across from him, watched also. I wondered what he was thinking. We were near the tree in the center of the Garden, the Tree of Knowledge, as it was called by the man.

The woman lay in the sun, combing her long raven hair. Satan came softly and sat down beside her. Then he spoke. I myself was astounded.

"Your hair is exquisite."

She did not hear him, and he grimaced at the realization. He could not communicate with her directly. I laughed to myself. So Satan truly was foiled. It was astonishing, but a joyful truth I instantly grasped and thanked Kyrie for.

Satan spoke again. "You are lovely."

But the woman only rolled onto her stomach, her hair dripping with dew on the grass. The shekinah clothed her in a glory that was marvelous to behold. Satan was right, even if he had been able to say it to her.

But why did he say such things?

"Because he wants to test her," a voice said behind me. I turned around. It was Cere. We embraced and I gladly held her hard.

"I have so missed you," I said.

"And I you." She smiled and the sparkle in her eyes made my heart thump.

We turned back to the scene. "What do you think will happen?"

"I am here to watch as much as you," Cere said.

"You believe Satan wants to test her?"

"To see if she will eat. I think he chooses the woman as his first prey, for the man is stronger. He will resist. But of course, if Satan cannot communicate with her, all his plans are foiled. Still, the test must happen somehow."

"What do you mean?" I turned away from the woman and looked into Cere's eyes. A moment later, Rune appeared and walked over. I greeted him enthusiastically. "We are all together again," I said.

"Except one," Rune answered.

I felt my face fall. "We will get him back," I said.

Rune nodded, but I could tell he did not believe I was correct. I looked back at Cere. "Why must they be tested?"

"I don't know," she said. "That's part of the mystery. But it must have to do with why Kyrie set up the test of obedience to begin with. He wants to see if they will obey Him on a point that, at some junctures, seems less than important."

"There are so many different kinds of fruit, though," I answered. "They will be content without tasting the one."

"Perhaps."

Cere knelt down to watch. "She is very beautiful. And they have so much that we do not."

"Are you envious?" I asked, stooping down next to her.

"No." She looked at Rune and laughed. "Their love is fascinating, but I do not envy it. I just don't understand it."

"I can agree to that."

Rune chuckled. "Then we are all agreed to something."

We all turned back to the woman.

She rose and walked, running her hands along the bushes, flicking back branches, playing. "I love the feel of warmth on my skin," she said and laughed. I felt her delight as a bolt of electricity through me, and I laughed myself. It was a joy to watch her angular, appealing motion, her lithe curves, her supple manner and personality. She was thinking of all that she and Adam would do this afternoon. I wondered at their love and their simplicity. I wondered if they could reason and think as we did.

I noticed one of the beasts walk by her. The serpent. A beautiful, comely beast with long sparkling silver hair, a wizened steady-eyed look, and a friendly desire to be with the woman. She touched the serpent and spoke to it. "You are such a lovely brute, Cignus. That is what I will call you, Cignus the Serpent." She nestled her face against the ruff at his shoulders and then rubbed her face in it playfully. The serpent fell to his side and kicked up his feet, inviting more play. She rolled with him on the grass, then tired of the play and got up, continued walking through the garden with the serpent beside her.

"She will make a pet of him," I said.

"Yes," Cere answered. "She's making pets of all of them. Giving them names like the man. But the man gives them a species name. She gives them personal names by which she calls them. It is interesting to watch the two and see the differences in their personalities and their manners."

"The man is sometimes gruff," said Rune. "But he is very gentle with her. He has real authority, though. All the beasts obey him—and her, too. But she does not command the way he does."

"And the woman revels in pretty things," Cere said. "Have you noticed that? She has a small collection of shiny rocks. And she has already made bracelets of grass and anklets of leaves. She is always making something."

"It is a wonder," I said.

We watched as the woman Eve pulled a peach off a tree and bit into it, throwing her head back. Her heart cried out a word of thanks to Kyrie. She listened and wondered if He was near. But suddenly she shook her head and took another bite. "I think the peach is my favorite," she murmured, then threw her hair back and walked along the already worn trail she and Adam used on their jaunts through the garden.

As she walked, I could see her concentrating, listening for her husband. Her desire was always for him, while his desire was for her, but also to rule well.

Soon, she heard Adam's singing, and she sprang forward toward the sound. When she saw him, she sneaked silently up behind him, then wrapped her arms around his back, sensually. In a moment, they were kissing and caressing one another.

After making love, he promised to bring some of a new fruit he had discovered to their meal. She told him to meet her in the center of the garden. The serpent stood far in among the fronds watching. When she left Adam, he followed her. The swishing noise of her light step and her singing were the only sounds. Two chickadees lit on her fingers and she threw them into the air, laughing. She paused to pet a lion and lioness, and watched two eagles climb the sky above her, swooping and rolling.

She reached the center of the garden, stooped to pat the grass and a pair of rabbits in her path. She sat and two sheep, a bear, and a giraffe sat with her. She sang to them, teaching them to baah, growl, and lisp as a part of her song.

Then the serpent was at her left hand again, and she ruffled its goaty beard, looked into its eyes and gave it a fresh, wet kiss on the forehead. The beast mewed with pleasure.

"I shall teach all of you to talk," Eve suddenly said. "Now say 'Adam.'"

The beasts all regarded her quizzically, obviously not understanding that she wanted them to speak.

"'Adam.' Say it. You can say it."

But the beasts all simply nuzzled her hand and drew closer, baahing and growling happily and mewing.

I grinned. "Nothing can destroy this," I said.

Rune answered me. "There is the meeting tonight on the Mount."

"Yes, and we will be late if we do not hurry."

"Satan will be there," he said.

"And Tyree," Cere replied, with a hint of pain in her voice.

I nodded. "Have you seen him?"

"Not since . . ." Rune's and Cere's voices trailed off together.

"We will get him back," I emphasized again.

"Perhaps," Cere said. "If you have finally made your choice."

I shook my head. "Kyrie has given me a great gift of time. I will not spurn it. I'm going to use it well."

"But how?" Cere answered, her eyes glistening. "It would be so much better if you were with us."

"I am with you," I said. "But I want to see more."

"I guess we must grant you that right," Cere said.

A moment later we passed through the doorway and we sped our way to the Mount.

34

"I desire leave to test them," Satan said as he pranced before Kyrie's throne, acting haughty and cocksure.

"You mean to tempt them," Kyrie said.

"Test? Tempt? They're the same. We wish to see if they're all You've proclaimed them to be. Obedience is not something to be laughed at."

"Nor to be mocked and scorned."

"I do not scorn it!" Lucifer cried. His lengthy dragonic form, scaly and wrinkled and powerful looking, gave the meeting a forbidding tone that I did not like. Now he was repeatedly pushing Kyrie to each limit and testing it himself. "I do not scorn it!" he said again. "I disavow it. I believe it is a pretense on Your part to suppose that all Your creatures will simply sally forth and obey Your every whim. Which is precisely what this Tree of Knowledge is. Whim cloaked in obeisance cloaked in tantalizing food for the soul. What would be a better way to see whether they love You or despise You?"

I watched as Lucifer and his fiends sought an opportunity to tempt the man and woman in the Garden. He had been frustrated in his efforts to communicate with her and did not like the position he was put in.

Kyrie said, "I will not put them into your hands."

"Then You have reneged on your agreement!" Satan shouted. "You said we shall have the right to test our theories of rule and so on. How can I test them if I can't even communicate with them? You have already won and not an argument has flown."

"The man and woman will confront the Tree soon enough," Kyrie said.

"Better sooner than later," Satan answered. "We should have the right to invite them to eat of the Tree. That is the whole point of this gamble of Yours, is it not? Then let's get on with it. Give me leave to test them."

"Tempt them."

"Tempt, test, what's the difference, as I said before? In the end it's all one and the same."

"Why should I grant this, Satan?"

For a moment, the adversary seemed dumbstruck, then he facilely spoke with that tongue of his slithering out like a rapier. "Because You are just, and good, and righteous, and it is a sham that they go on and on without confronting the very issue that keeps them from the full bliss of relationship with You."

"What do you know of that?"

"I know that if they succeed in the test—and why should they not?—that they will enter into a more intimate relationship with You, and an eternal one. That is the point, is it not?"

"It is."

I wondered how Satan knew this. But then I remembered that when Kyrie had first instructed the man and woman and the man asked why the two trees were there, Kyrie had answered, "One to ascertain your loyalties so that the other, which will grant eternal life and fellowship with Me, will not secure your eternal death."

"You shall not tempt them," Kyrie said suddenly. "They will face the tree on their own terms."

Satan roared off, howling about the injustice of Kyrie, and the rest of us watched in amazement. For once, Satan had not gotten something that he wanted.

Immediately, Rune said, "Let's go back and watch now."

As the meeting ended, we passed through the door and stepped into the Garden. We quickly found the man and woman staring up at the very Tree we had been discussing. Satan hid in the shadows, close to the serpent, who, with other beasts, stared on in the adoration and worship of their mutual masters.

"But what does it mean, Adam, that we shall die?"

"I do not know," the man said. "We shall be separated from God. I believe that. So we must simply avoid it. Don't go near this Tree anymore."

"But what is the knowledge that it gives?" Eve said. "Shouldn't we learn what that is?"

"If it was worth all that much, surely Kyrie would have given it to us another way. Now I say don't go near this Tree again! I don't want to find you looking at it, or sitting under it, or touching it."

"But that is foolish! Surely God wants us to look at it."

"You can look at it, but don't touch it!"

"Is that what God said? I thought He said we simply should not eat it."

"Yes, yes. But don't eat of it or touch it anyway. Lest we die! You don't want to die, do you?"

"Well, if I don't know what it is, I don't see how I can be that afraid of it."

"It is terrible, or He wouldn't have said so!"

"Adam, you're being unnecessarily hard."

The man's eyes softened and he held out his arms. They embraced and soon were kissing. "Dearest one, we cannot risk death. Though we may not know what it is, we do know that it means separation from Kyrie. Do you want that? I know you don't want that."

"But it's so lovely."

Adam turned and regarded the Tree a moment. "I do wonder what this knowledge is. Can we get the knowledge if we do not eat?"

"I suppose not," Eve said. "That's the problem. Kyrie says it imparts knowledge, but we don't really understand what knowledge that is—it's all so confusing."

"Kyrie would not give us a command unless He knew it was right."

"But if we don't understand it, it makes no sense."

Adam looked up at the tree and shielded his eyes from the sun. "Perhaps not understanding it is the whole point. If we obey Kyrie in this matter, then perhaps—I don't know." He regarded his wife with frustration. "All I know is that I do not want to lose what we have."

She wriggled in his arms, then embraced him fondly, sensually. Moments later they fell onto the grass and made love.

In the end, she gave the Tree one last look and said, "I love you, Adam."

"I love you. Let's go gather our dinner."

As they left, I heard a hissing behind the tree. It was Satan. The Dragon had taken a human form in the Garden, though not visible to the man or woman. "It's unjust! It's unfair!" he said with a scowl. "Kyrie is ruling with an iron hand and has reneged on everything He has ever said."

Satan's fellow consorts cringed before his rage. I had not seen Satan enraged before, and now he was pacing back and forth, gesturing, throwing his arms into the air, cursing, stomping, turning a moment to plead and cajole with his audience—who only answered in the most favorable terms— and then scorching off to more epithets and complaints against Kyrie.

Then with a sudden wave of his hand in abject anger, he launched himself into the air heading straight for the Door.

"Come on," cried Cere. "Let's hurry! He will be at Kyrie's throne again."

"But can he come unbidden?" I cried, leaping into the air with her.

"I don't know," Cere answered. "But we will find out. He's very angry now."

"Of course. For once he has not gotten his way."

"I'd say he has not gotten it much lately for anything," Rune murmured, haloed in the soft glow of his glorious attire and gentility of his nature.

"Kyrie has gotten hard and that's good," I said.

We sped for the Door and soon latched through it. Coming down onto the soft, grassy ground, I looked up at the Mount shining in the distance. Kyrie would be there now, conferring with different deputies and hearing their insights and suggestions.

Moments later we arrived, and Satan stood on the lawn in front of the throne on the Mount.

"I'll prove it to you," Satan shouted. He was shouting a great deal more these days, and I wondered if Kyrie would long allow it. "If you put them into my hands, they will do everything wrong. They'll eat the fruit and then they'll die. Give me leave to do that and I will prove it. No one will obey You when they think they won't be hurt. That's the whole trouble with you. Threats. Laws. Consequences. Strip away the consequences and what are You? An empty Potentate. The tyrant we've all come to know and hate! If not for the terror of You, they'd just as soon have nothing to do with You! You think they want to obey Your law? No, they are so frightened of the Tree they can't think. They avoid it. They don't want to deal with its true nature, they're simply afraid it will take away what they already possess. But take away Your dread death decree and I'll show You the truth. They'll lap it up like milk and biscuits!"

Kyrie regarded Satan with scorn and anger, but He said, "You believe that if their fear of death is removed, they will eat without a second thought? And how shall it be removed?"

"I shall remove it."

"How?"

"I have my ways. Just give me leave to tempt them. There, I said it. Tempt! Tempt! TEMPT! That's what I'll do. No more testing. I will tempt them, and they will fall because they don't want to obey You. No one does!"

Kyrie's lips twitched with anger. But suddenly He said, "Behold, they are in your hands. Do as you desire. Only you shall not touch them."

Satan's head snapped alert with a hideous grin on his face. He said, "And how am I to communicate with them if they cannot hear me? More of Your protection around them, which just shows You are quite afraid to let them stand on their own feet alone, without fear!"

"What do you propose?"

"I shall possess the serpent."

"And if the serpent refuses?"

"I shall arrange it. Give me leave to go."

"You shall bear your judgment, Satan. But I will give you leave to test the man and woman. The serpent will bear his own punishment if he allows you to possess him."

"Good!"

Satan leaped away and I, Rune, and Cere approached the throne. "Lord," I said. "You are giving Satan the right to destroy them?"

"Not the right. They are not destroyed."

"But he will find a way."

"Perhaps. That is yet to be seen. But he shall bear his judgment."

"And what of the man and woman? They are innocent."

"They must be tested."

"But why?"

"Because only when their loyalty is proven can I grant to them the greatest gift of all."

"And what is that?"

He smiled, and the singular humble reserve was back on His face. "That is another of those mysteries you must discover."

When He said it, I realized I was getting tired of this game we all seemed to be playing. "Lord, these are real lives. We cannot play with them as if it was a game."

"I am not playing with them," Kyrie answered, His eyes flickering with sudden passion. "I am giving them the opportunity for greatness and glory. But also death and damnation. Only when there is the first is there the last. If there was no death and damnation there would also be no glory. It is the price, but it is a price well worth paying."

I knew I could not disagree with that. But I said, "Why can't we gain glory without the specter of death looming over everything?"

"Because real glory is only attained at the point of a choice between the two great opposites. Embrace the one, and you triumph over the other. But embrace the other, and you lose all. If there was nothing to be lost, there also would be nothing to be gained."

I looked at Rune and Cere. "Do you understand these things?"

"I'm trying," Cere said.

"I too," Rune answered.

"It is all too befuddling."

"Yes," Rune said, "but let's hurry back. Satan may already be working his deception."

— 35

I watched, astonished and grieved. Cere was at my left and Rune at my right.

"Satan has taken the serpent," I commented, watching as Satan's slit-eyed demeanor overcovered that of the serpent.

"We know."

Rune said, "He will destroy them with his lies."

I turned my eyes back to the scene.

"We should stop him," Rune said.

"But Kyrie has not allowed it," Cere answered, and she took my hand and squeezed it. "We cannot intercede. Though that is not true for Aris."

"What can I do?" I said, suddenly willing to try something.

Cere said, "You cannot speak to her or the man, but you can speak to Satan."

"How?"

"Confuse him."

"I confuse Satan?"

Rune laughed. "Yes, I think that's impossible. But we cannot stand by and let him deceive her. We must at least make sure the truth comes out."

The serpent sidled up to the woman, brushing against her. Suddenly he said, low and unassuming, "A woman as beautiful as you must be a goddess."

Eve almost jumped, but then she peered at the serpent, knelt down in front of him and said, "You can talk?"

"Indeed," said Satan through the serpent, "I can talk, think, make propositions, reason, use logic—almost everything you can do." The obsidian eyes focused on the woman, giving her a shiver. His multicolored body seemed to change in the sunlight, from red to blue to orange to black to brown, and then back again. He was marvelous to the touch, almost slick, and his small head shone with intelligence and gravity.

Eve knotted her brow with wonder. "And where did you gain this ability? You never spoke before."

"I was a different creature then. But now I am changed."

"How have you changed?"

"I have eaten of the fruit of a tree that has great power." The serpent licked his teeth and responded to Eve's caress with a taut, lifted back. His small legs were perfect for climbing, the claws like a cat's.

"Show me this tree!" Eve cried.

The serpent pranced away and led her quickly to the forbidden tree. Eve gave a little cry when she looked up at it, covering her mouth with her hand. The serpent pointed to a hanging stem. "I climbed and ate. And now I am as you. If you ate, you would be a goddess. Alas, it will only allow me to rise as high as you and our master, I suspect."

"But I can't," Eve answered, almost biting her knuckles. "You are sure it was this tree?"

"Yes. Has Kyrie said you shall not eat from any of the trees of the garden?"

She turned, still startled and amazed. His question at first confused her, but as she thought about it, she realized what he meant. "Not all. He has said we may eat from any tree of the garden except the one in the center of the garden. Of that one Kyrie has said, 'You shall not eat from it or touch it, lest you die.'"

She turned away from the serpent to look up at the tree. The serpent climbed it nattily and slid out on a branch. "This fruit," it said, a vague sibilance in its voice. "This fruit is very good. It will not make you die! I have eaten it and I am not dead!"

Her eyes slowly opened wider, as if understanding was only beginning to register. She turned again, scrutinizing the face of the serpent, then looking at the fruit hanging under his right foot. She paused, then rose to the same height as the face of the serpent.

He almost shrank back, but said boldly, his eyes rolling over her, smooth and caressing, "Kyrie knows that when you eat from it your eyes will be opened, and you'll be like Kyrie, knowing good and evil. You will be a goddess, and you will need a god to appreciate your worth."

"Adam," she said abruptly.

"Yes. Both of you. Gods."

Eve lifted her hand and touched the fruit gingerly, as if she feared receiving a shock of some sort. She queried, "My eyes will be opened?"

The serpent nodded eagerly, its iridescent body shimmering. "Yes. You will know good and evil. You will be like God Himself."

As the conversation continued, I, Rune, and Cere watched with growing trepidation in the trees. In the serpent's eyes I saw the light of Lucifer. My heart pounded within me and I quaked, burning to act, to stop this charade. But I felt powerless, at a lack to know what to do.

Cere said, "Go, confuse him."

I stood, then strode forward. Satan saw me coming and regarded me angrily. "Do not come closer," he hissed, his stridency something I had not noticed before. "You have no cause here."

"And neither have you."

"I have freedom to act as I choose."

"But that doesn't give you the right to deceive."

"I do with my rights as I see fit."

Satan rose up to his full height, the sudden apparition of the dragon blazing before me behind the visage of the serpent. "Begone, guttersnipe!"

He ripped at me with his claw and swatted me back. Rune and Cere knelt down to help me.

"Do not come back!" Satan roared. "This is my place and my time. I will do as I please."

I clambered back on my feet, still dazed.

The woman continued regarding the fruit suspiciously. She said, "Why does God forbid it?"

The serpent, now fully in the claw of Satan, leaned forward, glanced around a moment, then pawed the bark of the tall Tree. "He does not want you to be like Him."

The woman wrinkled her nose and slit her eyes, then looked again at the fruit. With a sudden sigh, she walked to it, touched it again. She had never touched it before now, never seen it so close.

I wanted to shout something to her, but she could not hear me. I thought of taking some animal form like Satan had, but I did not know how. I sensed that Kyrie was nowhere near. The sun had momentarily disappeared behind a cloud. My heart boomed in my chest. Would Kyrie just let them die? Would He once again do nothing as Satan rampaged through His realm?

Eve stared at the fruit. It was beautiful, round, golden. She touched the surface and rubbed its smooth skin. She leaned to sniff it. The aroma reminded her of her husband's sweet breath after a meal of pomegranates. She pulled on the branch and the stem broke. Then she turned, holding it in her hand.

"It does look good for food."

The serpent nodded emphatically and stamped his clawed feet.

"It's certainly beautiful to the eyes, and it smells wonderful."

The serpent's eyes gleamed in the sunlight. "Indeed," it hissed.

"It will make me wise?" she asked, turning the fruit over and over in her hands.

When she looked up, the serpent whispered, "As wise as God Himself."

She brought the fruit to her lips and then stopped. "If God is that wise, then why didn't He let us eat it in the first place?"

For a moment, I thought she had him. But Satan's answer was smooth as silk. "He Himself has not eaten it, for He is afraid of it. So perhaps . . ." He drew out the *S* sound in a lengthy hiss. "Perhaps you shall even be wiser than God."

I could feel Cere steeling herself, and Rune had almost gone limp with apprehension. Behind Satan I saw Tyree and others. Tyree's form was mangled, cloven feet and gnarled facial features. But I recognized his spirit instantly.

The woman shrugged. "Then maybe He is all wrong about it." She bit into the fruit and chewed it meditatively. Then she said, "I don't feel any different."

The serpent said, "When your husband tastes it, you will both see as never before."

She continued eating the single piece, then plucked another fruit from a branch and ran to where she last saw Adam. He was still picking fruit from a peach tree, placing it into a small basket he had made of reeds.

We followed them through the garden. The serpent was still at her arm.

"You must taste this. We will become wise."

He stared at her, then at the fruit.

"This is the fruit that God for . . ."

She pushed it into his hands. "It will make us wise. I have already eaten it. When you eat, our eyes will be opened. We will not become wise unless you eat. I don't want to be the only one!"

Her body was beautiful in the sunlight. Her eyes were eager, earnest. But his heart thumped in his chest. He knew it was forbidden. As he paused, her eyes fell and she pouted. He remembered their lovemaking of only a few moments ago. He had not seen her look like this. Her face was almost dark now, angry. He gulped.

"We will not be wise unless you eat." Her voice had an edge to it. She folded her arms and stared at him now, her lips twisting into a half smile, challenging him.

Slowly, he moved the fruit to his mouth, closing his eyes. Then he bit into it, chewed, swallowed. Finally, he opened his eyes.

Her face was dark, horrified. She covered her breasts immediately and turned away. "Adam, we are naked! God made us naked!"

Immediately, I noticed that the glow of the shekinah light covering them had departed. Even I felt some horror at the vision. She was indeed naked, a nakedness that I had never witnessed before, one tinged with the acid of guilt and sting of shame.

Adam stared first at her, then at himself. A revulsion seared through him, then a hot humiliation. He quivered, then stalked down the path. "We will make something. How dare He do this to us!"

I looked on, horrified. The serpent pranced away, and I saw Satan break with it, his spirit crackling out of the iridescent back with a shimmer. As he rose, the triumph on his face gleamed like a flung coal. My eyes met his and I crumbled inside. Already, Kyrie had lost the first battle. In only a few words. It was impossible. Kyrie had to act now, to stop this. But the instant I thought it, I realized He would do nothing.

Others departed with the Dragon, clapping and laughing. I stood alone—though surrounded by many others—aghast, silent, stunned. Could it have been that easy?

I told myself, "Perhaps it is recoverable. Perhaps it was not as great an issue as we thought."

I watched as the man and woman hurried down the path. They obviously did not yet understand what had happened. I saw the darkness etched in their eyes. Adam shuddered. He touched her and she flinched away. He did not understand. She turned and said with rancor, "We are naked, Adam. All this time we have been naked. And He did it to us!"

"Come on," he said, "we'll find something to cover ourselves. To think He would do this and from the very beginning!"

"You find something," she said. "I will wait here."

His eyes fell. He hurried and came back with a sheaf of leaves from a fig tree. She remained angry and pouting. "I don't want to talk to Him, Adam."

He nodded. "We'll hide. He won't find us. We'll refuse to speak to Him. To think that He would make us naked, and ashamed, and not even aware of it, but ignorant, totally ignorant fools and children!"

"He deserves our anger!"

"Yes."

A moment later, she began weeping. "What are we to do, Adam? He will come for us. We will not be able to hide. He will punish us—with death!"

"We will hide!" Adam said, his eyes curiously flat and dull with dread. "I will protect you!"

"You can't! He is too powerful!" She slipped to the ground and wept, still covering herself with an arm. He tried to put his arm around her, but she pushed him away. "Don't touch me, please! I do not wish to be touched."

36

We all scattered. When we reached Heaven, Rune left. "I cannot talk right now," he said. Cere's eyes were red.

The pressure in my head built till I wanted to scream. Cere and I walked together to the River.

"Already, it is disfigured," she cried. "Already, Satan has won. And at so great a price. It's all foolishness!"

I slumped down beside her and stared at the waters. "It doesn't make any sense. Why did He let Satan do this?"

"You know what He said—Lucifer can test his ideas freely. So now he has tested them . . ."

". . . and they have proven powerful!"

Cere hung her head. "I feel a strong urge to join them."

I suddenly gripped her arm. "You cannot do that, Cere. It is death."

"But what is this?" she said vehemently. "Life? No, it's despair. What will come of it? And why did He do nothing?"

"Can we be so sure He did nothing?"

"He let them walk right into it."

I thought a moment, then I said, "Maybe He is up to something different, something we cannot yet understand."

Cere gazed at me skeptically, then she said, "I want to be alone now."

"Yes, so do I."

I walked back to my room in the Great City. My heart was heavy. The new creation suffered complete defeat before it had even begun. I wondered if it ever had a chance.

As I walked, I overheard other angels talking, as angry and upset as I was. Few seemed to understand, and many felt at the point of sedition themselves. I wondered what held us back? Curiosity, perhaps. Or a determined desire to hear Kyrie out in this argument, if you could call it that. Satan was bent on destroying Adam, Eve, and the whole world, or so I thought. And Kyrie was allowing him to do it.

What was Kyrie's purpose?

As I walked, it occurred to me that perhaps Kyrie could not have stopped the temptation. He had created this new world partly as a stage on which to test all the theories. But what were the theories? There were only two: Kyrie's way or another. Certainly, there could be many "other" ways, but really only one—that of the rebels. And within their rebellion, numerous arguments and apparent variations on the same theme.

And what was Kyrie's way?

The words echoed in my heart: "Obedience to His will."

Yes, that seemed to be the sum of it. But that felt so one-sided. Was there nothing in it for us, for those who were obedient?

Yes, there were other ways to put it. "To enjoy Him." "To partake of Him and His glory." "To share the kingdom and power." "To be a part of it with Him."

But if Kyrie was a fool—I flinched at the word as it echoed in my mind, but I had to let it stand: either Kyrie was far more brilliant and powerful than I thought, or He was a fool, playing repeatedly into the hands of an enemy He had created more dazzling than Himself, a seeming contradiction of terms—but if Kyrie was a fool, then I was right not to follow Him.

Already Satan had shown himself to be malevolent, determined to ruin Kyrie. What of Satan's own plans? How had he shown himself superior, able to tempt Kyrie's grandest creations to commit the same atrocious act of secession that he had?

It seemed to me a vast conundrum. But the answer, whatever there was of one, lay in remaining patient, willing to bear a loss or a few losses in order to establish something far greater. But what?

I reasoned that Kyrie had to have some idea of where it was going. He was omniscient, or so I was taught. He knew the end from the beginning. He knew Eve would be deceived and Adam would eat before He ever created them. So why had He created them in the first place, if He knew it would lead to holocaust?

All these questions nagged at my mind like nipping puppies that noisily tried to engage me in play. But I felt tired of all the argumentation.

Then suddenly, Tyree was at my side. I felt him before I saw him.

"Aris!"

He was as always: cool, friendly, ready to joke. He placed his clawed hand on my shoulder. "And how do you see it now that our illustrious leader has felled the crown of creation in one swift blow?"

"Tyree, it is only the beginning."

"You don't believe that. It is already the end. What can be accomplished from here? They will die soon and that will be the end. He will have to start over."

"I don't think Kyrie starts over." I looked at Tyree and my heart ached a moment. I wished for the old friend whose counsel I could trust and whose humor I could enjoy.

Tyree chuckled. "Yes, you're right. If He did, He would have already, and you and I might be no more."

"You more likely. Maybe me. But not all of us."

"Ah, yes. He would leave those loyal to Him alive. I tend to forget about that. Of course, one of those loyalists could always choose to see the error of his ways and start another rebellion. Eventually, Kyrie could whittle it all down to just one or two. Michael, and who else, do you think? Gabriel?"

I grimaced uneasily. "Let's just be friends again, Tyree. That's all I want."

"And that is why I have come. To invite you to the inner circle of Hell."

"The inner circle?"

"Well, really most of us, except a few of the lamebrains who would rather play and cavort than do battle. But the ones who count, yes, the inner circle, we will all be gathering to celebrate."

"Satan's victory?"

"Do not call him Satan."

"Then what?"

"Azraith. He will still answer to Lucifer. He likes what it means."

"And what does Azraith mean?"

Tyree chuckled. "'The one who has conquered.' We are creating our own language, making it up as we go along. It's really quite fun, if you'd give it a chance. Rebellion isn't as bad as it looks. We get the razzle-dazzle part of the battle, if you know what I mean. Kyrie does something, and we foul it up. It's pretty simple at the moment."

"And what of Satan's grand design? Is there no attention to that?"

"Of course. Azraith, please."

"I'll call him what I want."

"All right, that's fair. Stick to what makes sense. But come. Let's enter into the bliss of the adversary. I'll show you some things that will curl your eyebrows in a new direction. There's something good in every pot, even if some of them are burned!"

Tyree was still Tyree, even if he'd gone over. I watched as he turned and started walking through the City. He was allowed to be here as long as he did not trespass the laws of Heaven, which, fortunately for him, were few.

We walked through the streets, I at his back, and then he indicated to me to fly, and soon we stepped down into Satan's meeting place past the Outer Reaches. It was a huge gallery, something like the Mount itself, but dark and foreboding. The air echoed with the cries and cheers of the assembly. The demons gathered seemed drunk on the power that had just been manifested in the felling of the man and woman.

Speeches began and one sage rebel held court before the assembly with a fast fire series of jokes.

"'It looks good to eat,' says the woman. And our leader replies with a hiss, as if to say, 'Yes, my dear, the better to eat you with!'"

There was laughter all around.

"And Kyrie's prize says, 'I shall not die?' Not die? Of course not. You shall rot in place—so long as you do all that Kyrie says!"

More laughter.

I sat with Tyree, and we listened to several speeches until Satan rose up before the gathering. He had taken a more human guise, obviously preferring the glory of the crown of creation to his own dragonish form.

"Comrades, we now stand on the pinnacle of our greatest victory. Kyrie has shown Himself once again to be weak. He cannot control or govern His fondest creations. They all rebel against His rule as quickly as the laws themselves are laid. They rebel because they recognize the fickleness of His rules. To eat or not to eat. He is fickle, capricious. He makes a life or death law on the basis of eating a simple fruit. Why not make it something that really matters? But no, He in His simpleminded mindset chooses a piece of fruit. Either it's so brilliant it's beyond us, or it's the height of foolishness. What say you?"

"Foolishness!" the masses shouted back, warming to Satan's message. I simply sat and listened.

"Hear me, comrades. What have we achieved today? The end of the second creation? No, I tell you, now we rule in the second creation. Kyrie has been driven from the throne. The man and woman will no longer obey Him, for He must reject them by His own laws. He must kill them. And who will they belong to?"

"US!" demons all around me screamed.

"And what will we do with them?"

"Devour them!"

"Indeed!"

The cheers rose, until someone shouted, "Kyrie is in the Garden."

As if trap-sprung, even without a word from Satan, the singing heroes of the rebellion flung themselves for the Door.

37

Kyrie walked through the Garden quietly. The man and woman continued to hide, cowering, behind a palm tree. She whispered to Adam, "What will we tell Him?"

He brushed her away. "Just be quiet. He will go by."

But Kyrie paused, stopped, gazed in their direction. "Adam! Adam! Where are you?"

Adam remained silent, pressing his hand against the leaf apron he wore. It slipped and he was afraid it would fall off. The woman pressed her fingers into his arm.

"Adam! Come out!"

She trembled and whispered, "We cannot hide from Him. We must tell Him."

"No! Don't you know what the warning said? 'Death.' We will die."

She turned and gazed at the tall, august form of Kyrie, white and splendid, glimmering in the light. Something within her wanted to fly to Him and confess all. Something else wanted to run.

He stepped closer. "Adam! Where are you?" He was looking directly into Adam's eyes.

Adam rose. "I heard You in the garden."

"Then why didn't you come to Me?"

"I was afraid because I was naked."

She rose behind him, thinking He was angry now, and she cringed, expecting a blow. Adam set his jaw. He confessed to nothing.

Kyrie spoke, his voice like a rising wind over still water. "Who told you that you were naked? Have you eaten from the Tree I commanded you not to eat from?"

Adam stepped away from Eve, giving her a hard, bitter look. "It was the woman You gave me. She ate first, then gave it to me, so I ate."

With a cry of horror and anger, Eve stepped back, bunching her fist. "You blame it on me?"

Adam ignored her, keeping his eyes toward Kyrie.

She screeched again, "You blame it on me?"

Adam motioned to her to be quiet, and she turned embittered eyes forward to stare at Kyrie.

Next to me as we watched, Tyree snickered. "He knows what to say even without our master's suggestion. Bravo! Serves Kyrie right. The creature is all ours now."

I said, "Be still, Tyree. Kyrie has not finished His questioning."

"Yes, but why does He question them? Does He not already know the answers?" Tyree snorted with derision. "It's because He isn't omniscient as we were told. He is as ignorant as any of us."

"Don't be so sure."

"Oh, I am sure. Otherwise, why more of the charade? Why doesn't He simply kill them the way He promised?"

"Hush. Look."

Kyrie turned to the woman, His sharp gray eye fixing on her still-beauteous form. "What have you done?"

The woman's tongue was quick, and she gave her husband an irritated glance as she spoke. "The serpent deceived me! I ate from the tree because of the serpent." Giving her husband one final glance of triumph, she folded her arms and waited.

Tyree touched my arm. "See, she knows what to say, too! They both do. But now it is up to Kyrie. Watch. He will have to kill them now. And that will be the end of everything. Ruined before it was started."

"Just watch, Tyree," I said, wishing my friend was not so eager to see the sinners slain.

The sound of the serpent rustled in the trees behind them, but Kyrie paid him no attention. Kyrie's voice was even, low, controlled. The woman and man stood apart. Her thoughts told her never to let the man touch her again. The man stilled himself with the inner exhortation that he would never listen to her again.

I wondered if the man and woman would simply fall to the ground, dead, though before this we'd never seen anyone die, unless you considered what had happened with the rebels a kind of death, and I knew they did not look at it that way at all.

Kyrie did not strike them. First, He said to the serpent, "Because you have done this, cursed are you more than all cattle, and more than every beast of the field. On your belly shall you go, and dust you shall eat all the days of your life."

There was a murmur of approval among our company, but Satan and his supporters did not laugh. They were silent and angry.

"And I will put enmity between your seed and her seed; He shall bruise you on the head, and you shall bruise Him on the heel."

For a moment, everything went blurry, and then suddenly the serpent fell to the ground, his lithe, beautiful body a long coil. He was legless, and he slithered rapidly into the forest where I saw him no more.

"This is not what you said!" Satan shouted, but Kyrie gave him no recognition. Immediately, Satan rushed forward to speak directly into Kyrie's face, but he was stopped, halfway between the trees and the man and woman. He was held, suspended, his throat constricted and voiceless.

Kyrie regarded the woman with pain etched on his lips and face. "I will greatly multiply your pain in childbirth, in pain you shall bring forth children. Yet your desire shall be for your husband, and he shall rule over you."

Others behind Satan cried that this was not the bargain. They took up a chant. "Kill her! Kill her! Kill her!"

But a moment later, their voices were cut, and they were held the same way Satan was. They did not move. Tyree whispered to me, "Once again, Kyrie proves a liar!"

I said nothing in response, but only watched in fascination.

Kyrie looked at the man, His face a mask of broken torment. "Cursed is the ground because of you. In toil you shall eat of it all the days of your life. Both thorns and thistles it shall grow for you; and you shall eat the plants of the field; by the sweat of your face you shall eat bread, till you return to the ground, because from it you were taken; for you are dust, and to dust you shall return."

Both the man and woman were weeping now, and Satan and his followers were released from the power that had held them. Satan cried, "Lies! We have seen the lies! They are to die and die they must."

Kyrie, still ignoring Satan, motioned to Michael to slay one of the sheep. When the beast's blood mingled with the dirt of the earth, the angel skinned it and made garments of the skin for the man and woman. Then Kyrie sent one of the Cherubim to guard the Tree of Life so that neither Adam nor Eve could partake of it.

"You shall never live here again," Kyrie said to them. "Behold, you shall dwell in the land. Go now and begin your labor."

The woman wept. Adam bowed his head and waited. Two sheep came out next to him, some cattle, two dogs, chickens, other animals. They followed him into the rocky place, and beyond it he found a meadow with a brook. The man and woman sat by the brook. She gripped his arm and said, "I am afraid."

He nodded and blinked unhappily. "I think we will always be afraid."

"What have we done?"

He said nothing, but only tried to think of what he would do, where he would find food for both of them. As he rose for a better look, she said, "Has He forgiven us?"

For the first time he looked into her eyes. He pulled her into his arms. He did not think of time or age. He knew nothing of what death would mean. He knew only that what had been would never be again. He said, "I'm sorry."

She wept on his shoulder. She was still very beautiful, and she did not think of the curse. She was only afraid that he would desert her or hurt her. "What will we do?"

He held her tightly. "He will be with us. He has forgiven us. He will show us the way."

She gripped him and would not let go. She believed what her husband said, but the fear in her heart felt hard and tight as the stones beneath her feet. She tried to remember what Kyrie had said, but her only thought was where they would live and raise a family and find food.

And then something caught her eyes, a shining before her. A tree with fruit. She let go of Adam and ran eagerly toward it, to claim the fruit, to eat. As she pulled an apple from the tree, she saw Kyrie walk quietly away. For a moment, she hesitated, then she cried, "Lord?"

Kyrie stood before them. "Yes?"

"Thank you."

He smiled. The man and woman ate.

"He will help us," Adam said as he took an apple. "But we must obey Him."

He watched Kyrie pass back into the Garden, then he turned his eyes toward the meadow before him. As he watched the cows and sheep eat the grass, a tear burned in his eye. When Eve looked at him, he turned away and picked up a rock, thinking it might help him dig.

As I watched, I felt cool, refreshed, hopeful. Kyrie had indeed done something else. But then I heard a raspy, mangled ejaculation from the center of the Garden:

"Lies! It was all lies! And now they will pay!"

It was Satan. He tore back out of the Garden and through the Door. Moments later, he and the rest of us stood before Kyrie.

38

"They were to die. You said, 'If you eat of the Tree, you shall surely die.' And once again You have reneged! You are not trustworthy."

Kyrie sat on the throne, His chin on His hand. He was almost lolling, amused at this outburst. "There are different kinds of death, Satan."

"And You choose which one. I will not let it stand. You twist language. You do not mean what You say. And that is why no one trusts You. That is why we have rebelled. You do not say what You mean, and You certainly don't mean what You say. You speak in circles, and then You choose which circle You will land in, irrespective of what anyone actually believed about what You said."

"What I have done I have done. It will stand as is."

"Then You refuse to make this right?"

"It is already made right."

"You caused the serpent to go on its belly."

"Yes."

"That is unfair. It was I who possessed the serpent."

"And you shall also go on your belly and eat dust all the days of your life."

For a moment, Satan was silenced. I watched the spectacle with a strange mixture of anger. On one hand, I felt Satan was somewhat in the right. Kyrie had said the man and woman would die if they ate of the tree. Apparently, Kyrie meant they would die spiritually, and that was fair. But that was not the way most of us—including the man and woman—understood it. It seemed to me that Kyrie was using the obtuseness of language for His own purposes.

Was that fair? Who was to say? Kyrie was the law.

On the other hand, Satan's taunts and accusations had become habit. Repeatedly, Satan held Kyrie to His laws, but Satan did not obey his own laws, much less any others.

It seemed to me that it came down once again to a conundrum I couldn't solve. Whatever Kyrie did, He was right. He found ways to make it right in such a way that it couldn't be argued. No one could successfully dispute with Kyrie. He held all the cards, and with impunity He dealt from the bottom of the deck, so to speak. It was all written into the rules. He was allowed to deal that way because He was Kyrie. No one could subvert Him or overturn Him. He had it all wrapped in a tight little ball with no room for dissent. He was always right. Always.

Deep down, that realization irked me. I could respect Kyrie for His integrity. But it seemed to me at times that He resorted to the same tricks Satan used, twisting language to His own purpose.

But did He really?

That was the other viewpoint. That was Kyrie's. How did He see it? He had a rebellion on His hands. He had billions of beings who not only hated Him but would tell loud lies against Him without a flicker of the eyelids. Satan's argument seemed to me to be specious. Yes, Kyrie said they would die, but He did not say when. He did not say, "Immediately." He said, "Surely."

He did not specify what kind of death they would experience—physical, mental, spiritual, emotional. Undoubtedly, He was ambiguous because ultimately He meant all forms of death. And for the sake of brevity—Kyrie is unapologetically brief in all discussions—He did not specify which. Why should He? Adam could have asked, but he didn't. We could have asked. But we didn't. We just sat there hoping it would happen, and when it didn't, some of us went off in a rage accusing Him of lying.

But when it came down to it, He hadn't lied about anything.

That was the rub of it. He hadn't lied, but the truth was just liquid enough to flow both upstream and downstream. He always kept to the truth, but the truth was so big, and at times hard to nail down.

To be sure, I wasn't angry. Not like Satan, or Tyree, or the rest of them. Too often it seemed to me that now they were requiring of Kyrie a completeness of explanation that no amount of statement could clarify.

And I'm not even sure what that means.

Satan continued his assault on the deity. He said, "Then it is true that You are a liar and not to be trusted under any conditions."

"Begone, Satan," Kyrie said. "I do not owe you an explanation. I will hear you no more on this."

"You are a liar and a cheat!"

"I will hear you no more on this."

"You are . . ."

Kyrie waved his hand, and suddenly Satan collapsed on the ground, his dragonish form replaced by a serpentine, slithery creature, enormous and incandescent and wicked. Satan gnashed his teeth and his snout suddenly filled with dirt. Spewing it out, Satan screamed, "Is this a joke?"

"No," Kyrie responded fervently, "it is a judgment. More will be forthcoming if you do not depart."

Satan left the throne in a swirl of dragon skin and spittle. He disappeared into Hell with his cohorts. I followed with Tyree just to see what would happen.

Not much. There was plenty of loud boasting and railing and kicking at black cats, but really nothing came of it. I was beginning to feel that Satan was acting like an impotent blowhard.

Still, I had to credit him: he had foiled Kyrie against all odds and obtained an obvious victory in his quest for absolute power and freedom. He had brought it off deftly and competently, even if his whole modus operandi was temptation, deception, and outright lies.

Then there was a brief moment when Satan seemed to remember something, and he suddenly shouted, "What is this: 'I will put enmity between you and the woman, and between your seed and her seed'? And then: 'You will bruise him on the heel, but he shall bruise you on the head.'"

He gazed out over the gathering with yellow, sardonic eyes. "Do you believe it?"

"What is there to believe, Lord?" one of the angels said. "It is one more of Kyrie's little wordplays making no sense."

"Oh, it makes sense," Satan said, now twisting and slithering in front of us in his dragon form, looking herculean and dangerous as he spouted and fumed. "It will make sense in time. He speaks in riddles so that when it comes to pass in some fashion He will claim He predicted it. It will be one more of His insulting little word charades that we will spend all our time interpreting and then when it supposedly happens it will be as convincing and clear as fog. He'll have His day and make all these grandiose claims, and it will be one more mistranslated and misunderstood piece of trickery. So we are going to make sure it never happens."

There was a slight gasp, much reduced now because these antics were becoming commonplace. I looked at Tyree, and my demonic friend was leaning forward licking his lips with anticipation. I was trying to understand his position too, why he had followed Satan, and I think I was gaining an insight here: he simply found Satan the more interesting of two rather mismatched adversaries. Tyree would probably say simply, "It's more fun," but I had not yet heard him say that.

Satan said, "Therefore we will kill the woman ourselves."

Another gasp splintered out from our numbers, and I raised my eyebrows in no little wonder at the audacity of the statement.

"How will you do that, Sire?" someone said, echoing my own thought.

"I will find another opportunity to act against her."

"But will Kyrie grant it to you?"

"I do not need Him. We can now tempt at will. I have discovered something new."

Satan revealed what he had discovered: he and his cohorts had the ability to plant thoughts directly into the minds of the humans. "Merely sound a suggestion and the human hears it reverberate in his mind. By the power of suggestion, we will destroy all of them. And no one will bruise me on the head! No one!"

I returned to Heaven with a heavy, worried heart. Kyrie seemed to have retreated into silence and sudden judgments. Satan, on the other hand, was on an ever wider and broader offensive. I sensed that he wanted to make a quick end of everything. If he now had the power to plant these thoughts as he said, then he could not be stopped. If the humans fell as easily to other temptations as they did to the question of the fruit of the Tree, then there was nothing Satan could not accomplish.

The thing that was most befuddling was the apparent calm Kyrie displayed in the midst of this tragedy. He was obviously grieved. But He had dealt with it quickly and finally. No hesitation. No long harangues or consultations with the seven, Michael, or anyone else.

The abruptness and bluntness of it bothered me.

Yet, one thing did not escape my notice: Kyrie had redeemed the disaster. The man and woman were still alive. They were forgiven, and they had covenanted to live forever after in obedience to Him Great as the mistake was to eat the fruit, perhaps something greater had happened. I had seen Kyrie forgive and redeem.

The thought intrigued me. An animal had been killed, and then its skin had served as a covering for the man and woman. Why had Kyrie rejected the fig leaves? And why was a death necessary? Certainly, He had not authorized the death of one of His creations simply on whim. So there had to be purpose in it. But what purpose?

It struck me that Satan had missed this, or at least that he had not discussed it when I was present. Perhaps it didn't matter to him at all.

But I sensed that there was significance in all Kyrie was doing. Nothing that had happened had caught Him unaware, or even unprepared. He wanted us to believe that in the midst of all things that occurred in this world, He Himself would be working in them too, and around them, and behind them, and even, in some cases, through them. If I was to believe this, then I would also have to believe that ultimately He could have stopped the woman from sinning by eating of the Tree.

That was a terrible and tricky point.

Could He have stopped her? Presumably.

But He didn't. Why?

One answer was He saw that something better would result if she sinned. But if that was so, how was He any different from Satan? In fact, He was worse: He had, in some sense, used Satan to accomplish a dastardly and horrible deed so that somewhere down the road a "blessing" would result. That might be expected of someone like Satan, but Kyrie was honorable, adhering to His own laws of grace and goodness and righteousness. He could not purposely act to allow evil to happen and then claim He was entirely innocent and free of blame.

So that answer didn't work.

That brought me to the idea that perhaps Kyrie did not exercise the kind of control that I seemed to think. Perhaps Adam and Eve had acted freely, and though Kyrie knew what would happen and chose not to stop them, that was, in effect, what was required. If He had interceded, they would no longer be free.

It was an issue that I saw no answer to.

And then there were the various curses He had placed upon the serpent, the woman, and the man. It was in the same order as their respective involvements in the disobedience. The serpent had first allowed Satan to possess him. Then Eve had eaten. Finally, the man.

Which of the curses was the worst? Surely the serpent's, and ultimately the curse on Satan. Kyrie had prophesied his ultimate destruction, and he was right to take it seriously.

And what of Satan's threat to kill the woman?

I felt an urge to report this to Kyrie, but I suspected He probably already knew. So what would He do now?

39

I sat before Kyrie, nervous, fearful. I was angry. I wanted an answer. A complete answer. No more of this, "You must watch and learn." I'd already seen more than enough.

He sat down. "Speak."

"Kyrie, this is a great mistake."

"The garden and the test?"

"Yes. It has upended everything. Where can it lead from here? Satan will destroy it all, piece by piece, till nothing is left. Even now he is planning to kill the woman."

"I will not allow him to do that."

I stood. Now I was angry. I worked at controlling my voice. "You will not allow him to do that? But You just did! They ate of the tree. It was effortless. They barely argued. If it was that easy then, how much easier will it be now?"

"It will never be easy for them to sin," He said.

"But You saw what happened!" I began to pace. Never had I acted like this before Him. But things were all twisted up inside me. I had to speak about it. I had to settle it.

"I saw what happened, yes," He answered. "What do you think has happened?"

"They are cast out of Eden. They will die, eventually. Already, they are dead. I do not understand why You didn't prevent this!"

"Do you think I could prevent it?" His eyes met mine and for a moment I began to flinch away. But He held me.

"You couldn't prevent it, you mean?" I stared at Him, waiting.

He smiled. "Yes, I could have prevented it, I suppose, if you want to use those terms. But in reality, I could not interfere."

"Why not? Satan interfered!"

"It is not My way, Aris."

"Not Your way?"

"No, I would have had to violate My own nature to stop them, manacled them from doing what they chose to do."

"But why? Aren't you all powerful?"

"Yes."

"And wise?"

"Yes."

"And holy and righteous and just and good?"

"Yes."

"Then why did You not stop them?"

"Because to do so would violate Me and violate them."

"Satan has no trouble in doing that."

"I realize that."

"But it doesn't make sense. He does not have to play by Your rules while You do."

"That is correct." He smiled mirthfully.

"What are You smiling about?"

"I am enjoying your questions."

I stamped my foot impatiently. Did even He think this was a game?

"No," He said.

"No?"

"No, I don't think this is a game."

I felt my skin turn crimson. Now I was embarrassed. Somehow I pressed on. "If it is not a game, then what is it?"

"The most important matter in all of life."

"What is?"

"What we have seen. What we are discussing."

Now I was very frustrated. "You are talking in circles."

He coughed. "No, I am not talking in circles. Maybe in riddles. Maybe in complexities. Or maybe yet, with too great a simplicity."

"But how do you expect to win if Satan can do as he pleases, but You must do as You know is right?"

"This is not a matter of winning or losing. As I said, it is not a game."

I smacked my hand on my thigh with anger. "I don't understand this at all."

"You will."

"I will what?"

"You will understand."

"Ugh! This is nonsense."

He laughed. "You are a good debater, Aris. But this is not just debate. This gets at the very marrow of one's existence."

"What then is that marrow?"

"Choosing."

"Hateful word."

"No, a very solid term. A good word, and a worthy action. All of existence is about choosing, at least one level of it."

"So Adam and Eve made a wrong choice and now they are lost."

He cleared His throat, then stood to shake off His cloak. The pure whiteness of it nearly blinded me. "Their condition is not unrecoverable, Aris."

"But hardly suitable."

"At the moment, perhaps. That is a matter of debate."

I sighed audibly.

"You are frustrated."

"Very."

"Good."

"Good?"

He smiled again with a slight uptilt on the side of His mouth. He touched His beard as if to caress, then said with an almost professorial but generously friendly tone, "Frustration can lead to determination which leads to endurance which leads to a multitude of other good things too numerous to count."

"I'd rather not be frustrated."

"One day you won't be."

"You're still talking in circles."

"Perhaps."

I waited. Then I said, "What are *You* doing, Kyrie?"

He gazed at me a long time. Then He rose. "That is what you are in the midst of discovering. But I shall leave you with this. If I had prevented the choice that the humans have just made and, as a result, fallen into a pit from which none will ever be able to rescue himself, would things be better?"

There seemed a simple answer in my mind. "Of course."

"And how long should I have prevented it—till they were left to stand on their own?"

"As long as it took, till they were ready. That is what I would say." I looked at Him, trying to gauge the meaning of His words again, but somehow it all seemed elusive and distant. "You should at least have prepared them."

"Did I not prepare them by telling them the consequences of their choice?"

"But You only told them once! You should have repeated it!"

"They were reminded every time they went by the Tree. The Tree itself reminded them by its very existence. They were reminded every time they ate a piece of fruit. They were reminded every time they thought about the tree, or smelled the aroma of its splendor. I made sure all the reminders were there, constantly."

Again, I was frustrated and jammed my hand deep into my tunic. Rarely had I spoken to Him in this way, and yet something about it was so exhilarating, so racingly exciting, I almost did not want it to end. And still, in the midst of it all, was my dire frustration. I said, "Yes, but they didn't understand the real meaning of the consequences. If they had truly understood, they would not have been deceived."

He sighed and sat back down. "You are sure they didn't understand? Did not Eve think I was mistaken about My command? And did not Adam realize instantly that to eat was death?"

"Yes, but they didn't completely understand, that's what I mean. If they had known where they would end up, they wouldn't have ended up there."

"But I told them where they would end up. What you are saying is somehow I had to let them 'experience' death without actually dying so they would be convinced not to do it."

"Yes, that's exactly it." I grinned. Now we were onto something.

"A trial death, then?"

"Precisely."

"Perhaps then that is what is happening now."

I swallowed, trying to grasp His meaning. Then I said, "You mean this is the 'experience' stage now, to convince them?"

He smiled. "You tell Me the answer to that. Nonetheless, I cannot give you My answer in words. You also have to experience it to know it."

I laughed. "You speak in puzzles again."

"Perhaps because I also am puzzled."

I stared at Him. "About what?"

"About why they would choose this against all good logic, reason, spirit, soul, and heart, even their own experience of Me."

"You don't know why they would do that?" I was aghast.

He laughed. "It defies My own comprehension, yes. I have My theories, certainly. I have many thoughts on the issue. Knowing all does not mean I like and accept all, Aris. It still astonishes Me that they chose evil so simply."

If an angel could stand before Kyrie and be totally amazed beyond comprehension, that is where I stood. "It astonishes *You*?"

He nodded. "It is undoubtedly My greatest wonder."

I shook my head and decided I needed to speak with Cere and Rune and see what they were thinking. I said, "I think I need to meditate on these things for awhile."

He smiled. "That is a wise course of action."

Thus, we parted. But as I left the great room, I said, "I will come back to talk more of this."

"You are always welcome," He said, "any and all of you."

As He said it, a sudden and strange feeling crackled inside me. I could not name it. But it was something that made me want to know and understand Him better, something that so infused me with hope that I could not still it. I knew ultimately that a complete answer could only happen in time and through struggle. But I also knew He would not allow me to go through it alone. That sole truth gave me heart.

40

I wondered what Satan would do now that he had decided to try and kill the woman. I spent many days observing them in their life beyond the Garden. They struggled constantly. Food was ever a problem. Thorns and thistles were indeed Adam's bane of existence. But the two were gentle with one another, and loving. Several times Satan tempted Adam to anger about something, but he refused to resort to violence to gain his own way.

I spoke with Rune and Cere about it one day as I watched the man and woman eating in their hovel. She had just informed her husband she believed she was with child.

"My blood has stopped," she said.

He looked up from a meal of corn and fresh tomatoes. "You are going to have a child?"

"Yes."

He grinned, then stood and danced. "Finally, finally, I am to be a father. God has answered our prayers."

She stood and went to him, hugging him. "God has been so good. Now our joy will be full."

"As full as can be."

"Don't say it."

Adam inhaled deeply the warm air and then smiled ruefully. "I can't help but think what it might have been like were we bringing this child into a different world."

"We cannot forever regret what happened," she answered. "God has been good even with our sin."

"Yes, God has been good." He held her tightly and kissed her. They were both still very beautiful people, in the prime of their age, tanned from the sun and clear-eyed, willing to take their responsibility for the deed in the Garden and now face life in light of it.

She placed his hand on her abdomen. "You can feel. I am already growing."

"God has done a wonder."

Her lips parted as he touched her, and she flushed with passion. But just as quickly it was gone. He said, "I must go look at the wheat now. There are weeds in among the new blades again. It's very hard to keep ahead of it."

"But you do." She smiled sweetly and turned back to the low table where they knelt and ate. She brushed off the top with her hand and then began singing.

> *I will put enmity between your seed and her seed.*
> *He shall bruise you on the head,*
> *but you shall bruise him on the heel.*

She thought about the words often, and their meaning. They gave her a sense of direction and hope that their sad lot was not the end. She needed to believe that. The feelings of failure often came over her at night when they lay together, entwined in one another's arms, sometimes afraid of the many creatures that populated their land. They ruled the animals, yes, and there was always fear in the beasts' eyes when they were around. But she couldn't help but remember how it had been at first. At times she clutched at a memory, and tears came to her eyes. But she knew she couldn't keep going back to it. She had to face the future with a stout heart. And with a child coming, she didn't know what to think or say. She only knew for the first time she felt truly happy and not full of the remorse that had dogged her days since it had all happened.

In the shadows, we watched, Rune, Cere, and I, without speaking. I finally said, "Kyrie continues to protect them from Satan."

"Yes," Rune answered. "He calls it the hedge. Satan cannot touch them, though of course he sends various of his deputies to tempt them. More than once he has put the thought in one of their minds to strike the other. But always they resist."

"I should have thought after the Tree episode that they'd be much more susceptible to those temptations," I said. "But really, they've proven to be difficult subjects, from a certain point of view."

Cere nodded her head, her blonde hair tumbling around her shoulders and giving her an ethereal look. "They know about him now."

"Satan?" I answered.

"From the prophecy about the serpent. Adam spends much time thinking about the curses. His, and his wife's. But especially that of the serpent. He realizes now it wasn't the serpent himself who deceived her, but someone who possessed the serpent. He has an interesting theory."

"What is that?"

Cere sat down under a tree outside the small hovel of the man and woman and Rune and I sat with her, Indian style. "He believes there are spirits that cannot be seen. Bad spirits who want to destroy him."

"He is right," I said.

"He fears them, though," Rune said. "He has thought about making sacrifices to them instead of Kyrie."

"But he always sacrifices only to Kyrie," I said.

Cere said, "Satan is not tempting him. This time it is one of his deputies—Ismail, I believe. He thinks he can move the man to worship demons. They all believe it will be the final insult to Kyrie."

"If they don't succeed in killing her," Rune lamented.

"But they cannot. There is the hedge." I looked from Cere to Rune. "Satan is very angry about the hedge."

"Yes, more proof of his charges that Kyrie is unfair. But I'm glad of it," Cere replied. "They need protection. They have no comprehension of the forces that are arrayed against them. And yet with all their power, Kyrie's little hedge is unbreachable."

"What exactly is it?" I said.

"It's invisible to them—to the man and woman," Cere said. "But to the enemy it is like the brambles they love to see grow around Adam's gardens. It is so thick they cannot penetrate it."

"Except with their temptations."

"Yes, they can still attack them with such things."

"I saw one of them," Rune said, a smile cracking his normally sober face, "try to crack it by flying into it. He ended up scratched and scraped and nearly lost both wings completely. They are very frustrated. I understand Satan has many studying it, looking for an advantage."

"He also demands court with Kyrie about it daily," Cere said. "I wonder at his perseverance. He won't give up. Everyday it's a new argument: 'You are dealing unfairly with us.' Or, 'The man doesn't even know about it, so what thanks do You get for it?' And, 'Once again, You've proven to be a liar and a cheat, completely untrustworthy.'

"I think Kyrie almost laughs at these arguments now. Satan will have to find something much harsher or more inciting than that. I'm amazed at Kyrie's patience, though. He does not tell Satan he can't come to the throne anymore, which is something I would have done long ago."

Cere grinned. "I think the tide is turning anyway. The woman will have her child and I guess he will be the one to bruise the old dragon on the head. I'm quite eager to see that one happen."

We drifted off in the direction of the original Garden. Overgrown now, the Tree of Life still stood there with the Cherubim guarding it. I wondered what Kyrie would do with it now. Neither the man nor the woman had ever made any attempt to approach it, or eat of its fruit.

Finally, the day came when the child was born. The woman's pain was greater than I could bear and watch. But Cere stayed. Rune left after I did. I learned the child was a boy, and they had named him "Cain," which in their language meant "spear," the one who would slay the dragon.

Satan, of course, was very angry. But he was still impotent. The hedge surrounded them, and their land, and all that they owned. He could do nothing to impede their progress. We watched daily as the child grew. Of course, he was the first human we'd ever seen in infancy, and he was as beautiful as his parents.

It was not long before the woman informed Adam that she was pregnant again. I sensed that Kyrie had given them a great blessing, and I anticipated the day when the boy would bruise the Enemy on the head. But I wondered what it meant that Satan would bruise him on the heel.

We all spent much time looking into the prophecies and the curse and all else that had so far been revealed. I spent many sessions with Kyrie, asking questions and learning. He refused to say more than He'd already said in the curse itself. And I wondered at that. But He told me, "Too many words bring a fall. You must guard yourself against too much talk and not enough thought."

We were prone to that, running off with each new revelation to Goslin's Grove or somewhere else to talk and share insights. If the man and woman's sin in the Garden had done anything, one was sure: we certainly always had much to talk about. Kyrie was never better spoken of than as the author of this new creation, among the loyal anyway. It was an endless series of wonders, and we traveled the globe studying all His creatures and creations. Each new find seemed to spew forth a whole new array of revelation and ideation.

With the birth of the second son, Satan had two "seeds" to worry about, and we all wondered how and when this bruising on the head would happen. As the boys grew, we marveled at their simplicity, their penchant for play, the joyous companionship that happened among the members of the family. There were squabbles to be sure, and as the boys burst into youth and adulthood, their differences were all the more obvious.

Cain was a farmer, plowing the field, tilling the soil, planting and sowing, planting and sowing. He often sang as he worked, like his mother, and there was a certain earthy rambunctiousness about him, and yet a serious air. He did not seem to care for Adam's stories about the Garden and his mother's warnings to follow God without wavering. He was often the first to ask a question: "But why did you eat of the Tree if you knew it would bring death?"

His brother Abel answered for his father: "Because he did not want to leave Mama all alone in her choice."

"But maybe they would not have lost the Garden if he had not eaten. It's all Father's fault. I go out in the fields and what do I see? Weeds, thorns, thistles, tares, all those things come endlessly. There is no stopping it. If you had not eaten, we would not have to work so hard."

"Don't blame your father," Eve would chide him. "Neither of us understood the complete consequences of eating the fruit. And I was deceived by the serpent."

"But I was not," Adam said, leaning against the wall of their small hovel. "And I did understand the consequences."

"Then why did you eat, Father?" Abel asked.

"I don't know that I can explain it," Adam answered. He looked off into the distance where the sun was setting in a huge orange ball, flailing sprigs of light across the horizon. "I was aware that your mother had eaten and I had not, and I thought about that. But I knew that if I ate I would die. In a way, I didn't care. I was angry that I was put in that position. And suddenly I wanted to be free of God's laws, to break away and have no one commanding me what to do. It was a pure act of disobedience. I knew I was disobeying, but I didn't care. I thought maybe God would leave me alone then."

"But you always speak well of God now, Father," Abel argued. He was a light-skinned man, with long soft brown curly hair, a high forehead, and a strong straight nose. He was limber, fine of limb, as perfect a human as you could imagine. "You always speak well of Him now. Why would you think ill of Him then?"

"That was just it. I did not think ill of Him in any way. It's just as your mother held out that piece of fruit, as I stood there looking at her radiant face, her so sure she was doing something great and wonderful, a wild thought ran through my mind that just cried, 'Free, free! You shall be free!' And in that instant I thought I would know good and evil and even if I did die it would be worth it because I would have been free for just that moment."

"I can understand that," Cain commented.

"We are free now," Abel said.

"But God is our ruler," Cain answered.

"And what does He require? A sacrifice once a year? A little respect? Obedience to His laws? A few things, yes. But in the end, very little. We are free to come and go as we please. We are free to till the soil where we want. We can plant what bushes and trees and grain and vegetables we want. So how are we not free?"

Adam interrupted the two young men. "I did not understand then that freedom is not lawlessness or living how you want irrespective of good and right laws. Freedom is the power to live happily and joyfully within those laws. And I chose to disobey the only law that there was at that time. We are far less free than we were then."

"How so?" Cain answered.

"In this world we live with thorns and thistles as you said. And there's disease and sickness. Your mother had great pain in childbirth. And you and I must sweat every day just trying to wend from this soil the smallest, most shriveled products. If I had obeyed, all that would have come with little effort and I would have had more time for sublime things—naming the animals and plants, studying them, just walking in the Garden, for love and kissing and all the good things. No, we are a great deal less free now. If I had obeyed that one law I would have remained free, but I didn't, and so we find ourselves here today. Let us choose to obey God's laws now so that we do not lose more of our freedoms."

"I for one will fight against them as long as I live," Cain said.

Eve nearly jumped at him. "Don't say that. It will bring more curses."

"And who brings them? God! If it wasn't for Him, we would be free."

"If it wasn't for Him," Abel said, "we wouldn't exist."

"Better than this—weeds and thorns and diseased crops and emaciated fruit and vegetables. Sweat and pain and more sweat and an aching back. It shouldn't be this way!"

"Maybe if you'd just let Him speak to your heart," Abel said.

Cain whipped around, his fist waving. "Don't tell me more of your pious nonsense!" He stormed out of the house in a rage.

I was always surprised at these outbursts. The little family tried to get along, but it seemed that there were always differences pulling them apart.

Then came a fateful meeting of Satan and his master tempters, now organized and working in unison to achieve various important results. They had so far succeeded in setting a rift between Cain and Abel that revolved around Abel's love for God and Cain's indifference to Him.

I sat alone at that meeting. Tyree had received several promotions and was now part of a team working on the "Eve problem," the perennial issue of the "bruised head" that Satan was always so worried about. There had been arguments about that. Some said that God had failed already because neither Cain nor Abel were the kind of spiritual fighters who could defeat Satan in one-on-one combat. The issue had become submerged in the daily struggle just to befoul the relationships and render Kyrie's laws and encouragements useless. But it was still there, hanging over everything, and if Satan could snuff out the whole human race at the beginning he was bent on it.

One of Satan's chief tempters, a Hauker who had risen quickly through the ranks and came to be known as a sage, cerebral thought-planter named Hammal, began the speechifying that morning as we sat in a wood not far from the homes of the "little family," as they'd come to be called, with contempt, by most of Satan's number. He said, "We believe we have Cain on the edge of violence, and his brother so full of his pious nonsense that Cain can be easily incited. Abel is the stronger and larger. But he will not fight. He does not yet hate his brother, and because of that he is vulnerable. He is a bit too sure of himself, especially about matters involving Kyrie. We believe he has become proud and that pride irks Cain tremendously. We have them in the right position."

"What is your plan?" Satan asked, obviously pleased that his deputies were coming along so well.

"If we can get them fighting physically, their hatred will grow. It will divide the family—Eve's favorite is Abel, Adam's is Cain. Once violence has been manifested, we do not know where it can go, but we believe the results will be very good. The more anguish we create within the family, the greater the possibility of the family splitting, dividing, going their own ways. As they leave the protection of home and family, perhaps we will find a weakness in the hedge."

"How do you intend to get them to fight?"

"We are now studying them and constantly at the ready with thought-plants to begin an argument."

I was quite amazed at their audacity. Also, I was always astonished at their willingness to allow me in on their designs. I supposed they spoke differently when I wasn't there. That was possible. But they seemed very calm and calculated now and very sure of their success.

"What if there is a turnaround, Cain repenting or some disaster like that?" Satan seemed concerned to cover every possibility. It occurred to me that he looked older, more wizened, tougher, harder. His dragon guise was all the more imposing, and I had learned by now that he did not tolerate foolishness or failure, even though he'd had plenty of his own. Kyrie for once seemed to be on the winning side at this time. I thought the idea of violence between the two brothers a possibility, but the family still seemed to care greatly about one another.

Hammal replied to Satan's question, "We do not foresee that. Kyrie does not force His subjects to repent. He chooses to give them time to think and meditate and work through their difficulties, seeking Him in prayer. Cain has stopped praying for some time. He thinks it does no good, as all he prays is for a healthy, bounteous crop. Which, by now, we know is impossible in this land. At least Kyrie has proven faithful to His curse in its every detail."

There was laughter until Satan gave him a withering look. He had obviously forgotten the fundamental reference in the curse was the "bruised head" problem, but his eloquence obviously got away from him.

For a moment, I thought all was passed over, but Satan suddenly reared up over him. "There will be no jokes about the curse! Do you understand?"

"Yes. Yes, Sire. I had forgotten . . ."

"There is no forgetting. Until that prophecy is proven dead, there will be no rest on this matter. We are all set on one end, and that is the extinguishing of the power of Kyrie and His festering curse. Am I understood?"

His last sentence was a veritable roar, and all flattened back before it. Satan's rages were becoming more common, and no one dared arousing one if he could.

"You are dismissed, Hammal! What were you?"

"But, Sire, I . . ."

"What were you? I emphasize the *were* for you are no longer it!"

"A principality first, Sire."

"You are now a twelfth. This will teach those who dare to joke about such serious matters in my presence." There was a pause, and then the dragon roared, "Am I understood?"

They all chorused back immediately and with genuine fear, "Yes, Lord!"

"Get the woman and her seed!" Satan seethed, then vanished in an updraft of smoke.

41

The opportunity arrived soon enough. It was the time of year to offer Kyrie His sacrifices, a minor law of worship that was not so much stated as passed on from Adam and Eve. They had initiated the yearly sacrifices on the basis of a deep love for Kyrie and for His preservation of them after their sin. It was their way of saying thanks. The sacrifices were burned—fire had already been discovered in earlier years by Adam after a lightning storm— and the smoke curled up to Heaven in an aroma of sweet corn and wheat and, on occasion, the meat and blood of a lamb or calf. Adam was both farmer and herdsman and tried to alternate the yearly sacrifices as an appropriate expression of his abundance.

Cain resented the sacrifices. Adam had always brought the best of his labors to the altar. Abel followed in that tradition. But Cain brought the best only because he feared that anything less would bring God's wrath upon his field and thus yield less than perfect crops.

This year, though, a new thought-planter, an ardent up and comer named Tougal, deftly inserted a new idea into his vocabulary. "Why give Him the best? They're all just burned up. The result is the same. Bring to him the withered, useless ones from the edge of the field. He won't notice. He always pays far more attention to Abel anyway."

"That's right," Cain murmured as he went about collecting the food for the sacrifice.

"There, that one," the inner voice said, pointing out various of the more shriveled pieces.

Cain picked it up. "No, that one really is too shriveled. He might notice that. I'll mix in some good ones with the bad ones, just to be sure."

"That's the spirit."

Cain liked the sly inner voices that spoke inside his head. He believed they were his own thoughts, and indeed some of them were. There were several voices he especially liked: the self-congratulatory, mellow-toned friend who always pointed out his best efforts and reminded him that he was a far better farmer than his father and a better person than Abel in all respects. Then there was the supportive, encouraging mentor that often came into focus in his mind when he was in some argument with his family. "You were right. They just don't see it because you're far more intelligent than they."

There was another voice that he didn't like so much, though, and he had no explanation for it since the other voices were so much more inspiring. "You should not think that, Cain. That is sinful." And, "Why be nasty to your mother? She loves you as much as Abel, as much as herself."

He often had to shout that voice down in his mind with curses and threats, and he didn't understand why it wouldn't go away. Even as he selected the bitter, uneven, ugly specimens for the sacrifice, this voice railed away inside him.

"He should only get the best, and then you will inherit His blessing."

"What blessing?" Cain retorted to the voice. "There are still nothing but weeds, tares, and ugly vines growing everywhere."

"There are a great deal less as a result of the last few years' worthy sacrifices."

"A great deal less," Cain mumbled, "as a result of my efforts. Everything that has grown here is mine. I brought it forth and I have made it into what it has become. So why should I give it to Him?"

"Because He created it. He gave you the field. He gave you the rain and sunshine. All you have done is plant it!"

Cain bent to his work, now red-faced with anger. "Shut up! Planting it is a worthy pursuit and deserves much greater mention than you're giving it."

"Don't listen to it," another voice said, the encouraging one. "It's a sign of his jealous spirit. He always wants you to give the best to God. But God has not really done anything for you that He doesn't also do for everyone else! How has He blessed you personally?"

Cain listened as both voices argued back and forth in his head. Then he said, "I will do what I want to do. And I'm not giving Him the select peppers, corn, wheat, tomatoes, squash, and potatoes. That's the end of it!"

Abel, on the other hand, was not perfect, but he did have a heart for God. He also heard the voices in his mind, but was more successful at rebuffing the contentious voice that constantly counseled rebellion, hatred, and jealousy.

"Your brother is bringing a far better sacrifice than you are—he is bringing one like your father, the product of the field."

Abel shook his head. "That's foolish thinking," he said in answer as he checked the legs of one of his sheep for ticks. "God has always been kind to me about the lamb I bring. And this year, I am giving him the very best that I have ever seen. Not a wrinkle or a blemish on him. I would have liked to keep him as a pet."

"Then why don't you?"

"Because God deserves my best."

"He will not mind if you bring something less than the best. And who is a better judge? Perhaps God would prefer that you keep the best to mate and make more of such animals for the future."

"God will bless me if I bring the best. But even if He does not, I will still bring the best. If He didn't know—which is impossible—I would still know. And I will not compromise on that."

"You are so proud!"

For a moment, Abel leaned on his staff and sighed. "Yes, indeed I am. I am sorry for that. You are quite right. I must work on that one."

The voice turned sarcastic. "You are so spiritual. You must certainly be God's favorite!"

"Do not speak of such things! God has no favorites! He loves Cain and Mother and Father as much as myself. Do not say such a horrible thing!"

"Oh, you are so spiritual!"

"I hate that voice! I hate it!" Abel picked up the staff, and for a moment wanted to break it against a tree. But then he calmed himself and said, "I must fight the voice. I must not give in to it, as Father says. We all must battle the voice. It's the result of our sin and we must fight it."

"It is not the result of sin!" the voice suddenly cried, as if stung. "It is the voice of intelligence and reason!"

"Not the way I see it."

Then the other voice in his mind spoke, and Abel felt its calming warmth break over him. "You are doing well. Do not give up. There is always hope to him who will not give in to the pleas of sin."

"I am not sin!" the first voice retorted.

Abel shook his head. "I think I should just laugh now and continue caring for my sheep. That will take away the battle in my mind."

He walked out among his flock and, petting here and caressing there, he finally found the lamb which would become his sacrifice. He picked the lamb up and kissed it on the ear. "You are such a gentle creature. I am pained to have to sacrifice you, but God will give you new life again and you will be one of His greatest of all creations."

That evening, Abel went to the little altar he had made years before. It was fashioned of stones with one long flat piece on top. A pile of sticks, brambles, and leaves lay on top so that he could burn the sacrifice when it was prepared. He tied up the lamb's feet and lay the tiny creature on the altar. Then he knelt down before it. A sharp knife lay on the stone by the lamb, and it bleated helplessly as it lay wriggling in place.

"Be quiet, little one," Abel said, laying his hand on the lamb's head.

"You are proud again!" the voice inside his mind said.

But Abel prayed, "Please, God, do not let the voices hinder me. I come before you a sinner. Please forgive me for this year's many sins of thought, word, and deed. I have been angry at times with my brother and cursed him. I have fought with my father in words and not listened to his counsel. I have had bitter thoughts of blame toward You because of the storm that killed three of my sheep last winter. I have hated and been jealous. Forgive me, Father. I bring this sacrifice in thanks for Your many blessings, and I look forward to all You will do in the new year."

He stood and cradled the lamb's head in his lap, then picked up the knife.

As the lamb burned, he sniffed its sweet aroma and looked up into the heavens. The voice out of them spoke clear and low. "I am pleased, my son. You have done well."

"Thank you, Father."

"Go in the blessing of this your sacrifice and live free and right before Me all the days of this year."

"I will, Father."

Abel bowed and left the sacrifice burning. He would keep it burning all night until it was consumed. His heart sang.

As he walked along, he said, "Please send the same blessing to my parents as they offer their sacrifices, and to Cain, my brother."

The voice in the heavens didn't answer, but he felt its fond warmth beaming down upon him. He had a sense that God was always watching over them and, though their life was hard with sickness and stillbirths hurting the flock, he was doing well and happy. God supplied him a ready presence that he enjoyed and often conversed with, even when no voice from the heavens answered.

I slipped away and watched Adam and Eve as they prepared their own sacrifice from the fruit of the soil. It burned, and its aroma left its mark on their memory as a particularly fine year for sacrifice. They spent some time in prayer, and again the voice from the heavens spoke and assured them of His love. When they had finished, they embraced and decided to visit Abel and Cain to see the result of their respective activities.

I quickly moved on with Rune at my side to see what Cain had done. I immediately noticed his choice of the poor vegetables. Rune pointed to it. "He is becoming more recalcitrant," Rune said. "I see it now in his eyes. His heart is angry."

"Why is he so angry all the time?" I asked, watching Cain pile the sticks on top of his altar. The sheepskin bag of vegetables—Abel had given him the bag in exchange for daily pickings from his fields—lay at his feet. I walked over and peeked inside just to see what he had selected, and indeed they were not the best.

I stood up and watched the man clump the sticks together. He would light it from some coals of the fire he always kept lit. They had learned to preserve fire wherever they found it, and to keep at least one of their three cooking fires always lit.

Rune stooped down and looked through the vegetables. The man then turned and pulled out several. The good were mixed in with the bad, but when he pulled out a very nice looking piece of squash, he scowled and set it aside. "I'm not going to give the best of my fields this year at all," he muttered. "I don't care what the others do."

He took some coals from the fire in his hovel and lit the dry leaves and sticks on the pyre. Moments later, the fire was crackling and the rotten and shriveled vegetables singed and spit in the flames.

Cain did not kneel or pray.

Suddenly, the voice from the heavens spoke. "You have not done well, my son."

Cain looked up. "I have not done well. I . . ."

"You have not brought to Me a worthy sacrifice. I cannot accept it or give My blessing to such a sacrifice."

Cain's face fell and he grimaced with anger, clenching and unclenching his fists.

"Why are you angry?" God asked. "And why has your countenance fallen?"

Cain gave no answer, and his red, inflamed cheeks burned against the light of the fire. The aroma of the vegetables was smoky and not at all appetizing.

"If you do well," the Voice said, "will not your countenance be lifted up? And if you do not do well, sin is crouching at the door, and its desire is for you, but you must master it."

Cain suddenly looked up, set his lips with anger, and was about to speak, but then thought better of it. He kicked at the flames and the burning vegetables and soon the dying coals spread all over. Moments later, all the fire was gone. Cain looked at the clean, healthy vegetables in a pile off at the right. With a vicious kick, he sent all of them flying into the bushes. Then he turned and stalked off in the direction of Abel's flocks.

Immediately, another voice was in his mind, the sweet melodious syllables of Tougal filled his mind. "God had no right to reject your offering. Now you'll have to prepare another. That will take hours. And your fire went out."

"He expects too much," Cain seethed in response to the voice. "And He has done nothing this past year. He shouldn't have rejected my offering. He should know that I need the good ones for my own health!"

"Tell Abel! He will defend you!"

"Yes. Abel will understand. And he'll make things right with God. I need that blessing this year!"

I looked at Rune and we both followed, and suddenly I spotted a presence behind Cain. Tyree!

I called out to him, but he shook his head. I soon realized it was he and several others with Tougal who were planting the evil thoughts in Cain's mind. I shouted, "Stop, Tyree. He is already angry enough."

"Yes, we know. But he is right! Kyrie demands too much of the man. And Kyrie unfavorably compares him to his parents and his brother."

"Kyrie has not done that," Rune cried. "Kyrie made no comparisons!"

"Yes, He has, and that is His mistake." Tyree suddenly crooned into the mind of the angry Cain, "Kyrie has regard for the others' offerings, but not yours. He is showing favoritism once again. He always does. And that's not right. Kyrie is once again showing Himself and His true attitudes. He has shamed you before your brother and your parents."

"Abel had just better be on my side about this," Cain seethed as he trudged up the hill toward Abel's home.

Tyree answered, "But if he isn't, it doesn't matter. You are your own person. You will prove to them that you can achieve great results without God's blessing. And what is His blessing anyway? One more day of sunshine? You would rather live without it!"

"He had just better not go off talking about how kind and gentle God is with all of us," Cain yelled. This time, a flock of birds shot up at the sound, and he stopped and gaped around. He wore his stone knife for cutting the stems of vegetables at his side. He drew it from its sheath and scrutinized it closely.

Tyree said, "Give Abel a good scare if he doesn't come across."

"Yes!" Cain cried. "He'd just better not get all mouthy about this!"

I screamed at Tyree, "You are inciting him!"

"I am doing nothing but what I am commissioned to do!" Tyree shouted back. "Leave me alone and don't hinder me, or we'll incite him to worse!"

"This couldn't get worse," I answered, a bit stymied. But we all followed Tyree and his cohorts. Rune was right behind me.

"Be careful," he said to me. "Don't put ideas in their heads!"

In an hour, Cain stood at the edge of Abel's flock. Abel stooped among the sheep, stroking one's head and then checking a wound on another.

"Abel!" Cain called.

Abel stood, visored his eyes from the sun, and smiled. "My brother! What brings you this way?"

"Just taking a jaunt. Thought I'd stop by."

"Well, how goes it?"

"Very well. And you?"

Abel strode across through the sheep, extending his hand in greeting and embracing his brother. "I have thought about you many times. It was the time of the sacrifices, and I was worried . . ."

"Worried? About what?"

"You know. Last year, you were so angry. I hope it went well."

"As good as can be expected. How did it go with you?" Cain's open manner stunned me a moment. He was not usually this candid or friendly with his brother. Then for the first time one of the voices spoke in his mind.

"Be careful," it said. "Watch his every word. Don't tell him too much. He will tell you you're wrong if you're not careful."

I could hear Cain say in his mind, "I'm being careful."

"Don't expect much," the voice said again.

"I'm not."

Abel grinned broadly. "The sheep have been so restless. I was concerned about the one I had selected for the sacrifice. I thought it might get sick and then I would have to find another. There just weren't any like him."

"But he ended up being all right?" Cain said.

"Perfect. I think he was the best in all the years. Not a blemish on him. God was pleased. I think it will bring great blessing."

"God was pleased?"

"Oh, yes. I was so happy. Mother and Father told me their sacrifice went well, too."

"That's good."

Abel looked away at the sheep. Several had begun to baah, and he appeared concerned that a wild animal might be near. He started to walk over toward the trees when Cain said, "Don't you want to hear about my sacrifice?"

"Of course," Abel called behind him. "Come. You can talk while I check this little one."

Cain followed him, the anger rising. "Abel is always so perfect," he murmured.

"Yes, and he lets you know it, too," one of the voices said. Abel inspected one of the sheep. "Limping again," he said to Cain. "This one has developed a steady limp."

"Then you should have offered him as your sacrifice," Cain answered.

Abel stood and regarded his brother with an air of concern. "Cain, did you offer inferior vegetables to God?"

"What of it? I offer what I want."

"And did He accept them?"

"What business is that of yours?" Cain retorted. "I came up here just to visit, not to be questioned about things that are my business alone."

"All right. I won't question. Would you hand me that stick there?"

Cain bent down to pick up a long knobby stick that Abel used as a shepherd's crook. It did not have a hook on the end, but it was straight and hard. It would not break easily. Cain lifted it up and handed it to his brother. "God did not have regard for my offering," he said. "I have to offer another."

Abel gazed at Cain evenly. "I'm sorry," he said.

"It's all your fault!" Cain suddenly answered heatedly. "If you weren't always selecting the best in the flock, it wouldn't matter."

"That is the way Mother and Father taught us," Abel answered. "You know that."

"Well, they taught us wrong! There's no point in giving God the best of my vegetables. What is it? Smoke? A fire? A smell? Is that what makes Him feel so kindly toward you and so belligerent toward me?"

"God is not belligerent, I'm sure," Abel answered. He looked up at the sun and the sky. There were clouds, but it was always cloudy in that land. The morning grasses were fed by a mist that rose off the land and watered the ground. Later in the day, the sun would shine bright and warm.

"Your crops are well-watered," Abel said again. "And the sun shines plenty. Father does not have as good a gathering as you. Why do you resent the sacrifices? It's a small way to honor God and . . ."

"I don't resent them!"

"Then what would you call it? If you do well, you will be blessed!"

"That's just what He said."

"Who?"

"God! He said, 'If you do well, will not your countenance be lifted up?' Just like what you said."

"Well, isn't it true? I lift my face each morning now happy to know God is watching and caring and sending the rains and filling the streams and telling me . . ."

"Shut up! I don't want to hear about God!"

"Maybe you need to hear more!"

Cain stooped down and picked up a rock. "If I thought about it, I would not hesitate to throw this rock at you."

"Throw it," one of the voices cried in his mind.

Then the other voice: "Put down that rock! That's danger . . ."

Abel said firmly, "Put down that rock, Cain. You don't mean to fight me about this. We don't need this."

"Then take back what you said!"

"Take back what?"

"That if I do well, my countenance will be lifted up."

"I did not say that. God said that. You should listen to Him!"

"Say that again!" Cain said as he advanced menacingly. I and Rune and the others watched in dread and fascination. For the moment, the voices all seemed to be silenced with the sudden turn of mood. No one knew what was going to happen, but I sensed that no one, not Tyree or even Tougal, had expected this.

"Go ahead! Say it again!"

Abel turned away slowly. "Cain, we will speak no more about this. If you would merely listen to God . . ."

Cain hurled the stone at his brother. It struck in the small of Abel's back, knocking the wind out of him. He fell to his knees, trying to get his breath. He dropped the cudgel, and the sheep bleated, circling trying to get away from the angry man standing above their shepherd.

Getting his breath, Abel turned. "You should not have done that, Cain. I have not hurt you." His words came in labored breaths. The rock had hurt, possibly broken a vertebrae. "Your argument is with God, not me!"

Rage swept over Cain, and he leaped at his brother, grabbing the fallen rock and cracking it against his shoulder. Abel fell to the ground. He flailed out with his right hand, trying to ward off the next blow, but Cain was on top of him, with the rock in his hand. The next blow struck on Abel's temple. The rage so overcame him that he could not see through the blur in his mind. He struck, and struck, and struck. Soon his hands were dripping with blood.

Exhaustion finally overcame him and he stopped. "Do not . . . speak to me . . . again of God," Cain said between huffs of air as he tried to get his breath back. He slid off his brother's back and touched the younger man's shoulder. "Do you hear me?"

Slowly, his knees quivering and his whole body shaking, Cain stood, helping himself to his feet with Abel's crook. "Get up. You're not hurt that badly."

Abel didn't move.

Cain batted him gently on the thigh with the crook. "Get up, I say!"

The figure lay still and silent. Cain bent down to look at him more closely. He rolled him over, listened for breath.

"He is dead," one of the voices said inside his head.

"You have killed him," another voice answered.

Cain slapped his brother's face, pushed on his chest, kicked him. "Get up! Get up, you coward! Get up!"

One of the voices cried, "Quick, hide him, hide him or God will see. God will not like this. You will lose more than His blessing for this. Hide the God-lover!"

Swallowing hard, and then glancing around with terror, Cain dragged his brother's body across the yard.

"In the wood," the voices cried. "Hide him under the leaves and rocks! Quick! Hurry! God will see!"

Cain hid the body in less than ten minutes. Then he threw the cudgel as far into the woods as he could. Staring around and listening to make sure his parents hadn't seen, he ran.

But on the way, one of the voices suddenly said, "You will have to kill your mother and father now, or they will kill you!"

__ 42 __

I watched with growing horror as Cain ran back into the woods to find the cudgel. This time the voices were more insistent: "You must kill them now! Don't wait!"

"Kill them! Kill them!"

Cain caught his breath in the woods. He easily retrieved the cudgel, then stood looking across through the trees at the shallow grave where he'd hidden Abel. Another of the inner voices whispered, "You must not do this. This is evil. Evil! You are given over entirely to the power of evil!"

Cain winced and tried to breathe more slowly, in rhythm. "I'll return to the farm and make sure all is in order. I have to think!" he murmured. He noticed the blood still staining his hands and tunic. He had to wash them, too, or his parents might be warned. He had to wash and think about this. His father was strong, and even his mother would not be as easy as Abel unless he caught her completely off guard. But how soon would they know what he had done with Abel? And what about God?

"Surely, even God cannot see Abel that easily, can he?" Cain said to himself, staring at the rocks covering the body. He rushed back to the grave and piled more stones onto it, making sure every vestige of the murder was hidden from view.

"What will God do?" he kept asking as he held the cudgel, stalked by the milling, frightened sheep on the way to his farm. "I have to make like nothing is wrong," he said again. "I won't admit to anything. No one saw me. So who's to say a wild animal didn't kill him?"

He tried different lines of argument, but it all felt transparent to him. No, he had to act quickly and finally. He would go to the farm, clean up, put on the other sheepskin, then go to his parents' home, look for an opportunity. He had to do all that before they found out. They would know soon. Abel was always visiting, bringing them wool and other gifts. They would miss him, come looking.

"Just act like all is well," he said over and over.

At the farm, he passed by the little pile of good vegetables that he hadn't offered as a sacrifice and then realized how hungry he was. He gathered them quickly, took them inside the tiny hovel, and ate. He was still shaking, still terrified. And it was then that God spoke.

"Where is Abel, your brother?" the voice said. It was right in the cottage with him.

Cain looked about, took another bite, and blinked, telling himself he hadn't really heard the Voice of God.

"Where is Abel, your brother?" the voice repeated.

"I do not know," Cain answered, trying to smooth out the tremolo in his voice. "Am I my brother's keeper?"

Was the voice angry? Was God going to kill him, too?

One of the inner voices counseled, "Do not admit to anything! God cannot have seen the body already!"

But God said, "The voice of your brother's blood is crying to Me from the ground!"

Cain stood and started to speak, but then fell silent. He refused to hang his head, though. He would not be remorseful.

"It was right for you to kill him!" one of the inner voices said. "He was proud, arrogant! He deserved to die!"

The Voice of God said, "And now you are cursed from the ground, which has opened its mouth to receive your brother's blood from your hand. When you cultivate the ground, it shall no longer yield its strength to you."

Cain trembled. A tear burned into his eye, and he swiped angrily at it to wipe it away. The ground. The earth. That was what he loved, and God was taking it away from him.

The voice went on, "You shall be a vagrant and a wanderer on the earth all your days!"

Immediately, Cain looked up to heaven and cried, "My punishment is too great to bear!"

God did not answer, and Cain shook his head in anger. "You have driven me today from the face of the ground; and from Your face I shall be hidden. And I will be a vagrant and a wanderer on the earth. But it will end up that whoever finds me will kill me!"

There was a silence and Cain trembled again, closing his eyes and trying to control his breathing. The voice said, "Whoever kills Cain, vengeance will be taken on him sevenfold. Therefore I will give you a sign to prove that this is true."

A moment later, the whole room became dark. Cain rushed out, and the sun was gone from the sky. All was dark and chill. Then the sky exploded and a bolt of lightning ripped through the dark, breaking the silence with a groundshaking roll of thunder.

Moments later, the sun was shining, it was bright, and all was quiet. The sounds of birds and insects filled the air once again.

Cain swallowed, shaking even more from the tumultuous blast of thunder. He ran inside, grabbed a few things, and headed east of Eden, to a land he would call Nod.

Adam and Eve soon noticed that their two sons were missing. In a revelation, God told them the story of the murder and the banishment. They found Abel's body and gave it a proper burial. Eve's grief was great and was assuaged only when she again conceived.

Shortly after the murder, Tyree and I talked, for the first time confidentially and on terms as friendly as I could expect. I tried to avoid it, but I felt compelled to condemn him for inciting Cain to kill his brother.

Tyree replied, "We never thought he would kill him from the first. That was Cain's idea all along. Yes, we incited him with anger over the rejection of his sacrifice, but we weren't thinking in terms of him killing Abel. We thought only of ridding ourselves of all of them—Cain and Abel, and the woman—so that the curse could not be fulfilled."

I was astonished. "You mean you did not plan that he kill Abel?"

"Not at all. It just happened. In fact, we were displeased with the result. We wanted to keep Cain in the land so that he might fight with his father. Once we saw he was capable of murder, our plots grew increasingly murderous. We had no idea humans could take such actions."

"You really had no idea?"

"None."

"So now you will not stop at anything."

"No, we know now that humans are capable of doing far more in their own sinfulness than we are in tempting them. A new theory has come about among the tempters: that we need only plant small, even harmless temptations in their minds and they can then take them and make of them far more than we ever thought."

"Doesn't it trouble you, Tyree?" I searched my friend's dark face, looking for the least sign of remorse or regret.

"Why should we be troubled? We have done nothing to harm them personally. We plant a seed of doubt or fear and they turn it into murder. How can we be blamed for that?"

I shuddered at his capacity for self-deception. "You do not think Kyrie will call you to account for these deeds?"

"He has not yet. He has not even finished the curse. The woman's seed is now as good as dead. Cain is banished. Abel rots in the soil. Why should we worry about the future? When it comes, we will deal with it then."

"So you are wholly given over to your sin?" Even though I had not yet chosen Kyrie, I still had a conscience, but it appeared that Tyree had none.

"Sin? No, we do not call it sin. That's Kyrie's word, and we certainly do not have to agree to His definitions. We call it tactics in the great war for rulership, which our leader, Azraith, rightly holds. Kyrie made him chief administrator of all of creation, and now Kyrie has deposed him simply for trying to gain what Kyrie should rightly give us. If Kyrie will deal so unrighteously with us, then we will deal unrighteously with Him."

"So then it's all revenge, every bit of it?"

"Not revenge, Aris. We are trying to establish something."

"And what is that?"

"That Kyrie is not capable of effectively directing His universe. We are showing day by day that His rule is contrary, capricious, and criminal."

"But Kyrie does not incite His people to wrong, as you do. He doesn't counsel sin or vengeance or murder or lying, as you and your fellows do."

"That is only temporary. Kyrie has left us with no recourse but to go in that direction for now. That will change as we consolidate and gain a greater foothold in the realm. Once the threat of the curse is vanquished, Azraith will begin building a new order that will function within its own righteous laws. There will be a new and abiding realm which will never be extinguished, and that realm will be one of order, justice, and fairness for all. As it is now, there is little to work with, and we are simply weeding out those we can't trust to those we can."

"And this reasoning justifies something like the murder of Abel?"

Tyree chuckled, a gagged, choking laugh that I found completely insincere. But I made no mention of that. "Cain chose his own end in that matter."

I shook my head. "Tyree, will you ever come back to Kyrie?"

"Not now," he said, patting me on the back. "You are so sincere, Aris, and so sincerely trying to understand what Kyrie is doing. Well, it can all be summed up in one sentence. What Kyrie is doing is nothing. He does not know what to do. He could not stop Cain and he will not stop us. When that is established firmly in His mind, He will bargain for whatever He can redeem out of this wasteland. And then we will be in a position to get what we have wanted all along."

"Which is what?"

"Freedom to do as we please, without His interference. It's as simple as that."

"What of Satan's moods and angry outbursts?"

"Azraith is a great leader. He lives with tremendous tensions and threats. The threat of his own murder hangs over everything at the moment. Kyrie has made that threat and we take it most seriously. Kyrie is the one making such decrees. If He wants peace, then why doesn't He seek it? Instead, He bullies us with this prophecy: the very destruction of Azraith himself. You tell me how we are to respond to that."

"Make peace."

"And at what cost? Loss of the freedom we now have?"

"You do not have freedom."

Tyree laughed, and this time his laugh was a superior, condescending laugh that made me all the angrier. "We have greater freedom than any in Heaven."

"You are slaves of Satan!"

Tyree snorted with derision. "He lets us do as we please."

"There is a chain of command in your realm. What of that?"

"For the purposes of war. When it comes to our own time and efforts, we are free. You all are the servants of Kyrie—at least those who have followed Him. We are rulers with Azraith. Under rulers, if you want to get technical about it."

"You are vastly deluded, Tyree."

"Perhaps. And so are you."

We parted with no further comments. I returned to Heaven, eager to hear what Rune and Cere would say about things, but I could not find them.

__ 43

Time passed on earth, and Adam and Eve had other children. Cain returned to ask for one of his sisters as a wife. Seth, conceived soon after Cain fled, married another sister. Soon there were married children and grandchildren in the family. I watched now and then, but spent more time in Heaven puzzling over the events of years past. I still did not understand many things and thought much about the original sin of Adam and Eve and the death of Abel. Several generations had passed, and the earth's population was growing. I spent time now and then talking to Kyrie, and one day we spoke personally in the Temple.

I told Him outright, "Kyrie, I am weary and frustrated and I don't understand."

"What do you not understand, Aris?" Kyrie sat on the throne, His robe filling the Temple, and the Cherubim in motion above Him, their wheels and eyes flashing and burning.

"Satan repeatedly wins. You allowed him to tempt Eve and Adam, and now the whole world is plunged into sin. You allowed one of his cohorts to tempt Cain, and now Abel is dead. What is next? These things make no sense in any earthly or heavenly language. You say You can't prevent these things from happening if free people choose sin over what's right. But if that's the case, what good is anything? Your whole world will be turned into a cesspool any way you cut it. Is that what You want?"

"What I want, My son, cannot be coerced."

"You've told me that before."

"But you don't seem to understand it."

"What I don't understand is that You repeatedly do nothing."

"Are you so sure I have done nothing?"

I reconsidered a moment, giving myself just enough time to look contemplative. I replied, "What have You done?"

"There is the curse, which is teaching each and every being, including Satan, the fear of sin and respect for Me as Lord of creation. Every time Adam tugs a weed from the soil, every moment that sweat drips down his brow, he is reminded of what is and what might have been, and he longs for a return to a better day. He lives in hope of that day through My forgiveness and the redemption that took place following his sin. Everytime Eve or any other woman gives birth, there is a reminder of sin, and regret. But there is also a reminder of the gift of grace and that she lives on and new life comes into being because of My grace. Each year they bring sacrifices of worship. This is teaching them of Me and My kingdom, and though there is pain and more sin, there is also that single seed that brings forth beauteous fruit. If it takes a hundred seeds for only one to seek Me, then that is one more seed that will bear fruit than there otherwise might have been.

"So you are greatly mistaken, Aris. You have not studied closely enough. There is the prophecy that Satan will ultimately be defeated and with him the sin that permeates this world. There was the fervent faith of Abel, who, though he is dead himself, will live on in the memory of the world as a fragrant, radiant soul who transcended his own sin through genuine commitment to the truth. There is also the merciless, vengeful soul of Cain, who everywhere he goes will be a reminder that there is no joy or fulfillment in murder."

"But at what expense, Kyrie? Cain's soul? Abel's life?"

"I do not say these things have not come at a price. Very little in life does not come at a price that most humans will spurn to pay. But it is a price I am willing to pay. Those who will live by faith shall not remain there. They are not mired in the muck of the world so that they can never get out. Through faith in My promise, they shall live again, in a world where he who thrives on sin is smitten forever."

"Abel is dead, Kyrie."

"Yes, he is."

"So where does that leave it?"

"Abel is with Me now. All was not lost."

"Abel is with You?"

"All who have faith will live with Me forever. His spirit now worships at Heaven's altar, and one day he will have a new body and a new life that will never be extinguished by a vestige of sin."

"But still he is dead in the world."

"All in the world will die someday."

I shook my head. I felt as if I wasn't getting through. "So that justifies it? Abel died young by being murdered, but since he'd die anyway, that justifies everything? Is that it?"

"Sin is never justified, Aris."

"No, Kyrie, I mean You're saying because Abel now lives in this new world and all that, that justifies him being murdered."

"There is no justification for sin under any conditions, Aris. But I believe the question you're asking is this: Because Abel now lives with Me in Heaven, does that make it fair and right and good that he was murdered by his brother? And my answer is that murder, as perpetrated by Cain, can never be fair and right and good to anyone concerned. Sin is never good."

"But what it produced is good?"

"Ah, now you are saying that because of the results of the sin—a soul in Heaven with Me—the murder itself was good. And again, my answer is this: the sin did not produce the result. Murder is always evil and bad, whether it leads to anything good or not. I produced the good result by grace because I chose to redeem a terrible situation. There is nothing that says that a murder will produce any predefined result; it is only My grace and goodness that chooses to override the sin and produce a benefit to the one who lives by faith. But that choice remains Mine. I did not have to redeem it; I am under no obligation. But I have chosen to anyway, despite the terrible things that have been done, because Abel was a man of faith."

I sat there with my chin on my hands, wondering at the logic of what Kyrie was saying. I was still not sure that I understood it. But deep down, something inside me recognized His explanation as a point that would guide much of the rest of my days on earth. Sin was never good. But Kyrie could choose to work good in the midst of sin, not good predicated on the sin, but good that He chose to bring about simply because He is God and gracious and could bring it about.

It was a strangely warming concept, and for once I felt that we had gained some ground in my own search for truth.

Then I said, "But what might have been, Kyrie—if Adam and Eve had not sinned, if You had stepped in and prevented Satan from deceiving them? What might have been? How much better could it be?"

"What might have been, My son, is not for you or anyone to know. I do not tell what might have been; I tell only what is."

"But if we knew what might have been, perhaps we will be more careful in our choices."

"Then what might have been becomes what might be if I choose the right. And that is always worth considering—before the choice is made. Indeed, that is the very basis on which I build all My laws."

I sank back, still meditative. "This has been a good talk, Kyrie."

"I am glad in your joy."

I left, my heart rising inside me like a great ship on the crest of a frothy wave. For once, I felt as if there was some light in my discussions with my mentor, which was the way I now perceived Kyrie's role in my life. And for a moment, genuine love flickered in my soul. As I walked, I murmured, "You are worthy of my reverence, Kyrie. Let me not forget that."

I came around a corner and there stood Tyree, grinning as always. He immediately thrust his arm out around me and said, "I saw you go into the Temple and I am here to dispel your confusion."

"There is no confusion, Tyree."

"Then my confusion."

I stopped and looked at him. He was taller than me, a gray, wispy-haired apparition compared to his original form, and I felt his sour breath on my face. I chose not to flinch away for fear of embarrassing him. "Your confusion?"

"Yes. There are many things I do not understand."

"Pray tell what."

Tyree smirked. "I do not understand why you continue to try to skirt the issues and refuse to join the only movement that will matter in the end."

"What movement is that?"

"Our movement," Tyree said. "We will triumph in the end, and I have hoped you would be part of it."

"How will you triumph?"

"We will wear Him down with the sins of mankind. He will vomit them up, so great His revulsion will be. We will show Him over and over what He has created and then show Him over and over what His creatures do for sport, for fun, for revenge and malice and simple pleasure. We will show Him that, and then He will see how wrong He has been."

"What makes you think He will have that reaction?"

Tyree rubbed his chin, then shrugged. "We shall see, I suppose. But when He finally does grow sick of it all, will you then admit that I am right and you are wrong?"

"If Kyrie casts them all over, yes. I will join with you against Him, for then I will know He has been forever defeated."

"Good." Tyree clapped his hand on my back. "And now for some real fun. Remember the white stone?"

I regarded him with suspicion and then fear. "The one Sember guarded?"

"The very one."

"You stole it!"

"No, of course not. Not I!" Tyree smiled. "What do you think I am, a common thief? Never would I steal something so valuable. That's not my job anyway. I am a tempter, not a thiever!"

"Then what has become of it?"

"Come and see!"

She was a fair daughter of a granddaughter of Eve. Dark hair and eyes. Deeply tanned skin. Lithe and beautiful, the kind of woman that made us angels wish we were men.

I stood with Tyree in a wood by the small house. "So where is it?" I asked.

"Just watch."

We drew closer, and I saw a child playing in the yard, needling a little pig. Trees had been felled around the front of the cottage. Long, lush grasses grew about it. Cypress and teak trees grew on the skirts of the yard, and beyond that was a field where a man plowed. I heard him talking to his horse, but I did not pay him much attention.

The woman stepped out into the yard and called to the child, "Lamech, come in here. And stop hounding the pig!"

The small boy stood, rocked back and forth on his feet, then shambled forward. He was naked. I thought him to be three, maybe four, years old. He was handsome, with a small straight nose and crystal blue eyes. His hair was deep black and had been cropped short.

"Lamech, I told you not to devil the pigs. Now I want you to listen."

"Yes, Mama."

The boy slid through the door, protecting his rear end from a swipe, but the woman made no attempt to swat him. The pig oinked out in the yard, then trotted over to the weeds and found something to chew on. I watched as the woman combed the boy's hair by one of the windows. They were open, with slats like shutters that could be set in place from the outside. It was a crude dwelling, but in the few generations since mankind's birth much progress had been made. Already, some men had learned to smith iron, and some were trying to make iron implements to replace the wooden ones that did not last long. These people, though, had no iron, just the usual wood and stone tools that they used to cultivate the land and nurture their crops.

I listened as the woman began to sing. It was a song passed on from one of the daughters of Eve whom I knew had written many songs treasured and beloved by these people.

> *The Lord has forgiven,*
> *The Lord has forgiven,*
> *The Lord has forgiven,*
> *All our sin.*
> *So sin no longer, sin no longer.*

I noticed the boy touching something around the woman's neck, and I leaned closer to see more clearly. Instantly, I reeled back in shock. Around her neck, dangling from a leather thong was the white stone, presumably the same one that Sember had once cultivated at the heart of the mountain.

Tyree said, "Yes, she has it. Her son found it and was playing with it. She liked its color and shape, so she asked her husband to make it into a pendant."

"It is white, like a real stone."

"Yes. In Heaven, it is a shining white reflector of shekinah light, a small morsel of light that dances on the palm. In this world it is hard and crude. But you can still see the whorls and lines of the petals of the original flower."

I leaned closer, my head bending through the window now. Of course, neither the woman nor the boy could see me. But in the light, the stone shone with a matchless white radiance.

"Do they know?" I asked.

"Its power?" Tyree answered.

"Yes."

"I think not. They do not even know the tiny letters on the underside are letters for the sacred name. She only thinks it is pretty."

"But if she knew what could be done with it . . ."

"Then she could rise to rule the very world of men!" Tyree said, a slightly sinister tinge to his tone. I wondered why he was being so friendly now to me, and I longed a moment for the old days when we played and caroused together through the fields of Heaven.

"And her husband has no idea?" I asked again.

"He is an ignorant man," Tyree said. "I have been watching them for some time."

"Why?"

"To guard the white stone and make sure it does not fall into the wrong hands."

"And what would be the wrong hands?" I squinted at him and tried to take the stance of offering a reprimand. But he did not take the bait.

"The wrong hands would be anyone we did not want to have it. For the Cause."

"Oh, now it's called the Cause?"

Tyree laughed. "Come, Aris, you are always too serious. We have many names for our revolution, including that one. Cause. Movement. Rebellion. We are 'Freedom Fighters' and the 'Avengers of Azraith.' One picks and chooses which ones he likes and then sticks with it. So right now I'm calling it the Cause. Do you object?"

"No, only I wish you would be honest with yourself and call it by its right name."

"Which is?"

"The Rebellion, of course. For you are all rebels."

"You might find that term gains some glory one day. There will be those among men who might count themselves blessed to be on the side of a rebellion."

"I am quite sure of it," I said. "But what of the stone? How will you make it fall into the right hands, and what will the person do with it who receives it? Surely you don't think Kyrie will be willing to be used by evil powers just because they have learned one of His secret names, do you?"

"We don't know." Tyree studied the amulet as it swung on the thong around the woman's neck. She had finished combing her son's hair and had sent him skipping off to "devil the pig," or so I supposed. She stood there, gazing out the window, and suddenly her hand reached up to her throat and she clasped the amulet. She then untied the knot at the back of her neck and drew it off, holding it up to the light.

She said, "You have such interesting color. I have never seen anything like it. I wonder what you really are."

Tyree poked me in the side. "See, already it weaves its magic spell. She is tantalized by it. We believe the stone has the power to grip the mind of the owner so that he is compelled to search out the complete meaning of it. But we do not know that for sure."

"Why are you telling me this, Tyree?" I asked, still unsure of what his answer could be. Indeed, I could be considered by him to be one of the enemy.

"Because you are my friend, and because . . ." He did not finish the sentence. "It is not for me to discuss such things. It would be interesting to know all that the stone can do, though. We think that it intrigues the mind of the owner so that they are led to learn more of it. But what it will do among men, we do not know. We do not think all is bound up in knowing the name or using it. But this we must find out. Perhaps you know?" He regarded me as if expecting a cogent answer, and I just shrugged.

"I do not know such lore. You were always far better at such things than me."

"We will find out, though," Tyree said. "In time, one person will arise who will know."

I sank back into my own thoughts. The woman retied the necklace and left the window. She began preparing some gourds, raspberries, and red peppers for a meal. Tyree suddenly touched my shoulder and said, "I must be gone. We will continue this discussion."

I answered, "Yes. I will look forward to it."

"See what you can find out," he said. "I'm burning to know all I can learn about the stone. For I believe it holds a key to success, perhaps for all of us."

I watched him disappear in a twitch of light. I sat out by the house until evening, when the man came in for his supper, and I watched the woman again fingering the pendant. She said nothing to her husband about it, and I wondered if the stone's spell was working in her heart. I wanted to see what it would do and I resolved to watch for some time.

45

I had to leave my watch on the white stone soon thereafter. Meetings on the Mount of the Assembly kept us busy. Kyrie wanted to ask questions, Satan was there with his effete challenges. There seemed to be nothing left on his mind except to prove once and for all that Kyrie had cheated him of all that glittered or shone. He was more committed than ever to drowning Kyrie's laws and challenges into an inundation of nonsensical blather. I was losing interest in the whole matter. No one seemed to be winning or losing. It was a stalemate of one up, one down, and another around. Satan summarily wrecked Kyrie's every attempt at bringing mankind into a semblance of lawfulness.

Kyrie on the other hand seemed stymied but ever determined to launch his final sally that would vanquish the mite and silence him forever. Neither was succeeding. If Kyrie truly was omnipotent, omniscient, wise, and manifestly perfect, in my eyes He was failing pitiably. He should have long ago produced his head-basher and sent Satan to the depths. Satan strutted about ever more confidently, having turned humanity into a greedy, lust-swilling, rob-mongering, murder-loving mass of ingrates and common criminals. I was not impressed.

I had seen the death of Eve and then of Adam. Pitiful wretches at the end, mindlessly retramping their memories and wishing for an end to the regret. Their children, grandchildren and great-grandchildren heard their stories and dismissed them with a wave of the palm. "Myths," some said. And others, "The dreams of old men and women sucked dry of hope."

Lamech, the toddler son of the woman who had once owned the white stone, had grown up and made good on his threats to avenge himself seventy-sevenfold and had managed to become a killer par magnificence, if such a reputation was worth magnifying. He was the first to take more than one wife and had passed on the white stone to his grandson, a stolid warrior with the same fire in his eyes as Lamech himself. He was named Cain-Almalek. His ancestor Cain had long ago perished, an old man full of hatred and vengeance who had secured his place in history as the first murderer and had gone on to murder others with the same malice as the first.

I was now taking notes and watching this Cain-Almalek character, known to his friends (if you could call them friends) as Malek. I was studying this particular brand of miscreant when Kyrie was suddenly at my elbow.

"He is a courageous, corrupt man," Kyrie said, and I was almost too tongue-tied to respond.

But I said, "The white stone has given him special abilities."

"What ones have you seen?"

"Eloquence and the power to lead others. When he holds it as he speaks, it is a marvel to listen to him, even if what he speaks of is robbery and terror and destruction."

"Indeed, any good gift of Heaven can be corrupted."

"This is what has happened, Kyrie?"

"Yes. But there is much more the white stone can do. That is why I have come."

I turned to look at Him. Kyrie had the power, as did we all, to appear in various forms and guises, and I knew this was one of the forms He used when He wished to speak with one of us in an intimate, friendly, mutually-respectful fashion. He appeared just like one of us, and I felt His love burning through the light in His eyes as He spoke. "Aris, I have a special mission for you."

"Yes, Kyrie, I am here."

"I wish to recover the white stone."

"Recover it? To take back to Heaven?"

"No, it cannot be taken back now. But it can be placed in different hands. So far, Satan has managed to keep the stone in the hands of those who will do his bidding. You have seen the carnage from the beginning when it first fell into the hands of Methushael's wife, Aganah, who gave birth to Lamech. She turned into a witch of sorts who beguiled people and became rich on the harvest of their goods by telling fortunes that in many cases came true. She was entirely allied to the powers of darkness. She passed it on to Lamech, and now that vengeance-monger has given it to this warrior Malek, who is proving worse than all of them. It must be taken away from him, or he will soon be leading the whole world against those who would do right."

I said, "Kyrie, I will try to do as you say, but how?"

"You will become a man."

"A human being?"

"Yes."

"But how?"

Kyrie smiled. "It has always been in your power. When an angel passes through the door in Heaven separating our two worlds, he can go among men as an angel, and therefore invisible, or he can trek with them in their own form. It is all a matter of willful choice."

"Does Satan know this?"

"Yes. But I have prevented him from using it until now. Now I have chosen to use it Myself. And you will be the first to experience the transformation. You must use it wisely and well."

"But why me, Kyrie? I am not even allied to you."

"That is something I will not divulge now. Only know that I trust you enough to walk among men to do My bidding."

I bowed. "I will be circumspect about this, Kyrie. Thank you for the honor. I will not forget it."

He smiled and placed His weighty hand on my shoulder. "You are a different sort of angel, Aris, but at least a trustworthy one. And that is something I admire."

"Admire?" I almost laughed.

"Yes, Aris. I can admire. But now, you must go. You will walk into the wood for a hundred paces. There you will look to Heaven, raise your arms, and when you are ready you will say the words, 'I will become Aristes, a man.' And let your arms fall to your side. Instantly, you will be transformed into flesh and blood with clothing and something else—don't ask Me what, it will be a surprise. I like a surprise now and then, too." He smiled, and I felt His warmth toward me as a lance of sunlight into my heart.

He continued, "You cannot do anything that will compromise righteousness while you are in this form, Aris. And you cannot coerce anyone to do what you say. You can only help those who are My own, and you can, of course, try to retrieve the white stone. But you cannot kill or try to kill Malek or anyone else. Do you understand?"

"I understand."

"Beware, Aris. Do not fall in love with a woman."

"I will be careful."

"They are very beguiling. Mark Me on this. Do not look upon a woman to lust for her, or you will be ensnared and unable to do as I have asked."

"I will do as You say, Lord."

"Then go. And get the white stone. When you have it, you are to take it to house of one called Rellah. She is a good woman and will use it well."

"I will do as you say."

"Go, and beware."

I walked straight into the woods and moments later I was a slightly built, brown, tousled-haired young man, about twenty, with singing eyes and a small harp under my arm. I wondered if I was to use it and how, and I found it was not different from my Harpistrer from heaven. I stood and marveled at the emotion that rolled over me, and then I turned to peer back toward where I had last seen Malek. I crept cautiously out of the woods, moving my head in all directions wondering what the people would think seeing me in flesh and blood. I would be a stranger, and they certainly would be wary of me.

But as I walked, a song came into my mind, one of the songs of Heaven, and I smiled as I found I could sing as I walked. Suddenly, I realized that was my role. I would be a singer of songs and wend my way into their circles through music. I realized that this was a gift of Kyrie, and I looked briefly to Heaven, offering Kyrie a word of thanks. Then I stepped out of the wood, took a deep breath, and walked toward the circle of men gathered in front of Malek's house.

46

Several of the men drew their swords as I stepped closer to them. One fit an arrow to his bowstring.

"I come in peace!" I said immediately.

"Who are you?" Malek asked. He was a big-boned man with wide, blue eyes and an imperious manner. But it was easy to see why men followed him. Charisma oozed from every pore as he stood before the group, gripping the hilt of his sword. I would not want to fight him as an angel, certainly not as a man. I was slightly built, small-boned, with delicate features. I sensed that singing was appropriate for me, but I wondered how it would gain me an opportunity to get the white stone. Even now I saw it dangling from around his neck on a necklace with other stones on it. But none shone as brightly or as mysteriously as the white stone of Heaven.

I answered Malek without hesitation. "I am Aristes, from the north. I am a singer of songs."

Most of the men sheathed their swords and chuckled. One said, "Just what we need for our little band, a music maker. Can you filch wealth with that harp of yours?"

"No, but after a bold journey and theft I can provide relaxation and entertainment. I am looking for employ in a band such as yours." The words and ideas came into my mind effortlessly.

Malek remained silent as everyone turned to face their leader. There were over fifty of them. Then he said, "You are welcome here for as long as you prove useful. But your songs had better be jolly and full of sex."

I gulped. "I am sure you will find my songs . . . heavenly."

"Hah!" Malek mused. "Sing us one now and we will see."

I unstrung the harp from my side and touched a few of the strings. Plucking several, I began:

> He was strong and mighty,
> the grandest in all the realm.
> He guided the ship of men
> and stood sure around the helm.
> Like lightning he struck.
> With boldness he came.
> His friends called him Malek,
> but born with different name.

Instantly, the men were on their feet clapping and cheering. "Hear it for our leader!"

"A song of the brave."

"We will all sing it."

But Malek quieted them. "How do you know my name, singer of songs?"

"All have heard of Malek!" I said, suddenly realizing I might have said the wrong thing. Surely he would be suspicious.

Malek said, "And how do you know my given name?"

I shook my head. "Our father—all our fathers are the children of Cain. And always the great and first are named after our ancestor." I knew I was stretching it now, but I did not think Kyrie wanted me to reveal my true origins. "So I thought you must have another name."

"You are a prophet perhaps, then, and that will be very good for us." Malek walked forward, extending a muscular, hardened hand. I took it and he grinned at me. "You shall sing the songs of Malek, but we will also give you a sword, for each of us earns his keep by the plunder he gathers. Even tonight we are going on a raid, and we wish you to join us—first to help with the battle, and then to entertain us afterwards. What say you?"

I nodded, smiling at the men gathered around me.

"And now for feasting!" Malek cried. He clapped his hands and suddenly out of the woods appeared two elderly women.

One of them said, "The feast is ready, Sire!"

"And the women?"

"Yes!"

I had not yet seen any women with human eyes, and I briefly remembered Kyrie's words. I did not think this would be trouble. And then ten maidens appeared at the edge of the woods, their arms heavy with food, their bodies beautiful, dark, and mysterious in the brilliant light. I swallowed and one of them walked directly toward me.

As we took our seats on the earth, the maidens spread out among us. The one who came toward me was small, a tiny slip of a woman with beautiful red lips and eyes that seemed to look into my very heart.

I shuddered when she said, "I am Zillah." She handed me an apple and some vegetables cooked in oil. It looked like a tasty repast.

Zillah batted her lovely eyes at me and smiled demurely. "I am the second daughter of Malek."

I took some of the vegetables in my hand and ate. They were delicious, not as scintillating as the fruits of Heaven, but rough and wild in my mouth. I chewed happily, still looking at Zillah who watched me with a coy smile on her face.

"You are very handsome," she said. "You do not look like the rough men who go with my father."

"Zillah," one of the men cried. "He's not the only one here, you know!"

She turned. "Hush, I wish to speak with the new one."

"Zillah, you may speak with him when your work is done and his work is done," Malek said. "And then perhaps you can introduce him to the pleasures that Malek's family affords those who follow him."

A raucous laugh shot up around me, and I felt my heart thrumming in my chest. The sights and sounds around me were eerie with foreboding, and I did not know what to say or do. But the sight of Zillah had disturbed me. Kyrie's words resounded in my head. "Do not fall in love with a woman." And I knew already that I was close to being ensnared.

"I think the singer and poet has never seen a woman before," one of the brawny, thick-chested men gulping his food like water said. "Already his loins are burning. Zillah is like her father. She knows how to incite us!"

Everyone laughed, but I tried to pretend I did not hear. Zillah moved in and out among the men, giving each one of them endearing looks, but repeatedly her eyes came back to me and twice she winked. I tried not to return her gaze, but her eyes were so darkly beautiful that I was entranced.

As we ate, the men joked, and finally it came time for them to leave on their raid. I did not know how long it would take to procure the stone and what kind of fight Malek would put up against losing it. Furthermore, I had to find the woman Rellah and had no idea where to look. I sensed she must be somewhere near, but I would have to ask around. I was reluctant to ask any of the men I was with for fear they would know something of her that was unsavory by their standards and might alert them to my real purpose. I had not yet noticed Malek touching or holding the white stone in a way that indicated his sense of its power. But the power might simply be transmitted by him wearing it.

I finished my eating and Zillah walked over to me, swaying her slim, inviting hips as if to say to me, "You are mine tonight," and again I shivered. Her sexual power was altogether enchanting, and I did not know how to withstand it. Neither did most of the others.

"Zillah's hot tonight!" one of the men cried as he watched her sashay around picking up scraps.

Someone else cried, "Guess she's picked out her man for the evening." His eyes rested on me, and he leered provocatively as I tried to return a nonchalant shrug. He simply laughed and said robustly, "I think Zillah will find our new friend Aristes a hard case!"

Zillah just swung her hips all the more lusciously.

A moment later, Malek stood in front of me, handing me a knife. "We will see if you are really one of us tonight."

I stammered, "I have never used a knife, sir."

"Then tonight is your first time."

"But I have never even struck a man."

Malek regarded me with a squint of contempt. "Everyone in my band makes his own way."

"I will sing and entertain. That is important to men who have risked their lives."

"But I want to know what you will do when my back is to you. And the only way I can judge that is if a man will follow my orders. Will you?"

I groped fearfully for the right words. "I will sing, tell jokes, and dance whenever you want. But I should not kill."

"Why not?"

"Because it will corrupt me."

Malek stared at me a moment then burst into amazed laughter. "You are already corrupted by being with us."

"It will make me unable to sing, is what I meant to say." I was almost stuttering now, searching for whatever words would free me from this rank duty. I wondered again why Kyrie would choose me, and I was afraid of failing Him. But surely He knew this would happen.

Malek looked me up and down. "What? Do you want to stay with the women while we are gone?"

I shook my head vehemently. "I will go with you. I will guard the baggage. I will help the wounded. I have been known to heal people who are broken." (I don't know where that came from, but it popped out!). "I will help in any way I can. But please don't ask me to do those things that will destroy the only real gifts I have, which is to give men mirth after a hard day's work."

"So be it," Malek said, thumping me on the back with his iron hand. He knocked the wind out of me, and I almost tripped face forward into the dirt. He caught me. "You win, Aristes. We will call you Aristes the Arguer, for you are formidable with words. I will honor this request for now. But if I detect the slightest treachery in your words or deeds, I will dispatch you myself."

"It would be an honor," I said, biting my tongue.

"It is always an honor to be killed by Malek," he thundered to me and to the others. "Now we go. I will hear no more of songs until after we have pillaged the treasure of the Seraps!"

"Aye!" the men shouted together, waving their swords, spears, and bows in the air.

"We strike in the early morning when all are asleep," Malek said. "Now we march." He waved his arm and we all set out, walking single file. Malek sent runners out ahead, several of the younger men swift of foot and sharp of eye. As we left there were many hugs and kisses from the women, and Zillah stretched herself against me sensually, kissing me hard on the lips.

"I will sleep with you when you return," she whispered into my ear. I replied with only a brief nod and hoped I would not be coming back. I knew now I had to get the white stone before we returned.

47

The village of the Seraps was several miles south of us, on the other side of a brightly flowing stream. For a moment as we marched, I wondered where Eden was. I had not visited there since the early days after the casting out.

Malek marched in the middle of the group. I soon realized he kept his most loyal lieutenants close by. They were all heavily armed and each wore a woven sack of reeds on his back for bringing back the plunder. I learned that the Seraps had mined jewels from the caves of the mountain they lived by, and there was news of bronze weapons that Malek wanted for his men. There were also women they could take as concubines and children they could sell as slaves. From Malek's point of view, it looked like an excellent opportunity. I myself was filled with dread. What would I do if I was required to hurt someone, or kill them?

I tried not to think about it. We plodded through the quiet evening as long as the sun lasted. Soon, we were walking by starlight and moonlight. The glades we passed through were redolent with the aroma of cypress and cedar. I marveled at the effect the human olfactory system was having on my biology. Angels are quite used to aromatic scents in Heaven—scents that elevate the thoughts and move one to worship. Scents in the material world, though, aroused the emotions, made one feel hungry or thirsty, lifted a mood, or built a fire in your loins. I had no idea of their power, and I wondered if any man realized the beauty with which Kyrie had imbued their organic systems.

Sights and sounds also were a marvel. The twittering of a bird could shatter a silence and prickle one's back with fear or admiration. The crack of a limb or stick on the ground resounded in the air like what would later be known as gunfire. I found myself starting and jumping at each little sound, and the men around me found it hilarious.

"No need to worry about ambush," one told me, a heavyset man with a thick beard and deep green eyes that ran up and down a man's body as if immediately measuring off his ability in a fight. "They don't know we're comin'."

One of the younger men said, "I can't wait till I've hided out my first kill."

"So what will it be?" the brawny bearded one asked the younger. "A big-nosed warrior, or just some gimpy-eyed mongrel dog?"

The younger one squinted at the bearded man and said, "I'll take on the likes of you."

"No you won't, boy!" he answered. "You want a fight, you'll get plenty. But don't come after me. You'll end up dead."

"I could take you on."

One of the others immediately turned around and whispered, "Be quiet, you two. The enemy is several miles ahead, not here."

We walked on in silence then, only the snap of a twig and the rustle of leaves as we passed clouding the silence. There was an occasional cough, too, and I noticed several of the older men did not look well. I realized once more what Adam and Eve's failure had led the world to—murder, disease, and death, death, death. For a moment, I wondered if I was struck down in my human form, would I die? But I decided not to think about that, either.

Soon we reached a rocky area. Malek stopped us and stooped down, a twig in his mouth. "I smell their smoke," he said.

I noticed the acrid scent in the air of smoke from a signal or guard fire, perhaps close.

Malek pointed first one way, then the other. He divided the men into five patrols to make their way in a circle and come in on the other side. He drew on the ground with a stick. "The encampment is just over this rise," Malek said. "We move in at dawn. Take up our positions now. Each group will spread out and come in at the target all at once." He held up a little drum which one of the other men had been carrying. "When you hear four beats, rush in! We will wait till the first light of dawn. When it is gray. As the first gray strikes, we strike."

He held up his staff. On the top was a carved head. I had not seen it before. I knew of them, though. Many of the people throughout the world in other places had them in different forms. Some made them of stone, or out of a log they cut from a tall tree. It was their god. The people in this band had forgotten long ago the one true God, and now they worshiped an idol. Malek lifted the figure up, and all bowed down to him. "We sacrifice a man, woman, and child to Alish in thanks for good hunting. Look well to whom we choose. It must be the best."

All the men grunted heartily in response. I shivered again. When would my chance come to steal the white stone? It gleamed on the little necklace about Malek's neck. I watched him touch it several times as he laid out the plan.

When Malek was finished, he scratched out the drawing on the ground. He said, "Who will carry Alish?" It was a great honor.

"I will," one of the younger men said, the one who had been talking about his first kill.

"No, you will have other concerns. Usis, you will carry him." Usis was another of the older men, scarred, dark, scowling. I would not want him as an adversary.

"Now, to your places. Watch for the gray of dawn, and listen for the drum."

The five patrols began their long circle around the village. I remained with Malek and the main body. There were about twenty men left in it. We did not talk. Several sharpened their weapons in silence. Then Malek said, "We will creep forward. Remain low. Make no noises."

We began the trek up the hill through the rocks. Every few paces Malek stopped and listened. If there was a sentry, I did not see one. I wondered if the Seraps were known as people of peace and why Malek had selected them.

We stepped around the rocks, flitting from point to point, hiding, keeping our bodies out of the starlight. Soon, we crested the hill and saw the little village on the edge of the stream. There were mainly tents, a few wooden lodges. No one seemed to be about. All was quiet. One lone fire—just coals now—sent a thin tendril of smoke skyward. The air was cool. I almost felt cold—a new sensation, something an angel would never feel. I found myself beseeching Kyrie that I would not be required to kill. I had the knife that had been given to me. But I did not want to use it.

As we watched, one of the dogs in the village barked. Malek froze, as did the rest of us. The dog barked again, and the skin covering the door of one of the houses opened. A man stepped out with a spear in his hand. He walked over to the dog and spoke to him. I could understand most of what he said. The earth had one language then, though of course each tribe developed many of its own words as needs arose. He patted the dog's head and walked about the whole village—there were about twenty tents and three or four lodges made of poles with skins on them. The dog followed him. He stopped and listened many times. After several minutes of scouting, he stood on the edge of rocky slope looking up. I heard him say, "Protect us, Elohim, for we are few! Protect us this night."

The moment he said it, my heart quickened. The word he had used—"Elohim"—was the same that Kyrie had given to Adam and Eve when they first walked in the garden. It was the name only true believers used for God.

I quickly looked over the village with new eyes and saw no idol, no totem. Were these people true believers? And perhaps the very woman I was to give the white stone to lived here!

I watched the man go back to his tent. He said, "Be quiet, Lemm, or I'll have your tongue!" The dog just wagged its tail and lay down at the front of the tent flap, curled in a heap of fluff. In front of me, Malek grunted with approval.

"They are unsuspecting!" he whispered. "Just as I intended."

Now I did not know what to do. Attacking anyone like this was bad enough. But believers in Kyrie? And was this what Kyrie wanted?

I weighed the various choices of action, and then I noticed that my bladder had filled. I had to relieve myself—another human frailty, I thought. I crept up to Malek. "I need to go back among the trees," I said.

Malek looked at me like I was crazy. I pointed to my groin.

He grinned and shook his head. "Too modest for us, eh? Go. Hurry. Dawn will soon be breaking."

I rushed back toward the trees. There was less than an hour, I estimated, till dawn. There was not much time.

Wending my way through the trees I tried to think of ways I could warn them. Then suddenly it was clear: I could change back into my angelic form. Then I could go anywhere I wanted.

But could it be that simple? And would I have time? Would Malek miss me and come looking?

I had to take that chance.

Repeating the drill I had learned from Kyrie, I whispered, "I will to become Aris, an angel."

There was a rush of energy upon me and through me and suddenly I was invisible. My knife thunked to the ground beside me, but other than that, everything else including the clothes and harp were gone with the transformation. I sighed with relief at that. Then I sped for the tent of the man I had seen.

I stepped over the curled body of the dog, now sleeping. He gave no intimation of my presence. I stepped inside the tent. The man lay on some furs and was covered by furs. A woman lay next to him, and in a corner, two small children. A small fire burned in the middle, with the smoke rising up out of the hole in the roof. It gave enough light for all to be seen. I blinked, wondering how I might warn him without him crying out, and I realized I had to be swift.

Whispering again, I transformed myself. Instantly I was a man, fully clothed with my harp under my arm. The noise of my arrival must have stirred the man I had come to help, and he opened his eyes and saw me. He started to cry out, but I leaped at him and covered his mouth, speaking directly into his ear, "I am a friend."

His eyes popping at me, he did not fight me. I released him.

"Who are you?" he asked.

I indicated that he be quiet with a finger at my lips. I said, "I do not have much time. There's a band of fifty men scattered around your village. They are to attack at the first gray of dawn."

"Fifty!" he whispered, almost too loud. I put my finger to my lips.

"At least," I said. "Not many more, though. How many fighting men do you have?"

"That many, and another twenty boys who can wield the sword. We have bronze."

"Yes, that is why they have come. They want your weapons."

"But what can I do?"

I stared at him and thought fast. Next to me, his wife turned over on her bed, but she did not open her eyes. The children remained asleep, too. "Get up, and pretend that you cannot sleep. Go to several of the tents and step inside, as if you are checking on them. Warn them then. You cannot go to many or you will arouse suspicion. And perhaps . . ."

He gazed at me incredulously. "Perhaps?"

"Perhaps I can go, too. Maybe that would be better. I do not have much time, though."

He nodded. "I will go to several. Can you meet me back here in a short time?"

I shook my head. "I cannot come back. What is your name?"

"Hosta."

"Do you have a woman here named Rellah?"

His eyes grew wide. "My older daughter. She is with her man in another tent."

"Good. I will need to speak to her sometime."

"But who are you?"

"A friend."

He grabbed my hand. "Can you fight?"

I said, "I don't know. I have never done so."

"Then please help us. Most of our people are peaceful, though they can fight, but only because there are so many enemies."

"Then they must fight as if all they had were enemies."

"We will."

I said, "At the first sound of a drum, tell your people the attack is coming. Then let them wait in their tents till their enemy enters, and they must strike down the man while he is not prepared."

"Yes," he said. "That is a good plan for the first few."

I said, "Now please turn away."

He turned around, I spoke the words under my breath, and instantly I was an angel again. I stepped out of the tent and watched him open the door. He yawned, gave the dog a friendly caress, then walked lazily about as if he was simply thinking. A moment later, he went to the door of one of the other tents and stepped inside. It was all very well done. Perhaps he would not arouse too much suspicion. But I knew he could not do this often, or Malek would attack now.

I ran for the furthest tent on the far edge, wondering how close the marauders were. Once inside, I looked around, stepped close to the man lying asleep on the skins, and knelt. I made my transformation.

The young man had the same reaction, but I was able to assure him quickly of my friendship. They were very trusting people. I told him the plan. This time, though, his wife started, and seeing me, she started to scream, but her husband silenced her with a wave. Fortunately, the fire in the center shone brightly enough for her to see his intent.

Following this procedure, I managed to warn every tent where there were still sleepers. I stepped into two as an angel where Hosta had already been, and I did not transform. I knew time was running out but with the whole village alerted, I ran back to my place in the woods. My heart sank as I saw two of Malek's men standing over my knife.

"Where is he?"

"I don't know. Has he deserted?"

"We must tell Malek."

I hurried to a point further away and transformed myself. Then I ran toward the two men. "Hello!" I whispered.

"What were you doing back there?" one of them asked suspiciously.

"Relieving myself, of course." I suddenly realized I still had not done that now, too.

"You take a long time with it."

"Well, I had to take off my knife. No reason to take that with me." I said cheerily.

"Very strange," he said, eyeing me up and down. He was one of the younger men, one I had not yet spoken with but whom I heard joking shamelessly about the women earlier.

I strapped on the knife as quickly as I could.

"Awfully strange way of doing things," he said. "I think we should tell Malek."

"That's all right," I said. I prayed they did not want to see the spot where I had supposedly relieved myself. But they said nothing more, only grumbled under their breath and shambled back to the rocks. I took my time along behind them and when I reached the rocks, Malek scowled at me, but he seemed content.

"The chief went to several tents," he said. "But I think he was just checking his people. Little good that will do in a short time." He drew the edge of his sword made of flint over his lips and licked it. The saliva he left on the blade shone under the moonlight like the trail of a snail on a rock.

We crouched down and waited till the first gray of dawn appeared. Birds called in the trees, and Malek said, "Ready?"

The other men nodded.

"The drum," Malek answered. "Beat it loud!"

The man with the little drum held it up and waited on the command from Malek. The latter held up his sword, then swept it down in one hard, brawny stroke. The drum resounded.

Instantly, the men ran forward, and I could see the outermost tents surrounded as one or two started inside. Cries of surprise went up as I saw several of them driven through by the waiting villagers.

Moments later, the whole center of the village was teeming with fighters, men, women, and children rushing to and fro in the fray. The cries of Malek and his men went up, but I could see immediately that they were greatly surprised at the readiness of the encampment.

It was my time, now, I knew. And this time I knew what to do.

Uttering the transforming words, I was suddenly an angel. My knife fell to the ground at my feet as I stood. I ran for Malek.

He clashed swords with Hosta in the middle of the fray. I could see that Malek was stronger. But many of his fellow marauders were already dead or dying inside the tents where they were surprised, and now the men and women who had been inside had come out and taken on the rest.

In my angelic form, I leaped upon Malek's back and uttered the words. The moment I was transformed, he tried to throw the weight off, obviously amazed at my appearance. I tore at his neck and the necklace ripped off. It was in my hands.

But then Malek shook me off and I fell to the ground. My head struck a rock, and for a moment I lay helpless and stunned, the white stone in my hand.

Malek raised the sword. He intended to strike me down, but I immediately uttered the words. The white stone fell from my hand onto the ground. I disappeared and Hosta ran Malek through with his own sword.

Malek grunted with pain, then fell face down in the dirt. What was left of his band scurried off into the rocks and disappeared in the wood. I rolled out of the way, still an angel, and hurried back into the rocks, too. Once there, I transformed myself again, pulled on my knife, and huddled behind a rock, waiting for all of Malek's band to depart. When it was clear, I stood and hailed Hosta and the others.

They ran out to speak with me.

"Who are you?"

"How did you do that?"

"That was most brave!"

A girl looked up into my eyes, the most beautiful woman I had ever seen, and she said, "You are bleeding. Come. I will wash you."

Hosta led me back into the village while the other warriors and the women and children attended to their wounded. The girl, whose name was Alia, took me down to the stream and bathed my head. She covered my wound with a mossy substance which she said would quicken the healing. Then she took my hand and led me back to the camp.

Hosta introduced me, saying, "I do not even know your name."

"Aris," I said. "Aristes, I mean."

"But who are you, and how is it that you can disappear and appear at will?"

"I serve Elohim," I said. "That is all you need to know."

Looking around, I spotted the white stone still lying where I had dropped it. I walked over to it and picked it up. "Where is the woman called Rellah?"

Immediately, another of the very attractive women stepped forward. "I am Rellah."

"You serve Elohim, as do all your family and friends?"

"We do."

"Then this is a gift of Elohim. It is called 'the white stone.' It gives great power to him or her who will use it wisely. Will you take it?"

Rellah looked first at her husband and then at her father. She nodded yes.

I said, "It has until now been in the hands of Malek, the very evil man you see lying there dead. Now it is back in the hands of those who love and do righteously. Use it well."

She clutched it in her hand and said, "I will." I am sure she was still wondering at the events of the dawn and not at all sure what the white stone would mean for her and her family.

The girl who had doctored me stepped over to Hosta and said, "Can we invite Aristes to breakfast?"

I shook my head. "I am sorry. I must go now. My work here is done."

Before they could stop me, I turned and walked out to the rocks. Stopping there, I waved, then I took a few more steps and uttered the now familiar words. And instantly I was Aris again. My knife dropped and I left it there, hidden among the rocks.

I stood and watched them a long time, listened to them talk, heard the maiden weep over my departure, and walked about them as Rellah took the white stone and studied it. She spoke of how there were rumored to be stones of power from Heaven which no one had seen, and she wondered if this was one of them.

I did not stay long. I wanted to return to speak to Kyrie and learn if He considered my mission a success.

48

Tyree grabbed me just as I stepped through the Doorway. "What have you done?" he cried.

"Done?"

"The white stone. You stole it from Malek, gave it to the woman. You should not have done that. Azraith is extremely angry."

"That's his misfortune."

He glanced around him then gave me a confidential look. "Azraith is angry with me."

"With you? Why? You didn't do anything."

"Let's just say he's extremely angry—with me. What can I do?"

"You're not such a small angel. Do what you think you should do. If Satan is angry with you, then leave him. Come back to Kyrie. I'm sure you'll be welcomed with open arms."

"It's not that simple, Aris."

"Oh, there are troubles in Paradise, are there?"

"You don't know what his wrath is like. Demotions, imprisonments, guards in the pit, the fire. It's getting awful."

"Oh, now you have regrets, is that it?"

"No!" Tyree looked at me with grim, black-lined eyes. I could see he'd deteriorated. He seemed genuinely afraid, something I'd never seen in him before. "No," he said again. "It's just that he doesn't like failure. The same way Kyrie doesn't like failure!"

"Kyrie does not treat us like that."

"No, Kyrie only cast us out of Heaven forever. That's all Kyrie did!"

I could see the pain and anguish in his eyes. For a moment I wished I could help him. But helping him would have meant assisting the likes of Malek and his thugs commit their murder and plunder. Though in the back of my mind there was still the possibility that I might yet join the rebellion, I did not like the company Satan kept. He was the real tyrant. I could not understand how anyone could remain with him.

Tyree paced in front of me. "I have to do something to win back his favor. That's the point. Something." He regarded me with sudden new interest. "You have given us ideas, you know."

"What ideas?"

"About the ability to become human."

"You knew about that."

"Yes, but we did not know how to exercise it, nor did we have the right."

"And I don't think Kyrie will grant you that right."

"We have our ways." Tyree grinned. All the pain disappeared. All the regret was gone. He was scheming again, I could see that. Was that the only thing that amused him anymore: schemes, malevolent plans, evil tricks, hoaxes, and dark sins?

I said, "You should stop doing evil, Tyree. It will catch up to you one day. Kyrie says judgment is coming."

"Then why doesn't He make it come? His threats are meaningless. He does nothing, and His situation only gets worse. He has forced us into this position and all He does is sit up there on His throne issuing prophecies. They mean nothing to us, especially when He has no power to make them come to pass. You know about the one He gave to the serpent. Nothing has come of it. So why should we listen to Him?"

"Kyrie doesn't solve all problems in a single day, Tyree. Or perform all judgments."

"It's been centuries, Aris. How long does He need?"

"Maybe more than we think." I felt on the defensive again, and I didn't know what to say because this was the same thought that troubled me. "But," I quickly added, "Kyrie is not to be toyed with. I would rather trust Him than a hundred of your Satans!"

"So you trust Him now?"

I returned Tyree's piercing gaze, trying not to blink. I said, "I'm moving in that direction. I have seen things."

"What?"

"The people of Hosta. That was a change."

Staring at me with anger, Tyree looked me up and down as if gauging my ability to resist an attack. Then suddenly his grim eyes shone, and he was transfigured for a moment as if some elevating thought had just animated him. He cried, "We shall see about that!" His robes swished and he stepped past me to the Doorway. "Thanks for the talk, Aris. You have refreshed me."

"Refreshed you?"

"Yes! Thank you. Thank you. You don't know what you've done!"

"What have I done?"

Before the words were out of my mouth, he was gone, ripping off to the earth again. What did he mean? And what was he going to do?

I turned on my heels and headed into the Great City, perplexed and worried.

"You have done well, Aris," Kyrie said.

I knelt before Him. He seemed slightly distracted, though, and I thought to let my time with Him be brief. "Kyrie, thank you for giving me the opportunity to serve You."

"Then what conclusions have you come to, My son?"

"I feel near a decision, though I still do not understand all You are doing. Yet, after the incident with Malek, I feel I can see You acting to take some charge."

"It is not something I will often do."

I looked up at His face, a bewildered feeling coming over me. "But why?"

"It is not My way."

"But if You do nothing . . ."

"I do not do nothing, Aris. I only said I would not intervene or interfere like that frequently."

"But You have to. Faith on earth will not survive otherwise."

Kyrie regarded me with a weary look of inner sorrow. "I know it would be easier in some ways if I did. But not in the long run. I must always be thinking of the long run, Aris. Do you understand what I mean?"

"Perhaps if I knew how long, I could understand better."

"And if you knew how long precisely, how would that change it?"

I stopped and thought a moment. It seemed to me that it would change many things. If I knew how long, I would know instantly what it would take to stand firm. Furthermore, it might fortify me. I said, "It would help me stand the setbacks and make me feel that You truly do have it all in hand."

"But what if the time is far longer than you ever imagined, than you ever thought you could withstand?"

"How long could that be? Five hundred years? I am sure I could survive." I realized that if He would reveal to me how long, I would know something that perhaps no other angel knew. It was information that I'd either have to keep to myself, and that might be difficult, or else He'd have to give it to all of us. And what would that do? If we all knew how long . . .

"What if it is far greater?"

"Is it?"

"I'm only asking. If it is far more than five hundred or a thousand or ten thousand of earth's years, where would that leave you?"

For a moment, I couldn't imagine it. I finally said, "I guess I'd give up now if I knew it was that long."

He didn't stop with that, though. "And what if it is short, very short, only another year or so, how would that help you?"

"I'd be very excited."

"But you might feel what use was there in being vigilant. It is all going to end anyway, so why not just sit it out?"

I had to be honest, and I answered, "Yes, I suppose that could happen."

"If I reveal it to you alone, would you not fall in danger of pride, or thinking you are a favorite of some sort? And what pressure would it put on you to know and not be able to tell it? Wouldn't you ultimately either snap or tell, both of which would be deleterious to you?"

"Yes, that is possible."

"And finally, if I reveal it to all angels, then Satan also will know, and he will undoubtedly use it to his advantage. So not knowing keeps each of my loyal ones loyal and watching, and it also forces Satan and his cohorts to be ever fearful that this day might be their last."

I could not argue with Him, but I said, somewhat lamely, "It was just a thought."

"And a good one, Aris. But now you understand why it is better that no one know, for it builds vigilance, trust, patience, and a hundred other virtues that could not be developed under other conditions."

For a moment, I stared at Him in amazement, then I laughed. "You really have it all worked out, don't you?"

He shook His head slowly but deliberately. "And suppose even I don't know, Aris? Suppose in the end I will not have seen it till each of us sees it. Suppose it will not end, but will go on and on into eternity and there is nothing that I can do about it."

"But that is impossible." I stared at Him and gulped. He seemed utterly sincere, and His eyes glittered with the passion of what He was saying. I was charmed by His words. I felt as if I had entered yet another portal of His very soul. After a moment, I said meekly, "It is impossible, isn't it?"

"All things are possible with God," Kyrie said. "Go, think on what we have discussed, and again some day soon we will resume our talks."

"Please," I cried, "don't leave me like that! You do know where it is going, and when it will end, and where and why and how—do You not?"

"And what if I don't?" He gazed at me, his eyes gleaming with unusual liveliness. I realized He was not toying with me at all, but that He was enjoying me as I was enjoying Him. It was a powerful revelation and finally I smiled.

"Kyrie, You are enjoying this, aren't You?"

"Very much."

I shook my head with wonder. "You are a marvel," I said, almost mumbling, a bit embarrassed that He might hear and laugh.

"You did not answer My question," He said. "What if I don't know where it is all going and so on and so forth, as you have stated?"

"Then I suppose I would be forced to admit You are not omniscient as You say You are, that You are not wise, that You are not all-powerful, and that all those things are lies."

"Indeed, you lay it all out thickly. But that is the issue, isn't it: Do I or don't I? And that brings it all back to . . ."

"Trust."

"Yes, because I want you to trust Me that I do have it all well in hand."

"But there is always the wondering."

"Indeed." He smiled at me benevolently, and I realized for a moment that in some ways He was as angelic and human as any of us. He wanted our friendship as much as our love, and He enjoyed the simple act of hashing out an issue. He loved to teach, but at the same time He never exalted Himself over us. I had to admire Him for that.

"Aris," He said suddenly. "There is trouble now. Go back to your friend, Hosta. Go back immediately, and I give you leave to do what you can. There will be others to help you. But it may be . . ."

I stared at Him with horror at the words He was uttering. Tears formed ın His great eyes, and I swallowed. He waved me off. "Go! Hurry! There is no time to waste!"

49

Minutes later I crashed through the Doorway. Before me lay the whole earth, and I flew across the hills and valleys at lightning speed. I had no idea what had happened, but I knew Kyrie's words were not just unsolicited encouragement.

I sped along in my angelic form when suddenly I could see the camp ahead. There was a commotion, people fighting, swords clashing and spears being thrown. Just as I ran, I saw several people fall in the space of a few seconds. The tents were on fire, and the log houses sent smoke high into the sky.

I flew all the faster, ready to shout the words that would transform me when I was thrown headlong, spinning along the ground in unplanned cartwheels and body twists. I came face down in the dirt with a groan and rolled to stand again. I thought I had hit a rock or tree limb, but no rock or tree limb could have done that. I would have passed right through them.

Then I saw him. A towering Hauker with a sword. "Advance no further," he shouted.

"What do you want?" I drew my own sword. It appeared small and ineffective against what the Hauker held.

"You are going no further," he said. He swung the sword in front of him menacingly, and I stopped, momentarily stunned at his audacity. I had never been impeded by one of the enemy like this, though I had heard of such things happening.

I raised my sword. "I am on a mission from Kyrie."

"We do not recognize Him."

"That doesn't matter. He is still Lord even if you don't recognize Him." I spat the words at him.

"There is only one to be recognized in this world: our Lord, Azraith. Now begone or prepare to fight."

"And where will that get us? I can't kill you, and you can't kill me. So what is the point?"

The slow waving of his sword stopped, and he pointed it directly at me. His face was dark, his eyes looking yellow and dead. And yet there was fire in them, a kind of gasping, yellow, low-burning fire, but a fire just the same. I held my sword at chest height, and he said, "Killing isn't what this is about. Are you willing to withdraw?"

"No." I thought I could get around him. Surely I had some advantage, but as I sprinted to the left, he ran right with me. Then to the right. He was there in front of me. I flew up, down, sideways. He stayed right with me. I tried this for several minutes, speeding then slowing, feinting, thrusting at him without swords clashing.

It all had no effect. He was as fast as me in all respects. I could not defeat him by running, and certainly not by flying.

The battle in front of me intensified. I saw Hosta fighting off two then three assailants. There was no one close to him to help.

And then I saw Alia. She darted in and out among the fighters with a small sword. She looked small and frail, and blood ran from a slash on her upper arm.

The Hauker took a step toward me. "Go back," he said.

"I will change then."

He shook his head. "You cannot change as long as I stand here ready to strike."

I started to speak the words. Immediately, his sword sang and cracked against my upraised hilt. I fell to the ground. He hovered over me. "Go back!" he shouted again.

I rolled and jumped to my feet. Whirling my sword, I slashed at his feet. He down cut on my sword and broke its flight. Seconds later clangs of angelic steel on steel rang in the air. I thrust and slashed as hard as I could. But the Hauker was larger and stronger. I could not get past him.

Behind him, the battle raged. Hosta was on his knees now, deflecting blows from four who took turns slicing at him. Blood poured from numerous slashes on his chest. I could not see Alia.

The Hauker fought harder now. But he seemed only bent on keeping me from helping the believers. I prayed as I fought, but nothing changed. He remained in front of me.

Just as he swung his sword over his head for a defining blow, I cut at his belly. He fell back, wounded. I didn't wait for a second chance. I ran around him and spoke the words.

Immediately, I felt strong hands jerking me back. I had not transformed. The Hauker had me in a death grip.

I cried out. He twisted my head. I felt my neck breaking.

Then suddenly he screamed and relaxed his grip. I wriggled free and could see. It was Sember, the tiny angel who had once nurtured the white flower at the heart of the mountain. He shouted, "Go!" And with one more thrust, he split the Hauker's head in half.

I ran and spoke the words.

A moment later I stood at the edge of the encampment. The plunderers were already gone. Bodies lay everywhere. The whole camp was devastated.

I ran about looking for Hosta, Alia, Rellah. I found Alia by one of the smoking tents. Her throat had been cut. She was naked.

I stooped to throw a skin over her body, but I could find none. Her frail girlish face lay broken and lifeless in my hands.

Then I heard a voice. "Please. Help me." A woman.

I turned and peered over the encampment, searching for the voice. "Please. Over here."

I walked to the middle and found a woman. She had been disemboweled. Her life was going fast. "In the woods," she said. "My baby." I looked about me for water, but I saw none. A moment later, she died in my arms.

Hurrying to the woods, I listened for the cries of the little one. There were none. I found the baby a few minutes later. It had been stabbed through the chest. I picked up the tiny child and gripped him to my chest. "Kyrie, how can this have happened?" I said, tears filling my eyes.

I found Hosta dead of a multitude of wounds. And finally, I discovered Rellah. She was almost decapitated. The white stone was nowhere to be seen.

I sank to the ground, my heart like iron inside me. I could not breathe. There was no one left. I kept looking around, expecting the sounds of laughing children or men returning from fishing.

There were none. The only sound was that of crackling flames still licking up the sides of one of the tents.

I wept as I walked through the slaughter. I kept walking, checking here, there, until dusk. As all the fires died down to ashes, I looked about for something to dig with, to start burying the dead.

Then suddenly He was there.

I looked up into His eyes—He had taken human form. "Kyrie, I . . ." I burst into tears again, and He touched my still wet cheek and then sat down next to me.

I said, "Kyrie, why? Why? You had just sent me to help them days ago. And now they're all dead." I turned to face Him and His eyes glistened. His face looked haggard and broken, as if all the pain of Hosta's people was contained in His own heart. For a moment I was surprised, but I could say nothing to Him about it.

I closed my eyes and slumped, trying to gain some composure. Kyrie did not speak, and only the lift and ebb of His chest as great sobs wracked His breathing was evident. His thick long white hair stirred in the wind. Finally, He said, "It is a sad day."

I answered, "If only I had been able to get here. Perhaps . . ."

He folded his hands together and bowed, and for the first time I was aware of how small He seemed. Always before He appeared tall, strong, robust. But here I could see something had shaken Him.

"Kyrie," I said. "Are You all right?"

He nodded. I decided to remain silent.

Finally, after a long time He spoke, His fingers gripped and ungripped. They looked fragile and clean, but slightly withered as if old age had crept upon Him. He said, looking over the destroyed encampment and the crumpled bodies lying everywhere, "There is a sadness in My soul. All these . . ." He waved His hand over them. "All these are with Me now forever. But still there is a sadness in My soul."

"If only I had not been stopped," I murmured.

He shook His head. "You could not have stopped it. Not alone."

"But if others had been sent."

"There were no others except Sember."

"But there must be something that could have been done!" Now I was beginning to feel the old raw, blood-tinged anger well up inside me.

"Don't you understand!" He suddenly cried. "There is nothing that could have been done! Evil once again had its day, and it couldn't be stopped!"

"But why?" I said, astonished and aghast. "Aren't You all-powerful?"

"All-powerful does not mean I can summarily stop something simply because in My heart I wish to." He had ceased weeping now and stared over the clearing with haggard eyes. "They will come, and they will come, and they will come for so long, and there is no stopping them." He seemed to be talking to Himself, not to me—lamenting His own plight. "I must be witness to slaughters and destructions and holocausts, and their evil will only grow more evil and more malevolent, and I cannot stop it once and for all until the very end." He sobbed a moment and then looked at me with red, pain-wracked eyes. "I wish—how I wish—there could be another way, Aris. How many times I have wished that. But there is no other way."

I barely moved my head, still numb with the magnitude of the murders. Suddenly, I stood and shouted, "Then are there no answers to anything?"

He stood and embraced me. Then He said, "I am very sorry, Aris. I know you loved them." His eyes were still wet with tears, and He sighed. "All these things are so difficult."

I stared at Him. "Difficult?"

He turned and gave me that old rueful, far-off look I'd seen on His face a hundred times. It faded into a pensive sigh. The human form He had taken was that of a man in his sixties, with a trimmed white beard, curly hair, and deep blue eyes. He regarded me kindly, melancholy in the moonlight, and placed His hand on my shoulder. "Aris, if I offered to explain to you everything that would ever happen, including this monstrous tragedy, would you take the offer?"

I almost leaped up. "Yes! Yes!" I studied His eyes a moment, and they returned my gaze without blinking. I said, "I think so anyway."

"You are so sure about that?"

I hesitated only slightly. "I believe so, Lord."

He looked away, to the horizon where the sun still shone just as golden and trenchant as ever, and it was for a moment as if nothing in the world could matter but the great joyous fact of its shining intensity. He spoke after long thought. "Hosta was a man of faith and is still a man of faith. He does not condemn Me or the world or even those who took his life. In fact, he will beg for mercy upon them in their judgment, when it comes. He is a good man and I love him. So also Alia, your friend, and Rellah, and all of them. They were a simple people, one of the last remnants in the world who still worship Me—though there are yet others. And even more terrible days are coming, Aris. Days so tragic in their living that death shall be an eagerly sought friend to those who will endure them. It will all go on and on, even though it will in the end only have been a moment of time in proportion. But now it seems so long, so long and brutal and merciless. I would that it was not so, Aris. But there can be no denying evil its day."

He grasped me. "Aris, do not forget what you have seen. Do not let evil have its revisions in your memory. Do not let it grow old and boring and stale and forgotten. You must not—or it will never be conquered."

My face twitched and I was crying again. He held me, and I did not know how long we stood there. Then at the end we turned and began the task of digging a trench in which to bury Hosta and Rellah and Alia. We worked in silence and when it was over and we were ready to pass again through the Door, He said, "Aris, do not forget what you have seen here."

"I will not, Kyrie."

Instantly He was gone.

I was distraught for many days after that. I did not leave my room in Heaven to do anything. I resolved never to befriend a human being again, and I practiced on my Harpistrer as if we were to have a concert—though there were no more concerts—and I thought and wrote in my journal and meditated and wished for a better day. I kept coming back to His words about evil. I troubled over them, wondering at their meaning and where it would all go in the "long run," as He phrased it.

Finally I could sit no longer, and I went out into the shekinah of Heaven and walked in the gardens for days. They were so beautiful. I found myself saying over and over, "How can such beauty exist side by side with such evil?"

And I still had no answers.

50

Years passed. Time slipped away, and I watched and sometimes walked among people—those who were good, though they were fewer and fewer, and those who were bad. I tried to keep perspective, studying men and women and children and their ways as I had once studied the music of Heaven. There were no immediate conclusions, and I reconciled myself to enduring a great many more years of this than I had previously thought.

There was no sign of the one who would bruise Satan on the head, and it seemed that the adversary's own loyalists grew bored with the prophecy, alternately saying it had just been another boast that had not come to pass, or that its real meaning lay hidden from everyone so there was no point in trying to understand it.

As for Satan and his legions, they seemed far more bent on destroying every attempt by Kyrie to bring mankind under obedience than anything else. I wondered why they had not yet tried to establish their own rule, as they said they would, and so lead and guide the world into a new kingdom.

Then I realized that Satan was having as much trouble bringing people into submission to himself as Kyrie was. Humankind were a rascally, very independent sort that resisted any outside controls. Satan's deputies met daily to try and figure out ways to permanently secure a "people for their own possession," and they found it quite impossible. Humans simply went their own way, regardless of what suggestions and thought-plants the tempters managed to slip into their minds.

At times I found this laughable, and I suppose I entered a stage where I was cynical, skeptical, and feeling strongly that neither Kyrie nor Satan were worthy of anything except the most profound ridicule. My diary at that time is filled with exclamations such as "Kyrie fails again!" and "Once more Satan proves himself impotent!" and "The humans have managed to foil everyone to no one's pleasure but their own!"

I deliberated over the people of faith as much as anyone else and found that they were rarely more blessed than those who practiced evil. And all of them were still prone to sin in the most outrageous ways. A father could come in from prayer to Elohim, a glow on his face, and a minute later he might be abusing his son or daughter with curses and slaps to the face. It was common to find people who truly believed struggling far harder than any of those who believed nothing or worshiped one of Satan's idols. It was much more difficult going against the stream of sin, even with Kyrie's supposed blessing, than it was to run with it and still maintain a vestige of faith in the outside hope that Kyrie would reward them for the smallest obediences. Humankind had an amazing capacity for denial. One good act could cancel out hundreds of bad ones in their minds. And at the same time, a single bad deed could leave them guilty and emotionally distraught for days. I did not understand much about these passionate, oh-so-obstreperous creatures, and there were times when I rued the day that Kyrie had ever created them.

The worst part was caring for one of them. I would find someone whom I liked, who honestly seemed to pursue good and right and Kyrie Himself. I would try to nurture that faith, occasionally appearing in human guise to help them out of some trouble, and then they would catch a sickness and die young, or perish at the hands of the ever-growing bands of pirates and terrorists that plagued every land. Then I would be sick, accusing Kyrie of some foul deed, and then repenting of it when we finally talked it out.

The one thing that stands out in my memory of this time was that Kyrie and I had so many talks. We came back to the problem of evil over and over. I soon came to the conclusion that while He believed intensely that He would triumph over it in the end (He never wavered on that), still He grieved at times and His pain seemed so great that I feared for His sanity. That seems like a complete contradiction in terms, but that was my feeling. Could Kyrie crack under the pressure of all the evil coming at Him?

I did not know the answer to that. But I sensed that He felt far deeper about the smallest crimes against His children—He always referred to humankind whether evil or good as His children—than I ever did. The only thing I did not see in abundance was His wrath. He rarely lashed out at evil in the way I thought He should.

And then came the mating episode.

I was in Hell during a conclave of all the various tempters. I heard Tyree boast of the Hosta affair in which he'd gained revenge for Malek against the forces of Kyrie. He did not mention my role, though I suspected that everyone knew it. It had occurred to me after the second attack that Tyree might have been behind it, he himself bent on making a new beginning with his master, Satan. I had hoped it was not true, but despaired when I learned the facts of his involvement.

Satan, though, was not pleased with the progress of most of his tempters. He yelled and scorched up and down in front of them, his dragon/serpent form all the more horrible and distinct. He did not age, but he seemed more and more degraded. His many eyes had that yellow tint I'd seen in other devils. And his countenance was less eloquent, more forbidding. He railed and ranted—more harangue than anything else. At times he shrank into himself and muttered arguments back and forth in his own mind as if talking to others, but he was only talking to himself, and some of the devils around me were alarmed.

But most of them took no notice.

"This bruise thing, this murky prophecy, this half-truth out of the light," Satan ranted, "has got to be extinguished once and for all. There must be a way, a way to silence the seed. The woman is dead, but her seed is not."

Then: "Arghh! Horrible word: seed. I hate it. I hate it. Away with it. Do not mention it in my presence."

And again: "But we must think on it, analyze it, peruse it for its substance. What must it be? There is an answer. We will find it. Who will find it? Who?"

And once more: "No! We will not let Him triumph! Not ever. Never! It is impossible."

And then as if regaining his composure after awaking from a long sleep, he cleared his throat and said, "Let's get down to the business of the day. And that is vanquishing this accursed myth of the bruised head once and for all. I have some ideas, but I want to hear yours."

Beelzul, one of the Seraphs, said, "The prophecy has run its course. The seed was Abel, who was killed by Cain. There should be no more argument."

"No, I do not yet believe that," Satan said. "There were other seeds, Seth and the women, and many others. The whole world is populated with her seed."

"But we own most of them, Sire, as much as they can be owned."

"That is so. But there are still some of the faithful left. Enoch for one. I regard him as a most hated enemy and one who must be destroyed. There are others among them, hundreds I have seen praying and seeking His face. This must be stopped. Anyone of them could be the accursed seed that will strike me."

"But how can they strike you, Sire? So long as you remain in this world and not in theirs, there is no habitation by them of both."

Satan snorted with derision. "Do you think He will not find some way? He proves yet a powerful adversary, and though we are defeating Him in numbers, His loyalists still remain. Until they are all ours, I will not rest. This is sedition, Beelzul, and I will mark you for it."

The Seraph withdrew into the mass of Hell, hiding himself among the Kinderlings.

Others stepped forward and offered various suggestions, from wiping out the whole human race—which seemed improbable at this time—to seeking out and destroying every vestige of faith where it was found. But both of these ideas were already being worked on. Committees, sub-committees, and individuals all studied the possibilities and so far had only been successful in siphoning off about eighty percent of those who populated the earth. A recalcitrant twenty percent was still in Kyrie's hands.

Then my friend Tyree stepped forward. I could not have wished more that his creative energies would be spent on other works, but he seemed to thrive on every new imaginative way of corrupting the human race.

He said to Satan, "You all are aware of my recent sojourn on earth as one of them. Through it, I accomplished the destruction of Hosta and some seventy or more believers, all of them dead and their camp razed. That has led me to some sobering thinking. What if we sought to forever corrupt the race? What if we sowed our own seed among them? Would it not first of all produce aliens aligned to us? And second, aliens who might even be stronger and greater than the average human, so that humans would eventually be destroyed by the more superior angelic humans?"

"What do you mean?" Satan asked, stroking his chin and appearing once more in charge of things, but also excited and deeply curious.

"I am proposing that we send a force into the world, allow them to transform into human guise and mate with women."

There were hisses of derision all about, but Satan held up his hand for silence. "Go on," he said.

"If we can take human form, why wouldn't it be possible also to mate with women?"

"But what about Kyrie?" someone asked.

Satan seethed, "Do not utter that name in my presence!"

"What about the enemy?" the same devil rephrased the question.

"Would He permit it? Or wouldn't He more than likely stop it before it is started?"

"He has not stopped anything else!" Tyree cried. "And what is there to lose? If we can corrupt the human race with our own seed, then the woman's seed ceases to be. The curse is reversed!"

"How many of us would it take?" Satan asked.

Tyree cocked his head and said, "Several hundred? A thousand? One legion perhaps. The seed of our seed would be able to go on and destroy what males are left among the humans and then mate with their women till all entirely human species are erased. It might take a hundred years."

"More like five hundred," Satan said. "But it is a good plan. Who will go?"

Tyree's sword was up immediately, but as others clamored for the role, Satan eyed Tyree. "You shall not go, my friend. You are .. Let's just say I do not wish for you to go."

"But I will lead it!" Tyree cried.

"No, you are now first adviser in Hell. Cease and accept the honor."

Tyree bowed to his master. Then as others clamored for the privilege of going among humankind, Satan warned them, "This mission is not without peril. We do not know what the enemy will do when His wrath is kindled. And it will be kindled. Be prepared for the worst. But for Him, it will be too late. Go now and forever corrupt humanity!"

With a shriek and a yell, the legion disappeared from Hell and moments later passed through the Doorway.

51

In those days, I walked in the land as a human quite often. I took on different guises—that of the man Aristes, that of an old woman named Aristata, a girl named Arista, and a boy named Aristallis. I appeared only to help here and there and disappeared immediately so as not to arouse suspicion about my identity. It was during one of my sojourns that I met Motta.

She was a lovely maiden, one of the daughters of Enoch. I had been watching her father for many months. To say that he "walked with God" is far too simplistic for all that he did in the name of God. He was a man of great kindness, whose home welcomed travelers and his servants played the pipe and harp and often sang in the evening till the late hours. They sang of the exploits of their fathers—Enosh, who had vanquished the Giant of Umber in a terrible duel of strength and set free his people from the giant's oppression; Kenan, who prevented a multitude from stoning a man caught stealing sheep out of hunger, invited the man into his home where he preached the truth of God to him and he repented and became a loyal steward of all Kenan owned; Mahalalel, who halted the custom of sacrificing first sons to the idol of Moloch in his region and led the people into worship of God; and Jared, who marched into the hills with a contingent of his servants and rescued the beautiful Taura from the evil men who sought to rape and sell her.

One night I sang with them as a dusky traveler just passing through. Enoch and I shared a bowl of sweet fruits and spoke low and long of God and his love for Him.

"He has not failed me, ever," Enoch said as he stabbed his knife into the bowl of chunked fruit.

"And if He did?" I ask.

"There are different kinds of trust," Enoch said. "There is trust that all will go well before it happens. As at sowing time when we plant the fields. We trust God will give us rain and sunlight and a good harvest. We make our sacrifices and call upon Him to send good weather. And inevitably He does."

"But what if He didn't?"

Enoch laughed. "There has never been a time that He hasn't. Some years have been better than others, I give you that. But always the seasons bless us with much abundance. We have no needs."

I knew that Kyrie regarded Enoch as a special man and believer. He had placed around the good man a hedge of untold proportions, one that Satan called a rape and an atrocity. Satan even said to Kyrie, "Of course he believes as he does. You give him nothing but reason to. Give him a reason not to, such as an all-out attack upon his harvest and his possessions, and he will indeed reject You forever."

But Kyrie did not listen to such taunts, and He continued to build up and nurture His famed follower.

Enoch was a man of only eighty years then, still young among men, and he was tall, lean, his face almost gaunt with deepset gray eyes and a shock of brownish-red hair. He looked strong and fearless, and I knew he was not a man I would want to meet at the other end of a drawn sword. He spoke in a quiet way, not raising his voice, and his calm words made me feel at peace.

"Then there is the kind of trust when things go wrong," he was telling me. "Such as several years ago when the people of Adked attacked and tried to take away our livestock. Some of my people were killed—for there are always losses in these things. But Elohim always promises to vanquish the evil one once and for all, and we live for that day."

"When do you think it will happen?" I asked, realizing this was the first time I had heard a human speak of the curse upon Satan.

"It will happen when Elohim's time is right," Enoch said. "And that is a matter of trust, too. So you see, nearly everything comes back to trust. There are setbacks and problems, but ultimately God gives us wisdom, and He also promises to take us to His homeland after death."

"How do you know that?" I asked.

"It has always been His promise," Enoch said. "The spirit lives on."

"When did He make such a promise?" For I had not heard of it, though I knew there were those who believed it.

"He makes it to me every day that He speaks to my heart. When I walk in the yard, and when I till the field, and when I lead the donkey and the horse and the goat, He speaks to my heart. 'You are Mine, Enoch,' He says. 'All your children are Mine, and You will dwell with Me forever.' I do not know why He speaks so to me. There is no one I know to whom He speaks like that. But as I know my own heart, I know this is true, and I trust that His words will prove as mighty as His arm."

We ate in silence after that; I was not sure how to respond. His faith was firm, and he did not seem able to not believe. He was not plagued with doubts as I was, or as other men and women, and I respected him for it. How could a person be so sure?

And then I had a chance to see him prove it. As we ate, one of the servants rushed in and cried, "Master, raiders have come from the north and taken over a hundred of the horses and donkeys, and they have stolen the boy Methuselah and the girl Motta." His son and daughter, the ones who cared for the horses.

Enoch rose immediately, giving orders to the servant to gather his men. About ten of them appeared in minutes with spears and swords and bows. Enoch said to me, "You can come if you wish. It will be dangerous."

"I will come," I said, "but I don't have a weapon." They gave me a short sword made of bronze, with leather wrapped around the handle.

Several of the men hurried to gather the remaining horses. In a few minutes, a company of some twenty servants and relatives stood in the circle of their houses and tents.

Enoch held up his hands after he mounted his horse and cried, "Elohim of heaven, protect my children and grant us success!" All the men in the company shouted, "Amen!" Most of them climbed aboard their respective horses and gathered, jostling and clopping, in the open area. Several of the women wept for the loss of the two children, and one ran up to Enoch, crying, "Elohim will be with you!" She walked bravely to Enoch. Her face was dark and tanned, with a tracing of wrinkles at the edges of her eyes. I thought she must have been lovely in her earlier years, and I soon realized she was the mother of the two children. "I will be praying," she said.

Enoch answered as his mount pranced forward and back in anticipation of a good run, "They will be all right!"

I had never ridden a horse before, and when I tried to mount the beast given me, one of the young men still on the ground noticed my apprehension. He looked strong, with powerful shoulders, a chiseled face, short dark hair, a nose hooked just on the end, and bold, gleaming gray eyes. His name was Staro. He said to me, "This is how you do it!"

I followed his example and promptly plunked to the ground on my rear end. My tailbone struck a rock and when I rose, I winced with pain.

Staro said, "Come up behind me. Dark Star is strong enough for both of us. And you look light."

His tall, black thoroughbred with a diamond on its forehead reared a moment, then settled down as Staro pulled me up.

We galloped off behind the others. The horses did not wear saddles, but Staro held on with one hand to the light tan tuft of hair down the horse's neck and with the other he held the halter. The bit was wood and leather, and the horse responded to the slightest pressure of the leather thongs about his face with quick, tightly wound movements, as if the horse longed to get into the action.

We headed off in the direction the children and horses were last seen. Enoch shouted to us, "They think they have taken all our horses and will believe we are on foot. Thus, they will not be ready when we come upon them. That is our only hope. Quickly now!"

"They have attacked us often," Staro shouted above the thundering of the horses' hooves. "We will have to rout them all once and for all this time."

My heart seemed to roll over inside my chest. I simply held on as if the horse and rider would explode out from under me into a frenzied run at the stars. It was getting dark now, the late evening, and I did not know whether Enoch planned to wait till morning or not. Staro and I kept up well with the rest of the little army. I heard Enoch several times send out scouts ahead of us. I thought briefly of my friends Hosta and Alia and wondered if this would not turn out the same way. I prayed that it wouldn't.

By morning, we had not yet found them. They were traveling fast, obviously already using the horses. Enoch's scouts followed the trail easily. One of them came back and reported, "They have not stopped yet. But the horses will be tired and will need to graze. That might be when we will best find them. But our own horses are growing tired, too."

Enoch stopped us and said, "Let's take several hours rest. We cannot pursue all day and all night."

Staro stood guard while the rest of us slept fitfully. In my human form, I could sleep and it was a vivifying elixir to me. Rarely had I remained in human form long enough to have to sleep, and it was always an amazing experience. My dreams usually pictured the towering minarets and steeples of Heaven falling together into a great heap like wheat before the scythe. Then Satan would appear and glance at me and I would always wake up right then. Sometimes Tyree came to me in dreams and spoke of the joys of the rebellion and the need for angels like me, and I was never sure if he was really there or that it was the typical dream of human subconsciousness.

What seemed only minutes after I fell asleep, Enoch shook me. "Come on," he said to all of us. "The scouts have sighted the raiding party. They are moving quickly over the meadowlands, but we will catch them tonight. The boy and girl are still alive."

I had not seen either Motta or Methuselah, but Enoch's deep love was obvious. He said to me, "If they are harmed, I will never end my revenge upon them except at Elohim's word. I will hunt them to the end of the earth." For all his faith, he was a man of deep passion, and I could see that he would not easily forgive except at the point of real repentance. His face was locked with genuine anxiety, and I was tempted to ask him if he was still trusting God. But I knew that he might take me to be mocking him and I meant no such thing.

We rode hard all that day. The dust was thick on my face and hands and legs, all that was exposed. I wondered repeatedly how ten hard-ridden, weary men would defeat thirty or forty savages bent on theft and ritual murder. But I did not ask Enoch. Staro told me about other adventures with Enoch in which the man of faith had personally defeated several rabid swordsmen, had brought two murderers to justice (by hanging), and had freed over fifty slaves at one time from a pretend potentate of the realm.

"He is not a man to be toyed with," Staro said. "He has given me faith, but even more than that, he has given me the conviction that Elohim can and will work through him to do good." I listened in silence and made no comment of the bad odds that we were facing, and I began to think through some of my own strategies.

Finally, at dusk the scouts came back and reported that the encampment of the raiders was less than a furlong ahead. "They are feasting and rejoicing. Their women have joined them," the scout said. "They do not believe they have been followed this far."

"How close did you get?" Enoch asked.

"Close enough to see Methuselah's and Motta's faces. They have tied the boy to the crossbeam. They will burn one tonight, probably Methusaleh. Motta is held tied to a post. The women jeer at her and throw rotten vegetables, though I think the men would like to lie with her."

Enoch said, "May Elohim be with us not to let it happen!"

"There are forty-two of them besides the women, master," the scout said. "How are we to . . ."

"Enough!" Enoch answered, as if he didn't want to hear. "Our plan will come to us at the right time." He gathered his men. "We will attack soon. There is no time to waste. They may plan to sacrifice the children in thanks to their god, Molek, this evening. So we cannot wait till morning when the light is better."

We rode the horses to within a mile of the camp. Then we tied the horses in a grove of apple trees and went the rest of the way on foot. Coming up over a small hill, we looked over the encampment on the plain. It was a clear, moonlit night and we could see them dancing and feasting. There were two guard posts, at either end of the camp, and the area was largely clear, except for high grasses and the natural lay of the land in rolls and hills. There were plenty of trees, too, though they did not provide much cover.

Looking out over the land, Enoch stooped down and drew in the soil. He began talking through a plan, though he kept looking up, squinting, and shaking his head. "We will have to divide into three groups," he said finally.

"There are many of them. But this is the best we can do. Two groups of threes, and one of four." He drew in the soil, then sighed. "I don't think this will work." He looked around at the somber faces of the ten of us, then said, "Does anyone have an idea?"

"How will we get both of them?" one of the scouts asked, a tall lean man with a long white scar on his left cheek and a heavy mantle over his eyes. He looked hard, even ruthless, and for a moment I wondered that all men of faith do not look kind. He said, "Motta is tied up and guarded right by the fire. They are all there, telling stories and glutting themselves on fresh fruits they found along the way. Methuselah is tied to the crossbeam. They will undoubtedly . . ."

"We must get as close as we can and then . . ." Enoch looked over the encampment one more time. "If we can set up a diversion of some sort, perhaps . . ."

"Perhaps we can make them believe they are surrounded," Staro said. "We could spread out and beat sticks on sticks and make bird calls."

"They will not believe it," Enoch said. "They will consolidate and wait for the attack. And they might kill the two children."

"If we attack at three angles, run in, kill a few, we may be able to put them into disorder," one of the older men said, a thick burly man with a jutting chin and dull, worried eyes.

"They will know who it is," Enoch said, "and they will threaten with the lives of my children still."

"There is no way it can be done," one of the others murmured.

Enoch sighed and drew in the dirt once more, but suddenly I volunteered an idea. "I think I may be able to create a diversion, and quite an effective one at that."

Enoch regarded me a moment and said, "Go on."

I explained my thinking, and it was soon my plan they settled on. I was not sure it would work, but it was better than anything else we had, and it would most likely preserve the children because the raiders might think I was more madman than anything else.

Enoch said, "We will watch for our opening." He motioned to two of the older ones. "Mehael and Zok. You take a party of four to the point most advantageous to getting Motta. I should think the closer you can get to the last tent, the better. See if you can get directly behind it. I and Staro and the others will try to get close to Methuselah over there behind the trees. Do not hesitate to lop heads if necessary. Do not worry about the horses. Now we must let our friend Aristes do his little dance. Give us five minutes to get into position, Aristes."

"Of course."

I stooped behind a tree and waited as the others spread out. I could see them only for a few moments, and then they disappeared in the trees. I took off my sword and lay it on the dirt, then I disrobed down to my rough loin coverings. My heart drummed in my chest, and I found it hard to breathe. Why I had volunteered I did not know. But I was certainly better equipped to escape unscathed than most of the others. And they did need as many men as possible to work on saving the children.

I waited as long as I thought necessary, then crawled through the grass to the middle area between the two guard posts. The grass was rough, and little barbs caught at my skin and cut me in various places. I thought that would be good for the effect I wanted to create. I lay as quietly as possible, then grabbed two rocks in my hands.

Slowly I rose to my feet, hoping not yet to be noticed. I advanced to within fifty feet of the fire, when suddenly someone cried, "Who goes there?"

Immediately, others shouted and there was a tumult. I cried above the fray, "Elohim will save! His children live! You are dogs!" I just cried out whatever came into my head and threw one of the rocks at the first man who darted out toward me. The stone thudded against his chest and he stopped.

"Kill him!" someone cried.

I shouted, "Yes, kill me, kill me, but now you see me. Maybe in a moment, you won't."

Everyone seemed to be running every which way, some were shouting to guard the prisoners, others to quiet the horses. I threw the other stone. It clattered into the fire, sending sparks upward in a whoosh. I picked up another stone and several of the men advanced around me. They had me surrounded. The closest one was twenty feet away.

"Who are you, thief?"

"You ask who I am?" I shouted. "I am he who throws stones!" And I threw another one, a pebble this time. It rapped off the head of one of the men and he grabbed his eye.

"Get him!" the man shouted.

One of the others advanced slowly. I danced in place, playing the role of the madman. I hunched down and grabbed a handful of dirt in my right hand. "Now you see me!" I shrieked, trying to play the role of the crazy one, "And now you don't!"

I threw the wad of dirt into the eyes of the advancing swordsman, a thick-necked brawny man, balding with a wide bowl beard. He immediately screeched and tried to get the dirt out of his eyes.

"Shoot him with an arrow," someone else cried, and I whirled around, threw two more stones and taunted them. Others drew closer, swinging their swords and spears menacingly. But the plot was working. The guards were leaving their posts to see this madman who shouted and dribbled and spit at them like they were harmless.

I threw another rock, and one of the bronzed young men yelled, "I've had enough of this." He ran at me, whirling his sword like a dervish. At the last moment, I dove at his feet, knocking him over and sending him sprawling into the fray. I taunted him, "Can't catch me. Can't see me. Can't . . ."

He jumped up and came at me, this time slower, with a better feel for the kill. A ring of raiders surrounded me now. I kept looking for Enoch and the others, but I couldn't see whether they had yet done anything. "Get the children," I snarled under my breath, then said sweetly to the young man jabbing toward me with his sword, "You are a fool! Am I the fool? No! You are the fool!"

He lunged at me, and this time I knew it would be too late. Just as he reached me, I spoke the words in my mind, "I will be become Aris, an angel."

Immediately, I disappeared from their view.

They were astonished. "What happened to him?"

"Where did he go?"

"He just vanished!"

"Is he a magician?"

Twenty feet out from their circle and further away from the fire, I spoke again and was once more Aristes the Madman! I shouted at their backs. "Didn't you see me? I'm the spider. I weave my web, then wait for the flier!"

They all turned around as one and saw me. "How did you get there?"

"What on earth?"

"Grab him and hold him this time, Yacul!"

I picked up more rocks and threw them. But this time, four of them charged at me. I disappeared as I threw up a handful of dirt and sand. They all clattered to the ground around me—in my angelic form—and I could not help but laugh. The whole camp seemed to be trying to catch me. I ran about ten yards to their left—getting even further from the fire—and shouted, "Watch me, see me, bet you can't free me. I'm the bird. Fly in the sky and make girls cry." I hardly knew what I was saying, but they all ran at me as one this time.

"Surround him, and then squeeze. He can't get through us all."

I waited till they were all around me and I chanted, two rocks in my hands, "Whose head will I bash this time? I'll smash it and clash it and mash it to dirt."

I threw my stones, and with rage, they all screamed after me. I must have disappeared ten times, each time taking them further from their camp. Finally, after the last time, I ran back to the tents to look for the children. They were gone, and soon I caught up to Enoch and the others running through the high grass toward the trees. They had also freed the horses.

I was still in my angelic form and didn't change, but I decided to go back for one or two more diversions just to make sure Enoch and the others weren't caught.

The raiders were spread out, angry and bellowing about the "deceiver" and the "madman" and the "magician." They didn't know their prisoners and horses were set free until they realized I wasn't going to appear again. Then their rage only stoked higher, and they ran back to the camp to find their tents destroyed, their prisoners gone, and all their horses set free. I didn't stay to hear what horrid things they would say about me, but only laughed to myself at the ease with which it was all brought off.

I caught up to Enoch and the others at the horses. It was then I met Methuselah and Motta, both beautiful children, and not really children, but young people in their twenties and thirties. Methuselah stood straight, tall and tanned in the moonlight, an ardent young man of faith who immediately cried, "Thanks be to Elohim on High for His deliverance."

"And thanks be to our friend Aristes for his famous acting," Enoch said, gazing at me with wonder. "How did you do that? I saw you. You just seemed to disappear, right out of the air."

"Little trick I learned," I said, not wishing to talk further about my angelic transformations.

Motta brought me a skin of water. "You are very brave," she said, and looked into my eyes with affection. She was black-haired, with wide, bright eyes and high cheekbones. She looked like an Indian princess, and as she looked into my eyes, I found myself tongue-tied and unable to speak.

One of the men cried, "Already, Aristes is enamored of the beautiful Motta." Motta just batted her eyes and looked at my arm. "I saw the sword graze your arm. But you are not bleeding."

"I heal fast," I said, joking.

She regarded me fondly, then turned to her father. "We must give him a gift of one of the horses, Father," she said.

Enoch grunted. "More than that." Then he turned to the others. "It will take them till morning and longer to gather their horses," Enoch said, "so let us be off and back to our home." He mounted his horse, and already several of the freed horses had been captured and Methuselah took one, while Motta took another. This time I rode my own steed, a roan mare with a prancing, exuberant style that pleased me greatly.

We rode that night until dawn, then slept for several hours while others watched. I was tired and slept easily. Motta slept nearby, and when she rose, we talked for awhile by the fire. I found her talk captivating. Later in the conversation she told me of her fear that Elohim would abandon them to the raiders.

"I prayed over and over that my father would come. And then when he didn't, I prayed that Elohim would let me escape with Methuselah. But we were too closely guarded. They spoke every hour of the sacrifices, how pleased their god would be. They called him Molek. We had heard of him, a murderous, devilish god who required human sacrifice to satisfy his terrible desires and he would not give a blessing until they did. Why do people believe such things?"

I said, "They are led by evil forces beyond this world."

"That is what we have heard, in legends and things. But I have never seen such a being." She peered at me in the firelight. The flames danced light onto her face, giving her a dark, enchanting look. With her dark eyebrows, wide gray-green eyes, and thick, wonderfully soft-looking lips, I found myself drawn to her, wishing to kiss her hard. But with others around I would not do so. I knew my place. Kyrie had forbidden such contact. But it was a command difficult to obey. I listened to her, absorbed in watching her lips and the skin of her face move animatedly to her expressions.

She sighed. "I would like so much to know of Elohim, what He is like, where He dwells. We know so little. Only that one day He will break the curse that holds our land in spell of sweat and toil and a woman's childbirth pain."

I did not know what I could reveal. I said, "When do you think that will happen?"

"I hope soon," she said smiling. "Before I have to give birth to my first."

I laughed. "So you're planning already."

She answered, "I am not yet married. But who knows? Perhaps this year. Father has said that it is nearing the time. And I am . . ." She did not finish the sentence, but looked at me awkwardly, then her eyes slanted away.

"How old are you?"

"Twenty winters. I was born in the winter. I was difficult."

"Difficult?"

"So mother says. Very big."

"You are not so big now." I enjoyed talking with her. She had a natural, fluid style that made me feel liked, even admired. I liked the feeling.

"Yes," she said, standing and stretching so that the curvaceous lines of her body were accented by the moonlight. "My nickname is Almond, because I am small but look like I taste good." She blushed. "That is what the boys say, anyway."

I smiled. "Do you like that?"

"What can I say about it? Everyone in my family calls me that—when others aren't around. Otherwise, they call me Motta. But I'm not so sure how much I like Motta either."

"Maybe you should change it."

"Change it? How do you do that?"

I thought about it a moment. "Just announce to everyone concerned that you would like to be called something else."

She shook her head. "No, I really like Motta, and I like Almond, too. It's not often that you find loving families in our world. But Father loves Mother, and my younger brothers and sisters are always fun to play with. So I am content."

I picked up a stick on the edge of the fire and held it aloft. Its soft flame radiated across her face and she grinned quizzically.

"Are you going to set me afire?"

I said, forgetting my position, "No, it is you who set me afire."

She blushed and sat back down. "I would like to know how you managed to get my captors to come out and stare at you. From what I saw, it was a marvelous act, but each time they came near, you seemed to disappear. Are you a magician?"

I had hoped I would not be questioned too closely about this. And I only shrugged. "I am very quick on my feet."

"Far too quick for my eyes. I was watching you when you were close by.

They didn't know what to think. And then they were all so curious, they all left their guard posts. Foolish thing to do, but a very wise strategy on your part. How did you think of it?"

I wished we could turn to other things. I said, "It was nothing. Just trying to help."

"You don't like being a hero, is that it?" She smiled coyly, and her hand brushed my bare leg as she set it back in her lap. I did not know whether she noticed, but suddenly I felt bewitched with desire. This was what Kyrie had told me to avoid at all costs. And now I didn't know whether I could let go.

I looked off beyond the fire. Others in our band had lain down to sleep on skins. Enoch tended the fire and was roasting an apple from a tree we'd discovered along the escape route. He did not seem to be paying attention to us, but I said to him, "You have other daughters like this one, Enoch? Then you are a blessed man."

"Indeed," Enoch said, smiling across at me. "But I don't think you are interested in my other daughters."

This time I blushed. Motta slipped her arm through mine and said, "Let's go for a walk. My father's ears are too big for their own good."

"Is that all right with you?" I asked Enoch.

"Motta is a big girl now," Enoch said. "She can take care of herself. You are an honorable man. I trust you, and so does she."

"Perhaps you shouldn't—with such a beautiful creature." I looked at her again, and she pressed my arm, suggesting that I stand. Moments later, we walked back into the darkness of the small bluff that we had camped on. In the moonlight, her face appeared dark and mysterious. My heart thrummed within me like a bat's wings, and I found myself praying that it would never end.

"Have you ever been in love, Aristes?" she asked when we were far enough away from the camp that she wouldn't be overheard. "You are old enough to have had many experiences."

I wondered how old I looked—since I had no real age—and I said, "How old do you think I am?"

"Old enough to be married and have a family."

"I am not married, nor do I have a family."

"Why? You are handsome and brave and kind. What woman would not want you to be her husband?"

"I am a wanderer," I said.

She gripped my arm warmly, and suddenly she leaned against me, knocking me off balance. I quickly regained it and pushed back. Soon we were playfully trying to push one another off balance, gently though, and only at the shoulder. She laughed, and then poked me in the side. I wriggled away.

"Motta," I said suddenly. "We should not be doing this."

"And why not? I was just rescued from death. I am going to make the most of life from now on. It made me realize how quickly it can all be taken away." She pushed at me again, and the temptation only seemed to grow. I desperately wanted to kiss her, to hold her, to have her.

I knew now what had happened with the group of rebels from Hell who had gone to mate with human women. Kyrie's judgment had been swift and overwhelming. Those angels had been confined to the pit of pits and would never be let out till the final judgment, which, for all I knew, could be a million years from now. But none of that had happened before children were born to those women, and many of those children had turned into powerful, elite giants who were taking over much of the land in the south. They would be coming north, conquering everywhere they went. Even men as valiant as Enoch could not stand against them.

But it was the judgment of Kyrie that had terrified me. He warned us never to mate with women again, on pain of the starkest judgment.

Motta said to me, "Don't you think that is a wise way to come at it?"

I said, "At what?"

"At life. You have not been listening."

"Just thinking."

"About what?" She turned, took both my hands, and swung out in a circle. We danced about a moment, and she cried, "I love to dance!"

I needed to get away, to still my emotions, and to think. I said, "We should go back to the camp."

"Yes, but only after . . ." Suddenly, she stopped her dance and grabbed me about the neck and kissed me. Her lips were soft and titillating. Her breath on my face only magnified the excitement. I had never been kissed before. As she let go, she laughed gaily. "And now you know how I taste!" she cried, then spun and ran back toward the camp.

I stood out in the moonlight a long time, thinking, quieting my desire, and praying that Kyrie would not judge me for what had happened. Was this love? I did not know, but I liked the feeling, something perhaps no angel had ever felt before. I tried to tell myself to leave it behind, to leave now, to disappear back into my angelic form and never come back. But I couldn't.

__ 52 __

Motta sat on the edge of the stream, washing the skins and bowls and utensils we used for our meals. I watched her from afar. She was alone. She sang as she worked, and as I drew nearer, I could hear her.

The disappearer taunted and threw.
The rocks struck home, the crowd grew.

There was no way to catch him, he was far too quick.
Methuselah and Motta were saved by the trick.

She laughed and whapped the water with her hand, sending up a spray into the creek. I called to her from the bank. "Motta, did you make that song up?"

She whipped around and stared at me, obviously embarrassed. Her eyes fell and she blushed deeply. We had spent much time together the last few days, and I sensed something happening inside me that could not be stanched. I no longer cared what Kyrie or anyone else thought. I had even thought about never returning to my angelic form again.

Still blushing, she said, "It is not wise to sneak up on a maiden when she is alone. You may hear things you don't want to hear."

I stepped down, grinning and unafraid. "And what might I hear that I don't want to hear?"

She tried to give me a hard, angry look, but I could see the laughter edging out the bottom of her lip. Soon she motioned to me to come down and join her. But as I stepped down the bank, she walked out into the water, turned around, and sent a splash of water into my eyes.

"Motta!"

More splashes. I jumped into the creek and curled a sparkling wall of water at her. She stepped back with the wave, and sent more splashes my way. Soon we were soaking wet.

I was about to give up and started to turn, when she leaped at my legs and pulled me into the creek. We were both in the water, splashing and spitting and having quite a fine time of getting one another as wet as possible. My beard was soaked. My skins were wet all through.

"I'm going to dunk you!" she cried.

Then she leaped again on me like a cat. I let her push me under. When I came up, I sputtered water into her eyes, and she laughed happily. "I'm stronger than you any day!"

"Oh, I don't think so," I cried, and this time I dunked her under. Her dark hair fanned out in the water, and when she came up, it was all in her eyes. She pulled it all back and wiped her eyes with her fists. "All right," she said. "I give up. Let's lie on the bank and dry off."

"That's better!" I said, still grinning.

I turned to go, when she leaped on my back. "Ride, horsey!" she cried, and she pounded my shoulder.

I quickly warmed to the game and ran out of the water, galloped along the edge of the creek, then finally fell down in a roll of sand. She fell off, laughing. "You are so much fun, Aristes! Where did you learn to be fun? You must have had many brothers and sisters!"

I shook my head. "No, I learned it from you!"

She smiled and blushed again. "Well, I hope you don't lose it."

She took a comb out of her skin coverings and combed back the beautiful tresses. Her face was tanned and lovely in the sunlight so that I wanted to touch it. We had not kissed since the night on the hill when we were returning from the capture. Finishing her own hair, she glanced at me and said, "Would you like me to comb your hair?"

"That would be wonderful," I said. My blondish hair was long, reaching to my shoulders, and she stepped behind me as I sat on the sand. She began combing it straight back. She tried parting it several ways, and talked as she worked. "You have a majestic forehead," she said. "And your nose is perfect. But I think your hair should be shorter. You let it get tangled. You need to comb it more often."

I did not tell her that I had never remained in my human guise for longer than a few hours before. And here now I had done it for several days. I thought Kyrie would be angry with me, but I did not want to change back.

"I need someone like you to take care of me!" I said.

She smiled and ran her fingers around my head sensually, though I'm sure she was just concentrating on getting my hair right. She had no intent of sexual arousal. But I couldn't help it. And once again it was a new feeling. I did not know how to stop it or contain it. I only knew that soon I had to.

When she was done, she stretched out beside me, leaning on her left hand with her elbow on the sand. She poked me in the rib again, and I squirmed away. She laughed. "You are the most ticklish person I ever met."

"Oh, and you tickle all the young men, I suppose?" I meant it as a joke.

Her face darkened, though, and I could see she was suddenly pensive and perhaps pained. I said, "What is wrong?"

Her face clouded, and I could see the fear and worry in her beautiful dark eyes. I leaned closer. "Motta, what is the matter?" I felt her breath on my face, but she did not look into my eyes.

"Father is being very patient with me."

"How is that?"

"I am promised."

"Promised?"

"To marry Arondel, one of the young men. He lives in the next valley." She closed her eyes, and I could see small, hot tears form in the corners.

"What do you mean, Motta?"

"I am promised," she said very harshly. "Don't you understand what *promised* means?"

My heart fell. I had heard of how young women were given to young men in marriage, but I had not known about any such promise with Motta. Enoch would surely have mentioned it. Suddenly I could hardly breathe.

"You will marry him?"

She looked away and sobbed. "I should not have told you."

I grabbed her hand and stroked it. "Motta, you must tell me. Are you going to marry him?"

Her eyes fell, and suddenly a great weeping heave broke into her throat. "I do not want to. But there is no choice. Father spoke to me of it this morning."

The despair within me was black and cold and gripping. It had never occurred to me that she might be promised, but I knew that often in this land young girls, even before they had blossomed into women, were spoken for by fathers eager to ensure their daughter's life with a good mate. Enoch would be no different, and I don't know why I hadn't thought of it.

"So you did not know before?"

"No," she said, sniffling. "I knew. And I was prepared. Arondel is handsome and he seems kind. He would be a good mate. But that was all long before . . ."

I searched her eyes, looking for an indication of another way, but they reflected only the same despair in my own soul. "Motta, I love you," I said.

She nodded her head. "I love you, too, Aristes. But it cannot be."

"Isn't there some way? I want to marry you." I hardly knew what I was saying, but the sudden desperation of the moment impelled me towards it. I knew that what I said now might forever alter my destiny, but I didn't care. I only cared what would happen to Motta and myself.

She shook her head, still sobbing. "There is no way. I am promised. Promised!"

"But can't it be unpromised?"

"Only if Arondel dies before we are married."

She did not see my eyes flicker with the rush of a new plot through my brain. Could I do that—kill a man? For love? And what would Kyrie do? But I could not leave Motta. I was deeply in love with her. It was something I'd never before experienced, but the beauty of it was so great I could not let it go. Not now. Not ever.

Motta looked at me strangely, then she said, "There is another way."

"What? What?"

"If I am defiled." She said it quietly, but without a trembling in her voice. I knew immediately what she meant.

"But if you are defiled, what then?"

"I would be stoned."

I returned her steady, nerveless gaze, and I shuddered. "I would never allow that to happen to you, Motta. Never."

"Then there is one more way."

"Tell me!"

"We could run away together." She sobbed at the words and put her face in her hands. "And I would never see my family again."

I took her hands away from her face. "Motta, please, do not cry. I will talk to your father. Perhaps I can persuade him."

"I have been promised since my twelfth year, Aristes. Once each year they have come and I have talked with Arondel and his family. This is the year that I will be given to him, I am sure of it. It cannot be avoided."

"But if I speak to your father . . ."

"There is great shame in going back on a promise. He will not." She shook her head and wept again, and I drew her to my chest, holding her tightly.

"Surely, there is some way," I moaned, the darkness in my mind filling it like a spent moon. She cuddled and nuzzled against me, and I tasted her warmth, kissed her on the neck, and held her as if to never let go.

"There is only one way," she finally said.

"What?"

"If I go to my father and then to Arondel and tell them I am in love with another. Then perhaps they will release me from the promise. But it is only a last desperate effort. Otherwise, I am done for."

"Do not talk such a way. Kyrie will make a way." I said it suddenly, as if I really believed it, but I knew if anything Kyrie would never condone what I was doing. But I was willing to go to Him now, ask to be made a man forever and not go back. Would that that were possible. But was it? And would Kyrie relent? And would I then die as a man?

So many things had to be weighed and considered.

Suddenly, Motta unwrapped herself from me. "Take me, now, Aristes. Take me. Defile me and love me and I will die happy. Please!" She started to strip off the skin that covered her breasts and stomach, but I restrained her, suddenly terrified of what would happen if I did.

"No! It is not right!"

She hugged me close and placed my hand on her breast. "Please take me now and love me as no woman has ever been loved since the beginning of the world. Take me, Aristes. And then we will run away together."

I kissed her and a voice in my head suddenly whispered, "It is the right thing to do, Aris. You love her. It is right."

I listened to the voice and kissed Motta harder. She leaned back in my arms and I ravished her neck with more kisses. The voice in my mind cried, "Go into the trees. Then remove her clothing and lie with her. She will never go back to her people, and she will be yours forever."

"Yes," I whispered. I drew her to her feet. Her pupils were dilated with passion, and her flesh was on fire. I pressed her lips to my lips and we kissed hard and long. I was lost in it, unable to unravel myself now, and I knew that there was no going back. The voice in my head cried, "To the trees. To the trees. They are coming!"

I pulled away from Motta and grabbed her hand. "Come. Let's go into the trees where we cannot be seen or found."

She cried with excitement. "I love you so much, Aristes."

"I love you, Motta. We shall be together forever. I will fight for you."

"And I for you."

We ran through the creek and mounted the other bank. Soon we were hidden in the trees and the voice cried, "Here! Here! Now. Do not waste a moment."

I caressed Motta's cheek with my hand. We touched one another lovingly. My whole body was on fire, and her kisses only excited me more.

Then suddenly behind me a deep voice resounded. "Aris!"

I turned around. "What?"

Motta held me. "Who is it? I see no one."

"Aris!"

I could not see anyone, but I heard him. I remembered the voice, knew the voice.

"You are in grave danger, Aris!" the mysterious voice said.

Then the first voice, which I heard in my mind, cried, "Pay no attention to him. You are alone. Take the girl now. Take her now!"

"Aristes!" Motta cried. "What is it? Who is it? I don't see anyone."

I glanced around, a hysteria pressing me in my mind. Then I felt strong hands on my arms. Pulling. Pulling.

"Aris! You must stay with me! Now!"

Motta felt me being pulled away. She threw her arms around my neck and held me. "Aristes, what is happening? Tell me!"

I tried to speak, but already my voice was sinking deep into myself. I felt myself transforming.

"Aristes!" Motta wailed. "What is happening?"

For a moment, I was half angel, half man. And then I was jerked into the other realm with a force so powerful I could not resist. I stood there before two angels, Rune and Cere. Without a word, I reeled around and saw Motta, standing alone in the glade, weeping, shrieking for me, running about, and then crumpling to the ground in horror and terror. My eyes filled with tears and I turned to them. "Why did you force me . . ."

Rune said, "We were commanded. You must come now. You are wanted. At the throne."

"This is very serious, Aris," Cere said.

I looked at her face, as beautiful as Motta's, but there was no passion. I despaired that angels did not feel the passion of men. I cried, "I will to be a man, Aristes."

But nothing happened. The two angels simply stood there. Rune said quietly, "Come, Aris."

Then I felt another presence. I looked into the shadows and there I saw Tyree. And beside him, another whom I did not recognize. Tyree shouted, "You were almost there, partner. You are one of us, now."

I shook my head and looked one last time at Motta, now prostrate on the ground, crying out to Elohim to bring me back. And I knew there was no going back now. I cried out with despair, but strong arms gripped me again and I was pulled quickly, relentlessly toward the Doorway. The feeling in me was like something crushed deeply into the dirt and left for dead.

53

"Pay no attention to them, Aris; you did well. Next time you'll succeed!"

It was Tyree. But I didn't want a next time. "Let me go back!" I yelled. I could just see Motta far behind me in the trees. "Let me gooooo!"

The strong arms only grew stronger as we flew in sight of the Doorway. Tyree's laughter roiled out behind me in sarcastic chuffs. "Now you'll see what Kyrie really is! Now you'll understand!"

"Don't listen to him, Aris," Cere said to me. "He is a rebel!"

"Well, so am I now!"

"No, you're not! There is still time to recover it!"

"I don't want to recover it."

Cere's staid, unflappable tone should have had a calming effect on me. But Rune's dour unapproving silence angered me.

"I suppose you're both happy about this now that you've finally seen my true colors."

"We are only happy that we rescued you in time," Cere said.

"Rescued? I didn't need to be rescued."

"You did. You were on the verge of committing sin so awful you would have ended up in the pit of pits. Is that what you want?"

"Yes, it would be better than this. I love her!"

"And that is your grave mistake. Kyrie told you . . ."

"I don't care what Kyrie told me. He doesn't understand. He never understands. It's always this rule and that rule with Him. He doesn't understand! So let me go." I jerked around, trying to free myself from their arms, but a moment later we were through the Doorway and speeding toward the Mount. I cringed at the thought of a whole assembly.

I recoiled with even greater rage as we drew near. I knew I had become completely out of control, but something inside me bubbled and welled and blew and steamed like a boiling sea. I wanted to lash out at someone, at Kyrie, to tell Him and make Him feel what I was feeling.

We reached the Mount. It was only Kyrie, and of course the Cherubim and Seraphim and the Seven. The Son was there, too, and I felt His kind, empathetic eyes on me at the same time that Kyrie's stern gaze met my own inflamed stare. Immediately, I hated all of their concern and sympathy. I hated the way He would be there at my vulnerable moments. I hated the way He cared and loved and showed us the way. I just wanted to go back, to be with Motta and to live with her forever. I didn't want concern and love. I wanted freedom to do what I wanted to do.

"Aris," Kyrie said. "You have taken a man's form many times of late."

I didn't answer. I wasn't sure He even wanted an answer. He nodded, and Rune and Cere let me go and stepped back. I could feel Rune's forbidding eyes on my back, and Cere's gently pushing arms pleading that I just be honest with Him and admit my fault. I hated them, too.

"And now you have discovered the power of romantic love."

I looked up into His eyes. They told me He was not angry, and suddenly I thought perhaps I could win His support if I simply laid out my argument plain and simple before Him.

"Kyrie, I did not intend for this to happen. I was there to help."

"We know that you helped them. Enoch and his people are My beloved and I sent you there to help. I knew you would do well."

"That's exactly right. And I had no ideas to fall in love with anyone when I was there. I didn't even know what that was."

"You are not in love, Aris."

I swallowed, and His robe rustled as He shifted position on the throne. The Son did not move, but studied me with a friendly light in His eyes. I thought for a moment that perhaps the way to Kyrie was through Him. I started to look in His direction, but Kyrie said, "Aris, you are not in love. You were experiencing sexual passion and infatuation. It would not last. She would . . ."

"It would last. I love her. I would protect her. I . . ."

"She would grow old, Aris, and you would grow tired of her. Then you would look for another younger woman. And you would produce offspring that I have forbidden among men. They would not be fully human. You know that I can't let you transgress that boundary. It would destroy you, her, and their world."

"But Kyrie, she was so sweet and loving and I know I loved her. I know it."

"And I know just as surely that you have experienced a first love. You know what happened to the sons of God who transgressed the barrier and had relations with women and now their offspring roam the world and one day a judgment will have to come. When that judgment comes, would you want to be one of those who must be judged?"

"Kyrie, I don't want to be judged. I just want to go back to Motta."

"You cannot."

"Please, Kyrie. I will do anything You desire."

"Then do My will and do not transgress the boundary. You cannot fall in love with women or mate with them. That is My judgment."

"Kyrie, just this once. Please!"

"There is no once, Aris. Once and it will be the end. I cannot allow you once, Aris. You are not to transform into a grown man again."

I stared at Him, too stunned to speak. "That is not fair. That is not . . ."

"That is My judgment, Aris. Now return to the task you have been given."

"I have no task. I have nothing. I cannot live without her."

"You can live, and you can serve, and that you will do. You have not forgotten our agreement? Have you made a decision? You are a watcher. And at times I have given you special duties. It is time to return to what you have always been, Aris. You must remember who you are, what you are, and who and what Motta is. She will have a good marriage and bear loving, godly children, and she will be very happy. I assure you, I love her and I will bring about every blessing in her life. I will . . ."

"All I want is to be a human again and to remain that way, Kyrie. I will live and die a human. You can make me a human like that. I'm halfway there through the transformation. Just a few adjustments and I will be . . ."

"Aris!" A wrathful, dark look etched itself across His features. He regarded me evenly. I trembled and tried not to return His stare. But I could not help being held by His eyes. "I do not wish to make another judgment, Aris. Do not push Me in that direction. Do you understand?"

All the frustration and anger boiled out of me. "No, it's You who doesn't understand. You sit up there on Your majestic throne and everything that happens happens because You either allow it to happen or You make it happen. You can change things, but You don't. Instead, You wait up there for things to work out and when they don't work out and others decide to take action, You judge them. That's all You can do, isn't it? Sit up there and spew judgments out like they were all You have to do with Your time, and You tell us all what to do, and You decide if we don't do it, You'll crush us or send us to the pit or throw us out of Heaven forever. Well, I don't care anymore. I don't care what You do to me. I don't care if You put me in the pit. You'll have Your way anyway. That's what really kills me about You. You claim that ultimately Your will will be done. You claim to be all-powerful and all-knowing and perfectly loving and all that. And in the end everyone either does what You say or they get put in the pit.

"Well, it stinks. It reeks. Your world down there is a horrendous mess. There are people killing each other. And there's disease. And there is rape and pillage and slaughter and stealing and lying and illicit sex and men taking little girls and little boys, and You sit up here all high and mighty on Your throne and You say You're this and that and all-powerful and can do anything, and then You do nothing about most of it. Every now and then You send down an angel like me to make sure things don't get too bad, or else You do a miracle and fix some terrible situation, but You only do that very rarely because 'that's not Your way' and that's not the way to get the job done. No, You have to let them be, let them do as they see fit, and then as they mess it up and foul it up beyond comprehension, then You'll step in and judge them, throw all of them into the pit because they didn't do what You told them they should.

"And why don't they do what You say? Because You treat them like filth, You let them live in filth. You gave them one little thing they couldn't do—they couldn't eat of a certain tree in the garden. A stupid rule to begin with, totally stupid. Because all the other trees were there and it made no sense to anyone, especially the angels who were looking on and just hoping everything would turn out right. But still You gave them this stupid rule, and they didn't see the sense in it. In fact, You even made the rule so that it would play right into the hands of Satan, who You knew all along would tempt them and destroy them. And You just sat back there on that throne and let Satan do it.

"And You talk about trust. 'Just trust Me,' You say. As if we could. All You give us are reasons not to trust You, but You say the very essence of trusting You is trusting You when there's little or no physical, evident reasons to trust You. I don't get it. I guess I'm stupid. It would seem to me that You should get on down there and give all those poor hopeless people some reason to really trust You. Make their lives work out. Change their situation. Heal their diseases. Stop the murderers and the marauders.

"But what do You do? You let Hosta's people all get murdered. You let Cain kill Abel. You drive Adam and Eve out of the Garden.

"You want trust, but You have no idea how to get it. And that proves You're not worthy of our trust. It's very simple really. You show a person Your goodness and Your love and Your constant kindness. But You do none of that. Instead, all You talk about is holiness and righteousness and justice, most of which never happens down there in that world or in ours.

"Still, You expect us to trust You, to bow down and say, 'You are worthy, Almighty One.'

"Well, I for one can't do it! Not with what I've seen.

"What I've seen is that we have this terrible, horrid situation on the whole planet, and what You're going to do is sit up there on Your throne and judge them all. One by one. Each of them. Not one will escape.

"And You wouldn't dare put them out of their misery, or annihilate them so they don't have to feel the pain anymore. No, what You'll do is make them live forever, so the pain just gets bigger and stronger and more overwhelming, till they cry out for mercy. And then You'll say, 'It's too late for that,' and then You'll have Your revenge.

"That's what it's all about, isn't it? Revenge! Getting Your vengeance. You can't stand to have anyone want anything in the world but You. You can't stand to have anyone really happy with something unless You're the main thing. As long as You're the main thing, whatever else they want and have is all right. But if there's the slightest indication that You aren't Number One, then squash them, right? Grind them into the dirt. Kill them. Send them to Hell. Make sure they pay.

"So I guess then You'll be happy. Is that it? This is all to make You happy. Let You exercise Your awesome power and have all of us just lick your feet because You're so awesomely powerful. Well I, for one, won't do it anymore. I'm finished with Your little world and Your kingdom and Your all-powerful ways which amount to nothing but pain and suffering for all concerned. So do what You want! Strike me. Send me to the pit. I'd rather be there than where I am now. So that's how I feel. That's really how I feel."

There was silence all around, and it made me feel even better. "So no one answers. Where are your sarcastic little answers, angels? When are you going to shout me down and shout Him up? When are you all going to lay out those praises so that He can feel good about Himself again? Why are you so quiet? What's the matter—birdie took your tongue?"

I turned to look at Kyrie, actually feeling a whole lot better at this point. He finally spoke.

"Aris, you will not transform into a man again. That is My decree. Now it is time to go and get back to the things that are important."

"Oh, go go go! Is that it? That's what You want, me just to . . ."

"Aris! It is time for you to return to your work as a watcher. I will not hold these words you have said against you."

"Oh, Kyrie's largess once again comes through. A little mercy for the unruly, is that it? You'll give me a little mercy now, but have Your real

vengeance later, because You know it all—You knew it from the beginning.
That's how You can sit up there all smug and sure of Yourself. You knew
that it would come to this, and You know that later You'll really make me
pay for it. But You wouldn't have any real mercy. You wouldn't allow me
and Motta our moment of happiness together. No, You have to strip it all
away! You can't stand to see anyone really happy when what they're happy
with is not You!"

"Shut up, Aris!" Cere said.

Rune grabbed me. "Come with us!"

I tried to get away, but suddenly I felt too weak. I shouted, "Long live
the rebellion!"

And that was the last thing I remembered for a long time.

__ 54

When I awoke, I was in my room. All was quiet, the bright light through
the liquid glass that encased my quarters refracting rainbows all over the
walls. I was alone.

Angels do not normally sleep. But I had slept, and the refreshed feeling
that coursed through my limbs was pleasurable. I sat up on the couch,
studied my garden a moment—everything was perfect, as always—and
sighed deeply with a resonating inner thrill. I felt good, and alive.

And then I remembered.

The anger returned instantly. I stood, clenching and unclenching my fists,
feeling for my sword and wishing to withdraw it and lash at the shelves or
the desk, breaking them into shards. But my sword was not at my side.

I felt as if I'd been tricked. Indeed, I had been. I remembered my talk with
Kyrie and the fleeting last sensations of splendor with Motta. My eyes
burned with water, and I rubbed them at the memory. Why could I not
simply have been killed, forgotten, disintegrated in some pit somewhere and
never again spoken to? Why did immortality have to go on and on with the
pain only growing more primitive and punitive with each new venture?

There was no escaping it. I was bitter, lonely, pining for Motta. But I had
no idea how much time had passed and what might have happened in her
world. I almost shot out of the room and for the Doorway with that last
thought, but my instincts told me it would do no good. Motta was married
now, to her promised. Perhaps she even had children, and my reappearance
after my most abrupt and discomfiting departure would only tangle things
worse. I had to get on.

But on to what?

Finally, after drinking a cup of Vias Tea and making a repast of some sumptuous fruits left on my table, probably by Cere, I went out. I felt as if I was walking in a dream state. My senses felt pushed right out to the very limits of my fingertips, and everything in me tingled with the desire to move, run, whirl, and slide through space like a ballet prima donna who would never touch down from a leap. I did not feel joy so much as a penetrating, impelling push inside to get away, leave this place and think alone where there would be no one to argue away my most rebellious and bellicose thoughts. In a word, I wanted to hurt someone, and the energy that throbbed within me felt like a lion's mettle.

I walked through the streets, passing laughing groups and huddles of angels here and there talking, playing games, speaking low in corners, and eating small snacks from hidden pockets. Heaven had not changed in my absence, however long it was—maybe it had been only a few minutes, but I didn't think so—and everything appeared tinted with that golden glow that the shekinah glory drapes it in.

For a moment, it made me feel nauseous. What was I doing in Heaven? I did not belong here anymore. I was one of them now.

Or was I?

I didn't even know. But surely if I was, I would not have awakened in my room. I remembered with a cool inner chuckling my last cry: "Long live the rebellion!" Who did I think I was anyway? Had I really thought that I could hurt Kyrie by shouting something bitter and depraved like that?

In a flash, I realized that nothing could ultimately hurt Him. Not in an angelic or human sense. To be sure, He could experience frustration, anger, maybe even discouragement or despair, though I was sure the latter extreme was impossible. But my joining the ranks of Satan with the other third of Heaven could not wound Him in the way I wanted.

And what was that? To bring Him to His knees. To make Him plead for me to stop. To so afflict Him emotionally that He would give me anything in return for my favor and love.

Which all went back to Motta. I wanted Him to let me have her.

At least back then, whenever then was.

I stopped a lone Hauker walking along with a small Cruke under his arm and asked what day it was. He told me and I instantly calculated I'd been asleep over a month of Heaven's time. How had that happened? How was it possible?

I realized immediately that it was supernatural. Kyrie had given it to me to give me a chance to recover. But I didn't want to recover. Not now. Maybe there was still time to claim Motta.

I kept walking along drawing ever nearer to the Doorway, thinking about Kyrie's decree: I could not transform into a man. But how could He stop me? Was the power taken away? Or was it simply a command that I had a choice to obey or disobey?

I decided that I couldn't know until I tried it, and I set my mind on that end. Soon I saw the Doorway out on the edge of the City and walked to it with a steady, unswerving gait. I fully expected that someone would plop down and stop me, but no one appeared. The silence around me in the quiet fields of Heaven seemed preternatural, too. I did not quite understand it. Why were so few going through the Doorway? Normally, angels were passing through all the time, much as in later years people at rush hour would dart through turnstiles in the subway or train station.

Soon I stood before it. I hesitated a moment, looked across the vast green fields of Heaven, up into the sky to the clouds that ever covered our world and concealed Kyrie's home, and then I peered through the dark, shadowy quietude that glimmered in the Doorway itself. For a moment, I was afraid to go, afraid to find out what I must find out.

And then I stepped through.

Immediately, I found myself in a desert, arid land where the sunlight singed down like bars of iron just out of the furnace. I wanted to try the experiment immediately, and yet something told me to wait. I couldn't bear the truth just yet, if the truth was that I had no power to transform into a man.

Sprinting quickly across the soil, I took the hills and valleys in great leaps and soon I stood on a plain I recognized from its stately sycamores and locust trees, one not far from Motta's home. I hurried along, pausing only to shield my eyes from the sun and look across a long, wide valley where Enoch and his people dwelled. As I ran, I passed farms and gardens and herds. Then with a sudden jolt, I remembered that this was also the land of Arondel, Motta's promised. I thought perhaps I could stop by his farm and see if the bond had been sealed.

Meandering along now much more slowly, keeping to the creeks and rutted natural roads that had been carved into the valley, I found many different farms and paused only at each one to listen to enough conversation to find out whether it belonged to Arondel or not. But the people spoke of no such person, and I did not see Motta. Finally, I resolved simply to return to Enoch's patch of soil and see for myself what had come of it.

I followed the river and soon sat down on the very rocks where Motta and I had our last meeting, when I was so ignobly torn from my love. No one appeared, and I listened to the sounds of the stream, wishing to cast a rock into it or simply step into the rushing water without sandals and feel the lush, joyous flutter of cool clear water on my shins.

Then I heard voices and turned around. Two youthful maidens walked my way. They laughed and spoke gaily, their faces radiating the robust ruddy color of Enoch's people, their heart-shaped faces enraptured with girlish abandon. I envied them and listened carefully to their animated gossip. But nothing of Arondel or Motta was spoken.

I slid off my rock and stood quite close to them as they washed bowls and utensils in the crystalline waters. One splashed the other playfully, and soon they shouted and romped with the forgetful pleasure of the young. I felt very old watching them.

Finally I tired of their talk and walked back up toward the tents. Most of the men were missing; I was sure they were working in the fields or watching the herds. Then I saw Enoch. He led a limping donkey through the encampment. I could see the laughing but tired wrinkles at the corners of his eyes and the satirical downward pull of his mustache and beard. I wanted to talk with him, reminisce, sit about the campfire and dole out a passel of twinkling, golden stories that would keep everyone laughing and cheerful for hours.

I was just about set on transforming when Motta appeared. She caught up to her father and said, "Can't we wait just another month? He will return, I know it."

Enoch stopped to check the donkey's front right foot, he said, "Motta, I have told you I will hear no more on this. You were promised and married you shall be."

"But I love him, Father."

"He has disappeared, but even if he hadn't, it couldn't be. You were promised years ago, and I do not go back on my promises."

"But I don't love Arondel."

He stood and faced his daughter. Her thick, dark hair fell in sable tresses about her face. Her deep brown eyes wore a downcast affectation of inner pain. I looked away, too pained to scrutinize my love any closer.

Enoch said, "You will learn to love him, as all of us have learned to love our wives and husbands. It is our way, Motta. We don't even know if Aristes was a believer. He seemed to be, but he never revealed his own convictions to me."

"He was a believer, I know it." She stamped her bare foot, and her father sighed and turned around.

"I told you, tomorrow you are to be married. No more questioning of this."

"You are a tyrant!"

Enoch whipped around. "And you are acting like a biting, rabid cur! Please discipline yourself and learn to accept things as they are. No one knows what has happened to Aristes, and Arondel, your husband to be, waits eagerly for tomorrow."

"Father, I don't love him. I will never love him."

Enoch shook his head with a fond grin. He turned and began leading the donkey along, stopping every few paces to look at the lame hoof. The sun hammered down on their faces, and the hot air seemed to hang on the fields like an invisible mist. Before them the country lay green and comfortable in the sunshine. For a moment, I took it all in as I waited on Enoch's reply. I knew I had to do something. But what? If I did appear as Aristes, it might make matters far worse. And Kyrie had been adamant. There was no marrying between Heaven and earth.

Striding along ahead of his plaintive daughter, Enoch said no more till he reached the edge of the tents. She grabbed at his coat and cried again, "I don't love him, Father. I will never love him."

Enoch closed his eyes, clenching them tight with exasperation. He stood still, bunching his fists, and then slowly turning to face his demanding daughter. "Motta, no more. We do not marry for love. We marry for security, for companionship, because it is not good for a man to be alone, as Elohim told our ancestors. Arondel is a good man and he will protect you and love you as Elohim commanded, not as you think. Aristes, whatever he was, was a wanderer. You could never be happy with him, for wandering clearly is in his blood. He would use you and leave you."

"You don't know that!"

"I feel it in my heart, and for you. Tomorrow you belong to Arondel. I am finished with this."

Motta stood, trembling with an anger matched only by my own rage. How could Enoch know what was in my heart? He didn't even know what I was.

For a moment, I stood there seething. Then suddenly, Tyree was at my right hand. "Aris!"

I turned and greeted him, not sure whether I should be friendly or cautious.

"So you have borne the brunt of Kyrie's anger and survived."

"He was not angry."

"No, He simply judged you unjustly. But now is your chance."

"For what?"

"Transform! Take Motta and fly. Kyrie cannot stop you. He knows that. Simply transform and you will be free."

I stared at him a moment, amazed at the callous, bestial look that had come onto his visage in the last months. I said, "Why are you tempting me, Tyree?"

He chuckled. "I am not tempting you. I am only extending to you your right and destiny. If you do not take it now, you will never have another opportunity."

"Kyrie forbade me to transform into Aristes."

"And who is Kyrie—your master?"

"Yes."

"Then there is no hope for you."

I turned to look back down at the scene. Motta was walking toward the stream. I sauntered along behind her, still in my angelic guise.

"Transform, Aris."

I wanted to, but I said, "I cannot disobey Kyrie."

"And why not?"

I shook my head. "I don't know."

"I have disobeyed Him and look at me."

"You look awful."

"It's the light. In Hell, I look quite resplendent. But the point is that you are merely another one of His slaves. You have no choices anymore. You are no longer free to do what you want. That is what it has come to."

"I am free to do what is right."

"And what is that?"

I breathed in heavily. What was right here? What should I do—the thing that was kind and just and good? What was the thing that Kyrie would want me to do?

I struggled to grasp it.

Tyree said, "And what is that, Aris?" He was grinning malevolently, sure there was nothing I could do.

And then I knew. It was in my heart as solid as earthly gold. Something inside me throbbed with conviction, and I knew now I could not allow Motta to ruin her life. I loved her, but I knew Kyrie was right. I could not give her what another human could give her.

I said to Tyree, "Watch."

As I gazed upon her tear-streaked face, my heart felt as if it would cleave in two. I hurried out to the wood behind the tents and spoke the words, "I will be Aristata, a woman."

A second later, the transformation was complete. I was an old woman, wrinkled, thin, small, with a pale face full of wisdom and a tired, ancient air, one of the women whom young women would go to when in trouble. I did not like the form and I heard Tyree laugh, but I ignored him.

I found Motta at the creek, dipping in her fingers and playing with the tadpoles that swam to her for crumbs. I hobbled down over the bank to the water and stepped in. "Ahh, so refreshing."

Motta looked up at me. "Who are you?" she asked. Her tone was disinterested, and I don't think she even waited for my answer.

"I am a friend," I said.

She snorted, but I felt my face soften toward her. I wanted to tell her who I was and that I would always be close by. But I knew she could not understand and would only beg me if I truly was Aristes to become him and flee with her to the hills.

I cupped my hand and took a long draught of water, scooping up handfuls and sprinkling the clear stream like thrown jewels. I saw the tears in Motta's eyes and I said gently, "You are crying, child."

"My life is over," she said. She wiped at her eyes and her lips drooped at the corners despondently.

I sat down next to her, dangled my feet in the water and leaned back. Suddenly, I heard Tyree's voice behind me, "Do not do this, Aris. You are destroying yourself."

I shook it off with a shudder.

Motta glanced at me, suddenly searching my face. "Where are you from?" she said. "I have never seen you before."

"Far away," I said. "I am traveling to the north to find my family." I had no idea what to say in that regard, but the lie seemed to work and I did not feel guilty about it.

"You are very old," Motta said. "You remind me of Tira."

"Who is Tira?"

She told me about the ancient wise woman who accompanied their band and had created a thick, persimmon pudding that everyone loved. I did not like the idea that I looked that old and cadaverous, but I smiled at the idea, realizing that I was far older than any man now alive in the world.

I said to her, "You are sad, my child." I touched her face, and the soft skin of her cheek shone with a radiance that I burned to kiss and caress. "You have shed many tears in the last few days."

"For over a month."

"Has someone died?"

She leaned back and pursed her lips. "Not died. But he may as well have."

"Someone you love?"

"Very much."

"Who is he—or she?"

"Aristes, a young man who helped our people and saved my life." She turned to look at me. "Does any happiness come true in this world? Are we ever meant to be happy, or is it all cursed, as my father says?"

"There is a curse, yes," I said, thinking through an answer. "But the curse is lifted to those who will have faith."

"I had faith," she said, rubbing a small pebble between her fingers.

"You still have it. It is only buried now in your grief for your young man."

"Yes, and tomorrow I am to be married."

"To another young man?"

"Yes. I will never be happy with him. Never." She clenched her fist and fired the pebble at the other bank. It pinged off some stones and clattered into the reeds in the mud on the other side. A frog jumped, and we both watched it breaststroke through the water and then back to the bank.

"I wish I was that frog," she said bitterly. "Then maybe I would have a chance at happiness."

My heart felt like melted wax within me. I wanted to take her into my arms, cover her face with kisses, and be Aristes again. The thought mounted and shrieked within me and a tear burned into my eye. Motta looked at me and said, "You are crying."

"For all those who think they can never be happy again."

She gazed at me, her lips slightly parted, her dark brown eyes wide and expressive, the flawless straight nose pearl-colored and smooth. I wanted to possess her more than my own life. But I knew I could not. Kyrie had to have His way. I could never make Motta truly happy. I was an angel, immortal, of Heaven, and she was of earth. I knew if Kyrie had meant for the joining of our worlds to be, He would not have forbidden it. I doubted that I could ever be happy again myself, but I knew as I spoke with Motta that something about this set us both free.

"You are not happy yourself?"

I smiled glumly and wiped at my tears with the back of my hand. "Happiness is something that happens to us. When we are most happy, we are not thinking of happiness at all. We are most happy when we least think of ourselves and are thinking most how we can please others."

"I could please Aristes."

"But he is not here."

"If he was, I mean."

"But he is not here, my child, and he may never be here again."

"You don't know that," she said with sudden ferocity. I took her hand in mine and peered at the lines on her palm. I touched one of the lines, and she gazed down at it with interest.

"What do you see?" she said.

"There is nothing to be read in a palm. It is all read in the face and eyes." I looked away, toward Arondel's people and the place where Motta would soon be living.

"You will be happy with your man, Motta," I said.

"How do you know my name?"

I smiled. "I know many names."

Her eyes widened with wonder. "Are you Elohim?"

I shook my head. "No. I am just a friend."

She looked away, picked up another pebble, and passed it from hand to hand, dropping it from one to the other. "I thought if you were Elohim, you could bring him back for me."

"He will not be coming back, child. You must reckon with that."

"How do you know?" she said, the fierceness gone from her voice, but the pain renewed.

"I do not know it for certain," I said. "I only know that your happiness does not depend on your being with him."

"You don't know that!" she cried.

I took her hand again. "You must trust Elohim, that He is leading your father, Motta. Do you believe that your father loves you and loves Elohim?"

"Yes." She nodded and sniffled, and my eyes filled with tears.

"Sometimes we must trust Elohim even when we cannot see why or how," I said. I wasn't even sure why I was saying these things. But the words welled up within me as if from another source. "Sometimes trust means that we go ahead into the dark, believing that Elohim goes before us. Even though we cannot see Him, He is there, and He is leading. Perhaps He led your love Aristes away because He knew that you would never be happy with him, and he with you."

Tears rolled down her cheeks and I let go of her hand. She said, "I suppose you are right. But it is so hard to believe."

"Believing is never easy," I said.

She smiled at me, her lips slightly creased, and she looked into my eyes. Suddenly she gasped and stared at me in amazement. She said, "Your eyes look just like his!"

I recoiled slightly in shock, but I stammered, "Whose?"

"Aristes! He had dark gray eyes just like yours."

I said quickly, "It is only a coincidence, my child. I do not know him."

She put her head on my shoulder, and I draped my arm around her. Waves of regret and pain flooded through me, but the joy of simply being near her was so beautiful I ceased to feel my grief.

"I guess it happens to us all some day," she said.

"What is that?"

"Learning to trust in the dark."

"Yes, it is something we must all come to, or forsake, whichever seems wiser to us."

"I cannot not believe anymore," she said. "Elohim is too deep in me."

"Then let His thoughts fill your mind, my child. And trust that He will lead you."

She nodded, brushed off her cloak, and stood. "I must go to pick blackberries for my wedding tomorrow, much as I wish it was not to be. I have been so full of grief these last few days I have not been able to do anything. Would you like to come with me?"

"Certainly. I would enjoy that."

She held out her hand and we walked along, swinging hands and talking and then singing. My heart was full for reasons I don't even know. I was glad it was I who spoke to her. It had been hard, but perhaps my own words were my guide. And I didn't even know where they'd come from.

— 55

After that I stayed away from Kyrie and avoided Tyree as much as I could. My despair only seemed to grow. But I did watch Motta marry and change, have children and learn true happiness in Arondel's arms. He turned out to be a good man and husband, and Motta was blessed. I realized to some degree it was an unspoken agreement between myself and Kyrie: His blessing on her for my obedience.

The world became a much more violent place during that time. The giants who ruled in the south made their way north, leaving destroyed villages, raped women, and dead men and children in their path. Everywhere I looked I saw devastation. Occasionally, I appeared in my various guises to help a believer in need, or even an unbeliever. But believers had become scarce in the great mass of humanity, most of whom were bent on hatred, slander, lying, cheating, stealing, murder, rape, and every other sin imaginable. I attended various meetings in Hell and learned little. Satan cared only for destroying the work of Kyrie and for the worship of himself or his servants. He dotted the globe with his idolatries—from malignant, ritualistic animal cults to the far more dangerous and despicable child sacrifice and prostitution religions of the east and west. If anything of Kyrie was known, it was only that He was an impotent, distant prince who could not speak out of the silence, and who, in fact, had been silenced by the more powerful forces of darkness. The world was commanded and controlled by

Satan, and most believed it, though they did not call him Satan, but Belial, Beelzebub, Baal, Moloch, Azraith, Dagon, and numerous other names which belonged to various deputies and lieutenants in the enemy's hierarchy. Satan desired only that Kyrie not be known and worshiped. Anything else was all right.

I saw Motta die in her eight hundred and sixth year. I wept, but she was an old woman full of days who still remembered me and spoke my name on her deathbed. I wondered if she would ever learn what I really was.

I would not speak to Kyrie. In some ways I didn't even know why. I did not resent what had happened after my years of grief. I knew in my heart I had done the best thing, the right thing after all. And I knew that I would never again take the form of Aristes the wanderer, and I would never again touch a woman as I had touched Motta. In my travels I stopped at her grave many times, knelt and thanked Kyrie for her and for her life.

Then came a day when Kyrie summoned me to the throne. I stood before Him, feeling tired and wrung out, as if every syllable of praise had long been gouged out of my soul. I had not rebelled against Him as I had once thought I would. I was not even fighting Him. I simply ignored Him, and felt that He ignored me.

Of course I knew that was untrue. But I liked the silence between us. It was too painful to breach it.

And now I stood before Him, a bit disheveled. I would not look into His eyes and kept my eyes blank, unfocused. As I stood before Him, I waited. It was His place to speak first. But it seemed that He was waiting on me.

Finally I could not stand the quiet. "Kyrie, You summoned me."

"Yes, Aris."

"I am here."

"Yes, you are here."

The silence grew again until I finally had to lead again. "We have not been talking so much."

"Indeed, we have not. I have missed our conversations."

I laughed wryly. "Our last one was not exactly friendly."

"All conversations between Myself and others do not have to be friendly to be worthwhile."

"I suppose." It was a stupid answer, but I felt uncomfortable and tired. I wished for the kind of sleep I had experienced in the days after Motta and I were refused.

"Aris, I want to ask you a question and give you a task to perform."

I looked up at Him but not into His eyes. "Yes, Kyrie."

"First, the task. There is a woman who may be murdered. I want you to help her escape to a friend who will help her. It would be best for you to appear to her as a child, a girl of eleven winters. She lives by the Tigris River. You will find her in a hovel there with a baby. Her name is Daraana. She will go with you, but you must persuade her. She will be very afraid."

"I understand. And the question?"

"The question is this: Why does the lion not have spots?"

For the first time, I looked into His eyes, mystified and at the point of laughter. "'Why does the lion not have spots?' What kind of question is that?"

"A good question. One perhaps you can answer."

I didn't know whether He was serious, but then I had never known Him to joke, not like this. I stared up into the quixotic, ancient face as if I was looking into the eyes of a beloved friend and a hated enemy at the same time. I shuddered, then swallowed. "I don't know what You mean, Kyrie."

"The leopard has spots. The fawn has spots. The giraffe has spots and the jaguar and the cobra and the goat have spots. Why not the lion?"

"Because . . . Because . . . I guess it has something to do with protection. It conceals the weaker animals better from the predator."

"It also conceals the predator from the more vulnerable so that the predator can more easily catch its food."

"Yes, yes, I suppose. Then maybe . . ." I was stammering now, too flabbergasted to answer with any semblance of style. "It must have to do with . . . with . . . I don't know. Why do lions not have spots?"

"I wish you to think about it."

I felt foolish. Why was He doing this? "All right, let me think. Just let me think a second here . . .

"It must have to do with the way You originally created them. It must have to do with what You thought at the time and what You decided was best for the way the lion was to be constructed and how function best complemented design and all those things, I guess. I really don't . . ."

"Very good answer," Kyrie said, almost clapping His great hands with approval. "So you have learned something after all."

"I have?"

"Yes. You have seen that when I create, I am not whimsically fashioning beings and things on the basis of caprice and the mood of the moment, but that all I do is bred and born through research and insight. You are saying that I am not only an artist in My choice of color, size, form, beauty, and underlying structure, but also that I am much like an architect and engineer with other qualities well-suited to the process of creation."

"I am?"

He smiled in a good-humored, delighted way. "Not in so many words, but you are getting at the substance of it. I can't ask for much more at this time in your life. So why ultimately do you think the lion has no spots?"

I was still a bit flummoxed, but I said quickly and earnestly, "Because it pleased You to create the lion that way!"

This time He smacked His hand on the arm of His throne and grinned. "Bravo! It pleased Me to create it that way. A very powerful piece of wisdom. I think you can now take it and apply it to other circumstances."

I took a deep breath and waited, muddling over this seemingly vast insight and wondering what precisely I could do with it. But I did not voice my doubts to Him.

"Go now," He said. "You must help Daraana and her child, though you must understand that her child will die shortly after her rescue."

"I understand." Though my heart at that moment asked, "Must that be? Is there some way to avoid it?"

But He simply returned my stare and said nothing more. I exited and hurried to the Doorway, where I entered with a flourish and disappeared onto the planet.

Moments later I stood on the edge of a farm, a little girl of eleven, studying the farmhouse where Daraana lived.

56

And now we have come to where my story began. I know you have listened kindly and I appreciate that. Just let me say one more thing before I finish this day's proceeding. It has been long, and all I have said does not always make great sense. Some of the things I have done, I regret. But not much. Very little, in fact.

But now to Noah and the flood.

I learned the day of Daraana's rescue that Kyrie had decided to destroy the world. Noah would begin building an ark and Daraana would marry his son Japheth. The world was filled with violence, evil, hatred, extortion, murder, and every other sin imaginable. In many places, contests were held to invent a new sin that was satisfying and disgusting. Mankind scorned Kyrie especially and would listen to none of the preaching of Noah. As he built the ark, people assembled and watched, jeered and scolded him with derision.

At first I felt Kyrie had finally won the battle for mankind's soul. But as I watched the construction of the ark day by day, my heart seemed to harden and shiver and crack within me. I felt I was witnessing the complete disintegration of a great glory that would never return again. Of course, the glory, whatever there was of it, had long since passed. But I felt that Kyrie was admitting failure, and I could not imagine that He could fail. But I had only to think of Satan and his hordes and realize that He'd already experienced failure of a high magnitude. I supposed that in His mind He was starting over, not having failed per se, but having tried one way that didn't work and now veering off in a new direction that required working on a smaller scale.

I could easily justify it in my mind. Mankind had turned out to be a bitter, malevolent lot, not prone to obedience, worship, goodness, or even love in any form. They were by far His worst effort. With the angels, at least two-thirds had remained stalwart and loyal. In all mankind, He could find only eight souls worth preserving.

It was shortly before the rains began that I had another conversation with Kyrie. I also met with Rune, Cere, and occasionally Tyree, too, but they—especially Cere and Rune—were as mystified about the flood as any. Tyree continued to pursue and tempt me to join him and the rebels. I was pretty much beyond that now, just tired and weary and wishing for a long sleep. I found myself asking over and over what was the good of it, what was the good of anything. That life would go on wasn't good enough anymore. That somehow it would all work out in the end seemed a pipe dream. There was no end forthcoming. It was all simply pain and more pain.

I went to Kyrie feeling old and having done nothing of worth in my life. We were alone in the Temple with the Son. Kyrie gazed at me with those wise, fond eyes of His that always seemed to extend love even to His most abhorrent enemies. I had seen those eyes look that way upon Lucifer and Tyree and all of them. And yet, they all continued to reject Him, as, to some extent, I did.

"Kyrie," I finally said, my throat knotted with pain. "Will there ever be peace?"

"For those who believe, there is always peace."

"I mean for all of us."

"Alas, that may not be possible, My son."

"Then You have truly lost."

He smiled faintly. "That there are those who choose never to make peace does not mean I have lost, Aris. Or any of us. This is not a matter of winning or losing."

"It appears that You have lost to me."

"Appearances are not realities. Only when you have seen the end can you measure the beginning or the middle. You have not yet seen the end."

"But You have told us what the end is."

"Parts of it."

"The judgment of all."

"Yes. I have told you that."

"But that is not all of it?"

"No."

I decided to shift the focus of our conversation. "What am I expected to do now, Kyrie?"

He looked surprised. "Why, simply to trust Me."

"That is all You want from me?"

"What else can you give?"

"My service. My obedience. My allegiance."

"If you trust Me, all those things proceed from it."

"So it always comes back to trust."

"It always will. So long as you do not know all that I know—and you cannot ever know all—you will have to trust Me with that knowledge."

"And if I don't?"

"Already you have seen the consequences of that."

I nodded my head. I had. Lack of peace. Doubts. Fear. Hatred. Anger. I had rambled through it all.

"What do You want from me, Kyrie?"

He smiled kindly. "Must I answer again?"

"I just wish it were simpler."

"There is nothing more simple than trust, Aris. You can trust anywhere, anytime, in any guise. The small and humble can trust as well as the great and strong. There is nothing so universally operable as trust."

"So that is the key I have been looking for."

"One of them."

"Can it really be that simple?"

He laughed out loud. "On the one hand you ask Me to simplify, and then you protest that it may be too simple. You are not thinking straight, Aris."

"It seems to me that nothing is so simple and yet so large as trust, Kyrie. That's all."

"Indeed, that may be a fine description."

I stood and started to walk out. He called after me, "Will you exercise that trust, Aris?"

I turned, chewed my lip, ran through a hundred doubts and gave myself a hundred answers. Finally I said, "Yes, I am ready. But I won't."

"And why not?"

"I think you know, Kyrie."

"Yes. I know."

"Then why do You ask?"

"Because I wonder if You know."

I grinned for the first time. "I like You a lot, Kyrie. Perhaps I love You."

"And I you, Aris."

"Then let's let our love allow each of us to be ourselves."

He smiled with a transcendent gleam in His eyes. "Yes, I can do that."

"I will be watching, Kyrie."

"And so will I."

I walked out into the shekinah beauty of Heaven. I looked toward the Door, but I could not bear witnessing the death of millions in the flood. I would wait this time. Think, wait, and perhaps, above all, sleep. I longed for sleep. Thinking was so hard, and painful. I only wanted to forget everything for a moment, to not exist, but that, I knew, was the realm of dreams.

As I returned to my room, I remembered one more thing: the white stone with Daraana would be on the ark. Perhaps through it, one day there really would be peace on earth.

I did not know. And for the moment, I did not care. I sat down on my couch and closed my eyes. Briefly, there coursed the images of Tyree, Rune, Cere, Adam and Eve, Abel and Cain, Hosta, Motta. There were so many I cared about, even loved. And so many tragedies.

I wished for a final answer that would sum it all up. But none occurred to me.

As I closed my eyes, I whispered, "Trust, so simple. And yet . . ."

About the Author

Mark Littleton is the author of over twenty–five books including *Death Trip* (Moody Press), *The Crista Chronicles* (Harvest House Publishers), and *Stasia's Gift* (Crossway Books). He lives in Columbia, Maryland.